Alex Palmer was born in London in 1952. Her father abandoned her family when she was very young and they left England when she was five to live variously in South Africa, New Zealand, and Australia, arriving in Sydney in the late 1960s. Here, she studied English literature and language at Macquarie University and later sat for a postgraduate diploma in information management at the University of New South Wales.

Alex has travelled extensively in Australia and in Asia, Europe, Britain and North America. After a working life which has included occupations as diverse as geriatric nursing to automated systems design, she now writes full time. She is married and lives in Canberra.

BLOOD REDEMPTION

ALEX PALMER

HarperCollins*Publishers*

This project has been assisted by the Commonwealth Government through the Australia Council, its arts funding and advisory body.

'Live It Up' (words and music by Greedy Smith) as performed by Mental As Anything. Copyright © Syray Pty Ltd/Administered by Universal Music Publishing Pty Ltd. Lyric reproduced by kind permission of Greedy Smith/Syray Pty Ltd/Universal Music Publishing Pty Ltd.

All events, organisations, websites and individuals depicted in this novel are wholly fictional. Any resemblance to any actual event, organisation, website or individual, either existing or historical, is purely coincidental and unintentional.

HarperCollins*Publishers*

First published in Australia in 2002
by HarperCollins*Publishers* Pty Limited
This edition published in 2003 by HarperCollins*Publishers* Pty Ltd
ABN 36 009 913 517
A member of the HarperCollins*Publishers* (Australia) Pty Limited Group
www.harpercollins.com.au

Copyright © Alex Palmer 2002

The right of Alex Palmer to be identified as the moral rights
author of this work has been asserted by her in accordance with the
Copyright Amendment (Moral Rights) Act 2000 (Cth).

This book is copyright.
Apart from any fair dealing for the purposes of private study, research,
criticism or review, as permitted under the Copyright Act, no part may
be reproduced by any process without written permission.
Inquiries should be addressed to the publishers.

HarperCollins*Publishers*
25 Ryde Road, Pymble, Sydney NSW 2073, Australia
31 View Road, Glenfield, Auckland 10, New Zealand
77–85 Fulham Palace Road, London W6 8JB, United Kingdom
2 Bloor Street East, 20th floor, Toronto, Ontario M4W 1A8, Canada
10 East 53rd Street, New York NY 10022, USA

National Library of Australia Cataloguing-in-Publication data:

Palmer, Alex, 1952- .
 Blood redemption.
 ISBN 0 7322 7131 2.
 I. Title.
A823.4

Cover and internal design by Darian Causby, HarperCollins Design Studio
Cover photograph by Luke Causby; Author photograph by Hilary Wardhaugh
Typeset by HarperCollins in 10.5/13pt Sabon
Printed and bound in Australia by Griffin Press on 50gsm Bulky News

5 4 3 2 1   03 04 05 06

For Ches

So ye shall not pollute the land wherein ye are: for blood it defileth the land: and the land cannot be cleansed of the blood that is shed therein, but by the blood of him that shed it.

Numbers 35: 33

1

Blood, in this bleak light a shining, dark liquid, stained Grace Riordan's coat as she sat down with the boy in the gutter. She saw it brush from his clothes onto hers as she wound her arm around his thin waist and felt him cling onto her in reply. The curt orders from Harrigan still sounded in her head: Stay with that boy. Keep him with it because we need him. She let the blood lie there, damp and untouched on the fine black wool, and said, 'We're here, Matthew. You hold on to me. We'll have your mother in hospital as soon as we can.'

Grace was forcing calmness on them both as sirens screamed and a more human racket exploded around them. A rush of people stepping either side of the boy's shock, knocking on doors, stopping traffic, and searching the streets for a witness or a killer, whichever they might find first. Close to their feet, the paramedics treated Dr Agnes Liu where she lay on a wet road just now being strung with blue police ribbons, her breastbone broken open by a bullet. Grace did not have to tell the boy, probably only thirteen, that his mother held on by a thread. It was said in the blood on his school uniform and in the expression in his eyes, emotion displayed down to the bone, nakedness Grace chose not to look at too closely just then. She chose also not to think too much about the woman lying so near to them in the street. Later there would be time for her but not now.

'What are they doing? Why are they taking so long?'

She held Matthew Liu upright as he spoke, his compact body racked with tears. They sat in the speckling cold rain of a sun and showery day, in a dog-legged street of old terraces, warehouses of textile merchants and a red brick building hung with a discreet sign on its restored Art Deco facade: The Women's Whole Life Health Centres Inc., Administrative Offices, Chippendale. At a distance too close to them, the corralled media had begun to gather and howl for interviews and footage.

'They're doing everything they can, Matthew,' Grace replied, listening to her cliché. 'Don't think about anything except this minute right now.'

'I know why. I do know why. But not Dad. I don't understand Dad.'

'If you want to talk to me about that, Matthew, you go right ahead. I'll be with you all the way to the hospital and you can tell me everything you want to.'

As she spoke, she saw the boy turn to look past her, down the short distance along the street to where his father lay on the roadway. She stopped him, turning his head away and shielding his eyes with her hand.

'Don't. There's no point.'

'No, I should. I should be able to handle it.'

'No, Matthew. Don't. Don't do it to yourself.'

She might have to look but the boy did not. He had

seen it once already, when it happened, that should be enough for him whatever he thought. He did not fight with her.

She glanced back to where Paul Harrigan, with a number of other police, was standing over the boy's father. The man half sat, half lay on the street, his head resting against the front wheel of his car. Professor Henry Liu, late musicologist from the University of Sydney. Much of his face was gone but his eyes remained, open and human, staring upwards. As she watched, Harrigan reached into his pocket and taking out a large blue handkerchief dropped it over the man's face. The fabric clung and was stained immediately into a pattern of red. Grace blinked at the unexpected sight of the makeshift death mask and suppressed the recoil of her shock, the sudden in-drawing of her own breath.

Harrigan had turned away and was walking towards them through the moving crowds, a tall man with dark blond hair, preoccupied, apparently unmoved by the scene. He did not look at her but squatted down at eye level in front of the boy. He spoke in a neutral and uninflected voice, the tone of someone who is, and remains, detached from the events occurring around him.

'Matthew? Do you know who I am? My name's Paul Harrigan and I'm in charge of this investigation.'

In the face of a numbed response, Harrigan slipped his card into the pocket of the boy's stained school blazer. 'Keep that in case you need it. Now, I'm going to find who did this to your parents. That's a promise. I'm going to find them. But I'll need your help. I need to talk to you a little later on today about what's happened here. Can you do that?'

The boy nodded, his face set, his tears now dry. Harrigan put a hand on his shoulder.

'Okay. We'll get your mother into hospital first and I'll come and see you there. This lady will be with you all the way in the ambulance. I just need to speak to her for a moment. Over here.'

Grace followed him into a pocket of stillness within the constant movement of the crowd. She saw him glance down at the wet stains smudged onto her coat and then look past her, at Matthew, scanning the scene behind her for whatever was happening elsewhere. He spoke to her in the same neutral and unhurried voice he had used with the boy.

'That boy is your responsibility from here on in. You make sure you keep him afloat until I can get to speak to him. Call me if you need to.'

She did not have time to do more than nod before a paramedic pushed between them.

'We've got to go to St Vincent's. We've got to go now.'

'You'd better get on your way.'

Harrigan turned away as Dr Liu was lifted from the roadway, her son rushing towards her. Grace caught him by the hand and told herself, don't panic, keep the boy contained.

Keep everything contained, keep it moving. Moving someone from one place to another is only an exercise in practicality, even if they are dying and practicality is the only thing you have to offer them. She told herself this after she had followed Matthew into the ambulance. It raced through the city streets and he began to talk in an uncontrolled and jerky stream of words which she tried to record on her miniature cassette player. At the hospital, the reception party of hurrying people wheeling the injured woman through the corridors brought with it the strange atmosphere of emergency, of events whose outcomes are balanced on the finest, most fragile point.

At the entrance to the operating theatre, the doors were closed in both their faces. Matthew stared at them bewildered and let her put her arm around his shoulders and guide him to a small waiting room set aside for their use. A uniformed officer guarded the door. Marooned, the boy sat on a vinyl chair next to a low table covered with ancient *TV Week* magazines. He hunched forward, his hands in his thick black hair, dry-eyed and waiting. His head seemed too large for his small body, his fine bones should not carry the weight. Grace looked at him bent over the table and squeezed him lightly on the shoulder, just once.

'I'll be right back, Matthew. You just hang in there,' she said quietly, and stepped outside to call the boss.

Harrigan's voice came over the airways, thin and trivial through the compact instrument. 'How's the doc? Is she going to make it?'

His question came over as the original throwaway line. She paused, glancing around at the busy, echoing corridor.

'They don't know. I've been told she's going to be in surgery for quite a while and it could go either way.' She drew a breath to stop the catch in her voice from becoming too apparent. 'The boy's talked to me but he's not making much sense and he's not going to last. If you want to talk to him today, it has to happen soon.'

'I'll be on my way over there as soon as I can get away. Just keep him with it.'

'There is one thing he's said. He thinks he knows why.'

'Does he now? Okay. Be there shortly.'

In the brief interim, Grace had gathered courage.

'He shouldn't be crowded,' she said. 'He won't survive it.'

'He shouldn't be crowded,' Harrigan repeated. 'You don't say. I never would have thought of that. Thank you, Grace.'

Grace cut the connection on the edge of his sarcasm, thought to herself, you had to know, I had to say it, and dismissed him from her immediate concerns.

She had thought the waiting room would be a haven but it attracted people like flies. Doctors came to offer unwanted sympathy, nurses to suggest sedatives, auxiliaries to supply drinks. 'Keep them out,' she told the guard at the door. A little later there was a knock and a tall Caucasian woman was ushered into the room. Grey-haired and sixty-something, she was straight-backed and old-fashioned in her dress, which was both elegant and conservative and included a hat and gloves. She carried an armful of neatly folded clothes; there might have been no such thing as suitcases or even plastic bags left in the world.

'Miss Riordan? My name is Mrs Tsang. I am Agnes's mother. I've been asked to come down here and be with Matthew. I understand you are with the police but I'm afraid I must ask you to leave now. I have to see my grandson alone. I have been told his clothes are very badly stained with blood and I want him to change them. We can't do that while you are here.'

She spoke in an authoritative, almost mechanical voice, without stopping for breath. Matthew Liu gave voice to a gasp of some kind and held his head in his hands.

'Don't go,' he said.

Grace had stood up.

'I'm sorry, Mrs Tsang, but I can't leave either of you. I have to stay with you both until someone else takes over from me.'

As she spoke, Matthew suddenly shouted, outraged, 'Why do you — *why now*? Mum's dying! Why do you have to fucking think about that now?'

He might have run at his grandmother if Grace had not held him back in his chair.

'Don't, Matthew. Let it go. Just stay calm,' she said, holding onto him.

The woman herself had stepped back quickly, her face white but emotionless. She stood there in confusion, hugging the clothes she was carrying. Harrigan, arriving unaccompanied, walked into the room, timing it perfectly to see the chaos. There was a brief silence in which the boy subsided in his chair and Mrs Tsang stared at Harrigan, shrugging graceful if ageing shoulders.

'I do apologise,' she said to him with perfect manners. 'He should never use such language, certainly not in front of this young woman. It is always better to keep up an appearance. It will make things easier in the long run. But he won't listen to me ...'

'Do you want me to take those?' he replied, unfazed by anything she had said. He took the armful of clothes from her and set them on the table. 'Why don't you sit down over here? Would you like some water?'

Without argument, Mrs Tsang sat in a chair opposite Matthew. They did not look at each other, neither seemed to know what to do. Grace handed her a glass of water which she drained without stopping like an obedient child and then placed neatly and gently on the table. Harrigan sat near her and went through the etiquette, handing her his card.

'I'm going to talk to your grandson now, Mrs Tsang. You understand, this could be upsetting for you. If it's too much for you, you say so. Otherwise if you'd just like to sit there nice and quiet, that'd be the best thing. You need anything, you ask my officer here. She'll get it for you. Anything at all.'

His politeness combined the impossible with the normal, inviting them to accept that this was a completely usual situation, leaving the woman without an alternative.

'Yes, of course, I do understand. They told me ...'

Unable to speak further, she gestured her agreement and sat still with her hands folded in her lap.

'That's good,' he said. He turned to the boy and leaned forward.

Grace placed her miniature cassette recorder on the table amongst the torn photographs of soap opera stars, considering how the way Harrigan had soothed everyone down allowed for no dissent, and jotted into her memory how he had reduced her to a nameless role to help him keep the peace. Unasked, she stayed beside Matthew. The boy took her hand and held onto her tightly.

'I need you to take me through what happened, Matthew,' Harrigan was saying. 'Try and put it in some sort of order for me if you can. Take it as slow as you like.'

The boy waited before speaking. Grace felt his small fingers wound into her own and thought that Harrigan had to feel for him as well, but how would you ever know?

'I don't know why she shot Dad. I think she just wanted Mum. That girl — I didn't even see her, all of a sudden she was just there on the street. She shot Mum' — Grace saw Mrs Tsang close her eyes — 'and she sort of swung around and she shot Dad. It all took ... two seconds? Then she went back into that shop on the other side of the road — it's deserted, they used to sell peanuts there or something — I don't think she even saw me until she turned around. I thought, she's going to shoot me now. I don't know why she didn't. Why didn't she?'

He was shaking his head, wondering why he was still alive.

'Don't ask yourself why people do things like this, Matthew,' Harrigan replied. 'You don't want to know what they're thinking. It's not worth your time.'

'A fucking girl. Killed my dad. For no reason. You know her hands — she had these gloves on but her hands were really shaking. It's sort of mad, isn't it? You wouldn't think you'd notice anything but I could see her hands so clearly. She looked at me and I saw those mad eyes and that gun ...'

Grace felt him squeeze harder on her hand as he rubbed his forehead. His face was thinned down with remembered terror and he was shaking.

'It's okay, Matthew,' she said to him, looking at Harrigan, watching him wait his time.

'We found the gun, Matthew,' he said after a short pause. 'She dropped it around the back of the shop right where she'd parked her car. You don't have to think about her having it any more. So, can you tell me? Did you see her face at all?'

The boy shook his head. 'No, you couldn't really see her, she had this scarf thing on. And this blue coat. With a hood. There was blood all over it. She was little. She wasn't much taller than me. And thin. So fucking thin, because there was nothing of her, she was just so little. I'd know her. If you showed me a picture I'd know it was her right away. She was — I don't know — I didn't think she was old. Twenty?'

Mrs Tsang had drawn herself upright in her seat and seemed to be holding her breath, whether because of what Matthew had described or his language, Grace could not tell.

'You're sure it was a girl?' Harrigan asked.

'Yeah, I'm sure. I didn't believe it at first. But I'm sure.'

'My officer tells me you think you know why. Do you want to tell me about that?'

'It's Mum, it's what she does. She runs those Whole Life clinics — it's all women's stuff. They do these things, health care and abortions and things like that. She gets this mail — ultrasounds and letters saying she's a murderer and all that crapola. And she gets these idiot protesters hanging around the clinics. They keep saying things to her like "Murderer, God's going to strike you down." She's not a murderer, she saves lives, but they don't think about that, that's too hard for them — '

He stopped, staring at Harrigan. 'You don't care about that sort of thing, do you? You're not going to hold that against her?'

'No, Matthew, that doesn't affect me one way or the other. I don't think about it.'

'Mum's been getting this really gross hate mail lately — it was disgusting, it was death threats and dead babies. Dad kept saying to her, you've got to go to the police about it. But no, she said she wasn't going to do that, because you wouldn't do anything about it if she did. Then last night they had this incredible argument. He told her, you've got to go to the police because it's just the same —' He stopped, briefly. 'We were in the

States a couple of years ago when Dad was over at Berkeley, and Mum was working at this women's clinic. She got the same crap from some mad pro-life group over there and it was so dangerous for her. They had her picture all over the Net and they told everyone where she lived. They put these crosses on the front lawn for all the babies they said she'd killed. They'd camp out beside them and when she came out in the morning, they said to her she was going to end up dead herself one day, maybe today. She used to ask the people she worked with, do they mean it? And everyone told her, yeah, these people are psychos, you've got to be so careful about them. She had to wear this bulletproof vest when she went to work, and they had armed guards all over the place. Last night Dad said to her, it's like it's the same people and they're dangerous. You've got to go to the police. Call them now, he said. Oh no, she wasn't going to do that. I'll go to work and I'll call them tomorrow. That is just so like her. That's what he was doing out of the car. He was saying to her, are you going to call them? She said, yes, I'm going to call them. It was too late, wasn't it?'

Grace sat and let the boy hold on to her while he regained some calm. As she did, she saw Harrigan again wait and watch and then pursue his point.

'Do these people who stalked your mother in the States have a name?'

'I can't remember. I can tell you where she worked over there, they'd know all about them.'

'We'll talk to them. What about the ones who hang around the clinics here?'

'I don't think they've got a name, they're just loonies. But you might know something about them. They used to take pictures of women going into the clinics and

Mum used to call you in when they did. You'd come down sometimes and move them on. But that's all you ever did.'

The accusation glanced off Harrigan's hide.

'We'll check it,' he said. 'Did you see anyone else this morning, Matthew? We found some used syringes in the back of the shop and we're pretty certain there was at least one other person inside at the time. Did you see anyone else near that shop, before or afterwards?'

'I've seen smackheads come out of there sometimes. I know it gets used for that, but I didn't see anyone today other than her.'

The words sounded strange in his mouth, Grace thought, his nerve was about to break. There was a brief silence.

'Are you going to find her? You said you would.'

'Yes, I am,' Harrigan replied.

'Because she's a coward and she's a cold-blooded murderer and you've got to find her and put her away, you know, for ever.'

As he spoke, his grandmother leaned forward with her eyes closed, then sat upright again, appearing to force herself to listen. Grace's miniature cassette player, balanced on the low table, kept on recording.

'We'll find her.' Harrigan sounded disinterested. 'I don't want people like her out on the streets. I want her in a cell where she belongs for a good long time.' He paused. 'I've got some people outside who are going to stay with you both for a while. If you want anything, you just ask them for it. That's what they're here for. Do you want to get changed now, Matthew? Your grandmother brought these clothes in for you. You should get out of what you're wearing.'

'I'm not going to do that. You see this?' The boy let

go of Grace's hand and held out his arms where the blood had dried to fine caked dark crimson dust on his school blazer. 'This is real. This is what happened. I'm not going to change.'

'That's not going to make any difference for you, Matthew,' Harrigan said quietly. 'It's better if you clean away what you can. Why don't you let me and your grandmother give you a hand?'

There was a change of quality in the atmosphere; Grace felt a sense of the boy taking on an imposed restraint. He sat still for a few moments and then shrugged his acquiescence. She said her goodbyes to him, which he received with a confused vagueness, and waited outside while he changed. A little later, Mrs Tsang appeared in the corridor with Harrigan.

'I'll give you these now, Mrs Tsang. I think you'll want them,' he said and reaching into his inside jacket pocket handed the elderly woman a plastic bag with the dead man's effects: a gold watch, a tiepin, a wallet and a wedding ring.

'My husband gave Henry that watch. When he and Agnes were married,' she said in an ordinary voice, taking the package from him. Harrigan was guiding her gently back into the room as she spoke.

'Don't forget you can call me. Any time. Any of the numbers on my card.'

Grace, watching the waiting room door close on both Matthew and Mrs Tsang, allowed herself to breathe.

'Is that what he told you?'

They were on their way out to his car. She had stopped outside the hospital entrance to put on her coat against the wind, and stood in the wintry weather feeling stretched and dirty. Just then she would have paid good money for a cigarette but she had none with her, a self-imposed self-denial she was regretting badly. She frowned as she replied.

'Yeah, pretty much. He made a lot more sense that time around, he really lost it in the ambulance. Anyway, I've got it all on the tape. Both times.'

'Good for you, Grace.'

Neutrality gone, he snapped his reply at her. Grace felt the expression on her face harden as she looked at him and did not reply. What do you want me to do? Cry for Matthew? I can do that if you want but what's the point? He was watching her.

'You've cleaned your coat up,' he said.

She touched the still warm and damp black wool and felt a shift in her workaday realities. All the usual boundaries had been negated by a single morning's work.

'The hospital did that for me. It was nice of them to take the trouble.'

'Yeah, it was, wasn't it? Okay, we can't hang around here having a good time all day, we've got places to go. You drive, I hear?'

He was looking at her speculatively with the ghost of a grin.

'Of course I drive.'

'Yeah, I heard on the grapevine you were pretty speedy. You can drive me in that case.' He tossed her the car keys and she caught them one-handed with a perfect cricketer's catch. 'You don't mind, do you?'

She almost said that the grapevine was more speedy than she could hope to be. That morning, early, Grace had slipped her much loved car, her 1971 red Datsun 240Z, her stylish piece of retro culture on wheels, into a vacant parking space, zipping in ahead of a clapped-out Ford Cortina. The driver, a man of about fortyish or so with pronounced veins on his forehead and eyes popping with anger, had leaned out of his window and yelled at her that this was his spot, he always parked there, get out of it. Other spaces were vacant nearby and her stubbornness came up like a wall. 'Too late,' she'd said to him with her sweetest smile as she got out of her car and walked away. That was Jeffo, someone had told her later, he was on the team with her. He's nasty, you watch out for him.

'I don't care at all. Where to?' she replied honestly, with edge, tossing back some irritation of her own.

'The morgue. You know where that is? McMichael's managed to fit the professor in sooner rather than later. He's put some poor electrocuted woman and her broken-hearted husband on hold just for us. So let's feel privileged. You ready to go?'

'Sure.'

'A girl,' he said as she pulled out into the traffic. 'Little. Not old. Not much to know about someone who just shot both your parents in a back alley in Chippendale, is it? Why would she do something like that?'

'Obsession?' Grace replied, startled by the question and uncertain whether or not an answer was wanted from her. 'If you go after someone like that, you usually have to be obsessed with them in some way. It sounded to me like she had tunnel vision. She didn't even see Matthew until he was right there in front of her. I don't think she even twigged who he was.'

'I think that's spot on, Gracie. I don't think she saw anything at all except what was at the other end of that gun. When we find her, we'll ask her, won't we? I'll sit on one side of the table and she'll sit on the other and she won't tell me anything that makes any sense of this at all. We'll all just wonder why.'

He sat with his mobile phone in his hand, tapping it as he spoke, a strained, absorbed expression on his face. Grace looked at him sideways, surprised by what he had said. He didn't fit her preconception of the ferociously ambitious workaholic she had been warned to expect. She had thought he would be ragged and frenetic. Instead, his movements were unhurried and his expression was mainly indifferent. He was younger than she had expected and he had the kind of appearance an advertising agency might use to sell any make-believe Australian product from insecticide to financial services. The hair was receding a little at the temples, and there were suggestions of fatigue around the grey eyes. These and the possibility of a little too much preoccupation adding fault lines to his longish face were blemishes a marketing manager might balk at. But the clothes fitted. Suit, tie, colour, style, he must have spent time in front of the mirror adjusting them to be just right. It was a presentation for climbing ladders, a working disguise, you couldn't know what he was. She smiled faintly to herself. Are you a liar? And if you're not, then who are you? These were her first unspoken questions whenever she met anyone. He was watching her as she stopped at a set of traffic lights. Stop looking at me, she said to him in her mind, I get tired of being looked at.

'Don't mind me,' he said. 'I've got to make some phone calls. I'm not trying to be impolite.'

'There is just one thing,' she said. 'Do you mind not calling me Gracie? Thanks.'

Grace was not going to be Gracie to someone she had met for the first time that morning and who went by the title of her boss. Harrigan looked at her in some surprise.

'I don't care. Whatever you want. Do you mind if I get on with it?'

He gestured to his phone.

'Go for it,' she said very quietly, looking ahead.

I don't care either, pretend I'm not here. I'm the greenhorn, I'll just drive the car. I need my thoughts to myself for a little while anyway.

She needed this stretch of time to push out of her head, or at least appease, her visions of the last few hours, among them Matthew Liu locked into a tight, dry-eyed knot on his chair in a hospital waiting room. She had thought she was ready for this kind of extremity, had dusted off her rhino hide to take on this kind of violence. To face it and deal with it. She put this mantra on with her make-up every day together with all the other pieces of her armour. This morning, the sight of blood slicked on a city road had left a more poisonous aftershock than she had been prepared for. She thought of her coat, tossed carelessly onto the back seat of the car, remembering the touch of warm dampness where the stains had been cleaned away from the lapel, before focusing solely on the drive ahead.

2

The garage doors slid shut with the crash of sheet metal echoing into an empty space. Lucy Hurst listened as their reverberations stilled in an intensified silence. Around her, from the transom windows set up high in the brick walls, intermittent sunlight streaked dusty diamond shapes across the pearl-grey shadows. The thinned-out light touched on the stained concrete floor, the white Mazda she had parked in the centre of the deserted garage, and was then reflected as an oily, metallic brilliance as it passed over a deep trench of water near the car. Rain, seeping in under the wide metal doors, had flowed down the ramp to fill the garage pit over time. Lucy stopped beside the trench, calming her breathing.

As she stood there, the key to the garage doors slipped unhindered, almost unnoticed, from her hand and fell into the black water. The silence deepened as the barely perceptible sound of the splash faded. She stared down into the pit, watching as the obscure reflection of her own face was broken apart by the spreading concentric circles of water. Her breathing slowed as time stopped. The noise of distant traffic on Anzac Parade, several streets away, existed in another world. She listened, waiting. Under the continuous rumbling of the trucks and buses grinding their way through the city's external arteries, she heard another sound, a soft, pervasive sound, the faint calling voices of young children crying. It silenced every vibration, every other sound. She answered their crying in the silence of her own thoughts. I'm listening to you. Listen to me back. Listen to this. Listen to it. In her memory, the roar of the shots she had fired faded into stillness.

Now, in this drab place, even the shadows became comforting to her. She felt them fold about her as peaceably as a blanket, not necessarily soft or warm, but giving succour in the absence of any other shelter. She could breathe in the quiet, even with the smell of the dust and diesel. She felt an easing of her constrictions, the bindings which were usually pulled tight like a length of swaddling cloth or a shroud around her chest began to loosen and unwind. Briefly, she felt a sense of lightness new to her, a cleanness, the feeling that her body had dissolved.

Lucy drew in breath the way thirsty people drink water and walked towards the back of the garage. Here, a set of temporary offices had once been fashioned out of partitions made from grey painted wood and frosted glass. She went into one of these small rooms and turned on the bare light bulb. Opposite she saw a face in the pock-marked mirror above a washbasin, the likeness of some other unknown girl staring at her with fierce eyes. There were dark streaks on her forehead, across her eyebrows and into the line of her hair. Lucy brushed her fingers across her own forehead, watching as the reflection did likewise, and felt those dried, crumbling ridges in wonderment. She remembered, the flash of an achromatic image, her recall reducing blood to the texture of oil. The man's ruined face, his blood instantaneously on her face and clothes, touching her with the same sensation as warm viscous water. With a broken fingernail, she scratched at the dust this blood had become and stared at herself.

She was uncertain how long it was before she went to the basin and turned on the tap. Her hands hurt as she did so, both were grazed, she did not know how this had happened. Cold, rusty water came pouring out; she bent her head underneath the icy flow and let it wash the thin streaks of blood into the iron-coloured stream. In the mirror, water dripped from a face white as a carving out of bone.

I don't have a gun any more. Her thought was loud in the silence. Something essential to her was missing. She remembered. She had hurt her hands when she lost the gun; she had tripped on her way back to her car, landing heavily and tearing her cheap gloves. The gun had slipped out of her hand and skidded out of reach across the lane, the metal sparking on the rough bitumen, and she had not stopped to pick it up. It was there still, waiting for someone else to find it. She closed her eyes at the realisation and expunged all thoughts from her mind.

She pushed her short wet reddish-brown hair back from her high forehead and turned away. She had things to do, things she had to do. She sat on her crumpled sleeping bag on a pallet on the floor and changed her clothes, stripping away the outward signs of the shooting, leaving blood-stained shoes, torn jeans, her jacket in a crumpled heap on the floor, emerging in clean clothes to display a small body that possessed an elastic thinness. Work. She focused on this single word and looked at the table, where a stolen slimline notebook computer, with means to connect to the Internet through a mobile telephone, waited to be used. This was what she had come here to do: not to hide but to work. Things which were unfinished had to be cleaned up, closed off.

She sat down in front of the computer, hesitated and then hit the space bar. At the touch of a few keys, bright expensive software danced across the screen and Lucy began to re-energise her virtual world. She was travelling inwards, to a place of her own making, whose existence and shape, even the trajectory by which she reached it, had been fabricated by her alone. Light from the screen's radiance played on her face as she opened up onto the screen her kaleidoscope of moving shapes and colours. This world absorbed her, its geography was her visionary endgame. She had created it, building up its structures, moving the pieces about in patterned strategies whose outcomes she had known from the beginning.

At its heart was the foundation image, the centre onto which she had grafted all her other images of expanding complexity. Lucy had half believed that by some strange transference of events, Dr Liu might have been erased from the website as she, Lucy, had erased her from life that morning. Instead, the doctor remained where Lucy had placed her from the beginning, lying in a replica of the street she had lain in that morning in Chippendale, shot dead. In this familiar screen image, the buildings around the prone woman were burning and the street was littered with debris from a shattered landscape, everything shining with the green-ant glow of nuclear poison.

There were images missing from this crossover world, unforeseen events which Lucy had encountered in the actual world less than an hour ago. Events which she needed to build into her website to allow her electronic vision to replicate actuality, to ease the memory by binding them into a pictogram. The man with the ruined face also lying dead beside the woman on the roadway, and a boy, staring at her from a distance close enough for her to touch him. As she drew on this memory it took control of her, flooding her thoughts. Her hands on the keyboard became weighted, frozen in action.

She had intended to kill the woman. She had not thought she would ever have to use the gun on anyone else, she did not remember how she had. No one else was supposed to be there. The sound of the first shot had deafened her and she was caught in an airlock, breathless and vacant with the shock, staring at the red stain soaking into the woman's blue jacket. Then the man was there in front of her without warning, so close that he was almost in her face. As she stared at him, his face was suddenly and almost immediately unmade. She did not remember feeling the recoil of the gun.

She dropped a curtain in her mind over the memory. With a jerky, clumsy movement, she hit the close button and watched her other world fold back into its icon on the screen, collapsing inwards like a magician's stream of silk scarves. Its absence left behind a clear blue light which shone out of the computer like a benediction.

Lucy dived into the light, out onto the web, desperate.

Turtle, it's the Firewall. Are you out there? If you are, please talk to me, I need to talk turtle with you if you're there. Please say you are.

I'm here like I'm always here Firewall Wotzup??? Early 4u

For some few moments, Lucy did not type anything.

Firewall????

I did it.

U did wot???!!! Firewall u are joking U must be

No, I'm not.

U have 2 tell me u did not U are lying 2 me!

No, I did.

I don't believe u. It's not possible U couldn't do that

I did. Surf in and find out if you don't believe me because it's probably on the web by now. But I did it. In Chippendale, just like I said I would. And if you don't believe me, I can tell you things about it they probably won't want to tell you. But I did do it.

I don't get u. Why?????

I've already told you why. You don't have to ask me that.

I don't mean all that wild stuff u talk all the time I mean why? 4 real

Someone had to do it. That was me. It isn't any more complicated than that.

Bullshit!!! I know u I know wots in your head ok??? U didn't have 2 do this No way did u have 2 do this

Lucy sat staring at her keyboard, rubbing her forehead hard with her hands before typing again.

You say that but it's not true. It was something I had to do. All last night, I was here in my sleeping bag and I saw it so clearly in my mind. You know better than anyone what it's like to see things so clearly in your head like that. It was like that woman was standing in front of me in this blue light and I saw her for what she was. She was evil. I knew what I had to do. Your head takes you everywhere. But I can move, I can walk, and that means I have to do things. I have to go out into the world and I have to do things. I had to do what I did. It's that simple.

I had 2 do it I had 2 do it That's just a wall u put up. Nothing real U just say that because u can't tell me why u did do it

No, it did have to be done. It was horrible, okay? And it was. It was horrible. But it had to happen. But that isn't it, that's not what I wanted to tell you. Because I did something that really was wrong. Something I should never have done ever. And I don't know what to do about it now.

Wot could be worse???

Shooting someone else as well. He was right there in front of me. He was so close. Almost as close as my computer is now. I guess he wanted my gun, I didn't think about that before. I just fired. I didn't even know I had. But his face — Turtle, he looked — I didn't think it would look like that. I'm asking, what have I done?

Wot did u think it would look like????? Wot are u saying this 4??

There was a kid there. He saw everything. I don't know, Turtle. What do I do?

Go 2 police Now

I'm not doing that. What's the point of that? Everything I've done would be wasted.

It's wasted anyway Nothing but waste U can't say it's anything else It doesn't matter wot u do now Firewall This is never going away 4 u

Well, maybe I don't care. Maybe what I did to that

man and that boy is not so bad because maybe they deserved it. They knew what she did.

Bullshit U stop U stop right there U think I deserved being like this??? U want me 2 say that u deserved everything that's happened 2 u?? Do u want people 2 say that about u??? What do u think they're going 2 say u deserve right now?

I didn't say that. I'd never say you deserved what happened to you, Turtle. You can't think that. It isn't fair.

I said I know u Firewall U & me are both fucking cripples, right?? So fucking wot??? Doesn't mean we have 2 do things like this Do u want me 2 hate u for this? And say u deserve that? I could do that but I won't

It fucking is not the same. Anyway they're both dead now so what's the point of saying that?

Firewall u cant do this & walk away U cant

I can't keep talking now, I've got to go. I've got to get out into the air. I'm going but I'll be back. Love you, Turtle, love you always.

Lucy cut the connection before Turtle could reply and left her final words hanging in cyberspace.

'I have to get out of here.' She spoke aloud to the small room as she disconnected and folded up the notebook. She could not breathe, the quietness had begun to jangle. This place was haunted by her own ghosts, she could never come back here again. She pushed her sleeping bag and computer, her mobile phone, all her acquired and stolen things into her backpack. She walked out of the disused office quickly, leaving her stained clothes in a heap on the floor, and let herself out of the garage by a side door without once glancing at the stolen and now abandoned car.

* * *

She was ordinary, no one would look at her twice. Just a small young woman, nineteen perhaps, dressed in jeans and a white shirt, wearing a black hooded raincoat and lace-up shoes like a schoolgirl's, carrying a compact backpack. Stepping out into ruined streets where the houses had been demolished to make way for a new housing development. Walking through the rain past the cyclone wire fences, turning the corner towards the bus stop on Anzac Parade, passing a white-painted brick building sandwiched between a three-storey block of flats and a takeaway food bar. She paused to look at the white building as she went by, checking the red and white sign: The Women's Whole Life Health Centres Inc., Randwick Clinic. Then she was just anyone else, a student perhaps, catching the bus to Central Railway Station on a winter's day.

She sat next to a large woman in an orange coat who declared a boundary dispute by wedging her shopping basket against Lucy's legs. The skin of ordinary life settled over her like a muzzling cloth. The bus was full, the air steamy from the passengers' wet clothing, their tangled hair. The sound of the bus driver's radio fought against the noise of traffic and the softer voices of the packed-in travellers. Lucy listened to the talkback show host's relentless patter as the bus edged forward in the slow traffic. Her breathing was suspended as he began to announce in his clipped and angry voice: *Well, folks, this has just been put in front of me. I want you to know what sort of society we're living in today. A sick society, that's what. A man has just been shot dead outside a women's health clinic in Chippendale. And his wife, seriously, critically injured. So a man goes to* work, with his wife, and someone decides to walk up to him out of the blue and shoot him dead. What sort of a sick person does that? Do you think gaol's too good for someone who does that? Or maybe just this once we should be trying to make the punishment fit the crime? You ring and tell me. You know the number to call.

The woman beside Lucy stirred, snorted and muttered angrily to herself.

'People like that deserve anything they get. Useless, this government is. Why didn't Howard bring back the death penalty when he got in? None of them are good for anything. If they asked us what we wanted, we'd have it back today.'

Lucy raised her chin and stared at the back of the head of the passenger in front of her, a mass of damp black curls. What would they know? What would any of them know?

The bus had stopped near the Elizabeth Street entrance to Central Station. The woman was trying to get off and pushed vigorously against Lucy. 'Aren't you going to move?' she said.

Ignoring her, Lucy left the bus. The centres of her hands were wet, her grazed palms stung. A line of watchers sat on the low wall near the corner of Eddy Avenue, out-of-towners, the unemployed, derelicts. Near them, a busker sat with his back against the sandstone wall darkened by traffic fumes. His fair hair was tied back in a long ponytail and he played sweet tunes on a trumpet for the passers-by and the unending traffic.

Lucy walked past their collective watchful gaze, through the brown sandstone columns of the station entranceway, down into the concourse towards the ticket offices and the public toilets. People flowed either side of her. She felt that she had opened a door onto a room where someone should have been waiting for her but which in reality was so empty she might have been the very first person to step inside it. Her skin was scorched. The children's voices came rushing back into her head, their soft cries touching her cheek like the brush of tiny insects' wings before stinging her with their sharp acidic bites. She walked, weighted by this impossible duress, the noise in her head, fear and the constrictions of time binding her to this body, this place.

Her head cleared. The concourse, with its shifting crowds, came back to a washed-out reality. She was at the start of the open walkway that led past the florists, newspaper sellers and fast-food merchants down to Eddy Avenue. Indifferent commuters glanced at her as they made their way through the scrappy weather to the suburban trains. She remembered why she had chosen to come here. She went down to the roadway and crossed over to Belmore Park.

She saw who she was looking for in the gazebo under the Moreton Bay fig trees. A group of hungry boys who had climbed up onto the railings and were perched there, barely out of the weather, a chorus of ragged crows watching over the people who walked through the park. One of them, maybe fifteen and wearing a khaki coat and a dark red beanie over his straggling hair, climbed down as she walked towards them and came hurrying to meet her.

'Luce,' he said, quietly and urgently, 'where've you been? I was wondering if you were going to show up here. Look, I heard these two people got shot down near Broadway. You didn't do it, did you?'

'I did. Maybe a couple of hours ago? I don't know when. Yes, I did do it.'

Her voice shook as she spoke. She took hold of him

instinctively and he caught her by the shoulders. They hung on to each other desperately in the grey weather.

'Oh, Lucy, you didn't! Why? What did you come back here for? It's so close to where it happened. What if the pigs see you?'

'They don't know who I am. You're not going to tell them. I wanted to see you. I've got to sit down. I feel like I'm going to fall over.'

They sat on a bench at the edge of the open grass, close to each other in the damp cold. Lucy hugged her backpack, burying her face into it for a few short moments.

'It was just supposed to be her, Greg. But there was some man there and I shot him too.' She looked up at him, almost whispering. 'I didn't plan to do that but I just did. I don't know how. And he's dead now.'

He stared at her and then at the ground.

'Luce. Shit! Why did you? What are you going to do now?'

She shrugged.

'I don't know. I just don't know. And there was this kid there. Staring at me. I can still see him. And she isn't dead, that woman. I heard it on the radio. She's not dead.'

'Shit, Luce,' the boy said again. 'This ambulance went by here a while back and it was *screaming*! You don't reckon —'

They looked over towards the traffic on Eddy Avenue and the dark yellowish-brown façade of the railway colonnade on the other side of the road. The line of trees and the castle-like stone edifice of the station blocked out the grey sky.

'I don't know. I don't want to think about it. It was horrible, you know. There was all this blood and it was on me. It was just so horrible.'

'Fuck!' The boy was frightened. 'You get a car? Anyone see you?'

'No, that's okay, I did all that. And I got back to the garage okay. I left the car there and everything, like I said. But I lost the key to the garage, it fell out of my hand. It went in the pit. I didn't know what I was doing. It was really strange. It was horrible but it was just so easy as well. You know, you just do it and it happens, and that's it, it's over. Just like that, it's all over and done with? It's *so* quick. I thought it'd be different. I know Graeme said it'd happen really fast and I shouldn't worry about that, but I still thought there'd be more to it than that. I didn't think it would be like that.'

Her voice was shaking as she spoke. He looked at her once; after that they sat for a while in silence, staring at nothing.

'You want a smoke?' he asked.

'Yeah.'

He rolled a cigarette for each of them. Her hands were shaking too much to hold the match and he lit it for her. He sat beside her, frowning.

'Fuck you, Luce, why did you do it?' The words burst out of him too loudly. She tried to quieten him but he shook her off. 'Just because Graeme —'

'It's not "just because Graeme",' she replied in a tight, bitter voice.

'It is. Don't you say that to me. He put you up to this and you let him.'

'No. He didn't. I mean that, Greg. He didn't. I went after this. Me. I did. You can't change that.'

'Fucking bullshit!'

'No, it's true.' Lucy frowned. She dropped her barely smoked cigarette onto the wet ground. 'I can't smoke, I can't do anything. My throat's so tight, I can't breathe.'

'Why don't you come over to Wheelo's? You can hide out there for a while. He'll have something to loosen you up a bit.'

She shook her head.

'No, I don't want to do that. I've got to go back and have a look. I've got to make sure I really did it. Weird.'

They sat there for a few moments longer. People walking through the park glanced at them then looked away. A woman stared; the boy made a lewd face at her and she hurried on. Lucy stood up quickly, hoisting her backpack.

'I've got to go. And I've got to see Graeme as well, I promised him I'd go and see him. He said to me last night, you know, if your courage fails you, don't worry. You just come back here to me anyway and we'll talk and we'll see where we go from there. Well, I am. He's got to tell me this is okay.'

'Oh yeah, and it's got nothing to do with him —'

'You don't understand it.'

'I don't want to. You didn't have to do this. You shouldn't have, Luce. You're the one who gets to live with it, not him. You know, for the rest of your life, when you wake up in the morning, you're always going to know you did this. But he's not. He's just going to lie there and jerk himself off and not give a shit. Anyway, it's too fucking dangerous. They put you away for ever for things like this.'

There was a silence in which they looked at each other.

'No,' she said, 'it wasn't Graeme. It's me. All right? It's me.'

'*It fucking is not!*'

The boy threw his own cigarette on the ground. She looked around, not knowing what to say. For the first time, she thought she might cry.

'When am I going to see you next?' he asked.

'Later on. This evening. I'll see Graeme and I'll come by Wheelo's later. I might sleep there if that's okay.'

'Yeah, that's okay. I'll see you there. I'm not going back to the refuge now. There's no way I'm going to stay at Preacher Graeme's community fucking refuge ever again after this. I don't care if I am supposed to be living there. I don't care what you say about him, that guy just fucking scares me so much, I don't like going near him anyway. But I am never going anywhere near him again after this. You shouldn't have let him do this to you, Luce. Not ever.' He was shaking his head angrily. 'You promise me you'll be there tonight?'

'Yeah, I promise.'

'Okay.'

He rubbed his face. The anger had gone out of his voice, now he was only sad.

'Fuck you, Luce, the things you do. You be there. We've got to work out what we're going to do now.'

'I'll be there.'

She walked away, back across the park to the street, turning to wave goodbye to him as she went, and saw him, still seated and waving back to her, as she waited to cross the road.

3

In Railway Square the traffic flowed in a solid roar and the rainy air smelled of petrol. Lucy, lost in her thoughts, barely saw the crowds around her. No, Greg, it's not just Graeme. You should know that, you know me, we've been together for a while now. We've slept in doorways, under bridges, anywhere there was a bit of warmth. You and me hanging on to each other with nothing but old clothes and newspapers between us. You've seen me when I'm wasted and the only thing I want to feel is nothing. When the only thing that keeps me going is the blood pumping through my veins because I can't fucking stop it. Sometimes I want that blood to run down the nearest drain and take me with it. But it's not just mine any more, it's someone else's as well. I think it must be painted all over the sky.

She looked up, breaking out of her trance; the expanse of sky above the station was grey. The roadway opened into George Street, taking the traffic past the verdigris steeple of Christ Church St Laurence before moving on towards the harbour. She was travelling in the opposite direction, past the ugly, squared tower of the University of Technology. In the last year, she had spent hours inside its student computer rooms, out of the heat or the chill of the day, opening up new worlds through a false student account. Knock on the right door at UTS after hours and someone who was just a boy, white-faced and quietly spoken, would give you a log-on ID and a password for nothing, with no questions asked. Lucy had not tried to guess his reasons for doing this; she no longer asked herself why anyone did what they did. That question had been replaced in her mind a long time ago by others. Are there any limits to what people do? Why do they like to be so cruel to each other? When she asked this aloud, people laughed and called her stupid.

The questions drove her as she gained skill in using the software and built her own website, both in the computer rooms and on her own stolen machine. Everything she fashioned worked around this insoluble puzzle, which never gave ground to her. Duplicating the things she had met with in her life and seen out on the Sydney streets — beatings, robberies, rape — and fixing them as electronic impulses on a screen, she transformed them into something she could suspend out of time. She was safe in the computer rooms and the events she recreated on her website were controlled, they could not hurt her. She studied the images she built, remaking them if she needed to, trying to understand what it must mean to hurt someone or to shoot them dead.

Today she did not stop, her restless, jerky energy drove her on past the pubs, restaurants and takeaway bars to the serrated wall of the Carlton brewery.

Further up Broadway, close to the park, stood two old, ornate buildings with elaborate clock towers supporting translucent spheres like fragile crystal worlds. In the middle distance, Lucy saw what she had come to find. The usually swift flow of traffic down Broadway was forced to slow before negotiating a hazard marked by a string of plastic blue police ribbons snapping in the wind. Access to a particular side street had been cordoned off and police cars were parked on the road and the footpath.

Although she had been waiting to see it, she stopped abruptly to lean against the rough wall of the brewery and wait until the blood had stopped pounding in her head. Images from her website began to surge through her mind. In her electronic world, the counterfeit Lucy pulled the trigger, the woman doctor died under the gun, and once that switch was thrown, catastrophe was initiated. The buildings around the doctor began to burn, the sky was split open to rain down green fire, nuclear flame burst out onto Broadway and all the buildings that surrounded Lucy where she stood now, exploded. A fireball roared the breadth of the roadway and ate up stick figures and toy cars.

Outside of her head, in the ordinary daylight, she watched the world move on routinely around her. She was alien to everyone passing her by, someone the crowds would turn on if they knew what she had done. She held the contrasting visions side by side in her head but the electronic images were her true reference points. What existed around her — these buildings, everyday life, tangible things and immovable structures — were hollow, they had no reliable substance. They hid something that stank to her, something that was dead and rotting.

She crossed against the traffic to the other side of the road, just another student from one of the universities. A small crowd had gathered opposite the police cordon, watching and talking underneath the yellow sign outside of St Barnabas's Church that told the passing parade, 'Forgiveness means not having to pretend any more.' Lucy stopped amongst them, looking on, listening.

'Two of them. Someone shot two people. And their boy was there watching.'

The words were taken up by the crowd and spread like an echo from an uncertain source.

That was me. I shot her. I waited for her inside that empty shop and then I went out into the street and I shot her. I shot the both of them.

No one turned on her for her unspoken words. The surrounding buildings were unchanged from their daily aspect. The uniformed police guarding the street looked around at the crowd, their faces expressionless with boredom. She could walk up to them and say, 'You want me. I did that.' Why didn't she? They might only laugh at her, or even become angry, and then wave her on her way. Lucy waited for a few moments longer and then, there being nothing else to do, walked on.

She sat on a bench in Victoria Park, her backpack propped beside her, and stared at the ornamental ponds where the seagulls and ducks huddled in close to the shore. Brief sunlight brought a drab flush of yellow to the thin grass. Lucy glanced back towards Broadway, to the wide intersection where City Road fed its vehicles into the traffic. As the sunlight faded and the weather became dreary and dark, she saw the sporadic glow of headlights from the passing cars and the occasional gleam of neon from the shop fronts on the far side of the road. These lights were the only brightness to touch her; her visionary other-world had grown drab, its vivid dye had bled out of her into the watery air. From here she could see nothing of the police ribbons. She was isolated here. She could pretend that the shooting had never happened; and then, curiously, understood that she did not want to let her act of execution go, however bloody it had turned out to be.

The noise of surrounding traffic hung in suspension. The preternatural quiet held her in a sense of anticipation, she waited as the atmosphere became strangely claustrophobic, strangely lonely. She was chasing another memory down this emptiness. There was sunlight warming her, the sound of magpies carolling in the background, and Graeme's voice as he spoke to her, rich as honey. They were sitting opposite each other at a picnic table someone had set out on the back lawn of a small private hospital.

'Why, Lucy? Why do you need to go and live on the streets the way you do? You've been to school, you have an education. You're an intelligent girl. Why do this to yourself?'

'I'm playing a game. I call it dancing with death. I like doing that. Didn't you know that?'

'Why death? Why not life?'

'Why anything? I can do anything I like, you know.'

There was no other reason why she should have been at that tiny private hospital on the northwestern edge of the city, Greenwood Convalescent, a run-down place with few patients and an ageing doctor. She had been living rough and bingeing, deliberately chancing her luck with heroin. Pushing it, marrying lethal exhilaration with the thought that this rush might be her last chance to see daylight. Grinning to herself each time that she came back to the light and thought, well, I'm still here, maybe next time I won't be. I won't know, will I? Do I care?

Detox was an option forced on her by Greg with the help of Ria, the woman from the Family Services Commission. Greenwood was the only place where she had been able to find Lucy a bed at short notice, tracked down after endless frantic phone calls to unresponsive agencies, none of whom had any space available. Lucy had agreed to go there on the fall of a coin.

Even so, Greenwood was a strange place in which to come to earth. When Graeme introduced himself to her as her counsellor, he was the first normal-looking person she had met. He sat with her when she was in the throes of cold turkey while she told herself this was all the same roller coaster ride, the same coin, just another side, and she could get through it, she could survive anything. The underlying rule of Lucy's game was that she took the consequences of her actions full on. She hung on to every ache and sweat, every gripping pain, as a gift. Pain *was* a gift, something in the fibre of her body which could be relied upon to assert her existence when everything else had deserted her. On the streets, anything was a currency and pain could be traded along with everything else. Plenty of people dealt in pain for the pleasure of it, looking for people to hurt, setting traps in public toilets and on empty beaches, boasting later, did you see what I did to them? She'd never had the stomach for that. Her pride lay in what she could endure. If you couldn't give pain, you took it: took it without showing you felt it and that made you as good as anyone else.

When the mists cleared and her roller coaster ride

came to an end, she began to spend time with Graeme in the hospital garden, an overgrown place shaded by white eucalyptus trees. She was shaky from the brutal process, groggy with tranquillisers, smoking cigarettes one after the other. Graeme sat on the other side of the table, smiling as they talked. She watched him cynically through the spirals of cigarette smoke.

'What are you doing here?' she asked, insolently throwing back his own questions. 'Why should you give a shit about me? You're being paid to care, aren't you? Because Ria sent me here from Family Services. You get paid for it.'

'No, Lucy. I'm not being paid by anyone. You being here is a purely private arrangement. I actually do care what happens to you,' he replied. 'But if you want to know, I'm rebuilding my life as well. I'm just back from many happy years in the United States, the last few in California. The sun gets to you there, it wears you out a little. It's a bit like here. But, of course, this is home.'

'Yeah, I guess,' she said indifferently.

California was a mythical location for her, some gaudy place on the other side of the ocean made up of names known to her through television shows but whose physical reality was indistinct: Santa Monica Beach, Beverley Hills, Sunset Strip. Out of some strange ghost of politeness, she named these places to him and he smiled again.

'Yes. I've been to all those places. Santa Monica's a beautiful beach. Perhaps you'll go there one day.'

'Yeah, one day maybe I will.'

She looked at him with contempt for the suggestion.

'Why not?' he asked. 'Why shouldn't you?'

She did not bother to reply. She stubbed out her cigarette, and then lit another.

'You didn't answer my question, Lucy. Why are you out there?'

She shrugged. 'Because the world's a piece of shit? Because everyone lives off everybody else? What does it matter what I do? So fucking what.'

'Do you mean that, Lucy? Is that what you really think?'

'Yeah. Don't you think that way sometimes? Don't you want to smash things up?'

She stopped, suddenly energyless. He waited for some moments after she had finished talking, looking at her.

'Yes, Lucy, I do. There are many times when I feel like that.'

'Do you?'

His reply sent a jolt of white anger into her head. 'Well, I do it. Smash things. You can do a fucking lot with a brick if you're aiming it at a car. And it's even better if you can get hold of a bit of metal pipe. What do you do? Anything?'

'In my own way, I do quite a lot of things,' he replied. 'I've dedicated my life to it. I know what you mean when you say the world is empty. I understand that.'

'I didn't say empty. I said shit.'

'The meaning doesn't change. The world is rotten. Its decay reaches up to Heaven. It's that decay you smell, all the stench that is the world's corruption.'

She shrugged again, surprised, uncertain how to reply.

'And you are out there, Lucy, because the world is shit, as you call it?'

'Yeah, I am,' she said, very softly.

Her cigarette was finished again. She rubbed her eyes before lighting another. There was a pause and she began to talk as she rarely did.

'I get sick of being out there though. You get hungry. I don't stay out there all the time now, I come and go. I get rooms to live in, sometimes I can get the dole. And I work too. I've had jobs. Even me.' She laughed cynically. 'But you know how I mostly live? I steal. It's the only thing I am good at. I've never been caught. I get tired though. I keep thinking, why am I out here, what am I going to do now?'

There was silence as she smoked.

'In the end I just go back there. I keep going back because there isn't anywhere else. I think that really is where I'm supposed to be.'

'There's something you're not telling me, Lucy. Why are you so badly hurt? What happened to you?'

He seemed to speak out of genuine concern. Lucy had a test for people who said they were concerned for her, she knew how to prove they were liars. She reached into the pocket of her jeans and took out a small plastic wallet which contained a square of shiny dark blue material. She unwrapped the material and placed on the table a torn scrap of letterhead.

Because of this. Because this was the day. When she had thought, this is the end of the world for me, they can't do this to me any more.

'You really want to know about me?' she asked. 'Okay. You look at this. And you go and work it out. If you know so much.'

She pushed the piece of paper towards him and he picked it up.

'You be careful with it,' she snapped.

Her words, deliberately cryptic, were intended to make it clear to him that he couldn't know, he couldn't understand. No one could; it was knowledge privileged to her. No one could have the gall to pretend they knew. She looked at him. Go on. I dare you. I just fucking dare you.

He smoothed the torn paper flat onto the table. A scrap Lucy had ripped from a doctor's note pad when no one was looking. Dr Agnes Liu. MB, BS (Syd.), FRACOG, MRCOG. The Women's Whole Life Health Centres Inc.

'I know this woman,' he said eventually. 'I know her very well.'

'You can't.'

'But I do, Lucy. Why shouldn't I? I know what this woman is, better than most. But not, I think, better than you. She's an abortionist. A murderer. And someone took you to her, didn't they? You didn't go yourself. Someone took you there for the slaughter, Lucy. Because that's what it was. A dual murder. You and your child. Isn't that what happened?'

His clear eyes had become almost expressionless as he spoke to her. She had nodded, unable to speak at first. She thought that she was feeling nothing.

'My mother. Dragged me there. Twice. Didn't even tell me where we were going. The first time they sent me on to hospital because I had this miscarriage right there in the reception. The second time round I worked out for myself what was going to happen.'

It was as much as she could say to begin with. He waited for her to continue. She spoke again, quickly, her words tripping over each other, as unstoppable and irretrievable as the gush of opened veins.

'It was my dad. Did it to my little sister as well. Tried to anyway. I couldn't stop him. Stevie did though. He's my brother. He's not as big as Dad so he didn't help me. But when I left and he worked out what Dad was trying to do to Mel, he said he couldn't handle it. He knocked Dad right out of the door, said he'd kill him if he touched her. He told me Mum just stood there with her mouth open. Dad's a coward, you know. He never went near Mel again.'

Lucy laughed with relief as she talked.

'Do you know my dad's got cancer now? Did I tell you that? Stevie told me he hasn't got that long to go. He's playing around with dying too now. I can say to him, hey, Dad it's you and me now. We're both at the same game. How do you feel about that?'

Her voice was shaking.

'And your mother took you to this woman.' Graeme tapped the piece of paper. 'And she helped your mother and your father hide from the world what he had done to you. Because that is what this woman is. Someone who has no conscience. Let me tell you what happened to you in there, Lucy, in that clinic — and let's give it its true name, a Hellhole. She raped you once more. That's what happened to you there. An evil, evil thing.'

The words entered her memory, fixing themselves as unconditional and unshakable truth, as tangible to her as the scrap of paper she always carried with her. The images of her memory converged. The fixed injury impressed onto her by her father — still felt, to the point that she wanted sometimes to scrub away her skin — coalesced into its parallel remembrance, the entry of steel into her vagina.

'Yeah. That's exactly what she did. You don't know what happens in there. They hook you up, she cleans you out — it's like you're fucking nothing. And no one cared. They didn't give a shit. How could she do that?'

Lucy had taken back the scrap of paper and begun folding it up, compressing it. Her actions were repetitive, compulsive. She did not cry. Relief was spilling through her, her heart had opened out. She felt a strange lightness, an intoxication. Her mouth was open, her breathing sharp and shallow, breath that did not get down into her lungs.

'Do you know what she said to my mum when we were driving away? She came out after us — Mum said she almost ran her down in the car park. Do you know what she said?' She was staring at the piece of paper that she had folded small. 'About me. She said to my mother, she can't have sex for a fortnight. I thought, fuck you. No one is ever coming near me again, I don't care what you say. I was gone after that. As soon as I got home and I could get out of there. I was gone.'

'Let me have that piece of paper, Lucy,' he said to her gently. 'You can trust me with it. I promise.'

She held it, her hands still shaking, feeling that to give it away was to give up some essential piece of herself. Even so, she handed it to him as he had asked.

'You've got to be careful with that,' she said. 'The second time I was there, at that clinic, I took it. It's to remind me that's when I said, I'm out of here, I'm gone for ever. You can't lose it.'

'I will be careful with it. This is a very precious piece of paper, Lucy. Wait here for me. Trust me.'

After he had gone, she lit another cigarette. Her hands continued to shake. When he came back, he placed a file on the table and took out of it a photograph of a woman's face, scrawled with the word 'Murderer' and splashed with a translucent red dye.

'This is her, isn't it?' he asked.

'Yeah, it is.'

He smoothed out the torn paper and attached it to the photograph on the file, then set the documents between them.

'Yes,' he said, 'this piece of paper is very important. You see, Lucy, this woman and you, you are connected. And that connection is indissoluble. This is her fate, Lucy, this scrap of paper. This paper is her crime against you, against God, against the world, and it is also her fate.'

He spoke as though they were two old friends who had always understood each other and who alone knew the real truth. He tapped the stains on the photograph.

'Do you see the blood on this woman? This is your blood. She can't escape you now because you know what she is. A mass murderer. A serial killer. You are one of her survivors. You can accuse her. You can stand up before the world and say, this woman is my murderer. Someone who is paid to kill and takes pleasure in it. Someone who smiles each time another victim walks out of her abortuary carrying the same scars that torment you now. But she doesn't care. It was your blood that she spilt, Lucy, your blood and the blood of your child. But she doesn't care.'

The vehemence with which he spoke surprised her.

'It was my dad too. And my garbage mother. It wasn't just her.'

'But your mother is a weak and foolish woman. And your father has been accounted for now, hasn't he? He will answer for what he has done to you very soon. But not this woman. She is still out there, still free and practising her trade. On young girls like you.'

Lucy said nothing. Her cigarette hung from her fingers, burning, ash falling on the table.

'She could have been worse,' she said after a while. 'Tried not to hurt me, I guess.'

'That isn't the point, is it?'

No, it wasn't. Lucy looked at the rough surface of the picnic table. Cruelty. This was her word, she sought it out and repeated it to herself, it carried the weight of her memory. The doctor asking her all those so-what questions. *Is this what you want?* How do I fucking know? She had said only the quietest word in reply. Yes. She just wanted it over with.

She did not say any of this. She sat there shaking these thoughts out of her head while he watched her. She dropped her cigarette to the ground and did not crush it out. She could not speak, she sat with her hands in front of her mouth. He looked at her with his clear and gentle eyes.

'I hate her, you know, for what she did to me. I hate them all. Mum, Dad. You shouldn't do that sort of thing to people.'

'She does what she does, Lucy, because she's a murderer, pure and simple. She killed your child and tried to kill your spirit. But in your strength, you survived to bear witness. She should fear you. Because you know her.'

'You know what I hear sometimes?' Lucy said after a few moments. 'I don't know why. Kids crying, little kids. I hear them in my head. They stay with me. Sometimes I think they are me.'

He smiled at her and closed the file.

'I know of others who have been tormented like that. They don't let you rest, do they? We'll find a way to make them go away. You see, Lucy, here you are with people who understand you. Sit there. Try and relax your spine.'

He stood behind her and placed his hands on her shoulders. He began to massage her neck, working at the tight knot of muscles. She felt his closeness, the human warmth, the imprint of his reassuring hands.

'Listen to me. Those voices in your head. They are the

voices of your heart as you say. But they're your children as well.'

'No,' she said, 'they didn't ever exist. I don't want them to.'

'But they did exist. They were living. They were your children and they are still living. You and they are indivisible, it's their grief that you're hearing.'

'I just wish they weren't there. I want them to leave me alone, that's all.'

'No, Lucy. Listen to them. They are asking you to give them rest. You can do for them what was never done for you: you can give them redress. Vengeance is mine, says the Lord. You have a right to vengeance, Lucy.'

He continued the slow massaging for some moments, then stopped and rested his hands lightly on her shoulders.

'We know who Agnes Liu is, Lucy. We've known about her for a long, long time. It's not chance that's brought you here. This is ordained. You came here to be made clean and you will be. You came here for peace of mind and you will find it. Now you wait here. You just wait.'

When he came back, he placed a gun, compact and metal blue, on the table in front of her. She looked at it for some moments. She shook her head to say she did not understand.

'Have you ever fired a gun before?' he asked.

'No,' she said. 'I know about them being out there and all that, and people getting hold of them. But I've never had to do that.'

He picked up the gun and loaded it with two bullets.

'This is a very special gun. It's one that I had made. I want you to try and use it. Come with me,' he said, 'I'll show you how to fire it.'

He led her to the centre of the lawn and stood behind her as he folded both her hands around the gun. He was not a tall man and her body fitted against his without discomfort, his strength seemed to cushion her. In this serenity and the closeness of his human presence, she had felt a suspension of time, a sense of the peacefulness he had promised. She let her body relax.

'When you're ready,' Graeme said to her soothingly. 'No one can hear us out here. Call on your strength. And then fire. Twice. You can do it.' He stepped away from her.

The shots crashed out, she rocked on her feet. Graeme did not quite laugh as he watched her trying to shake the ringing sound out of her head.

'It's a little noisy but you get used to it,' he said. 'Let's sit down and talk, Lucy.'

They had sat down on a stretch of grass much more lush than the winter-starved turf that surrounded her now in the public park. The blue metal finish of the gun lying between them gleamed in the sun. Graeme was a young-looking man with clear brown eyes but as she looked at him Lucy had thought that maybe he was older than he liked to appear. This did not worry her, he had a good-looking face, a comfortable face, and dark hair which had not yet turned grey. She had picked up the gun and weighed it in her hand.

'You have to understand, Lucy, that when you have that gun in your hands, the way you do now, you have the power. No one else owns it, it belongs to you. And then you control whatever happens to you, not the reverse. You need to remember that.'

She did remember, both that and the strange lightness of spirit she had felt in counterbalance to the weight in her hand. He had continued to speak as she held the pistol balanced in her palm.

'You can take this gun and find redress for the sins committed against you, against your unborn children. You, Lucy, are a very strong young woman. You take this gun and you will show the world how strong you are.'

She had sat holding the gun for some moments longer.

'Do you want to load it for me again?' she asked.

'And if I do, what will you do?'

'I'll shoot at that tree.'

'And that's all?'

'What else am I going to do?'

'Guns are there to be used, Lucy. That's why they were created. But you have to use them carefully. They have their designated targets. Your target has already been chosen for you, but I think you know that.'

He reloaded the gun. She looked at the tree and imagined the doctor at the car door, speaking to her mother. She emptied the gun into both imaginary figures, firing as quickly as she could, feeling the force of the bullets as they thudded into the tree.

'I don't want to hurt anyone,' she said, once the gun was empty. 'I don't like hurting people.'

'You won't be hurting anyone,' he replied. 'She'll feel nothing at all, there will be none of the pain she has inflicted on you. You will be cutting a thread, it will be clean and merciful. Blood will wash away blood. You will be left clean. When it's over you will feel nothing except the most blessed relief. The voices of your children will be silent for ever. They, and you, will be at peace.'

She held the gun, unable to prevent herself from feeling a faint emotional rush at possessing it, a sense of swelling that she had somehow grown stronger.

'It's empty again,' she said.

'Yes.'

'So I can't use it on myself then?' she asked suddenly.

'Please don't do that, Lucy,' he said in his softest voice, smiling at her. 'I care about you. Please don't do that to me.'

On the park bench beside the pools of cold water, Lucy's thoughts momentarily gained clarity. No, that would have spoiled everything, wouldn't it? That would have put the kybosh on everything.

The quiet was shaken by a blast from the horn of a truck rumbling past University Hall. The noise shattered the glass shell containing Lucy and her thoughts. She got to her feet and hoisted her backpack on her shoulders, turning her back against the chill wind.

I've used that gun now, Graeme, just like you showed me. Now I'm going to come and talk to you about it, and maybe you can tell me for a second time why I did it.

She walked across the park towards City Road and King Street, a small figure overshadowed by the university buildings crowded onto the perimeter of the parklands. Unnoticed by almost everyone.

4

There were certain things Grace knew she could never do. The sectioning of the dead was one of them, even though the postmortems she had attended were always such matter of fact events. It was only this remaking of dissection as an everyday occurrence which made it bearable for her. Today, that this was just regular, paid work for them all, had the opposite effect, she did not know why.

She watched the attendant wheel Henry Liu to the stainless-steel table then saw him jerk his thumb at the corpse and ask it to get up on the table now if it didn't mind, mate, because they were all in a hurry. Grace felt the joke was on her. She glanced at Harrigan beside her but did not see a flicker of reaction in his face. How did he do it?

The pathologist appeared, Kenneth McMichael, shambling angel of death, a massive man in his surgical gown. Dressed and groomed by St Vinnie's, his coke bottle glasses were flecked with flakes of dandruff from his oily black hair. He leaned over the corpse and took its head in his huge, dexterous hands, turning it this way and that as he studied the wound, as delicately as if he were holding a child.

'Now,' he said, and the word was almost a sigh, 'this is not something you'd be expecting when you got out of bed this morning. Are we dealing with a regular firearm here?' His voice was soft and dry like the crunch of fine sand.

'No, we're not, Ken,' Harrigan replied matter of factly. 'This is very much a one-off. Specially modified to do the maximum amount of damage close up.'

'You can put it down as succeeding in that case,' the pathologist said, with a slightly ironic raising of his eyebrows. 'All right. Let's start.'

Harrigan's expression did not change but Grace was surprised to notice him suppress a recoil to this comment.

On the steel table, technicians stripped the body of its clothes, peeling it to indiscriminate nakedness before charting its fragile geography by x-ray.

'He's not going out dancing tonight,' one said, removing the shirt.

'Not without a makeover,' the other replied.

The pathologist grinned as they spoke and briefly hummed *cha-cha-cha*. With gentle finesse, he welcomed his subject into its permanent silence by sectioning it down to piecework, his soft voice speaking his findings into a cassette recorder. As Henry Liu's body was opened out into its layered complexity, Grace smelled a pervasive odour she had never noticed so vividly before: old blood. It stank, there was no other word for it. She stepped back, giddy on her feet, swallowing. Briefly she thought she would faint.

'Are you all right? Leave if you have to,' Harrigan said.

'No, I'm okay. I'll stay.'

'Is your companion feeling this, Harrigan?'

McMichael was looking at her, unsmiling, for some reason angered. She shook her head.

'Yes, you are,' he said. 'Now why is that? You could even say this is beautiful.'

He gestured to the open cavity of skull on the table in front of them, where the interior bloomed pink and grey into the open air. The attendants were also watching her.

'He was murdered,' she replied. 'People do feel for the dead.'

'Do they?' he asked and leaned on the table, supporting himself with both hands. He smiled at her. 'Autopsy. From the Greek. *Auto*, self. *Optes*, witness. Navel-gazing in other words.' He straightened up and gestured to the corpse with his large hands. 'This is all of us, madam. Remember that, because you'll be here soon enough. You are looking at yourself, that's what's bothering you.'

Grace felt another sickness at the memory of events that might well have placed her here on a table like this, but which, in their final washup, had not. She was alive and standing, but she was also cold to the bone in this steel and tile room where the living mixed with the dead. She stared back at the pathologist: And what would you know about people who can still breathe?

'Ken, we're not in one of your lectures now. Give my officer a break, thanks,' Harrigan interrupted testily. 'Let's move on. We've only got so much time.'

The pathologist smiled as he went back to work in silence. Grace stood still. When McMichael and his assistants were finished, the dead man lay naked on the table, his palms upwards, his eyes still open and staring at the ceiling. What had to be presented to the living had been stitched back together with an easy skill. He had become a figure which, other than to be disposed of, was finished with in every sense. Grace could not make any of the usual connections. If these pieces were not living now, how had they ever been alive? Why couldn't Henry Liu get up, get dressed and walk away? Briefly, the fact of death did not make sense to her, she could not understand it.

'We're finished,' McMichael said. 'Something you can tell your lady friend, Harrigan. We don't do anything wonderful like getting people back on their feet again. Sorry to disappoint her.'

Harrigan was unruffled. 'Thanks, Ken. I'll need your report ASAP, you know that. I'll be waiting on it.'

'I'll see you outside,' Grace said.

She was gone so quickly she left Harrigan slightly confused. He followed her out into the hallway and found himself in the less than congenial position of loitering outside the door to the women's toilet. He stopped a female technician in the corridor.

'I think my officer is in there and she's probably feeling a little light on her feet. Could you check for me if she's okay? Tell her I've gone to the café to get something to eat. She can catch up with me there when she feels up to it.'

'I can do that,' the woman replied, smiling sympathetically.

Grace was holding onto the white porcelain basin for support and looking into the mirror when the technician opened the door and asked her if she was all right.

'Yes,' she replied, trying to smile but otherwise unable to move. 'I'm just redoing my face, that's all.'

'Your boss said to say he's gone over to the Street Café to get something to eat and you might want to join him when you feel like it.'

'Thanks. I'll be there in a little while.'

She spoke with effort, her cheeks pale beneath her façade. The young woman smiled at her in the mirror and went out again.

'Why do I do this?' Grace said to herself, shaking her head and leaning on the basin. She had refused to faint but she had been sick. She looked into the mirror to check her face. Another mirror behind her returned the reflection: she saw the white mask of her make-up repeated in a series of ever diminishing images until it disappeared into the dark. Pulling herself upright, she and the other reflections faced each other as she drew a careful line around her mouth with her dark red lipstick.

'Just look the world in the eye, okay, Gracie? Walk tall,' she said, mocking her own melodrama. She straightened her jacket to give the final touch to her armour and then went out to find the cigarette machine, her coat and the boss, in that order, with that priority.

He must never leave that mobile phone alone. All the way here, he had been talking to somebody or other. Now he was on the phone to someone else again as she walked up to him with a cup of coffee in one hand and a sandwich in the other. His coffee was cooling on the table in front of him, a half-eaten roll beside it.

'How are you?' he asked, returning the persistent object to its holder on his belt. She wondered if he ever thought of turning it off or throwing it away.

'I'm okay,' she replied. 'Do you mind if we sit outside so I can have a cigarette? I know it's a bit cold.'

'You smoke, do you? We're in the right place for you then, you must have a death wish. No, I don't mind just so long as you don't want to smoke in the car. My car's been a cigarette-free zone ever since I gave them away myself.'

I wouldn't dream of it, boss, she thought.

They found a table under an awning, out of the scattered rain and sheltered from the wind which harried litter in small gusts across the tiny stretch of open ground.

'Did you pass out?' he asked as they sat down.

'No.'

'I wouldn't worry about it if you did. It's going to happen to you at least once if you've got half a brain.'

He sounded almost sympathetic. Grace, on the other hand, was reminded of the last few hours and felt an immediate return of nausea. She put down her sandwich and drank coffee instead.

'I'm not lying, I didn't pass out,' she said. 'I felt a little queasy, that's all. I just needed something to eat.'

He drank his own coffee and watched her force her way through the leftovers of her sun-dried tomato and ham sandwich.

'I'm sure you did,' he said when she had finished. 'But want me to tell you the reason you're feeling it now? You saw something of the man. Everything about that boy made his father more real to you. You've got to remember, it's not a person you're dealing with. Whoever they were, they don't exist any more, it's good night for them. A body's nothing, it's a throwaway. See it that way and it can't hurt you.'

He spoke dispassionately, a giver of useful advice. A

brief shower of rain fell on the awning, a sound like a hush as Grace brushed away the crumbs and lit her first cigarette of the day with relief. She glanced out at the passing rain and felt cold at heart.

'Do you have to see it like that?' she replied. 'A body isn't just nothing. Not to the people who cared about him.'

'You're not those people and you can't afford to think like that. Not in there.'

'No? Because if I do, the pathologist will stick the knife into me instead? "This is all of us, madam. Remember that, because you'll be here soon enough."' She heard herself mimicking McMichael's soft dry voice with savage accuracy. 'What a horrible creep he was! Is he always like that?'

To her surprise, Harrigan laughed, much more than what she had said called for. She wondered how much tension he had stored away in there.

'Yeah. He is. A horrible creep,' he said, still laughing. 'And yes, he is always like that. I don't know how often I've heard him give that little speech. He's got a filthy temper. He's reliable, that's the only thing you can say about him. You wouldn't ask him round for dinner.'

He wiped his eyes.

'You've had quite a day, haven't you? We didn't even have to organise it for you. We just tossed you in at the deep end.'

'It's okay, it's not a big deal. This isn't my first job.'

This solicitude embarrassed her, she wanted to brush it away.

'Either way, I wouldn't worry about it. You've handled it well.'

'Thanks,' she replied concisely, blushing faintly under her make-up.

She had always dealt badly with praise. Unconsciously, she touched the raised line of a scar on her neck, a straight thread-like mark beginning with a fish hook near her pulse and finishing above the line of her breast bone. It was a habit all her self-discipline could not suppress. The touch of her fingers wanted to soothe away both the scar and the indelible physical memory of the cut itself. She saw his gaze follow the movement of her hand and, realising what she was doing, stopped. She wondered if he would ask her about it, people did from time to time. There was no point in Harrigan asking her anything: she had no explanations to give, not to anyone, ever. Eight years ago, an ex-lover had held her down and cut that scar into her neck in a few short moments which she had thought would be her last on this earth. She had carried the impression of his body ever since: first inside her, brutally, as he raped her and then his fist in her face until she lost consciousness. He was her personal demon. Time after time she unpeeled him from her memory, only to find him back again when she least expected him, dragging that smell of old bad blood after him, the same odour she had smelled in the dissection room.

'Are you okay to drive?' Harrigan asked, watching her with a slight frown. 'Do you want me to?'

'No, it's fine,' she said. 'Driving's good, I like it. It'll clear my head. Where to this time?'

'Downtown. I've been summoned to a press conference with the Area Commander and sundry other dignitaries. The Area Commander's known as the Tooth for your information, Grace, Marvin Tooth. If you haven't met him yet, that's a joy you can look forward to. Don't forget to count your fingers after you've shaken his hand. You'll probably find a couple missing.'

'I can hardly wait,' she replied with a faint smile. Tell me about him. I already know. She stubbed out her cigarette and reached for the car keys.

'You do have a reason for being in this job, don't you, Grace? I'm sure you do,' he said, as they walked to the car.

Grace had spelled out her reasons for wanting to be here on her enrolment forms ad nauseam.

'I think that's all on file,' she replied.

'I'm not asking you to tell me what they are. It's just that, whatever you think you're doing here, this is just a job. This is how you earn your dough. When you go home at night, you do whatever else you do with your life. You try and turn it into much more than that and you can end up in a lot of trouble. It's not a good idea to put too much pressure on yourself. Other people will do that for you soon enough.'

Maybe they already have. Maybe I've found that out for myself already. Don't be modest, Harrigan, you've made a pretty good fist of it yourself so far today. And if everything I've heard about you is true, since when did you ever act like this is just a job?

In reply, she smiled at him and said nothing. He seemed to be speaking to her in a less detached and more personal way than was usual for him in her brief experience. Even so, she thought it would be a mistake to see this concern as any particular compliment to her. Her information said that ambition drove his interest in other people's welfare. He was known for caring how well his people coped with their work because he wanted outcomes, bottom lines accounted for to those he had to answer to. Grace surmised that his advice was just an expression of his famed 'team approach', summed up as mutual survival, a way of keeping all their heads above water. She was happy to keep everything businesslike. It made life so much easier.

As Grace drove them down Parramatta Road, Paul Harrigan remembered. Or, more accurately, could not stop himself remembering. A hot summer night, twenty-one years ago. A small room with walls painted a dull green and splashed with blood. Bright dark hair (just like his hair), matted and straggling onto the linoleum. In the fluorescent light, how bright that blood was, how liquid, how shining and iridescent, like smudges of engine oil. (You think these things when you're eighteen and you've never seen anyone dead before.) He could not see his mother's face, she lay staring at the skirting board. In the dull light, his father had turned around, still holding the .38 Smith & Wesson revolver. Paul had walked into the room and turned his mother over to look into her face. In the present, he closed his eyes again. For whatever reason, at the trial the jury had accepted his father's plea of an accidental killing. Standing in the dock after the verdict, Jim Harrigan had said in a clear, if shaking voice, 'I never meant to kill Helen. I wish I was dead along with her.'

No, father mine, it wasn't going to happen like that. I made sure you got to live with that memory for the rest of your life. The way I still do. That was the point.

Harrigan drew in his breath too sharply and noticed Grace glance at him curiously. He came back to the world, clearing away his thoughts, that memory. He didn't want to start another day this way again in a hurry. The events he encountered as part of his job didn't usually trouble him like this. He watched and dealt with them as objectively as McMichael dissected his subjects, with a meticulous, almost gentle and uninvolved touch. His approach was like his careful dressing every morning, matching the right colour shirt with the right cut suit, dabbing on the Givenchy aftershave lotion, making sure the exterior he presented to the world was faultless. It was nothing essential to himself, just something to keep out the daily dirt. Today the boy's shock had been too close to the bone. Harrigan's careful separations were contaminated, by the dead man's face painting itself in reverse onto his blue handkerchief (burned to ashes, he hoped, in some incinerator in the morgue) and the streaks of blood down his newest recruit's black coat. As the car came to a smooth halt at a set of lights, he said to himself, as he'd thought at the time: We'll find this person, Matthew, this girl, whatever she is. I will get her. Whatever it takes, I will get her. I will see her locked away for as long as I can.

'Once you've dropped me off at this press conference, Grace, take the car and get over to the hospital again. See if you can find out how the doc's going, and check up on Matthew as well. He felt safe with you. I'd like you to keep an eye on him over the next few weeks. See if you can help him stay with it.'

'Okay,' she said. 'Poor kid. Having to live with seeing that for the rest of his life.'

Her words matched the anger he felt within himself. Often anger just left him drained, but today it'd had a nice clean feel to it. In his own territory, almost under his eyes, someone had blown away two people going about their daily business and left it to him to pick up the pieces. He could see it as an insult to himself as much as anything else if he chose to, an affront to the order he liked to see kept out there. He remembered his own advice to his recruit: see it that way and it can't hurt you.

The lights changed, the traffic moved. He looked sideways at Grace; as she glanced around to check the blind spot, he studied the scar down her neck. A neat scar and a neat cut. Put there, in his opinion, by someone who knew exactly what they were doing. A millimetre to the right and she wouldn't have been driving this or any other car right now. Why would anyone want to do that to her? You have a lovely face, he thought. Not many people who come knocking on my door look anything like you. So why are you bothering with this shit job? You could do anything you wanted. And why do you bother with all that paint? How long did it take her to put it on in the morning? Her hair was braided back from her face, her white make-up picking out its shape like some finely made china mask. Her eyes were dark brown, the eyebrows equally dark, a little thicker than they should have been, her mouth dark red with lipstick. He'd watched her back in the café as she ashed her cigarette and noticed that she hadn't left a mark on the filter or on the rim of her coffee cup. He disliked the imprint of a woman's lip on leftover butts or china, the sight of it left him with a sense of sleaziness he could not shake off. No, she needed a little less paint and some more hair, something to give her face some softness, to make it something you'd want to touch. Everything about her now prickled with 'Don't touch me'. It was a pity.

He wanted to talk to her but could think of nothing vaguely sensible to say. Instead, he turned his gaze out at the city streets. He knew these streets, this drive downtown, as well as he knew anything, just as he knew the shoreline of the harbour from the Coat

Hanger through to Iron Cove. Old industrial landscapes, superimposed on the ancient yellow ochre foreshores of a drowned river, which were changing even as he watched them. He had grown up at the heart of them, on the Balmain peninsula, with a view of the White Bay power station, close to the container wharves and the White Bay Hotel on the crest of the hill, overlooking the timber yards and the wharves and the curve of Victoria Road with its unbroken traffic. The streets around his home were crowded with old pubs, thin, narrow terraces on high foundations, irregular wooden houses and rows of identical single-storey cottages. On certain days in those treeless streets, the sun had cast a wrung-out yellow light, thin and brittle as a light bulb. When he was a child, this washed-out emptiness had left him with a sense of bleak contentment. He had felt secure near the shadow of the bulk of the White Bay power station and its rusted conveyer belts, whether it was outlined against a hot summer sky or, in weather like today's, standing desolate in the grey rain.

He no longer lived in that part of the peninsula and Balmain had changed. Houses had been bought up, renovated and had become expensive. The patina of how things used to be had been polished away or covered with the unfamiliar shininess of fresh paint. A matching change and demolition had occurred in the city, in ways which gave familiar landmarks — such as the clock tower at Central Station, which they now passed, and the ugly chiselled colonnade on Eddy Avenue — the status of what was left behind. He often mused that the fate of the city's landscape was not unlike that of many of the people he had met in his sixteen years on the job. They had either been tarted up out of recognition or had rotted away to ruin; or were dead and buried under the concrete foundations of the office towers and apartment buildings which had sprouted across the surrounding streets.

Occasionally, he liked to think of himself as a survivor from another time but he knew this was hardly true. He had changed as the times and the places around him had changed. He had dressed himself up as well. Promotions he once would never have expected to achieve had become possible these last few years, and he had gone after them, hungrily, successfully. Somehow he had hung around long enough to climb ladders, to have the prospect of further promotion. He had acquired influence and he liked it, he liked using it, it was a nice change. It was a consolation prize, something to make up the balance, an antidote to his occasional black moods, like the one today.

'Is just here okay?'

Grace's clear voice broke into his reverie.

'Yeah, this is fine, thanks. I'll see you back here a bit later. Call me if you've got any serious info on the doc.'

'Sure,' she said with a smile.

He watched her pilot the car back out into the traffic. He thought about her hands on the steering wheel, her nails painted dark red, the colour of her lipstick. Hard colours. Softness wasn't a qualification for the job.

He arrived just in time to take his seat at the table before the questioning started. At any press conference, he always felt like one of the three wise monkeys sitting in a row. He would have claimed the right to speak no evil as the safest possible option. Do otherwise and a man could fall into a crevasse; as he had done once, spectacularly, in his career, lucky to escape with a seven-year transfer to a small town near the Riverina and a smashed jaw. Both accomplishments had been courtesy of a fellow officer who had taken a strong exception to Harrigan's interference in his personal business affairs, as he saw it. Both had been preferable to their alternative: becoming the statistic of an officer shot dead while on duty. That would have earned him impressive funeral rites but little else. Apart from any other benefit, the whole affair had been a lesson to Harrigan that it was unwise to bait someone quite that far. He could still remember the embarrassed faces of the senior officers who had visited him while he was recovering in hospital to offer him either resignation or exile. Exile was only on offer because of the scandal the affair had caused in the media; and it was one way of making sure he kept his mouth shut (which he had done, obligingly).

The officer who had almost shot him dead, one Michael Casatt, had gone down in flames a few years ago, following the latest royal commission into police corruption, the same commission which had opened up the possibilities of Harrigan's own advancement. It had been sweet entertainment to think of the man squirming in front of the video in the courtroom, but while the exile might be over, the sporadic ache in Harrigan's reconstructed jaw was there still. A useful reminder for him to be a little more subtle about how he went about his own business in future.

He brought himself back to the present, to pay attention as the Assistant Commissioner expressed public condolences for the loss of a citizen loved, respected and admired. He admired the man's calm as he refused to be drawn on questions of how the shooting might affect the government's law and order campaign in the upcoming state election. With an equally straight face, Harrigan listened as the Tooth spoke portentously on the pooling of area command resources with Harrigan's specialist crime task force. Such persuasive lies. They'd be lucky to get one free beer out of the man for Christmas. The Tooth did not double as Santa Claus, or as the tooth fairy for that matter. He was good material for the cameras, a smiling man with a fleshy face and neatly cut hair silvered grey, his soft distended stomach hidden by the table. At first glance, he appeared benign, even pliable, but to Harrigan's certain knowledge he could outmanoeuvre the best of them.

Then the pack turned on Harrigan and the two men beside him sat back and let him deal with it. In Harrigan's estimation the media were parasites: they drank other people's blood to stay alive. They were useful only occasionally, if you wanted something out of them. He stonewalled. Initial information suggested the intended victim had not been Professor Henry Liu but his wife, Dr Agnes Liu. At last report her condition was critical but stable. The motive was unclear. The murder weapon had been found, investigations were continuing. After this he deflected questions until the Assistant Commissioner wound things up.

Outside in the corridor, Harrigan was disturbed to find the Tooth bearing down on him in an apparently friendly manner, his smile revealing a line of even, very white teeth which would have done a dentist proud. It was a smile designed to make you complicit, to make you grin like an idiot in reply, while the 'How are you?' that went with it made Harrigan marvel at how Marvin could make a casual greeting sound like a death threat.

'Paul. You handled the boys and girls very nicely in there. Of course, we may have to get together sometime and talk a little more frankly about resources — unfortunately I do have other commitments and this job could be a bit of a squeeze. Meanwhile, a quick word with you now? There's a question I wanted to ask.'

The man moved him towards a window by the elbow; Harrigan stepped aside from his touch.

'You had a recruit from the Graduate Entry Scheme start with you today? Grace Riordan? Is that right?'

'Yeah, that's right,' Harrigan replied, managing not to look surprised.

'Yes, she hasn't been out of the Academy all that long — eight, nine months perhaps? I know there are recent academic qualifications of some kind in criminology but *really* ... ' He paused as if expressing their agreed contempt. 'Public Affairs needs a body. Why don't you let them consider her? There are other people I could let you have. As I understand it, her only outstanding quality is that she flaunts herself.'

Ouch, Harrigan thought.

'She hasn't in front of me.' He spoke casually, pacing his words. 'No, I don't want to do that, thanks, Marvin. She handled herself well today. She's got a brain and she uses it. It's nice to see. It's rare enough.'

'Have it your own way. But there are other people. And you can always be in touch with me later if you want to change your mind. Perhaps we can come to some arrangement the next time you drop by to discuss your resource allocations. She may not be your most honest recruit. I dare say you'll find that out in time.'

'I guess time will tell us a lot of things. I wouldn't have any reason to think that way about her now. I'll see you later, mate. Give my regards to Joan.'

They smiled at each other with equivalent insincerity before separating and walking away. Harrigan stopped to watch with distaste as the Tooth's broad back disappeared into the open elevator, and wondered why he was so anxious to sink his fangs all over his new starter. She was lucky he never let Marvin decide who ought to work for him, simply as a matter of self-preservation. He could never be sure who the Tooth might want to salt onto his team or why. Still, if Marvin did not like her, then probably he could trust her. Bright skies, mate, he said to himself ironically, if a little sourly. Always look for the bright skies while you negotiate the tightropes strung over the crevasse beneath.

He walked along the corridors back to his office softly whistling, 'Always look on the bright side of life'.

5

As Lucy moved through the alternations of urban devastation and bright, lively bazaar which made up King Street, her destination became her sole external focus. Her surroundings were immaterial, they could have been something made up out of fog. She found herself not far from the railway station, like someone who, after a night of drunkenness, cannot remember how they came home intact. Cutting through familiar narrow streets past the old police station, she followed the curve of the hill down towards Parramatta Road, to where a small, old-fashioned picture theatre, square, squat and flat-roofed, stood on the corner of a laneway. A sign — The New Life Ministries Temple, Pastoral Care and Community Youth Refuge, the Preacher Graeme Fredericksen — had been attached to the façade of the theatre against a backdrop of weathered film posters. Its companion building, the refuge, a large terraced house with a closed-in veranda, stood on the other side of the narrow lane.

The front door to the theatre was always locked. Lucy went down the laneway to the back of the hall. Here, there was an open expanse of ground where two houses had been demolished some months ago, leading to a protest which had left the site undeveloped. The back door was also locked and she let herself inside, dropping her keys into her jacket pocket and leaving the door on the latch behind her. She stood in a small hallway where bare bulbs hung unlit from the high ceiling on their long cords. There was a set of stairs leading up to a mezzanine area, with a door beside them. She opened the door and looked into the untidy office beyond but it was empty. She walked down the short hallway and opening the heavy wooden door that led into the small auditorium she called out 'Hello?' A vacant echo was the only response. She stepped inside, shutting the door behind her.

A single row of small navy-blue rectangular windows near the ceiling locked out the light on the laneway side of the building. They created darkness, cutting out the sound and sight of the outside world. A painted Christ was projected onto an ancient film screen at the back of the auditorium. Beams of light from the projection illuminated the slow circling fall of specks of dust. In the unlit room, the figure's face and garments were luminous and seemed to float above the tiny stage, with hands held out in blessing towards the watcher. White plastic chairs were set in concentric circles in the middle of the auditorium, centred underneath its gaze.

Lucy's heart beat more quickly as she looked around her. She took off her backpack and placed it on a chair. Then the door next to the stage opened silently and Graeme, dressed in black trousers and a grey striped shirt, came into the room.

'Lucy,' he said, 'I have been so worried about you. I was beginning to think I wasn't going to see you at all today. I heard it all on the radio. Congratulations. I can't say it enough: I am so proud of you, I am so very, very proud of you. I knew you had the courage, I knew you could do it. But how are you? You are coping? You do know that now you've done this, you've nothing to fear?'

He had been walking towards her with his hands held out to take hold of hers, but something in her face made him stop where he was.

'How am I? I'm fine, Graeme! I just shot two people and I killed one of them, but beside that, I'm just fine. How do you think I am?'

The fury of her emotion came up from a depth of revulsion she only now acknowledged.

He sounded shaken as he replied. 'You were brave, Lucy. You were very, very brave. You did what had to be done.'

'Yeah?'

She began to move restlessly through the circles of chairs.

'Yeah, I was brave. You always say that. I am always so fucking brave.'

She stopped and kicked over a chair and then another and another. They clattered against the wall. The preacher watched her, unmoving.

'Just so fucking, fucking brave. You know what? There was some kid there. I don't know who he was, her kid or something, I don't know, but he was watching me. He saw everything I did. And nothing's changed, has it? I thought it would. You said it would. You said everything would change. I'd just feel relief. I'd feel ... clean. Well I did, maybe for five minutes, I felt like, yeah, I'm glad I did it. But I don't feel that any more. And nothing's changed. Nothing. The world's just rolling on and I don't feel any different. No, that's not true. I feel like shit!'

'Lucy ...' he moved towards her slowly, 'you must calm yourself. You're upset, of course you are. An action like this asks so much of you. And it is unpleasant. There's nothing to rejoice about in carrying out a task like this, no one said there was. But it is a cleansing process and it has to be done —'

'You stop right there, Graeme!'

He did stop and she saw his face briefly distort with a passing flash of anger. She registered the emotion with surprise.

'I said that to Greg, you know? I said to him, it had to be done. And I did it. And you know what he said to me?' She laughed. 'Bullshit. That's what he said. They put you away for ever for things like this.'

She stopped to draw breath. In her mind, she saw the Turtle's electronic words: *That's just a wall u put up Nothing real*. She closed her eyes.

'They will never find you, Lucy,' the preacher was saying. 'Never. No one's ever going to tell them who you are. Except for Greg himself, perhaps. I have no idea why you had to tell him so much about this in the first place. I thought we'd agreed you wouldn't. Greg is in my charge, Lucy, the government has made him my responsibility. He may be your friend but I know him. How do you know he won't bring the world in here?'

'No,' she said, shaking her head. 'You don't know him better than I do. There's no one in the world I'd trust more than Greg, because, you know, we're one and one. There's nothing he doesn't know about me, he could tell people all sorts of things. Nothing like this though.'

The preacher's face was very pale, his expression fixed; the sight of it disturbed her. She fell silent and sat down next to her backpack, and then leaned forward, as though her nerve strings were cut. Graeme stood at a distance, hesitating.

'What did you do with the car?' he asked eventually.

'It's where it's supposed to be, it's in the garage. I left everything there, like you said, the jacket and the gloves, the whole thing. But I lost the gun.'

'You shouldn't have done that. That was very careless of you.'

'It's in that back lane somewhere, I don't know exactly. I guess they've found it by now. I tripped. I didn't remember at first. I ripped my gloves.' She looked down at her grazed hands and then up at him. 'I want you to give me another gun now, Graeme. Now I've lost that one. I like having it. I didn't think I would, but I do. It makes me feel safe.'

'That was a very special gun, Lucy. You shouldn't have lost it. I don't know if it can be replaced just like that.'

'Well, you'd better find me one. Because I want it.'

The preacher took another hesitant step towards her.

'Guns are fine so long as you use them for righteous purposes, Lucy. But not if you don't. You should remember that.' He paused. 'I'll see what I can do for you.'

She was no longer listening. She was leaning forward, staring at the floor, chewing a fingernail. Then she looked up at him.

'You know something? I wish I'd never done it. I told myself just what you said, that I had to do this. And I know it sounds really mad but I still believe that. I still believe something like this had to happen. But now that

I've done it ... Blood's all the same colour. It's all just the same, it doesn't matter if it's mine or theirs.'

She stared at him, trying to give voice to what was in her mind.

'The thing is, I didn't know what it was going to be like. I didn't really know what they'd look like when I'd shot them. But when I say that, I think well, *why* didn't I know that?' Her voice rose to a shout. 'It's not forgivable, not to realise how it was going to look when I did it. I should have known that all along. Before I even thought about doing it. Just so I knew what it meant.'

'I don't understand you, Lucy. What should you have known? That there was going to be blood? That woman lived in blood. Your blood, for one. You can't let these details get in your way. You have to push them out of your mind.'

'You didn't see them. You didn't see what that man looked like. You know what I want to do? I want to go down there now and say to the police, I did that. I almost did it. I walked past them on my way here and I thought, I just have to go over there and say to those police, "It was me. I'm sorry I did it, but I did. So where do we go from here?" And I almost did do that. Except you can't turn time back, can you? I wish I could. I can still hear the shots, you know. I'll never forget that.'

In her electronic world, the shots were a trigger. Once they were fired, time stopped and the world was split apart, burned and broken, to be remade as something clean. Out in the real world, the shots had stopped time for her and the three other people who had been there with her. She and the two survivors were fixed in those split seconds, connected to each other for as long as their memories survived. Only the dead man had got away.

She chased these thoughts, slippery as fish in her mind, absorbed in a prolonged silence while the preacher stood quite still in the half dark watching her. When he spoke, his voice had acquired its usual gentleness.

'And if you do do that, Lucy, if you do go to the police, what happens to everyone here? What happens to me?'

She shrugged, looking away. 'Well, everyone's got to make up their own mind, don't they? They've got to live with themselves too. I'm not going to dob anyone in. You don't have to worry about that.'

'You'll still bring the world in here, Lucy. There will be no way of avoiding that.'

She shook her head. 'No, that wouldn't happen. I wouldn't let it,' she said.

The preacher sat on a chair and they faced each other in the obscurity. He leaned forward.

'Lucy, you poor child. I am so sorry. We have asked too much of you. I should never have let you go out there alone, I should have realised what it would demand of you. I am sorry, I am so very sorry that I have done this to you. You need to rest. Because what you're feeling — I've seen it before, often. This is a war and you are a soldier. And the fighting is hard and sometimes you have to do things that you wish you'd never had to do at all. You need to rest and then to wake in the morning and see how you feel then. And by then I think these things will look very different to you.'

'Rest?' Lucy leaned back in her chair. 'I am tired. I'm really tired. But I don't see that's going to make any difference. How can it? Because I did this, okay? All right, we talked about it. But I did it. You didn't. I know what I'm feeling, Graeme. I just don't know where to go from here. I know I can't leave it like this. I'm going to have to do something. I'll tell everyone why I did it. I'll stand up and I'll tell them why so at least they'll know that much.'

'What makes you think they'll understand you?'

'I don't give a shit if they understand me! They'll know. They'll have to, because they won't be able to pretend this didn't happen. Then maybe they won't want to hang me from the nearest tree —'

She had got to her feet and was roaming about in a small space; she stopped now to stand with her hands on her hips, and shook her head.

'They'll know,' she repeated. 'They'll know that I never really wanted to hurt anyone. I just wanted — a bit of peace, I suppose — something . . .'

'Lucy.'

The preacher's voice called her back to herself.

'Lucy, you are exhausted. When did you last have anything to eat and drink? Tell me that.'

'I don't know.'

'Wait here,' he said.

She sat down as he left the room. He returned shortly afterwards with a mug of coffee from the jug that he always kept brewing in his office. It was thick with milk.

'I've sweetened it,' he said, 'I think you need the energy. Drink it. You need something.'

She did not argue. She sat in her chair, sipping the warm milky liquid.

'Lucy, we have to try and focus on the necessities. Those at least we can deal with. You need rest, you need food. Then we work out what we do next.'

'I don't think I can eat.'

'Come and try. You need food, Lucy. God created us that way, in case you hadn't noticed. Eat and rest and then we'll see what we can do. Come into the office and I'll get you something to eat.'

He was close to her now. She finished her coffee quickly. He took the mug from her, she collected her backpack and followed him through to his office behind the auditorium. It was a small room, heated by a two-bar radiator close to his desk. He sat her down in a chair near the heater.

'You get warm while I make us something to eat.'

He went into the tiny makeshift kitchen behind the office. She heard the sounds of food being prepared as she waited. He called out to her, his voice a little muffled.

'Lucy, you must trust me on this. Things will look very different to you tomorrow. Whatever you think now.'

Lucy was looking at a poster on the wall that displayed the image of a pale pink foetus floating in the womb. Its sightless eyes were closed and its small hands were curled up to its mouth. The poster was stamped with the words: Abortion is Murder.

'No, Graeme, I don't think it will. Because right now I can't see how it's any different. What that woman did and what I just did. It's the same thing when you come down to it. It's murder.'

'Are you sure about that?'

'Oh, I'm sure.'

She was sitting upright, her arms tight about her midriff, when he came back into the room carrying a tray of sandwiches. He put them in front of her on the desk and then poured a mug of coffee for himself. 'Do you want another?' he asked, and she shook her head.

On the wall behind him was another poster, this one of the sun glowing through clouds over the sea with the legend: You must be reborn in the spirit. At the sight of this, she felt equal amounts of anger and revulsion.

'Eat,' he said.

She took a tiny bite out of a sandwich, chewed and swallowed it with difficulty, then put the sandwich back down on the plate.

'Can't eat. My throat — it's really tight. I don't want it, Graeme. I'm so tired all of a sudden.'

'Lucy, you ask so much of yourself. Did you sleep at all last night? I told you you'd need to. You can't do these things without being at your fullest strength.'

She smiled grimly before replying. 'No, I didn't sleep much. I tried to but...' She shrugged. 'I was so scared and I just kept thinking about her. I kept seeing her in my head. It was weird. She looked so real somehow, she was so powerful. And when I saw her today, I thought — is that really her? She doesn't look like anybody. She didn't look real.' Lucy closed her eyes, shaking her head. 'That man — the one who was there — I thought you said it was only ever her. I don't even know why I fired at him. I must have just kept firing. Why?'

'I said you should be prepared for anything. This man, he was her accomplice. He was as guilty as she is. What difference does it make if you did shoot him?'

'It makes a big difference to me.'

'Why? He knew who and what his wife was. He watched her go off to do what she did every day. He lived on her money. Why is he any less guilty than she is? You tell me that, Lucy.'

'It isn't them, Graeme. It's me. I'm the one who did this. It isn't who they are. It's what I did that's in my mind.'

They faced each other, angry, stubborn.

'This was an execution, Lucy, clean and merciful. That's the only way you need to see it.' He sounded irritated.

'No, it wasn't, it wasn't anything like that. It wasn't clean, that's for sure.'

She shook her head and opened her mouth to say something else, but as she did, she felt the grip of some kind of drug travelling her veins, a numbing sensation growing stronger by the second. She stared at his expressionless face opposite her.

'You ... Did you ... Is that ... '

Her voice seemed to dry up. She leaned forward on the desk to support herself, shaking her head.

'Why did you do that — you didn't need to...' she managed to say before falling back in her chair.

He put his mug down and stood up. He was businesslike. Nothing unusual was happening, this was just the daily round.

'We'll take you upstairs, Lucy. You need to rest. You've overdone it, as usual. You can use my room, no one will bother you up there. However, there is just one thing I need from you first ...'

He searched her pockets for her keys to the building. Finding them, he smiled at her. He dropped them into his own pocket before pulling her upright to take her upstairs. She tried to fight him but could only flop about like a landed fish.

His room was on the mezzanine level behind the auditorium, just above the office. Its louvred windows, covered by steel security grilles, looked over the patch of ground where the two houses had been demolished and to the street the beyond. He sat her on the bed and pulled back the blankets for her.

'Graeme,' she forced out, 'you didn't have to ...'

'It's all right, Lucy. Just rest easy.'

He took off her shoes, put them neatly to the side, and manoeuvred her into the bed and covered her with blankets. She could not stop him, her body was rubbery. The ache of the drug came bearing down on her as her head fell back on the pillow and her eyes began to close.

'No, you can't...' she said, and then slipped away into an airless darkness. She seemed to dream that she was back at her father's house on the northern edge of the city, standing behind the disused sleep-out on the edge of the small escarpment that was the shared boundary between her father's block of land and the national park. She was looking out to the north where the eucalyptus forest began its descent over sandstone rock to the Hawkesbury River. The sky was a clear blue; she felt cold wind on her face and heard the drawn-out whistling of currawongs. 'I'm safe here,' she said in her dream, so vividly she believed she had spoken aloud.

Her eyes opened onto the small bedroom. She felt her back and her neck cold with sweat, her body paralysed and her breath shallow. In this swimming nausea, she saw Graeme looking down at her in that gentle way of his, his face unsmiling but not unkind. There was a roaring in her ears and then, as the roaring stopped, she heard him say clearly, 'Yes, you are safe here. You always have been. Soon you'll be safe for ever, Lucy, you'll reach a home that's not on the streets of this city but on the streets of the city of eternal life. Greg can join you there, you can be happy together, you and he can be as one in Christ for ever. I promised you that you'd find peace and I'm going to keep my promise. I always do. The river of death is cold but it is narrow, and once you're there you will be at peace. You can rest.'

'You can't...' she heard herself say before there was a noise from a distance, the phone downstairs ringing. He left the room.

Stay awake, she told herself, fighting the waves of the drug, stay awake. She had struggled into a half-sitting position when Graeme came back. Gently he pushed her back down onto the pillow.

'You shouldn't fight it, Lucy. Just go with it, as you sometimes say. That was Mrs Lindley. She's expecting me to dinner, she's already sent the car to pick me up. It should be here very shortly. I will be back later on tonight because I have a few other things to do as well. I think you'll sleep through till then. You rest now. You've earned it.'

I'm not going to let you do this to me.

Just as she slid away she heard a door banging somewhere, a voice calling out. She thought there was something she should recognise about this voice. Then she had the final fleeting perception of Graeme hurriedly leaving the room.

6

'I'm just a little puzzled, my friend, as to why,' the preacher was saying with a slightly baffled, slightly anxious smile. 'Here you are, knocking at my door, the only door that was open to Lucy in the past, yet I don't recall you ever showing any noticeable concern for her before today. Is there any particular reason why you should come around here looking for her now?'

Stephen Hurst was surprised to find himself playing mind games with a man he'd thought would be only too happy to help him. When he had first knocked on the door to this office, the preacher had appeared behind him from out of nowhere. He had ushered him in, cleared away the remains of a meal from his desk and then sat Stephen down with a perfunctory smile. Everything about him radiated a tired patience while he generously displayed tolerance towards someone who was wasting his time. He was not someone Stephen would have picked as Lucy's chosen saviour, even though, from everything she had told him these last few months, this was just who he was.

'No offence,' Stephen said, mildly enough in his high-pitched, boyish voice, 'but I don't see why I have to give you a reason for wanting to talk to my own sister.'

In reply, the man's smile was beatific.

'I always care for my flock, Stephen. I have no idea whether she wants to see you or not, and that is a very important consideration for me. Has she been in touch with you lately?'

Stephen adjusted his round metal-rimmed glasses, watching the man's face, unable to work out where he was coming from.

'Yes, she has,' he replied after a short pause. 'She rang me last week. She knows what this is about. From what she said, I thought she'd have told you all about it.'

'No, I'm afraid not.'

'I need to find her,' Stephen said. 'She needs to think about coming home for a little bit. I've got to talk to her about that.'

'Is that what she wants?'

'Well, I have to ask her.'

'And home is — where?'

'Didn't she tell you? I would have thought you'd know.' Stephen saw a slight flush of red cross the preacher's face.

'I don't know that I can help you, Stephen, unfortunately,' he replied, leaning forward. 'I am sure you know that Lucy lives a very nomadic sort of existence. In my experience, she finds you. Perhaps that's what she'll do if she wants to. Find you. Perhaps she'll call you again.'

'Lucy told me that if I ever needed to find her, this is where I should start looking. She said I just had to ask you and you'd help me out. I can wait around if you like. Just to see if she turns up.'

The preacher smiled and shook his head. He stood up and walked to the door of his office and opened it.

'I'm afraid not. This is private property. People come here to pray and I can't have them disturbed. I have to say I'm a little surprised at the way you invaded the place. I didn't realise the back door was unlocked. You should have rung the front door bell, that's how most people announce themselves to me. But I'll show you out the way you came. I don't want you to get lost.'

The combination of his smile and gaze compelled Stephen to his feet. At the door, he hesitated.

'No, I'll wait for her,' he said, taking courage. 'She said she'd be here some time and I've got the time to wait. I need to find her. I don't want to just walk away from her. You never know what Lucy's up to or what's she's doing to herself. I'll wait.'

To his surprise, the man reached over and took hold of his wrist.

'No, Stephen. I don't think you should wait. I think you should leave now. As it happens, I have to go out very shortly myself.'

Stephen tried to pull away but the man had a numbingly tight grip; he was still smiling, as though nothing unusual was happening. Under the man's gaze, Stephen was trapped in inaction, unable to say something so simple as 'let me go'. It was either leave now or fight, but he had no energy and no words of protest to help him. He blinked a little behind his glasses and chose to leave.

'Just this way,' the preacher said.

He led Stephen through the short hallway to the back door. As soon as they stepped outside, he let him go.

Stephen looked at his wrist and saw that it had been squeezed white at the bone. He stared at the preacher in shock.

'You walk uncomfortably, Stephen. You have a limp,' he said. 'Why is that?'

Stephen answered the question, speaking haltingly. 'It's my knee, it got smashed up when I was fifteen. I've had three operations to fix it.'

'How unfortunate for you. I do sympathise,' the preacher replied. 'And believe me, Stephen, I understand your misgivings concerning Lucy only too well. I have always had grave concerns for her safety. I know what a troubled young woman she is. She lives on the edge, falls in and out of addiction and puts herself in terrible danger. I fear for her very much and I often wonder what the next phone call is going to tell me. But I cannot be with her twenty-four hours a day. That is for you to do and I am afraid you have let her down very badly there. Perhaps you should go to the police and tell them how afraid you are for her welfare. No one wants the worst to happen. No one wants her to be found one morning lying in a laneway, taken from all of us who care for her because she has overdosed.'

The preacher's voice seemed to drop down to a strange mechanical whisper in Stephen's ear, as quiet as the inner voice of self-doubt. Stephen could not reply. The preacher turned and went back into the theatre, locking the door behind him.

Stephen's wrist began to ache as the blood flowed back. He stood for a few moments nursing it then walked down the laneway back out to the street. He got into his car and drove to a place where he was certain the doors would be open to him: the Hampshire Hotel on Parramatta Road.

* * *

Stephen sat solitary in the saloon bar and, over a beer and a cigarette, tried to weigh up the man he had just met. The preacher had spun his words out well, like a spruiker fronting a sex show, or a used-car salesman or a politician. Just like his father. They all had that same sideways calculating and slightly anxious glance, asking the question, have I got away with it? They all had the gift of the gab, that inviting smile. They got under your skin and, once they had, they took more than they gave.

Stephen contemplated without joy how he was caught between two of them. On the one hand, there was his father, the local butcher. A successful man with a large and profitable shop and money in the bank, who had always greeted his customers with a grin and a slogan, something picked up from the radio that appealed to him: *We're pleased to meet you and we've got meat to please you. What can we do for you today?* George Hurst's patter was all picked up from here and there, scraps of wit glued together, a dazzling patchwork. He made the housewives laugh, and some of his regulars had cried when they heard he had cancer. His father's days of persuasion were over now, he could not sweet-talk the disease out of his bones as the substance of his body consumed itself.

And on the other side was the preacher, a man with a cold fish smile who left behind an after-chill which grew stronger the more you thought about him. Stephen nursed his wrist and wondered: who and what are you? What does Lucy want with you?

He ground out his cigarette in the ashtray and held up his glass for a refill. The man beside him got up and left the afternoon paper behind on the bar. Stephen took another cigarette, reading the banner headlines and the opening paragraph of the story without moving his head. For a few short seconds, the cigarette hung from his mouth unlit. Then he pulled the newspaper towards him and read it over again.

When the beer arrived, the barmaid said, 'That's such a shocking thing, isn't it? And just up the road here too. You don't feel you're safe any more, do you?'

'No, that's right, you don't,' he replied perfunctorily and lit his cigarette at last, staring across the bar at the music machine in a darkened corner.

There had to be certain things Lucy could never do, no matter what she had told him during these last few months. Stephen had to believe this, he did not have a choice when the alternative was unthinkable. He preferred things to remain unsaid: he found they were easier to deal with that way, and later he could forget they had ever happened. He thought about the preacher again. Lucy, you get yourself involved with some fucking weirdos. When are you going to realise no one out there is going to give you what you want? The words snapped angrily in his mind.

He pushed the newspaper away and sipped his second beer. He wanted to be practical, to stop thinking, to find her. To bring her home safely and bury the past with his father's death, to have it finished with once and for all. To make it something he never had to think about again.

He finished his beer quickly and stood up to leave.

7

'Amazing Grace. We don't get many people like you in here. Come and talk to me. You're going to like me. I'm a real sensitive New Age guy.'

Ian Enright, thirty-something and a gym junkie and one of Harrigan's team, grinned to people around him as he spoke. Grace had just walked into the office and put her bag down on her desk, which was some distance away from his. She saw the small group watching her speculatively and wondered if they were manufacturing gossip, then told herself not to be so thin-skinned.

Harrigan's 2IC, Trevor Gabriel, appeared beside them, calling out to the room, 'Better get a move on, people, it's show time. It's on in the big room, not out here.'

People got to their feet. Grace waved to Trevor across the busy office, a gesture he returned with a smile.

'You know her?' Ian asked.

'Known her for fucking centuries, mate. She's an old friend. I was at uni with her once upon a time.'

'Introduce me. I'd like to get friendly with her too.'

Trevor glanced at him darkly and was already moving away. He joined Grace by her desk, leaving the others to watch and wonder.

Trev, a substantial man with no neck and shoulders like a wrestler, had black hair shorn to stubble. Known to be gay, he was the subject of occasional to frequent nasty remarks but was too formidable for anyone sensible to bait to his face. No one could credibly spread the rumour that he and Grace were sleeping together, but if they were friends it could be said that she was here only on his recommendation. In the rounds of gossip, this particular slant on her arrival had already become currency. There was some slender truth to it. Trevor had suggested Grace as a possible recruit and was her informant about life on the team and Harrigan in particular.

In the midst of this, Harrigan himself arrived to marshal his team for a recap of the day's events. He stopped at Grace's desk to let her know that he intended introducing her to the troops once they were inside the incident room, if that was all right with her.

'Sure,' she replied with a polite smile, a response the watchers searched for hidden meanings.

The incident room was the engine room. Everything that was worth watching happened in this ugly elongated piece of open space without windows and where the walls were lined with imitation wood panelling. It was a public place, where people arrived as at a theatre, where accounts of rape, assault and murder were thrashed out in detached detail, and competition and aggression acted out free of charge.

People came here to hatch out ideas, discover what they might be asked to do next, or find fodder for something to talk about.

'Okay,' Harrigan said, calling for quiet. 'Before we start — most of you have already met Grace Riordan. Grace started here today, I've already told her she's lucky we could turn on something like this for her. We've tossed her in the deep end but she's handled it. And she's still smiling. You can't ask for much more than that. Welcome, Grace.'

'Thanks,' she replied, her clear voice carrying across the room. 'I've got to say that I never once had to wonder what I was going to do next today, which is not something you can complain about. And it's nice to be here. Thanks for the welcome.'

There was some laughter and applause.

'That doesn't change, Grace,' Ian called out. 'You never stop working around here.'

'It's my concern for your welfare, mate. I don't want you to get bored,' Harrigan said. 'We'll give you a proper welcome with a few ales down at the Maryborough as soon as we can, Grace, but just now we don't have the time, I'm sorry. We've got work to do.'

With the social niceties out of the way, he looked over a sheaf of photographs which he'd laid down on the metal table in front of him. Everyone waited as he gathered his thoughts. He looked up to address the room.

'Something I want you all to remember as soon as you wake up in the morning, as soon as you get in to work every day: we have no time to spare. This job has priority over everything else we do from now on, no matter what it is, and that includes our social lives.

We've got someone very sick out there on the streets, armed or unarmed we don't know, and we have to find her. She is not going to walk away from this. I want this girl. I want her as soon as we can get her.

'All right. To start.' He held up the sheaf of photographs. 'These were all posted in the Haymarket over the last three months. There's nothing of much use to us here but they are somewhere to start. This is our girl's mind at work.'

He began to pin reproductions of Dr Agnes Liu's hate mail onto a cork board that covered half the length of the wall. 'Oh, gross,' someone called out as the images began to appear. A display of foetuses in miniature white coffins with the phrase 'Holocaust Victims' written across them. Dr Liu's picture covered with a wash of red ink, the words 'Satanist Mass Murderer STOP NOW' scrawled across her face. Then ultrasounds and more photographs of aborted foetuses. A text in what appeared to be a child's handwriting: '*So ye shall not pollute the land wherein ye are: for blood it defileth the land: and the land cannot be cleansed of the blood that is shed therein, but by the blood of him that shed it.*'

'How sick is all that?' someone else said.

'As sick as the mind that went looking for all that,' responded an older woman with a cracked and broken voice. 'Someone who likes to occupy themselves with that sort of thing. A really happy mind, wouldn't you say?'

'Louise is still sober and it's after five. What do you know?' Grace heard someone mutter. Jeffo, the man who had shouted at her in the car park that morning, was standing a little too close to her.

'Women do that sort of thing to themselves?' he called out loudly then, in her ear, 'Turns your stomach.'

Grace did not bite, she was studying the glossy pictures. She recognised one of them, the mildest, the famous photograph of the tiny feet of a foetus between a man's thumb and forefinger. Eight months ago, a female protester from a ragged group waving placards on the street had pushed it into Grace's hands as she made her way into a Whole Life Health Centre clinic to have an abortion herself.

'I don't give a shit what they do, mate,' Harrigan responded with professional indifference. 'That's not our business.'

'They're fucking asking for trouble if you ask me,' Jeffo said.

No one replied to him. The gibe had changed the atmosphere, there was a creeping sense of tension and anger in the room. Harrigan paused.

'Let's get something clear right now,' he said. 'Point one. Like I just said, I do not give a shit what happens in those clinics. That goes for everyone else in this room. Point two. We're looking for a murderer. That's all we need to think about. End of story.'

Grace remembered the woman protester snaring her at the clinic door, ear-bashing her all the way inside until Grace had taken her by the arm and hustled her back out onto the street. There she had flashed her warrant card under the woman's nose. 'You see this?' she had said. 'Do you want me to arrest you? Do you want to spend the night in the lock-up? Or do you want to get out of here right now?' The woman had stared open-mouthed at the card for some moments, before walking away with a strange, almost satisfied expression on her face. When Grace went back inside the clinic, Dr Agnes Liu had come to thank her before showing her into the operating theatre. The woman had been bothering them all week, she told Grace, they were so grateful she had moved her on. All facts that Grace had no intention of ever sharing with anyone in this particular room.

'This is the important bit of mail,' Harrigan was saying. 'The doc didn't get to see this, it was waiting for her this morning at the clinic. So we can assume this wasn't for her; it's meant for us or whoever else was going to clean things up. I want to know where this photograph came from and I want to know who the woman is. It looks like it's been taken from off the web somewhere but there's nothing to locate it for us. Louise is going to track it down if she can. If it's still out there.'

Those assembled looked on silently at the photograph of a woman lying face down in front of an open doorway, shot dead. The words 'You can run but you can't hide' were written across the image. Streams of blood flowed from her head down a small set of steps onto a pathway. A small winged figure carrying a sword was etched into one corner.

'I want to know who thinks they've got the right to make that decision about someone else,' Harrigan said, tapping the photograph before turning away.

'They're on a mission from God, Boss.' Louise spoke out again. 'They can do what they like. They do — that's who they are.'

'You find them, Lou,' Harrigan replied.

'Do my best,' she said, with a grin as cracked as her voice.

'Now, our home-grown protesters. They're on a mission from God as well. You can start with these nosey people, Ian. They make a habit of photographing the women who go into the clinics and then sending them letters afterwards, saying things like you're a murderer, we know where you live, and so on and so forth. Question: How do they get the information about who the women are and where they live? We've had a couple of these women ring the hot line already, you can talk to them as well.'

'Can I get some help?' Ian asked.

'Yeah, you can find someone to help you out. You can organise that.' Harrigan sounded a little surprised.

'I thought Grace here might like to learn the ropes. She can work with me.'

There were some smirks and suppressed laughter at this, while Grace glanced at him with pity, shaking her head.

'No, mate, you can find someone else,' Harrigan replied, with a touch of astringency. 'Grace is going to be occupied with Matthew Liu, apart from anything else she might have to do. We've already agreed on that. Now, America — Trevor's going to follow up that connection. And the gun. It's a pistol, not exactly home-made but something close to it ...'

No, she wasn't working with Ian. Grace brushed off the silly grins, they did not concern her. She couldn't work with Ian because she was one of *those women*, as Harrigan had called them. When she left the clinic, the strange woman and a man had appeared out of nowhere and taken her photograph before disappearing just as quickly into the city streets. Not long afterwards, the print, splashed with red ink, and an ultrasound had arrived in the post. They came with an unsigned letter saying they knew what she was, a murderer, and they could find her if they wanted to, she had better be afraid. She had thrown it all into the rubbish bin. She knew she should walk into Harrigan's office and tell him this, her training said she should, but the idea of doing so was repulsive to her. Apart from being forced to reveal herself in this way, he might take her off the job, even send her off the team, back out into Area Command, straight into the arms of the Tooth. No, she was keeping her head down, staying here, staying out of sight.

Harrigan spoke over her thoughts. 'What troubles me most is what this girl might do next. We have to hope she doesn't have another gun like the one she used today back home under the bed. She might decide she wants to use it on someone else. Now, before we all go ...'

He pinned up onto the board a picture of Matthew Liu in his school uniform, smiling for the camera.

'This is to keep everyone's mind focused on what we're doing here. Think about this boy. He's had something killed in him today as well. And remember — we don't have any time to spare. We work and we keep working until we find her. Let's get on with it.'

'If she has got another gun, Boss, she'll shoot herself in the foot with it first,' Trevor said to Harrigan as they left the room together. 'She's mad. Probably doesn't know how to fart properly.'

Harrigan was half smiling when Jeffo pushed in beside them.

'I reckon that gun belonged to someone who likes to sit on their back porch and pick off cats for target practice, because they splatter. I knew a bloke who used to do that,' he said, grinning.

There was a brief silence in which neither man replied. Jeffo turned suddenly to Grace who was walking a little behind Trevor.

'I hear your claim to fame is that you shoot,' he said. 'You've won trophies or something. Is that right?'

She looked at him deadpan, feeling a chill of aversion. 'That's right. Mainly at my club.'

'You shoot?' Ian said, appearing at her elbow. 'I've got a pretty good average myself. We should get together for a little friendly competition sometime.'

Grace did not reply to Ian's attempts at self-promotion other than with her politest smile.

'Hit anything but a target?' Jeffo was asking her. She shook her head. 'Just kids' stuff. Wait till you aim at something real.'

'I can always start on you if you want,' she replied sweetly as she walked away. People nearby laughed, while Harrigan seemed to be trying to suppress a grin. Jeffo flushed brick-red before disappearing without a word.

Later, after most people had gone and as Grace herself was readying to leave, Harrigan appeared at her desk and spoke to her quietly.

'A private word if you don't mind, Grace. In my office.'

Out of the corner of her eye, Grace saw Trev watch them walk into Harrigan's glassed-in eyrie in the corner of the room.

'Do I need to shut the door?' she asked, a little puzzled, wondering if he was about to lecture her for swapping insults with a supposed colleague.

'No. Don't give anyone around here anything else to talk about, they don't need it. Sit down. Keep your voice down if you can, this is between us. I take it you already know Marvin Tooth.'

Grace went cold down her spine.

'We've met once. Very briefly.'

'So he wouldn't have any particular reason for asking me to move you out of here?'

'Did he do that? So what does this really mean? Are you asking me to clear my desk?'

'No, I'm not asking you to do that. I'm going to be blunt with you about this, Grace. I want to know why he's got it in for you. Is this personal?'

She shook her head, her face pale underneath her make-up.

'Would it make any difference if it was?'

Harrigan was looking at her directly.

'Yeah, it would. For a start, he'd want to make things nasty for us all. And very nasty for you. I'd like to avoid that if I can.'

'You do want me to go. You want me to say I'll go for everyone else's benefit.'

He frowned, shaking his head.

'No, Grace. Listen to me. I've already said I don't want to do that. I want people I can rely on. I could rely on you today. I don't care what's behind this, I don't want it to reach in here and make life difficult. If that's going to happen, I need to know about it. That's all.'

Grace wondered how she could know whether to trust him or not. How she could know what was really in his head?

'No,' she said, 'it's nothing. Nothing like what you might think.'

And what's that, Harrigan thought. He hadn't been trying to find out if Marvin had put the hard word on her. He decided it would be better if he didn't say this to her.

'Okay, fine,' he said, and then as she got up to go, 'Watch your back. He's a bad enemy to have. Come and talk to me if you change your mind.'

She smiled in reply, a slightly crooked smile, full of self-parody and with a sudden sadness that surprised him.

'Thanks,' she said and was gone, heading for the lifts.

Outside in the corridor she stopped. She was leaning against the wall, shaking with relief, when Trev appeared.

'You right, Gracie?' he asked.

'I'm fine, I just need a cigarette.'

'Don't smoke one in here. You'll set the smoke detectors off.'

She smiled. Trev took a proprietorial interest in his friends whether they liked it or not; he was inclined to feel responsible for the unprotected. Once, in the very early morning outside a Sydney nightclub, Grace had seen him wade into a street-bashing, shouting, 'I'm gay. Hit me too.' When the attackers turned on him, he swatted one of them to the footpath with a single punch. The others had turned and run while he shouted after them.

'That was about the Tooth. He's asked Harrigan to move me out of here.'

'And is he going to?'

'No, he says he wants me to stay on. I thought I was gone.'

Somehow this did not lessen her anxiety, the extent of the Tooth's reach left her feeling gloomy and vulnerable. Like it said on the picture of the dead woman in the incident room: you can run but you can't hide, they were still out there waiting for you.

Trev moved closer. 'You'll be fine, mate. You don't want to worry. Get yourself home and get some sleep.'

Just then, Harrigan appeared in the corridor and saw them standing there. They looked at him and then looked away as he headed into the Gents.

'Yeah,' Grace said. 'Everything's going to be okay, isn't it? I'll see you tomorrow.'

'Sure it is. See you, mate. You take care now.'

She left in the elevator. After she had gone, Trevor went into the Gents after Harrigan.

Harrigan looked at him as he walked in the door.

'What have you got to say, Trev?' he asked as Trevor came and stood beside him.

'I hear the Tooth's been talking to you about Gracie. You shouldn't believe what he says about her.'

Harrigan raised his eyebrows in slight surprise, thinking that, by him at least, she didn't like being called Gracie.

'Look, mate, I don't. What's so special about it for you? I know she's your friend.'

'It's my fault she's in the job, isn't it? I'm the fool who talked her into applying in the first place. She hadn't thought about it till then.'

Harrigan gave a short laugh. 'She won't be thanking you for it now she's got Marvin gunning for her.'

Trevor smiled without humour.

Harrigan went to wash his hands and stopped to look in the mirror. As he approached his fortieth birthday, he was still holding down his age. There were no grey hairs visible yet and he was keeping his weight under control, staying fit. He put his hand on his stomach, breathing in a little. Trevor's moon face appeared in the mirror alongside his own.

'I was just wondering if you were planning on pissing her off on the quiet. That's what you'd normally do, isn't it?'

Harrigan was combing his hair.

'No. Why should I? Unless you know something I don't and you want to tell me about it. For starters, did Marvin try and get her in the sack?'

Trevor, who had no more dress sense than a fly, straightened his ugly tie in the mirror and then smoothed down his thick, black moustache. Harrigan glanced at him, waiting. Trev only shrugged.

'No, mate, it wasn't anything like that. Talk to her about it. She'll tell you if she wants to.'

There was silence.

'Is she a single lady? Has she got someone in her life?' Harrigan asked.

In the mirror, Trevor gave his reflection a sideways glance.

'You don't know, mate, she might be a dyke. But if she is, I haven't seen her at a Sleaze Ball yet. No, I don't think she has.'

'I told her she needs to watch her back.' Harrigan was slightly embarrassed, parrying with a touch of self-justification.

'I've already told her that myself,' Trev replied. 'Half a dozen times at least.'

8

Grace left the overhead light switched off in her tiny flat near Bondi Beach and trod her way across its small square of living space by the light of the street lamps outside. Newly renovated studio apartment, the advertisement had said, living and bedroom in one. Grace thought that radical austerity combined with New Age squalor was a better description, with the harsh green carpet ruffed up with steel wool as a matching design feature. She had her priorities, accommodation was not one of them. This was somewhere to sleep, to get dressed in. She was here for the scenery outside, for the sight of the headlands with their white and orange buildings and the strip along the beach front just at dawn, both momentarily transformed in a clean wash of light. To drink takeaway coffee on the beach and watch the sea, a cold, marbled green at this time of year, and feel the salt air on her face before she was obliged to paint on the day's make-up.

Her flat had other useful attributes which were not to be sneezed at: a secure car park you needed a keycard to get into, doors which were programmed to your own personal combination lock. Her ex-lover, her own personal demon, made his reappearance in her life (as well as in her memory) from time to time. She saw him trailing behind her in the street sometimes, or standing at a distance from her building, watching her windows. She had taken some discreet steps for her own protection, obtaining a handgun illegally, something that would not bear examination in her current line of work. There was no other defence she could rely on. Tonight, there was no one out there on the cold and misty street, which proved that even personal demons can be driven away by bad weather. Relieved, she sat at her table, put down her bag and lit a cigarette, kicking off her shoes.

'I am so tired,' she said aloud to the rustle of the undrawn curtains. 'I am so tired.'

In this moment of sudden relaxation, the vision of Henry Liu naked on a steel table came into her mind. She saw him with a handkerchief over his face and then without, and remembered the stink of old blood which had attached itself to her during the autopsy. In her memory, the smell had the same vividness and she felt, briefly, the same sickness. She swallowed. In the clinic, Dr Liu's hands had been gentle, she had comforted Grace while she sat in the recovery room unexpectedly crying once her abortion was over. Agnes Liu did not carry that smell of blood, nothing like it, she was not the thing those people said she was.

Grace put her cigarette in the ashtray and closed her eyes. She pressed her head between her hands, stretching and then arching her backbone against the chair before relaxing again. She pushed her fingers into her hair and squeezed her scalp. I want, she thought, loosening the knots in her spine, I want. Body warmth to push that cold and ugly picture out of her head. Some sex, now that would be nice. To come home to some beautiful man, thin and muscular, with smooth skin and a smooth stomach, who could make her forget what she had seen during the day. The thought made her smile. She should be so lucky. These days, when she had no one serious to concern herself with, she chose to be casual about it. Keeping sex for when the impulse, the fancy, took her, rarely inviting anyone here into her plain sanctuary.

She shook the appetite away, expunging it. Grace was inclined, from time to time, to move from abstinence to indulgence and back again. She was in no mood for either state just now, or for the emotional press that went with wanting someone a bit too hungrily. She only wanted to keep her thoughts to herself, on her work, to see how long she could persist in her job among the minefields the Tooth kept laying for her. It was just a game, *Survival at Work*, where the rules spelled out that you took no prisoners. She did not have to keep playing if it came to that; she could walk away whenever she wanted to.

She allowed herself a few more moments of rest as she finished her cigarette, before the pleasure of stripping away the day's make-up and letting out her hair.

On the other side of the city, Harrigan stood on the pier in Snails Bay and looked out over the black water towards the lighted span of the Harbour Bridge. He was there in the hope of emptying out his mind and feeling the constraints which cramped his body during the day disappear. Often he did not sleep and, if he lay in bed, could spend hours filling the shadows with his night thoughts, phantasms of failure, scraps of bad memory, old grief. This was a hazardous chemistry for his waking dreams at any time: depression followed after them like a promise. On his dangerous white nights, he came out here where he could think freely. Caught up in the quietness of the night noises, and watching the movement of the lights on the water, he might eventually relax enough to be able to sleep as soon as he lay down.

Tonight, nothing could shift the memory of the professor's face or Matthew's Liu's dazed confusion. They touched him more than the thought of Agnes Liu in St Vincent's Hospital, surviving on the faint lines of green light generated by her life support system. He wondered who else might be dying out there in the luminous darkness of the city. He could be called out at any time to deal with any stranger's death. To resolve it, if it could be resolved, for whoever wanted to know; sometimes for no one other than himself.

He kept this simple word *why* in his mind as he worked through whatever case he had to hand, even if the *why*, when discovered, had no sense to it. He always questioned where any death might lead you, ever since his father had shot his mother and handed Harrigan the gun with shaking hands saying: 'Shoot me, Paulie. I don't want to live.' He had fired once, knocking his father back into a chair, to hear him say, 'That won't do it. Shoot me again.' Harrigan had discovered that he could not pull the trigger for a second time, a notch in his mind marking what he could and couldn't do. His father had taken responsibility for the gunshot wound on himself, pleading a botched suicide attempt. Once again, the court had believed him.

Years ago, Harrigan had gone up-market with everybody else, moving from White Bay across to the inner harbour, just up and over Darling Street — which ran like a spine along the Balmain peninsula — and down the other side of the hill. Not so very far from his boyhood home, a distance you could walk. These days, it was another world altogether. As he walked along the edge of Birchgrove Park under the Moreton Bay fig trees, he looked up at his house not far from the water's edge, a pale brick two-storeyed terrace more than a century old with an apron of white lace on the upstairs veranda. 'How did you afford that, mate?' A question often asked with the implication, 'since you're only a copper?' 'By the sweat of my brow,' he always replied with a grin. It had belonged to his aunt, his father's sister, a relationship soured by years of arguments too rancorous to be forgiven. She had inherited it from an uncle, much to his father's chagrin, who had expected that it would come to them both. Harrigan *had* earned it: she had made him pay for it with sweat and blood in more ways than one.

'Oh, you are my beautiful boy, aren't you?' His aunt's unnaturally cooing voice sounded in his head. He had never said yes to her question, not even as a child when she sat him up on her knee and dug her bony fingers into his ribs. An unmarried woman with her fiancé dead in the war and a compulsive churchgoer, she had talked about his becoming a priest, something that he'd never wanted to be. 'We have to make sure he has a good education. You don't want him to work on the docks, Ellie. You don't want him to be like Jim,' he had listened to her tell his mother. 'I will get him into St

Ignatius for you. I will pay the entry fees. But you will have to contribute.'

'I will. You wait and see,' his mother had replied, condemning herself to work at two jobs morning and night for years to keep him there. She'd finally had the reward of seeing him through a year at university, returning to her old haunt in the parlour of the West End on Mullens Street to boast to her friends over a cigarette and a gin that her son wouldn't work on the docks, he was studying law.

Don't you want to ask me what I want? As the two women had decided his fate, he had said nothing. Silence which had left him for six years in a place where he had learned to survive as an outsider, watching everything he said and did. A privilege for which his two sisters still had not forgiven him, both of whom had been packed off at fifteen to work for Woolworths and earn their keep. Life had changed since then. These days, he often saw boys in the Iggie's uniform crossing Birchgrove Park. Back then he had been the only pupil at the school with this address. In another way, life remained the same. He was still a survivor in an institution with fixed rules that could make him feel unwelcome when it wanted to.

'Paulie was always Mum and Auntie's Maeve's *fave*,' his oldest sister, Ronnie, liked to say at family gatherings, scruffing up his hair boisterously. 'That was a curse, Ronnie,' he'd reply. 'You shouldn't worry. You haven't done too badly for yourself.' Life in a waterside mansion on the Georges River should be as good as living on Snails Bay.

When his aunt had died, just after his sixteenth birthday, she had left him the house, to be held in his mother's trust until he was eighteen. His father never forgave his sister for the public insult and refused to attend her requiem mass. He was an atheist in any case, a union man, a member of the Communist Party, all good reasons for her to disinherit him. The day they had all moved in, he had gone from room to room, cursing her ghost. Her insult festered in the house for years, provoking arguments between his parents so savage Harrigan had wished they would both die. He assumed that this was what his aunt had intended, she'd done enough damage for it to be premeditated. When he laid out the blame for his mother's death, he put his aunt there (among others) as surely as if she'd loaded the bullet herself.

Harrigan walked in the gate to his back garden and looked up at the darkened windows of his house. All their ghosts were gone, he had excised them, making the place his own. He had gutted it in his spare hours, removing the room in which his mother had died, working his own carpentry. He painted the walls a smooth pale texture, like the unbroken membrane on the interior of an egg, which magnified and softened the light and made the space appear larger. He walked into this space now as someone relieved to be home, although the expanse of room and freedom had not been intended just for him. He had built it as much for his own son, in the inverse shape of Toby's body, which was not straight but twisted and which had locked a good mind into a wheelchair and kept his boy in care all his life. He did not have the energy to think about his son tonight. He was tired, tomorrow would do, tomorrow he would go and see him.

He went into the kitchen to mix himself a whisky and water and saw that his ancient cat had struggled up onto the table, settling itself down on the papers he had left there. No one knew how old the cat was, it had walked in off the street one day when his father was still alive, a scabrous, savage, yellow tom who fought with every other cat in the street and littered the neighbourhood with kittens. His father thought it was ugly and nasty and named it Menzies as a posthumous insult to a man he'd hated all his life. Now Menzies was toothless, too decrepit to do more than flex claws which were no longer sharp. He hissed impotently as Harrigan moved him aside, then sank back into sleep.

As Harrigan sipped his drink, Grace's resumé, her smiling photograph, looked up at him from the table. He had read it before but now sat down to look it over with more interest. The daughter of a very senior army officer, she had spent her early life in New Guinea and was boarding-school-educated before the family had returned to the Central Coast when she was about fourteen. She had left school not long after, at sixteen, for life in Sydney, eventually working as a singer. Or so the resumé said: Gracie Riordan & Wasted Daze. Really? So who were they? In his working life, he had met a lot of women who called themselves singers. She hadn't returned from that stratosphere until she had taken herself off to university in her mid twenties.

Harrigan knew the Central Coast, his father used to take him fishing up there when he was a boy. He remembered him marooned among the mangrove swamps in the sun, an unsuccessful fisherman but happy for being on neither shore nor sea. Grace hadn't been a surfer girl if she'd left it all behind that quickly. Here it was: Member, Eastern Suburbs Pistol Club. Winner, Combined Clubs Trophy, Open Category, two years in a row. That's how she got the job, never mind the degree. Not many women shoot well enough to earn trophies two years in a row. Now that he'd met her, he would never have thought she was the type.

Handguns. He sat back in his chair. She'd been there today, she knew what a handgun could do. Why do you shoot? he wanted to ask her. Don't tell me it's a thrill for you. He had his own handgun, not his service revolver but the Smith & Wesson .38 that had killed his mother, hidden down in his tiny cellar behind a loose sandstone block. The gun was memory made real, something in the order of a personal gravestone, a means of holding onto the event and seeking for some solution to it when the actual memory was too painful to recall. There had been occasions when he'd thought about eating it. Occasions not so long after he'd had his jaw broken, when he spent his spare time sitting in a drab hotel room in the country town they had sent him to, playing Russian roulette in the early hours. It was a gamble that had excited him in a way not much else had back then. Not any more. It wasn't what he wanted, if it ever had been. He hankered for a bit of life, not the reverse.

He closed Grace's resumé and decided to try his luck at sleeping. He turned out the light and went upstairs to bed.

As usual, he lay there thinking. There was a black hole at the heart of that resumé, something she wasn't telling anyone, two or three dead years starting when she was just twenty-one. That was young to end up nowhere. How was she living then? The dole? Some other way? He told himself to stick to the tangibles; recruitment had passed her. People have gaps in their lives, he had a few of his own. The real question was: could he trust her, could she do the job? Nothing else mattered. On this thought, he drifted away to sleep.

9

Lucy Hurst raised her head from her pillow in a darkened room made strange by the streaked glow of streetlights through the open louvre windows above the bed. She sat up slowly to see a face in the wardrobe mirror opposite shadowed to a dull, luminous white, bloodless as silicate and surrounded by a stiff mix of dark tentacled curls. She touched her hair and saw the figure in the mirror do likewise. Some event, impossible and unavoidable, that she could not immediately remember, was pressing in on her. The room was empty of any hint of what this might be or why she was here. It was a territory without reference points, static in its unfamiliarity.

She remembered. It was the first time that she had had to remember, a vision possessing a precise and surreal clarity, as indifferent to her as it was to the other three figures at the heart of it. In her mind, silently as a dream, she saw the woman and the man falling one after the other to the roadway, saw the stain on the woman's blue jacket, the man's unshakable stillness, his face, and the boy so close, staring at her. She saw this with a shock of unreality, with only the ordinary room, and its arrangement of an ancient wardrobe, chair and bedside table, to remind her how real it was. She stared at the image in her mind, sickened at heart, unbelieving.

She lay back, actually winded, and then felt that the bed was damp. She touched the warmth in which she was lying and raising her hand into the white light saw a dark liquid on her hands. It was her menstrual blood, not the blood of a wound. It was darker and flowed less freely but had still soaked through her clothes into the bed. She could not understand it, she had not bled for months, had been pleased that she had not bled for months. She had short-circuited her cycle, spiking it with a thin diet and nervous energy, feeling its connective, circular rhythm replaced by the equivalent of a blank sheet of paper, a perfect and disinfected emptiness without the need or the capacity for change. She pushed back the bedclothes and sat up again, scrunching the sheets with her hand to clean it, uncertain what she should do. A giddiness took hold of her. She shook off the mists of sickness, noticed the sour aftertaste of a drug in her mouth, and remembered why she was in this bed.

She had to get out of here. Moving as quickly as she could, she got up, put on and laced up her shoes. As she put on her coat, she again saw the image of the three people in her mind and this time took possession of it angrily, holding onto the fact in its impossibility and extremity. I did that, she told herself. Never forget that. I took those people apart like that. That's mine,

I'm never going to forget that. She looked at the bed with its blankets pulled back to display blood splashed between the ribs of light, dark butterflies on the white sheets. Like the action of a narcotic, she felt a numbness set in, a severance from the surrounding world. She left the room but then was forced to go into the bathroom next door. She sat on the throne, acutely aware of various wastes purging themselves out of her body and feeling the ache of menstrual cramps. She did not know why she should need to bleed when she had schooled every other need — food or warmth or shelter — down to its fundamentals. She cleaned herself as well as she could when she was finished but could only find a hand towel to soak up the flow of her blood. She washed herself again, almost compulsively, and then, badly dehydrated, drank copious handfuls of water from the tap.

She had no perception of what time it might be, she only wanted to find her backpack and then leave the Temple as soon as she could. She left the bathroom and went down the stairs. Silence was diffused like an undisturbed sleep throughout the darkened building, she could not even hear cockroaches scuttling. She tried the back door but it was locked. The Temple was difficult to get into or out of once the doors were shut against you: it was a place of thick walls, barred windows and strong locks. She stopped outside the office and listened for any sound to suggest there might be someone in there, but heard nothing. Opening the door carefully, she saw by the streetlights through the bare windows that the room was empty. She found her pack, placed out of sight inside the tiny windowless kitchen. It was open and had been searched, the contents disturbed. As she looked around, she saw a blister packet emptied of all its tablets on the bench next to the sink. She picked it up. Rohypnol 2 mg. She did not quite laugh as she stared at it. She thought: I need a gun.

She knew things that Graeme did not realise she knew. Under the floorboards in his office, she found his own insurance as he called it: a solitary gun and a good supply of ammunition. She took both, putting the ammunition into her pack after loading the gun with the expertise he had taught her. It was larger and heavier than the one he had originally given her. She weighed the gun in her hand and felt an immediate relief to have it, knowing that, of all things, it was something she could rely on. Because if you can use a gun once, then you know how to use it again. This last thought was a negative whisper in her mind.

The office computer, a powerful and expensive machine, had been left on; its tiny orange lights were intermittent pinpricks in the dark as the monitor slept in power-saving mode. She glanced towards the open door but saw and heard no one. The whole building had a sense of abandonment. Holding onto her gun, she woke the screen and went out on the Net, quickly.

Turtle, are you out there? It's the Firewall. Are you there?

Firewall??? I've been waiting 4 HOURS 2 hear from u Where are u???

You don't want to know. Out here. With a gun in my hand. For real. I'm holding it right now. I'm holding it because I think I might need to use it. It's just so strange to know that.

U can't do that U just can't

I don't know what else to do now. I need the protection.

Who from???? They should be afraid of u!!!

There are worse people than me out here, Turtle. And yeah, I am frightened of them. You can believe I am.

I wish I wasn't stuck here I would help u if I could but I'm stuck Wot are u up 2 now? Can't I do something?

No, this is not you, this is me. I don't want you to take this on. But I don't know. I really don't know what I'm going to do. I've got nowhere to go now.

U can go 2 the police

I said before, there's no point in doing that. Anyway if you do go to the police, all they do is bash you up.

They don't all do that

The ones I know do. No, I've got nowhere to go. Except maybe ...

Except maybe where????

Home? It's the only place left on earth now, isn't it? And it's the worst place to be. My brother rang me the other day. He wants me to come home. But if I do go back there now it's because everything I've done has taken me back there, not for any other reason.

You don't have to go back there do u?

Maybe. If they want me, maybe I will. I was just thinking about it really, that's all. There just isn't anywhere else now.

I've been thinking all day I don't believe it was u who did that U pulled the trigger but your head was somewhere else It has 2 be U just couldnt do that

No, Turtle. I did do it. And I did it because I thought she was evil. But I woke up just now and all I could see in my head was all that blood and what those people looked like. And I think — I have to think this, don't I — if that's what she is, then what about me?

Aren't we both the same now? Aren't we both killers? I don't want to be like her. But I am. So what does that mean? I don't know where my head is any more.

Everything u say — it all says that u aren't like that OK??? I know its not u When I talk 2 u — U are not like that It was some mad thing but not u

But that mad thing is me. I wonder, would I feel like this if I'd only shot her and not that man? I just don't know what to think.

As she typed this, Lucy looked up to see the refuge van, with its lights dimmed, drive across the open space at the back of the picture theatre and come to a halt in the shadow of the building.

Got to go. Love you, she added quickly.

No wait Firewall dont do anything stupid U cant

Lucy shut down the connection. She saw Graeme's figure pass the window and knew that she did not have time to get out of the back door. She moved quickly into the auditorium, hoisting her pack and holding the gun ready. Leaving the door slightly ajar, she stood watching through the crack.

The back door opened and he appeared there in silhouette. He was looking, it seemed, straight at her. She was certain that he had seen her and raised her gun, waiting for him to come towards her. He did not. He shut and locked the door behind him and walked quickly up the stairs, to his room. In the half light she could see that he was carrying a small white paper bag, something round and compact. A fit, was Lucy's instinctive thought, the kind you get free and anonymously from the needle exchange. She was certain that it was intended for her.

She did not wait. She went to the back door and shot the lock open, stepped out into the cold night air and sprinted down the alleyway towards the street, still holding onto her gun. As she reached the end of the lane, she heard what seemed to be a shout behind her, a strange guttural sound, but she did not stop to look back. She cut her way breathlessly past narrow rows of terraced houses, sprinting silently on the tips of her toes. As she ran, she heard a car behind her, its engine suddenly engaged. Its lights caught her briefly as she ran and she sped up, reaching the Peace Park on Church Street, coming through a small grove of eucalyptus trees to the sandstone wall bordering the cemetery at St Stephen's Church. There she lost the strength to run any further. She collapsed on the ground, dropping her pack, and leaned against the wall, curling into the stone out of the light.

She crouched there, gathering breath and looking back at the small grove of trees but no one appeared after her. Her lungs were burning. Still on the edge of panic she thought of Greg, and putting down her gun she reached into an outside pocket of her pack for her mobile phone. Her hands shaking she rang Wheelo's, more out of hope than expectation that Greg would be there. She looked around at the empty park with its sparse lights as she waited for someone to answer her call. Someone would answer sometime, they always did. Someone was always awake. With her free hand, she held onto the butt of her gun.

'Yeah?' a female voice eventually said.

'I was looking for Greg,' she replied.

'Yeah, who's this?'

'It's Luce. Is that Jade?'

'Yeah. He's not here, Luce. He went out with Wheelo. He said he was going for a joy ride, he knew this car he could get hold of. They were going to torch it, I think. That's what I thought I heard them say, anyway.'

Shit! Lucy thought. 'When?'

'I dunno. A while ago now. But I think the pigs got Greg, because some of them came sniffing around here for Wheelo just this little while back. Mick told me to stay out of the way but I think that's what I heard them saying. So if they got Greggie, that means he's going back in again. So you can't get him. Unless you want to go and see him up at Kariong.'

Lucy was silent.

'You still there, Luce?' said the voice.

'When you see Wheelo, you tell him from me that I rang looking for Greggie, okay? And if he sees Greggie, he should tell him that he's got to be careful. Really careful. Tell him he's not to go back to the refuge ever again, okay? Tell him exactly that. Just say it's not safe.'

Jade sounded surprised. 'Yeah, if you want.'

Lucy did not believe Jade would remember to do any of this. She cut the connection without another word. She had no energy left and her head was bathed in sweat.

Back to the cells for you now, Greggie. I can't get to you there, it's too dangerous. Just believe I'm thinking about you in there. They'll shave your head again and they'll take away your beanie and, if you're lucky, they'll give it back to you when they let you go again. Whenever that is. Graeme won't be able to get you out of there this time. This time, for the first time, you might even be safer in there. Just for now anyway.

Someone would tell Graeme what had happened; it wouldn't be her. The woman from Family Services, Ria, would call him if no one else. Or the police. He would be angry when he was told, very angry. Thinking of this, she almost smiled. Then a giddiness took hold of her and she leaned back against the wall. She felt cold, a residual wave of the drug was travelling through her bloodstream. The telephone slipped out of her hand and fell to the ground. Having nowhere else to put it, she pushed her gun into the outer pocket of her backpack and buttoned her jacket tightly around her, hugging herself. She wanted to run but could only sit there unable to move, feeling her eyes closing against her will. She had no strength.

She was breathing deeply and was part way between waking and unconsciousness when, even in the dark, she became aware that there was a shadow across her face and someone was leaning over her. She could hear and then feel their breath. She forced herself awake, not quite screaming, plucking desperately at her pack.

'Luce! What do you think you're doing? It's only me.'

Stephen's voice and her perception of who it was were simultaneous. Unnerved, she sat up slowly.

'Stevie, please don't ever do that to me again,' she said. 'I was so frightened just then.'

'You frightened me too.'

He smiled nervously and hunkered down close to her. The empty park and the dark streets of Newtown stretched around them.

'Shit, Luce. Look at you. What have you done to yourself?' he said, and touched her forehead which was damp with perspiration. 'Are you all right? You look like — I thought you were clean. Has that all changed, has it?'

She did not immediately answer him. She tried to smile but could not.

'No,' she said, 'this was something I really didn't want to take.'

This particular truth sounded strange in her mouth, like the taste of metal on the tongue.

'God, Luce, you take some risks. I never know what I'm going to hear about you next.'

'I do, don't I?' she said a little shakily. 'Chasing me around, are you?'

'I must be.' He spoke quietly, looking around them. 'You know that guy you told me about, the preacher? I went and saw him yesterday evening but he said you weren't around. He threw me out, I thought he was going to break my wrist. Where were you?'

Lucy said nothing. She swallowed some leftover fear and shook her head. Stephen's glasses had slipped down over the bridge of his nose. He pushed them back.

'When you came out of there,' he said, 'you were running so fast. I tried to get after you in the car but you just ran. I thought I saw — did you have something in your hand? I didn't know if ...'

He stopped.

'No. That was just me being me,' Lucy said. 'I was being paranoid. I get like that.'

'I heard — I don't know ... Did you hear a shot or something? Was I dreaming? Did you hear —'

'I didn't hear anything, Stevie. I wasn't listening.'

He looked at her where she sat against the wall, her jacket pulled around her, then sat on the grass beside her, stretching out his damaged leg. The glow of the park lights touched on his pronounced forehead, his straight dark hair.

'I've got to deal with Dad, Luce. And he's dying. I don't have the energy for anything else. You have to tell me that you're not in any sort of trouble and there's nothing that's going to make the shit hit the fan. I can't deal with it if there is.'

'Dad?' Lucy interrupted him. 'He sent you running around town looking for me? Wouldn't you know it? He wasn't going to come looking for me himself.'

'He can't, Luce. He can hardly move. He says he wants to see you before he dies. He keeps at it, he won't let it go. If you don't come, it'll be the last thing he ever says to anyone. We'll all be standing around and the only thing he'll say is that you're not there.'

'What does he think he's going to say to me?'

'I don't know. I don't think he knows either. He wants to see you. That's all he's told me.'

'And what if it had been me that was dead instead of him? It could have been. It almost was once or twice. What was he going to do then? Was he going to worry about me? Or was he just going to say, oh, she didn't come and see me before she died?'

'I don't know, Luce. Okay? I can't answer that question. You want me to tell you the truth? I'm here because it's going to make things easier for us if you do come home. And I'm at the point where I just can't handle much more.'

Her father had never come looking for her when he had been well, why should she expect him to now? She looked down the slope of open grass to the narrow streets below, where the small houses and white factory buildings slept on in a pattern of streetlights. The scene was so still; it seemed that no world existed beyond the reach of the streetlights, only darkness without end on the other side of a wide glass bowl.

'All right, I'll come home,' she said after some moments. 'I'll talk to him. Because *I* want to talk to him.'

Twenty-four hours ago nothing would have made her go home, but yesterday, just after dawn when she had fired those shots, she had slipped between a hair space in time. Every thought she had, everything she did, dragged her back to that moment. Her mother and father were waiting for her there, like two spectators in the cheap seats, eating popcorn. Thoughts formed in her mind like words spoken out of the shadows to those two expressionless figures, munching as they watched her. I want to see you. For the first time I want to see you, I want to ask you something. She wanted to look at her father and her mother and ask if either of them had ever woken in the night, the way she just had, and thought: I did that, what am I going to do now that I've done something as horrible as that? She wanted to ask them: don't you feel like that, just a bit? For what you did to me? Give me an answer, because you owe me one.

'Will you promise me you won't fight with him?' Stephen asked, pushing his glasses back on his nose again. 'Because if you do, he'll just take it out on everybody else.'

'No, it'll be okay, Stevie. If he doesn't say what I want to hear, I'll just go again.'

She spoke with a false bravado. Stephen's relief was all too obvious. He stood up quickly.

'Let's get out of here then, I don't like it here. Have you got everything? You don't have to go back and get any stuff out of that place?'

He jerked his thumb over his shoulder in the general direction of the Temple.

'Oh, no,' she replied.

No, she wasn't going back in there.

'Is this yours?' he asked.

He had as good as trodden on her mobile phone and was holding up the shiny blue object.

'Yeah, I must have dropped it.'

Even in the half dark, his face expressed the question that he was never going to ask her: where did you get it?

'Does it work?' he asked instead.

'Used to,' she said, with something of a smile.

'Do you mind if I use it?' he asked. 'I should call Mel, just to let her know we're coming.'

'Keep it if you want.' She was dismissive. 'It's just a bit of nothing. It's never hard to get hold of bits of nothing like that.'

'It's okay, Luce. You can have it back when I've finished.'

She stood up slowly, looking around her. Her head was still bathed in sweat and she did not know if this was because she had been drugged or because she was afraid. She had the perception that they were being watched, and that the person out there watching them was dangerous.

'Hi, Mel, it's Stevie. I'm sorry I got you out of bed. No, I've found her, she's coming home. Yes, I know — it's okay. Could you get something ready for us, something to eat? I'm starving and I don't know when Luce last ate anything. And can you get some clean clothes or something for her? She needs them. And some ... napkins, whatever ... I don't know. She's a mess. Forty minutes? There's no traffic. Okay. I'll see you.'

He handed the phone back to her. She switched it off and stowed it away, then hoisted her pack, swaying on her feet under its weight.

'You all right? Do you want me to carry that?'

'No,' she said. You don't get to carry this, Stevie, I do.

'You look like death, Luce,' he said, his own face grey in the unnatural light.

Yes.

The park seemed deserted as they walked back to

Stephen's car in a nearby street, near the small grove of trees and opposite the blue and yellow swirls of a mural painted with the caption 'Simultaneous Lovin', Baby'. As the car turned an arc, she thought she saw the outline of a figure in the dark, Graeme standing in the shadows of the trees. It was only a glimpse but she looked away quickly nonetheless.

They drove through the empty streets, out onto the highway. She curled up in the corner of the seat but was too jangled to sleep. The electric outlines of the city came to meet them: high-rise, shop fronts, service stations, the curve of the Gladesville Bridge over the dark river. As they passed, the array of ghostly structures faded away either side of the thin white line. She began to feel icy cold as they drove further and further towards the edge of the urban sprawl; the substance Graeme had given her had left her body embalmed in a chill sweat.

'What time is it?' she asked.

Stephen glanced at his watch. 'Twenty past four. Almost time to get up.' Then, 'That guy at the theatre — he doesn't know where home is? He wouldn't try and come looking for you out here, would he?'

Lucy looked at Stephen and decided not to ask why this possibility might worry him.

'Graeme?' She felt uneasy simply saying his name. 'No, I never told him where I came from. He never asked. We didn't really talk that much about me after a while,' she added, in an oddly halting voice.

'What are you saying?'

She shook her head. 'Just what we talked about, that's all.'

No, their months of conversation, one on one, had been fixed towards another point completely. Everything she had said to him, he had directed elsewhere, away from her — something which in itself had been a relief at the time — towards a single action. That of her firing a gun at the specified target he had presented to her. In her mind, these actions were reduced to their sharp outlines, recall came in disconnected flashes: Graeme's smiling face, the recoil of the gun as she fired it at a tree, the recoil as she fired it at a person. Then all the players were caught in her act of execution, the woman and the man and finally the boy, staring at her with horror in his face. She asked herself how often she was going to see this. She glanced at Stephen next to her. What would you think about me if you knew, Stevie? What's it going to do to you when you find out? You and Mel? I never asked myself. I didn't even ask myself that.

When she considered the preacher, she realised she no longer had a way of describing him to herself. The image in her mind was of the man standing over her, watching her with his gentle and serene gaze while she was in the grip of the drug, saying that he intended to kill both her and someone she loved.

You can't get to me, Graeme, and anyway I can look after myself. And you can't get to Greg, and that's really all that matters. But just to make sure, I'm going to ring Ria. She can warn Greg, even if no one else can.

'What are you thinking about, Luce?' Stephen asked, a strange tone in his voice.

'Nothing,' she replied, unaware of the expression on her face or the shiver that went down Stephen's spine as he looked at her. He sped up, accelerating past a convoy of trucks rumbling northwards along the highway, a monstrous force tricked out in a delicate rigging of many-coloured lights, taking on the force of their jet stream, passing them at speed.

* * *

They had reached the streets close to home, the far northern edge of the city. There was no moon. Lucy looked out at large houses newly built in the old bushland, where occasional groves of trees had been left behind for decoration. All were pale silver in the reflected light of the city.

'None of this was here before,' she said.

'They just keep subdividing. There won't be anything left soon. We've got houses almost up to our front door now. We get real-estate agents ringing us all the time. *If you want to sell, we'll get you a good price.* I feel like telling them, you don't know what you're buying, mate. You don't have that much money.'

Their double-storey ninety-forties brick house came into view, built by their grandfather several years after he had been demobbed. In the photographs that Lucy had seen, there had once been a four-roomed, wooden tongue-and-groove house in this place, one that her great-grandfather had built here not long after he had cleared the original forest. Their grandfather had told them how he had demolished it and built this pile in its place, going up in the world.

Stephen turned off the engine to slide noiselessly down the gentle slope of their driveway, halting just before the garage.

'You're home,' he said.

Yes.

In the pale light, they walked across a rectangle of spongy couch grass. A dog came out of her kennel, her chain rattling. Lucy knelt beside her, rubbing her head.

'Hello, Dora. Hello, girl. Look, she remembers me. Why is she chained up? She never used to be.'

'It's just something that's happened. Dad said to chain her up. The neighbours don't like her. They say she's dangerous, she bails up their kids.'

'She wouldn't do anybody any harm. Poor old thing.'

At the back door Lucy hesitated. She stood listening to the rustle of the bushland around the house, too frightened to walk inside.

'It's okay,' Stephen said. 'Mum's asleep and Dad's out to it just about every night these days. It's only Mel. Come on.'

The kitchen, a large room, smelled of toast, coffee and milk, a comforting and safe smell. In the bright fluorescent light, Mel was putting breakfast dishes on the table. She looked at her older sister without smiling, her face seemed deliberately emptied of emotion. Short like her brother, she stood bare-legged in a tight denim skirt and sweatshirt, her hair tightly curled and dyed a pale red.

'Hi, Mel,' Lucy said, with half a smile.

Mel looked back at her, still unsmiling, refusing a greeting. Her eyes were sleepy.

'I made your bed up. Do you want to go and have your shower now? You need one, you look awful. There's some napkins in the bathroom if you want them. When you've finished, can you put your dirty clothes in the laundry for me right away because I've got to get them washed and dry as soon as I can. I've got to wash Dad's sheets every day so I haven't got time to do your washing as well.'

With this, she went back to the bench where she was preparing breakfast. Lucy said nothing. She turned away but then stopped at the doorway that led into the rest of the house.

'It's okay, Luce.' Stephen said. 'Want me to walk you in?'

Lucy looked back and saw that Mel was watching this concern with contempt.

'No,' she said to him, holding tightly onto her pack. 'I'm all right.' In the hallway, and on the stairs up to her room which were lit by a night-light, everything was as it had always been. The house was rambling, a collection of airless rooms with small windows, all stacked with an accumulation of things. Lucy's mother, Vera, never threw anything out. In her thinking, everything, if kept long enough, might one day have a use, and if broken might one day be repaired. Ancient leftovers were buried in the permafrost of the freezer; old clothes and toys were crammed under the beds; newspapers, cardboard boxes, aluminium cans were stacked in the hallways. Lucy walked along the upstairs hallway that smelled of naphthalene and used goods, a bite of mould and cobwebs, odours which were only dispelled in the heat of summer when the house baked in the sun.

'It hasn't changed. Nothing's changed,' she said to herself, almost in bewilderment.

Opening the door to her bedroom and turning on the light, she was surprised by its unfamiliarity, how faded it was at first glance. She shut the door softly behind her and put her backpack next to the bed, then looked around her uneasily. The walls were covered with posters torn from magazines: pop stars she had forgotten about, golden-eyed tigers swimming in tropical rivers. The ceiling was painted blue, the skirting boards and cornice, silver. The arc of gold stars she had glued onto a window was still there. It was a world with nothing on its surface to indicate the events which had once occurred regularly in here.

Her father used to tell her in the afternoon what he intended to do that evening. When he walked into her room, he simply said, 'Strip.' It was the only thing he said to her, from the first moment to the last, from the first time to the last. There was another memory: about ten days after she had become too sick to eat in the mornings, her mother saying to her, 'Hurry up, we're going into the city now. He'll give us a ride to Hornsby and we'll get the train from there.'

Lucy spoke aloud, to herself, 'You don't want to worry. It's what Turtle said — he ought to be frightened of you now. So should she.'

She was on the verge of something that was not quite panic. She sat on the bed, holding herself and rocking backwards and forwards. She took her gun out of her pack and held onto it tightly, breathing deeply, drawing on its security.

'I'll keep you with me,' she said, 'and then I'll be okay.'

In the bathroom, Lucy locked the door behind her and placed the gun on the basin within reach. In the shower, she felt the warm water ease her spine and watched as her own blood was washed into its spiral at her feet. She shook her head at the peculiarity of having a body that felt and bled. She dried her clean skin, drawing each of her limbs into existence as she polished herself with the towel, reconnecting her nerve endings. She saw herself in a full-length mirror, in a small pool of white light. Her body had gained strength since she had broken with her addiction. Despite her lean diet, it was wiry rather than thin and she had acquired some cushioning softness and muscle. She saw a body that — without her noticing — had gained some womanliness. 'That's me,' she said with a compelling sense of dislocation. After she had dressed, she looked at herself again. She saw her reflection silvered in light, a figure made of metal, clean as purified air.

'I couldn't have stayed here,' she said to her reflection, 'I couldn't have. What else was I going to do but go?'

She smoothed her wet hair back from her forehead. Her face in the mirror and the light were extinguished at the same moment.

Reluctantly, she put the gun back in her pack before she went downstairs. It had grown light when she came back to the kitchen. There, she heard Stephen and Melanie arguing. Mel's voice was quick, breathless and angry. Lucy stopped to listen until she did not want to hear any more.

'I don't see why I have to be nice to her,' Melanie was saying. 'She was a bitch. She went off and left me, she didn't care, she didn't wait around. Now she's out there all the time, doing whatever she wants to do, and I stay here and I have to wash for him and I have to wash *him* as well and I cook for him and I look after him while all Mum does is sit around and watch TV all day. And then she just comes back here when she wants to and you say to me *I* have to be —'

Mel stopped short as Lucy appeared in the doorway, and turned away. Stevie was sitting at the table, smoking. He greeted Lucy with the faintest shrug. She stood there, awkward, wishing that she was carrying the gun and could feel its metal pressing against her waist. For a brief moment anger seethed in her head.

You shouldn't talk about me like that, Mel, it's not fair. I couldn't do anything back then. If anyone tried to hurt you now, I'd kill them. I would. Then you wouldn't be able to say that about me.

'Sit down and eat your breakfast,' Melanie said to her without turning around.

The silence weighed on them all as Lucy and Stephen ate slowly. Two thirds of the way through the meal, Lucy stopped.

'I can't eat any more,' she said. 'My throat feels like it's full of broken bones. I've got to go and sleep.'

'Are you all right?' Stephen asked.

'Yeah. I'm just really tired.'

She got to her feet. At the door, she turned to look at them, Melanie with her angry face, and Stephen's, with his guard let down, showing intense exhaustion.

I can't tell either of you what I've done, I'll never be able to tell you.

'I'll see you later,' she said.

In her room, her sense of fear returned powerfully. She slipped her gun under the pillow and then pushed a chair against the door. Forcing herself to make the effort, she sat on the bed and made her call to Ria. The woman answered almost immediately, over a line that shifted and roared with static.

'Yes,' she said, in a crackling voice.

'It's Luce, Ria.'

There was a pause.

'What do you want?'

The woman spoke sharply through the interference.

'I've got a message for Greg. The police have got him, haven't they?'

Lucy heard the woman laugh angrily.

'Your information's good. Yeah, they have, they just rang me. I wish I could keep track of him the way you do ...'

The line broke up. In the crackling, Lucy heard the words 'can't believe', which faded and then came back strongly as 'accessory' and 'murder'. Hearing this, Lucy spoke softly to the airways with a twist of bitterness in her voice.

'Well, they wouldn't know anything, would they?

They'd just pick on whoever they could find. They never get the real killers.'

'What's your message, Lucy?'

The woman's voice came through suddenly clear, sounding wary and disturbed.

'You tell him from me that whatever he does, he can't go back to the refuge. That's all. He's not to go anywhere near it again, ever. He'll know what I mean.'

There was silence.

'Lucy,' the woman said, 'I don't want you to say anything else to me. I'm hanging up on you now. Whatever you do, don't ring me again.'

Lucy said nothing else. She turned off her phone and tossed it onto her old desk. She crawled into bed exhausted, without undressing, and slept with one hand holding onto her gun.

10

In the winter morning light, Paul Harrigan was countermanding his own instruction that the job took precedence over everything and nothing else mattered. He drove against the traffic to make the short journey from Birchgrove to Cotswold House at Drummoyne, stealing the first hour before work to see his son. He may not get the chance again for some time.

Toby was the product of a briefly sweet marriage, contracted when Harrigan was barely twenty-one, while he had been wandering the countryside, working as a boxer and a fruit picker. His marriage had had the unusual effect of leaving him holding the baby while his wife had disappeared, rejecting a child permanently injured during the hours of his birth, a tiny baby left weighted down for life with the medical terms choreoathetosis and dysathria. Her action was truly unforgivable in Harrigan's eyes. They'd divorced years ago; Sara lived in Western Australia now with some other man. He did not give her a voluntary thought, she had never tried to see her son. She had never even sent money, although if she had, he would not have taken it. She was another figure he had excised ruthlessly from his past.

This morning, as he crossed the Iron Cove Bridge, Harrigan watched his night thoughts disappear in the dawn over the harbour to become the daylight certainty that there were possibilities for happiness after all. Among other things, life had its pleasures in the early glitter of the sun on the harbour and the sight of the black cormorants fishing from their perches on the old wooden piers. At Cotswold House, built on the shore overlooking Cockatoo and Spectacle Islands with their disused shipyards, he was let in and greeted by the house manager, Susie Pavic.

'Good morning, Paul,' she said. 'We all sat with Toby and watched you on TV last night. What a terrible thing.'

'Yeah, it is. But we're working on it. We'll get there.'

Although he liked Susie, he spoke to stop the conversation, with a quick smile, not wanting work to come between him and his son. Down a short shining hallway, he saw Toby being wheeled out of his room by his therapist.

'Paul. I didn't think you were going to make it today.'

Toby's therapist, Tim Masson, fussed too much in Harrigan's opinion.

'No, I'm right on time as far as I know. I'm here now, that's what matters. Hi, Toby. How are you?'

Using his one good hand, Toby squeezed his father's offered hand for a few moments. Masson withdrew to the activity room to make them all coffee, while Harrigan left his coat and tie in his son's room. He took hold of the chair and set off down the corridor to the bathroom, a large room with walls and floor covered with shining white tiles and a wide spa bath with chrome fittings. Toby stubbornly pulled one-handed at his nightclothes as his father knelt by the tub, turning on the taps, swirling the water around. Steam began to rise in clouds, the noise of running water concealing their mutual silence.

'Let me help you,' Harrigan said, standing up.

He felt the night warmth of his son's body as he carefully removed the unresisting garments. Toby's dysfunctional body and his inability to speak connected Harrigan to his son, body to body, human to human. Sex did not necessarily give him this closeness. Toby was made in his father's image: his height, the shape of his body, the paleness of his skin, could have been — would have been — Harrigan's own. Their physical capacities were different, only that. Harrigan carried this sense of loss as something that was as unchanging as Toby's disability; his feelings made him gentle with his son. He dropped the side rail on the chair, slid one arm around his son's shoulders, another under his knees, and lifted Toby, an action which these days took all his strength. One day, very soon, he would not be able to lift him at all.

'I've got you,' he said. 'Here we go.'

He lowered his son into the wide bath and let the warm water bubbling up from the light spa support and ease his body. Toby slid out to almost his full length in the water, his fixed arm crooked at an angle across his breastbone, one leg hooked a little over the other.

'Are you comfortable there?' Harrigan asked, and saw Toby's silent response, the yes flicker of the fingers of his good hand.

Toby could speak a little, and sometimes did, but it took much effort to get out even a single word. His words lived as thoughts, or became bits of light which he tapped out one-handed onto a computer screen. Their conversations were silent, today expressed through the movement of Harrigan's hands as he washed his son's hair and felt the weight of Toby's head in his hands in reply. He massaged his son's shoulders, working at the unyielding muscle with slow, patient hands before washing the rest of his body. He began to soap around his son's genitals, which were partially erect. They had their own young boy's perfection and were pale as the skin on the rest of his body. As he did so, he felt Toby hitting him on the arm with his good hand.

'I hurt you, did I? I'm sorry, I thought I was being careful. That hurts, does it? Okay, I won't do that.'

Harrigan rinsed the soap away and saw no sign of injury or inflammation. Some minor infection? The ache you get when there isn't any means of relief? Or is it that you don't want me washing you any more, you're too old? I have to, Toby, it's the only way we can do this.

He stopped and looked at his son. His hand was resting on the edge of the bath and Toby took hold of it. He held on to Harrigan with a tight grip. What is it? Harrigan thought. Tell me what's locked in your head. Used to this silence between them, Harrigan was unaware that he had said nothing. They held onto each other for some moments and then his son let go. The connection broken, Harrigan went to get the bath towels, to get Toby out of the bath (an action which would require Tim Masson's help, Harrigan had to admit this) and then dried and dressed.

'Are you hungry?' he said. 'I could use some breakfast myself.'

As he looked back, he saw Toby looking at him, an odd, indefinable expression in his eyes. He did not know whether it was his son's helplessness as he lay there in the water or some other quality that he could not define, but the expression left him troubled. He dried Toby, dressed him, dried and brushed his hair, and in the dining room fed him and wiped his mouth clean. Toby sucked orange juice through a straw out of the drinking receptacle Harrigan held for him. I'm here, Toby. I'm always here.

'What's on your mind, Toby?' he said. 'Something's bothering you. I've got to go to work now but I'll drop by again as soon as I can. I'll see if I can't get here tonight. You can tell me then if you want.'

Toby flickered 'okay' with his good hand, a gesture that was neither inviting nor repelling. They said goodbye in their mutual silence, with Toby squeezing his hand.

He went to see the house manager in her office on his way out. Susie, plump and fair-haired, sparkled in the sunlight through the windows, her make-up rainbow-like.

'Do you need to worry?' she said. 'His health is good, he's eating well. His school marks are very good, he's up there with the best of them, Paul. He has been spending a bit of time on the Net lately, but I don't see that's a bad thing. It all takes him out of himself. He's doing really well. I feel we should be pleased.'

'No, Susie.' Harrigan shook his head. 'There's something troubling him. I want to know what it is. Now either you or Tim should be able to tell me that.' That's what I pay you for. He let the words hang in the air unspoken.

Susie's opalescent blue fingernails glinted in the light. In reply, she spoke with the care of someone who made a living walking tightropes.

'Well, I don't think you need me to tell you any of this. He's seventeen at his next birthday. In some ways he's older than most boys his age, but he's a lot younger in others. If he doesn't want you washing him any more, I'd say that's probably all there is to that. He does need to feel his body's his own. But he needs his head space more. That's where he lives. You know better than anyone, Paul, he's got people around him all the time, he has to have. Usually he's never alone except in his head. We don't have the right to intrude in there without him letting us. If there's something on his mind, he'll tell you when he's ready to.'

He did not reply, her words had left him almost breathless. They looked at each other across her desk.

'He still needs me, Susie. He's always going to need me.'

'Yes, he will. But that isn't what I said.'

He stood up.

'We'll have to talk about this some other time. I can't hang around here now, I should have been at work half an hour ago. I didn't really have the time to come here in the first place. I'm only here for him.'

She smiled at him professionally in reply. He walked out without thanking her or saying goodbye. Did she think she knew his son better than he did? He could not talk to her, he could not look at her.

Harrigan went out into the morning sunlight and stopped by his car. Toby was with his therapist in the activity room, sitting in the sun and watching him through the wide windows. He waved and saw the flicker of Toby's fingers in reply. As things were now, Toby was with him for life. Oh, there was money enough. Harrigan had sued the hospital where Toby had been born for everything he could think of, taking their drunk and incapable doctor through every level of appeal. The exercise had got him the law degree he was supposed to have had a decade earlier, and while it had taken years, in the end they had paid, had been forced to pay, much more than he had ever expected or hoped for. Money was no longer the point. *He does need me, Susie. Who else is going to love you, Toby, the way I do?*

There was never an escape. Trevor Gabriel tracked him down on his mobile phone as he loitered in the traffic on his way back into the city, worrying at his concerns for Toby in the no-man's land between work and not-work, almost as if he was unemployed.

'Morning, Boss,' Trevor said cheerily. 'Good news, we've found the car. A couple of juveniles were caught trying to torch it in the wee small hours down near Macdonaldtown Station. We've got one of them in custody now.'

'Just the one? What happened to the other?'

'Still in full cry. He went up a wall and over the train lines and away.'

'Yeah?' Harrigan tried to picture it. 'Lucky he didn't get smacked by the state rolling stock. Who have we got?'

'Ours is a Greg Smith. He's fifteen and he's got a file the size of a phone book down at Family Services. And another one at Juvenile Justice to go with it.'

Harrigan manoeuvred through the traffic as he traversed the steel spider's web of what he still called the new Glebe Island Bridge. On his left, the Balmain peninsula looked like an island in a glittering mirror of water, edged in a scattered green amongst the container wharves. The Romanesque colonnaded church tower of

St Augustine's, the tallest of the towers and steeples, was outlined against the clear air.

'Have we checked any known associates for this other boy?'

'The patrol went around knocking on a few doors early this morning but they didn't find anybody. I've got a couple of the guys out looking at the moment.'

'Is anyone with the car? Do we know anything about it?'

'Ian should over be there by now. The owner is a Christine Van Aalst. She reported it missing from outside of her house in Enmore at 7.08 a.m. yesterday. She checks out. I'd say she was just unlucky.'

'I'll go over there now and take a look. In the meantime, don't let anyone pester this boy. Keep him on ice till I get there.'

'No rush,' Trevor replied. 'The boy's in the care of some character called the Preacher Graeme Fredericksen, whoever he is. We can't raise him from anywhere, he's not at home and he's not answering any of his phones. And we're still waiting for the case worker from Family Services to get here. I don't know what she's doing with herself but she's bloody slow too.'

While Trevor spoke, Harrigan was watching the glass walls of the city's office towers ranged in the near distance with the pale sky behind them. The sunlight glanced off the sides of the buildings with the sharpness of new steel.

'Nobody wants this boy,' he said. 'Check up on that preacher or whatever he is, would you? He should be there if no one else is. I'll be there as soon as I can.'

He began to drive with purpose, making a detour through the city's arterial roads to the other side of

Newtown. At the scene, a small group of bystanders had gathered to watch on a nearby street corner. They looked at him curiously as he let himself in under the blue ribbons. The houses roundabout were the same as the one he'd grown up in near White Bay: narrow single-storey cottages with a lone front window opening onto a tiny porch. These ones had been painted in bright colours and had second storeys extended into the roof line, with bars placed over the windows for security. Trees had been planted along the street to shade them, bottle brush and jasmine lined the laneways close by. In summer, these plants would provide the illusion of coolness.

The car, a late model white Mazda sedan, had been parked in a narrow lane between the back fences of the houses and the retaining wall bordering the railway line. At first sight, it appeared largely undamaged. There was a fire engine standing close by at the end of the lane. He saw Ian at a short distance from the car, watching the forensic team at work.

'Hi, Boss,' he said as Harrigan walked up.

'Morning, mate. What's happened here?'

'The kid we've got in custody was splashing petrol around in the boot when he got jumped on by a couple of the locals. Apparently a car got torched down here a while ago and half their garages and the fences along here almost went up in smoke. So the neighbours got together and put in a silent alarm. Lucky they did, that car is fucking drenched. I think it would've exploded if anyone had lit it up.'

'And the one we didn't get went up that wall?'

Harrigan looked up at the dark-stained and uneven stone wall rising above their heads. A suburban train rattled past at speed on one of the further tracks.

'That's what I've been told. Up, up and away. He must have done because no one's found him yet. You might want to take a look in the boot while you're here, there's some interesting things in there.'

Harrigan walked over to the car with Ian and greeted the head of the forensic team. They stopped work and stood aside for him. Tossed inside the boot was a small collection of blood-stained clothes: jeans, jacket, gloves and a scarf.

'I see what you mean,' Harrigan said, wrinkling his nose, 'the sweet odour of petrol.'

'Can you tell us anything about this?' he asked the forensic team leader, a middle-aged woman with purple hair.

'So far?' the woman replied. 'Whoever she is, if she got into these clothes, she's very small. She took a tumble, a bad one. It must have hurt. She landed on her hands and knees and she tore her gloves. I'm fairly certain we should get some skin fragments for you. If we do, we can tie the gun to the glove to the hand without too much argument. There's a lot of blood on these clothes as well.' She smiled at him. 'An embarrassment of riches.'

'You could say that,' Harrigan replied a little dryly. 'Thank you.'

They moved back, out of the way.

'That's how she dropped her gun,' Ian said, 'tripped coming out of the shop. Our girl can't know what she's doing. I don't think she could have made any more mistakes if she'd tried.'

'We know everything we need to know about her except who she is. And she's still out there,' Harrigan replied. 'You're staying on to see this through?'

'Yeah, I'll be here.'

Before leaving the scene, Harrigan stopped once again to look up at the high retaining wall with its sparse toeholds of tenacious vegetation. The other boy must have been pissing himself to get up there, but fear has a leverage all its own. He knew this from his own experience of sheer terror: the moment in a back alley in Marrickville one night ten years ago, when Michael Casatt had pushed Harrigan's own gun into his mouth and forced his hand onto it with the succinct words, 'You're dead, mate.' That microsecond of time was set to be his permanent hiatus when it was broken by some brave, brave soul that he had never met and thanked, who had shone their car lights onto them at high beam. The moment had had a depth of emotion Harrigan would not have thought possible if he had not experienced it. His body might have vaporised, he might have already been dead. Then the gun butt hit his jaw and his jaw hit the ground, almost in the same instant. After that, he had felt nothing except atrocious pain, which, for a short space of time, was the most welcome feeling he'd ever had. At least he was still alive.

Maybe this was the reason he had never taken any pleasure from seeing fear work on the people he interviewed in his job, the way some of his colleagues did. He watched his subjects twisting in its grip and felt nothing other than repugnance for the humiliation. He dealt with it by telling himself that fear was like anything that was human. What mattered was how you used it.

He took out his phone and rang Trevor. 'What have you got Grace doing this morning?' he asked.

'She's doing what you wanted her to do. She's over at the hospital checking up on Matthew and the doc. Why?'

'She was good with that boy yesterday. I'd like to see how she might go with this one today. Get her back in for me, would you?'

'You want Grace? Sure you don't want Louise? After all, she's already here. Look, Boss, you don't want to be sexist about this — you could always get one of the guys.'

'Louise will breathe stale booze all over him and she'll scare him. So will all of the rest of your ugly mugs. Get Grace. Get her to meet me outside the interview room. Tell her I'll brief her myself and I'm going to sit in on it.'

'Lucky Grace. I'll get her right away.'

Ignoring the sarcasm, Harrigan hung up. Yes, get Grace. She can chat to this boy in that nice voice of hers and smile at him with that smile. Sweet-talk him, soothe him down. Maybe even put him off his guard long enough to make him open up.

The forensic team began to remove the clothes from the boot just as he walked away to his car. He always thought that blood, whether it was dried on clothes or walls, had an inconsequential look to it, something that could be brushed off and the slightly more stubborn stains washed away. The boy they had in custody had wanted to burn these rags into non-existence, even at the risk of obliterating himself. Grace could use this fact to squeeze him in a gentle enough way if she tried. He was curious to see if she would do it, whether she had the backbone. It was a pleasant thought, the idea of spending some time with her to find this out. It was already brightening up his day.

11

Grace stood beside him outside the interview room, her long hair in a single plait over one shoulder, waiting while he checked his watch once more. Harrigan had not expected to waste quite this much time hanging around.

'I just love cooling my heels like this,' he said to her with a grin. 'Nice to know I've got nothing better to do with my time. What is this woman doing? Writing the boy's obituary?'

She smiled ironically in reply. 'Here we go. At last,' she said.

The case worker finally appeared in the corridor, a big woman in a shapeless black dress wearing round glasses and with bright earrings in the shape of parrots. Harrigan turned to greet her with a smile and an outstretched hand.

'Ria Allard? I'm pleased to meet you,' he said. 'I'm Paul Harrigan and this is my colleague, Grace Riordan. How are you?'

The sociability was wasted. She brushed past him, ignoring his offered hand, and returned his introduction by looking them both up and down as though they had dropped in for the day from outer space.

'Do you mind if we don't bother with all the crap,' she said. 'I need to talk to Greg for a few moments alone first but I'd like to get this over and done with as soon as we can if you don't mind. I have got other things to do today.'

'Be my guest, Ria. I'll even open the door for you,' Harrigan replied affably.

'How would you like to be locked in a small room with her?' Grace commented, after the interview room door closed on the case worker's back.

Harrigan grinned. 'Yeah, she's a real charmer. Don't let her throw you, Grace — I'm assuming that's what she's up to. Whatever she does, you take your time and you take it gently. Just keep coaxing him. I'll keep her in line.'

'Okay,' she replied.

They waited around a little longer until the door was finally opened to them.

'I've already told him who you are,' Ria Allard said, as they came inside. 'You don't have to bother with that. He knows your names and why you're here.'

'We have to tell him anyway, Ria. I'm sure you know that,' Harrigan replied, smiling in a businesslike way.

Harrigan went through the ritual, giving Grace the opportunity to look the case worker over. Her hair was dyed too black for her ageing face and she had reduced her eyebrows to a thin painted line. Anger was her most obvious quality; she sat beside Greg Smith seething with unspoken rage. The introductions finished, Harrigan sat back a little from the table, leaving it to Grace.

'Hi, Greg,' she said. 'How are you?'

'How do you think he is?' the case worker answered for him. 'You've hauled him in here on some wild pretext, he's hardly had any breakfast. What do you think he's feeling like?'

'Maybe he'd like to tell me that for himself,' Grace replied with her tough, sweet smile, and then repeated for him, 'How are you?'

The boy shrugged. He had a long, thin face that was hollowed out from the nose across to the cheekbones and his hair straggled onto his shoulders. He twisted his red beanie in his hands and glanced quickly from one person to the next. The room was lit with bright lights which left no shadows in the corners. Everything in his edgy movements told Grace that the walls were closing in on him.

'I'm okay,' he said eventually.

'I'll start by asking you about the car, Greg. Okay?'

'Whatever you want,' he replied quickly.

In the background, the case worker snorted in contempt.

'Where did you find it?'

'It was just on the road. Nowhere.'

'Nowhere? You can't remember where it was?'

'No.'

'What about the other boy? What can you tell us about him?'

'He was just there. I don't know anything about him. I never saw him before.'

The boy gave a loose smile, quick and unconvincing. Grace waited for a moment.

'Why did you take it down to Macdonaldtown Station to torch it? Is it because you live near there?'

'Good place for it,' he replied, shrugging and trying to grin. 'That's all.'

'In the New Life Ministries refuge,' Grace continued, 'just up and over the hill. That's where your guardian, Preacher Graeme Fredericksen, lives as well. He's not here today, he's not answering his phone. Do you know why that is?'

'Why are you asking him that?' the case worker asked.

'Just let him answer, Ria,' Harrigan said quietly.

'I don't know. He's busy, I guess. I don't care, I don't want to fucking see him.'

The boy's hands were twisting at his beanie and he was shaking.

'Why not? We'd like to see him if we could find him.'

At this, there was a change in the boy. He became still, glancing from Grace to Harrigan, an indefinable expression on his face.

'Are you afraid of him, Greg?' Grace asked.

'No.'

The word had an echo in the small room. The boy seemed almost to smile as he said it.

'Did you like living in the refuge?' Grace asked in the silence.

The case worker stirred a little in her seat but did not intervene. The boy glanced at her sideways.

'It's just a place,' he said, speaking in a flat voice. 'I'm not going back there again, so what does it fucking matter?'

'No, you're not,' Grace replied, watching his face and trying to pin down whatever he was feeling. 'Why did you want to torch the car?'

'I wanted to see it burn.'

'You like that?'

'Yeah,' he said, throwing it back at her, 'I do. I like seeing that. It makes me feel good.'

'You like it,' she said very gently. 'Do you like being in rooms like this too? Being questioned like this. You like being in Kariong? Does that make you feel good?'

'Yeah,' he said, picking at his fingernails, 'I fucking love it.'

He looked up at her, smiling. She was silent at the sight of the desolation in his face.

'You don't have to live like this, Greg,' she said, leaning towards him. 'You really don't.'

'You say that. And that's all you fucking know. What's going to fucking change in my life? Nothing. There's nowhere I can go where anyone wants me. Except here.'

His body language said that he was worn out. Grace felt a nudge in her feelings, a sudden realisation as she looked at him.

'Where anyone wants you,' she said. 'Does no one want you?'

'No, they fucking don't,' he said quietly.

'Don't bully him.'

The case worker interrupted, sounding as if she had just remembered that she should put in her two cents worth. Harrigan almost smiled but did not speak.

'You would have seen the car burn, Greg,' Grace continued. 'There was enough petrol on it. It would have gone up like a Christmas tree. There would have been nothing left. And maybe nothing left of you, if you'd been standing close enough. You did that because someone does want you.'

The boy looked at her but did not answer.

'Those clothes in the boot,' she continued, 'put them together and you know what you have? A young girl. That's what those pieces add up to. She wants you. That's why you wanted those clothes to disappear off the planet. So you could protect her. Where did you find them? Were they already in the car? Or did you put them in the boot so you could burn everything in one go?'

'They were just there. I never touched them.'

'So when we check them or the boot or anything about them, will we find your fingerprints? Anything that ties them to you?'

'It doesn't matter if you do,' he replied, quite calm.

'Why not?'

He shrugged, ever so slightly, looking to the side.

'Because. It just doesn't matter. Whatever you say. Nothing matters.'

'Yes, it does. You matter. And she does. She matters. She matters to you, you matter to her,' Grace said. 'She's smaller than you. Small and thin. Just a little girl. When did you see her last? After yesterday morning?'

He became absolutely still, there was just the soft sound of his breath.

'She fell. When she was running away. Did you know that? Did she tell you? She landed quite hard,' Grace said. 'She landed on her hands and knees. She tore her gloves and she scraped her hands. It must have hurt.'

'I didn't know that,' he said very quietly.

'She didn't tell you.'

'That's entrapment,' Ria said, quickly. 'Don't you say anything, Greg.'

The boy did not reply to either of them.

'There's a lot of blood on those clothes, Greg. I saw the shooting later and that was the first thing I thought. How much blood there was.'

'So fucking what if there was blood?'

Grace leaned closer to him. She spoke to him directly, cutting everyone else out.

'This is not something she can walk away from, Greg. This is something that means people come after her until they find her, no matter what. You must know that. Maybe you even told her that — you can't walk away from this because it's going to find you wherever you go. What matters is how you deal with it.'

Again there was silence.

'Do you want to leave her out there? What do you think might happen to her if you do? Is she going to end up dead?'

The boy leaned forward, pressing his elbows on the table and bracing his fists against his forehead. He looked up at Grace once, his mouth a thin pressed line, and then looked down again. He shook his head from side to side.

'Just tell me,' Grace said. 'Tell me who she is. Just do that and we can put a line under this. You can and she can. Before something does happen to her.'

He shook his head again.

'Yes,' she said, speaking urgently, 'finish it now. Stop it where it is. Just tell me who she is.'

Again he shook his head slowly. No. No.

'Why not?' Grace asked. 'Why not? Who are you going to save? You can't save her from this. It's too late for that. It was too late as soon as she pulled that trigger. The only thing you can do is salvage what you can for her. That's the only way you can help her and help yourself. You can do that for yourself. You can salvage something for you.'

He began to hit the sides of his head with his fists.

'Don't do that,' she said, 'don't hurt yourself.'

'No,' he said, his voice strained with tears, 'I am not fucking going to do it. No.'

He repeated no, no, no and then leaning forward,

struck his forehead hard on the table several times, quickly. Ria Allard stood up at once and ran back quickly towards the wall while Harrigan hit the emergency button.

'You stop that *now*!' Grace was standing up, stretching across the table, shoving him back hard with both hands. He stopped like a bird in mid flight at her touch. He had blood on his forehead where he had split open his skin.

Harrigan stood back, watching. When the uniformed officers arrived, he waved them to stay back, indicating they should wait.

'That was stupid,' Grace said to the boy, genuinely angry. 'Do you see this? Look at that — I don't want this from you.' She reached forward and wiped the blood from his forehead with a tissue and showed it to him, throwing it on the table. 'Do you think anybody really cares if you make yourself bleed? No, they don't. They *love* seeing it happen. They stand around and they watch and they cheer. They say, oh, do that again, please, a bit more blood this time, thanks, and a lot more pain. The more you do it, the more they like it, they get hooked on it. Do you really want to give anyone that satisfaction? No, you don't. Never do that to yourself. Never, never do that.'

The tension was gone from the air as the boy sat staring at her. He shrugged, a gesture closer to despair than aggression. She sat down again.

'I do what I fucking like,' he said, speaking only to her, 'because it doesn't matter. I've got to get that into your head. You're not going to know who I am if you don't know that.'

'No,' she said, leaning forward again, 'things do matter. They do. You matter.'

'No.' He spoke with finality.

'You can't believe that about yourself.'

This time he didn't reply.

The case worker moved forward to stand behind him. 'The interview is over,' she said.

'We're just getting started, Ria,' Harrigan replied.

'No. He needs a doctor. This interview is over.'

'I didn't mean him. I meant you. Sit down,' he said.

'What?'

'Sit down, Ria. This won't take long.'

'Can you get this boy to the medical officer, thanks,' Harrigan said to the waiting officers. 'This lady will join him a little later when she's finished here.'

'I get to go now, do I?' Greg asked.

'You do,' Harrigan replied, his face expressionless.

Grace took one of her cards out of her jacket pocket and underlined her name before passing it the boy.

'That's my name and number. If you want to talk to me, you can call me.'

'Why?' he asked, looking at it.

'Just take it. Just in case. You never know when you might need something.'

He shrugged and pocketed it.

'Don't hurt yourself,' she said.

He looked at her, directly in her eyes, and smiled. She understood him.

'Don't,' she said but he only kept smiling to himself as he left the room.

'What did you mean by going on with all that bumf? *It matters*,' the case worker mocked Grace, after the door had closed behind Greg.

'I mean, he should be on suicide watch,' Grace snapped, her colour high under her daily paint.

'You're panicking a bit there, aren't you? He's always

like that.' Ria was dismissive. 'Or are you worried you might be responsible?'

Grace had opened her mouth to reply when Harrigan forestalled her.

'Okay, Ria,' he said quickly, 'just a few quick questions. It won't take long. He knows her, doesn't he? He knows who this girl is. So I think it's a fair bet you do as well. I'm asking you. Who is she?'

'No, I don't know. Why should I?'

'You're such a good friend of his, Ria,' Grace said, needling. 'He would have confided in you, surely?'

'No. Why should he? He doesn't trust anyone.'

She looked away when she said this, her voice shaking a little.

'What's her name?' Harrigan asked.

'Whose name?'

'This girl. The one who shot two people in a back alley yesterday. What's her name? You know who she is. You know who he hangs out with.'

Harrigan was making it clear he did not want to be pissed about. The woman almost shouted at him in reply.

'No, I don't. I do not know that. No way are you putting that one on me.'

'Ria, I thought those people might be a matter of concern to you. The way they are to us.' Harrigan was calm in response to her anger.

The case worker stared at him with a look of unashamed and intense fury.

'Yeah, well. They matter, don't they? I get to concern myself with the people who don't. But why are you asking me all this stuff? Why aren't you out there going after Mr Preacher Graeme Fredericksen? He's supposed to know these things too, you know. He's even supposed to care. Why don't you talk to him?'

'We're trying. He's not answering his phone at the moment,' Harrigan replied after a short pause.

'Is that right? I am so surprised.'

She spoke softly, with an unexpected depth of hatred. They were both momentarily silent, watching her.

'Not someone you'd want to call a friend in that case, Ria,' Grace said, disturbed by the woman's expression.

'Fredericksen? Of course he's my friend. He's everybody's friend. He's our latest wonder boy. He wowed the high-ups in the Commission, they think he walks on water. They gave him everything he wanted. Approved his charity, got him his operating grant.' She drew breath, as if about to cry. 'But you never know. Never know with anyone, do you? People lie to you all the time.'

Don't they, though, Grace thought without compassion.

'He's your wonder boy? They're rare. I've never been able to find one,' she fished.

'No? People like him are going to solve all our problems. And they're not going to spend any money doing it either. Oh, no, they're going to make money. They're going to go out there and they're going to save all the lives we couldn't. And the rest of us can just pack up our tents and go home.'

Grace thought that a white toxic fury had consumed every portion of energy Allard had to offer. Harrigan watched the case worker, repelled by a degree of anger that he saw as uncontrolled and useless. They sat in unrelenting silence, looking at each other.

'Is that it?' Ria asked. 'Can I go and see to Greg now?'

'That's it.' Harrigan stood up and opened the door quickly. 'I'm sure he's waiting for you. You can go.'

She was gone immediately. When they stepped out into the corridor after her, she was already moving away at a fast pace, her escort hurrying behind her. There was an awkward pause as they watched her disappearing back.

'Nice try, Grace,' Harrigan said. 'For a moment there, I thought you had him.'

'Yeah. But I didn't quite get there,' Grace replied, thinking, no, he was never going to tell me, there had been no point in tormenting him the way she had.

'You shouldn't have let her bait you,' he was saying with that detached look of his. 'You stay out of any games they want to play. You don't give them anything.'

Grace felt a little more heat in her cheeks underneath her make-up.

'Maybe not,' she replied, 'but it is his life. He should still be on suicide watch, whatever she says.'

'Do you think so?'

'Yes, I do. I meant that.'

'All right, if that's what you think, we'll look into it. I don't want a dead witness. I'll get Trev to call them, they should pay attention to him.'

It was not a put-down. She had no clout, she knew it.

'Do I get to talk to him again?' she asked, as they walked down the corridor.

'Yes, you do. You got to him and we need to make use of that. That was a good start, we'll see how we go from here. It'll be easier the next time around. For one thing, you probably won't have her breathing down your neck. I think you'll get it out of him.'

He seemed pleased at the thought and pleased with her. I got to him, Grace thought but did not say. Is that really all I was doing in there? Nothing else? Didn't that boy matter more than that? She would have liked to ask Harrigan the question but she did not want to push her luck. Right now, she only wanted to escape for a desperately needed cigarette.

12

Afternoon light was coming in through the chinks in the curtains covering the small square window when Lucy woke. She was surprised to find herself once again in her own bed. She lay watching the patterns of light on the wall, remembering, once again remembering. This time, the shootings of the previous day and the past events that had occurred in this room coalesced in her mind, without forming a single, clear picture. For a few moments, she felt detached from them both. The memory of her father was part of her, it had been for some time. The memory of the shooting was becoming part of her as well, or she was becoming part of it. With her head buried in the pillow, she thought: this is who I am. I own this, this is my action, this is me.

Lying there, she began to feel afraid in a quiet sort of way. There was a sense of expectation in the quietness, the beginning rustle of voices in her mind like sounds heard behind a heavy curtain. She lay without moving, trying to find protection in stillness. As she did, she tightened her grip on something hard and metallic under her pillow. This metallic object came into being as a handgun and she sat up slowly, still holding onto it. She let it fall onto the bed and stretched her hand which was cramped and stiff. She sat with her head in her hands, emptying her mind until her thoughts were quiet.

She felt a compulsion to clean herself and went to the bathroom and washed. She dressed herself in different clothes, jeans and a T-shirt under a loose and heavy sweatshirt that came down past her hips. She pushed her gun awkwardly into the waistband of her jeans. In the mirror, she looked like a small, lumpy child.

When she came down the stairs she heard the television in the lounge room, the sound turned up high, and guessed this was where she would find her parents. She did not go in there, she did not have the stomach. She walked through to the kitchen, where she made herself instant coffee and ate leftovers from the refrigerator. Melanie appeared just as she finished eating. They looked at each other and did not speak. Melanie went to the bench where she began sorting medications before crushing tablets with the back of a spoon.

'Are they for Dad?' Lucy asked, swallowing both food and trepidation.

'Who else do you think they're for?' Melanie replied. 'Don't you want to go and talk to him? He's in the lounge room with Mum, they know you're here. Stevie told them.'

'No, not yet,' Lucy said, cold at the thought.

Melanie shrugged.

'Where's Stevie?'

'He's at work. He spent the whole night out looking for you but he still had to go to work today. I don't suppose you care about that.'

'It's not my fault, Mel,' Lucy said.

'I didn't say anything was your fault,' Mel replied. 'Anyway, I can't talk to you now, I've got things I've got to do. I had to leave school, you know, so I could look after Dad. So I've got to do that.'

'They didn't do that,' Lucy said, shocked.

'Yes, they did. So I've got work to do.'

'Why didn't you just say no? Why didn't Stevie say no?' Lucy asked, immediately furious.

'Because no one else was going to do it. Mum wasn't, that's for sure. She was just going to let him die.'

'We could pay someone, couldn't we?'

'You think Dad is going to spend his money like that? Don't be stupid! He won't do that even now he's dying. He and Mum are never going to do that, not while they can get me to do it for nothing. Why should you care? You left when you didn't even have to.'

Melanie walked out of the kitchen, carrying a tray of medications, without waiting for a reply.

'I did have to,' Lucy said softly.

Lucy walked out to the back garden, where the air was still fresh from yesterday's rain, needing the relief of some open space. She stopped to let the dog off the chain, rubbing her head and noticing how the fur on her neck had been worn thin by her collar. Dora hesitated at the entrance to her kennel and then pushed forward, uncertain that she was free. She came and sat beside Lucy who stood looking down the slope of her father's block of land towards the boundary of the national park.

'Let's go, girl,' she said to the dog. 'Let's go for a walk. Let's go check things out.'

There had once been a garden on this slope, brought into life by Lucy's grandmother. Granny Hurst had been a big woman, with her fingernails split and ingrained with earth. Lucy remembered that she had always been there, ever since Lucy was small, although she rarely spoke and never seemed to talk to anyone directly. She never looked at Lucy when she talked to her but kept her gaze focused on a point in the distance, somewhere past her granddaughter's head. Over the years, Granny Hurst had shaped the ground into a series of shallow terraces linked by wooden steps and brick paths. She had grown gardenias, azaleas, camellias and rhododendrons, their flowers ivory white, dark crimson, cerise and shell pink; cultivated beds of blue and white English violets, snow-in-summer and pale yellow bearded iris. Lucy used to follow her through the garden, spending hours with her, watching and helping her. They had, in this silent way, been very close to each other. If for some reason Lucy was not there on some days, her grandmother would come looking for her, always speaking to that same distant point behind her and saying, 'Where were you today? I was waiting for you and you didn't come.' Lucy collected the flowers as her grandmother cut them and then carried them up to the house. She put them into jars of water, stroking the petals gently, fascinated by their colours and the softness of their textures.

At other times, her grandmother used to sit on the step of the uppermost terrace, wearing her ugly brown and orange dress, her legs set comfortably apart, smoking menthol cigarettes and talking to the three of them, Stephen, Lucy and Melanie. She told them about her own grandfather who had cleared this block of land of its original forest. 'There were big trees here,' she said, 'the biggest he ever saw before he cut them down.' He had worked first as a blacksmith, and then kept dairy cows, and had then grown cabbages, but had never made any money, not even from selling the original timber from his land. Her own father had been the one who made the money, starting out by selling second-hand clothes at the Haymarket, holding on to every penny he got his hands on. 'Just like my son,' she said, meaning Lucy's father, 'he won't spend a cent either. But he doesn't sell clothes, he's a meat dealer. That's what he likes.' Her slightly acid voice was still clear in Lucy's mind, she saw her sitting on the step dropping her cigarette butts into a tin rather than let them litter her garden.

Her garden had gone to seed in the years since she had died of diabetes, when Stephen had been fourteen, Lucy thirteen and Mel just ten. Only the camellias and the rhododendrons in her garden continued to flower, all the rest had been reduced to a tangle of dead and living plants, small crowns of green on otherwise dead branches.

Lucy pushed down through this tangle, following the dog, finding the old paths and steps, reaching the small sleep-out near the escarpment that looked out over the park. Her grandmother had lived in this sleep-out during the last four years of her life, after their grandfather had died, unconcerned by the winter weather and happy, she had said to them, with the sight of her garden and the bush outside her windows. From here, it was possible to see where small stands of flowering eucalyptus and mustard yellow acacias had begun to push their way back over the boundary of the park, even in the short time since Lucy had left.

The sleep-out had been abandoned since Granny Hurst had died, its sliding aluminium doors left jammed open to the weather. Lucy went to look inside a building that now smelled of fresh earth. Dora nosed past her, leaving a trail of paw prints on the dusty floor. Camellia bushes that had grown up close to the external walls pressed their dark leaves against the windows, leaving the pattern of their shape on glass filmed with rain-washed dirt and spiders' webs. Camellia flowers had drifted through the open doorway, leaving behind pale scatterings of detached pink and red petals. Lucy walked into a pool of silence, following the footfall of the old dog. In the bathroom, soft dirty cobwebs covered the face of the cabinet mirror, while leaves and imperfect flowers had filled the white plastic bathtub to a shallow depth. The bathroom was dry. The taps shuddered when Lucy turned them on but no water flowed out. It was a place cracking open under the slow crush of the plants that surrounded it, they strangled it with root and branch as it subsided into the ground. Lucy drank in the silence.

'Hi, Gran,' she said to no one.

She walked back outside into the afternoon light and listened to the clear sounds of the birds calling to each other in the surrounding bushland. Small waterfalls from the previous day's rain flowed down over the honeycomb-coloured rock into a gully at the foot of the escarpment. The dog preceded her through the ferns down the short slope and then along a track that bordered a creek. After a short walk, Lucy crossed the stream to a rock overhang opposite, where the shadows and faint outlines of hand prints had been painted onto the sandstone. Their grandmother had told them they had been put there a long time ago by the blacks.

'There were blacks around here when your great-granddaddy came here,' she had said to them once, 'he gave them work clearing the land. They lived along the river in shacks, so it wasn't that far for them to come up here. We used to play down there together when we were kids.'

Gran had painted her own hand on the rock when she was a child, with a date and her initials. Once, she had taken the three of them to see it and they had painted their own hands among the others on the rock face. Lucy found the child's drawing of her hand and covered it over with her adult palm. The dog came and sat near her. Leaning against the rock, Lucy emptied her mind of any thoughts, listening to the rhythm of her breathing and nothing else.

Four months after her grandmother's funeral, and not long before Lucy's fourteenth birthday, her father had walked into her bedroom one evening for the first time. When he left, Lucy's bedsheets were dirtied with blood. The next day at breakfast, Lucy had looked up at her mother, uncertain whether she should tell her that they needed to be washed. Her mother refused to meet her eye and Lucy stayed silent. She went to school as usual and came home to find that there were clean sheets on her bed. Nothing was said. Always, the sheets were changed with nothing being said. Except for those times when Lucy's mother had taken her to visit the clinic on the other side of the city, everything had gone on as usual. Until the day Lucy had picked up her pack and walked out of the door. And today, when she had come back.

Just then, Lucy felt that there was no other world in existence anywhere, that this stretch of land was the only place that was real. This place here on the edge of the park, where her family were caught in a house with a tangled garden, where everything was detached and out of whack. As she leaned against the rock, she felt the gun pressing into her waist. It was a reality of a kind, bringing her back to the present. She sat by the side of the creek, gathering strength, fighting fear. The dog stayed with her, until something in the nearby scrub attracted her attention and she got to her feet and disappeared into the bush, leaving Lucy by herself. Lucy took her gun out of her waistband and aimed it at the shrubs on the opposite bank, firing pretend shots. It was a long time, and had grown dark and cold, before she felt brave enough to go back into the house.

13

The message that hit Harrigan's desk later that afternoon summed up the day for him. Greg Smith would not be available for further questioning until the Department of Juvenile Justice had completed its own urgent psychiatric assessment of the boy. It was the price they had to pay for requesting earlier that day that he be put on a suicide watch. It was not failure, only frustration; something that stretched all their energies a little further. Controlling either time or events in Harrigan's business was a war of attrition: you had to know when to wait and when to let things happen. If he let the anger he felt drive his work, then he could put everything at risk. In the interval, he needed to break the tension.

He walked out of his office and announced to his people that it was time for a refresher. A brief hour at the Maryborough, money on the bar from the social club matched by an equivalent amount from Grace, to welcome her to the team before they all got back to it again. It might be the last time they had the chance for some days or even weeks.

'Just don't let Marvin get wind of this,' he said to everyone as he made his announcement. 'If he does, he'll be burning my ears about it from now until doomsday.'

There was a ripple of laughter as people collected their coats. It was all very amiable but Harrigan also had some unfinished business of his own.

At the Maryborough, the publican, on notice from Harrigan, would reserve the back bar for him and his team. They arrived in a group to take possession of it.

'What'll you have?' Harrigan asked Grace, as she put her money down according to tradition.

'Lime and soda,' she replied with a smile, abstinence that he noted but decided not to comment on.

'Get the lady what she wants,' he said to the barman. 'I'll have a whisky and water.'

In the initial mêlée around the bar, Ian had already ordered a schooner of Old. As she waited for her drink, Grace watched the white froth ooze down the glass while the smell filled the air around her like a wash. She felt an undercurrent of nausea, a prickle of sweat at the back of her neck.

'Don't you drink?' Ian asked her.

'No, mate,' Trevor intervened unsubtly, shoving up against the bar. 'No vices for my mate here. Just the occasional fag, hey, Gracie.'

'Plenty of them around here,' Jeffo observed *sotto voce,* a bait which Trevor ignored. 'Hey, Gracie,' he said then, flashing her a toothy grin, 'I hear you had fun with that kid today. But you don't need all that half-arsed psychology. With a kid like that, all you need is a couple of phone books and half an hour and he'll tell you everything you want to know.'

Grace returned Jeffo a glacial smile but could not be bothered answering. He was winding up for another comment when Harrigan snapped in his ear.

'Spare us the sparkling wit, mate. No one's in the mood, including me.'

Drink in hand, he moved away from the bar while Jeffo made a face at his back.

'That's a bitch, you not drinking.' Louise appeared and ordered gin. She was a chunky woman with greying hair flaring back from her forehead and broken veins across her cheeks. 'I was hoping we might have a few sessions together. Us girls should stick together.'

Louise, fifty-something, was a software engineer of repute. She drained her glass of gin with slightly shaking hands. Her fingers were heavy with ornate rings, red and white stones serving as glittering knuckle-dusters alongside her wedding band. Grace heard the empty gin glass chink down on the counter as she asked immediately for a second. Grace did not drink, not any more. Alcohol had once flooded her veins with its metallic, poisonous edge, irritating a portion of her mind to unpredictable furies and mawkish self-pity. She turned away, lime and soda in hand, to find Ian lying in wait for her.

'I hear you used to be a rock star,' he said. 'Is that really what you used to do?'

'Me?' she laughed. 'No, I wish I had been, I'd never have to work again. All I did was sing with a band for a little while. All we ever did was work really hard for almost nothing and deal with lowlifes who just wanted to rip us off all the time.'

'And you liked it so much, you joined the force so you could keep doing it,' he said.

'That's right, I'm right back where I started from. That's life. I'm just going to go and find the cigarette machine,' she replied.

She found the machine in the hallway past the gaming room and hummed to herself as she punched in her coins. She reflected with black humour on various episodes of disaster in her not so overwhelmingly successful career in rock and roll, from broken-down vans to audiences so frightening she had been reduced to climbing out the back window of the women's toilet to escape them. What was so fearsome about this job?

Turning to go back, she saw Harrigan standing just inside the door to the gaming room, catching up on the last race for the day, watching as on the big screen the barriers were opened and the horses were away. He was alone, absorbed by the sight, his whole attention focused on the race, his body tense with excitement. 'Yes!' he was saying as the horses came in, hitting one fist into his palm. Then he turned and saw her there watching him.

'Do you bet?' she asked, caught out.

'I don't bet that much as it happens, Grace. I just like to pick them. What about you?'

He picked up his drink from a nearby table and walked out to join her.

'I don't even know how to read the form guide,' she replied.

'No? In this business, that could be a serious deficiency. A lot of things go on down at the track.'

'But do you need to know how to read the form guide to work them out?'

'Not always. It depends on what your interest is. How the horses are running. How they ought to run. Who's betting.' He was smiling as he spoke to her, relaxed in a way that he usually was not. 'Haven't you ever been to the races? Racing's life.'

'Is it? Why?'

'It's a magic moment watching them come down the straight just before the finish. Just the sound they make when their hooves hit the ground. It is, it's magic. There's nothing like it. Horses are beautiful to watch when they're racing well.'

Harrigan had been going to the track since he was a boy, it had been his passion ever since. On race day, his mother used to get out her good dress with the shoes and the hat and the make-up. And those heavy clip-on earrings that made her ears throb by the end of the day, which she would slip off on the bus home and drop into her handbag with a sigh of relief. She would dress him up as well and they would go out together for the day. It was her indulgence; he thought she was happiest there. Her favourite bookies always greeted her by name. Hello, Helen, how are you betting today? How's your boy? To a couple of the old-timers out at Royal Randwick, he was still Helen Harrigan's boy, even if these days he frequented the Members' Bar as well as the track side.

'I don't think I've ever put a bet on in my life. Not even on Melbourne Cup Day,' Grace was saying, an odd tone in her voice. 'My father used to, though. He used to take my mother to the races.'

She was somewhere else, remembering a childhood in New Guinea, a place dreamlike and beautiful in her memory. A road in the highlands one hot day, sitting beside her father as the Land Rover made its slow way along the dirt road, through its stream of villagers going about their business. An ancient, worked landscape stretching up into the hills, thin, sharp, irregular picket fences surrounding thatched houses. An intricate pattern of vivid greens; she had not realised how vivid until she again saw the parched and bled out grasslands when she was on her way back to Brisbane for the start of the school year. Another world. Yes, it was magic.

'You should come along sometime during the Spring Carnival. You might enjoy it,' Harrigan was saying to her.

'I should. I might need the relaxation if I get to deal with any more people like Ria Allard.'

'Yeah, you might,' he said, looking at her. 'Glad you found me, Grace. Come and talk to me.'

'What about?' she asked.

'Nothing dramatic,' he replied as they walked back into the bar. 'Just the way you did that interview today.'

'Yeah, I wanted to ask — have we got hold of the Preacher Graeme Fredericksen yet?'

She spoke lightly, full of foreboding for what he might want to say to her.

'No, we haven't. He's too elusive for my taste. He should have been knocking on our door first thing, not the other way around. I'll be glad when we run him to earth. That wasn't what I wanted to talk to you about. Did you know that Greg Smith's not available until the Department does its own psychiatric assessment?'

He was sipping whisky. She smelled the odour of the spirit as something almost sweetish, all pervasive, bringing back to her the memory of a stale alcoholic sweat on her numbed skin, a counterpart to liquid the colour of caramelised onions in the glass. She lit a cigarette to cover the smell, he stepped back a little from her smoke.

'Is that a problem?' she said. 'Like you said, we can't talk to him if he's dead.'

'No,' he said, not quite grinning at her reply. 'No, it's not a problem. It just adds to the time, that's all. What I want to know is, what did you think you were doing in there today? Can you keep that up, putting yourself out the way you did for that boy?'

'I wasn't putting myself out,' she said. 'As far as I was concerned, it was just him and me talking to each other.'

'Yeah, that got to be pretty obvious. But it's not just him and you. There's a whole apparatus out there that you can't ignore and the only place it's going to take him in the end is Silverwater. And one day, it could be your business to put him there. He knows that, he told you so. So do you want the information he's got? Or do you want to save his life? What makes you think the two go together in the first place?'

'Then what do I do?' she asked. 'Isn't this Catch–22? You say to me, coax it out of him. So I do. I go and talk to him from where he's coming from, because that's the only way I can do that. But now you say I'm putting myself out too much. That doesn't leave me any room.'

'You weren't talking to him from where he was coming from. You were talking to him from some place in your own mind. And you wanted him in there with you, that's what you were doing.'

'That boy's on the edge. He's not going to talk to me if I don't get down there with him.'

He looked past her to the crowd behind her.

'That's what you have to learn, Grace. To make him open up without doing that. Because you've got no business getting down there with him. You don't take on what other people bring into the interview room. That's the road to hell. You don't go where they are. What you do is draw a line.'

'Maybe it's not like that for me,' she replied. 'Maybe I am just talking to people one on one, without taking it on the way you say I am. I can do that without it hurting me, I can meet them there. Maybe that's a difference between us.'

He looked down into his drink, smiling in an odd way.

'Do you know you get to people? You're good at it. I think that every time I see you talk to someone. You let that woman bait you today and then five minutes later you got right back into her.'

Without even trying, you can pick on all the right nerve points just like you know exactly where they are, he could have said to her. You must have x-ray vision.

'People say I get to them,' she replied, shaking her head and moving her plait of thick brown hair from one shoulder to the other. 'I don't try to do it.'

'You don't have to. I've got a son, you know,' he said suddenly, 'there's only me to look after him, his mother dumped him. He's got cerebral palsy. Can't walk, can't talk. He's got a really good mind but he's stuck in a wheelchair. He will be all his life. He just wants to live. You have that kid there, and even with everything that's against him, he could still do something with his life. He just wants to throw it away. I don't like seeing people dead, Grace. But some people — you can't save them, they don't want to be saved. If you go after them, they just want to take you with them. That kid is one of them, he doesn't want to be saved. He told you that too.'

'I heard him say that. I don't like throwing people away. I get stubborn.'

She was embarrassed by his confidence, moved by his description of his son. She threw her cigarette butt into a nearby ashtray. Harrigan put his empty glass on a table.

'I didn't know any of that about your son,' she said, feeling that she owed Harrigan this courtesy at the least. 'I'm sorry. I wasn't trying to find anything out. I don't do that.'

'I didn't think you were. I don't usually talk about it. No one talks about it,' he replied, looking past her, avoiding her gaze. They might have thought, mutually, that it was the sole thing not discussed exhaustively by the team.

'Well, I won't say anything to anyone,' she said quickly, wanting to move on. 'So — are you in this job to draw that line? Is that what you do every day?'

'Me?' It was unusual to find himself on the other end of the question. He grinned. 'No, I'm here because I couldn't think of anything else to do with my life. I needed a job to support my son and this was the only thing I thought I could stick at for more than a fortnight. Sixteen years later I'm still here.'

It was the truth as far as it went, a diversionary tactic rather than a lie. His presence here was the result of a half-formed thought brought into being by his father's irritated gibe one night in the kitchen: 'Why don't you be a fucking walloper? You're always telling people what to do.' Not long afterwards, a serving policeman, an old mate of his father's, had called him with an offer.

'It's chance sometimes, isn't it,' Grace replied. 'You never know where your life is going to take you.'

He smiled in agreement; she smiled back in the same way.

'You are stubborn,' he said quietly. 'What are you really trying to do here?'

'I'm brave and foolish,' she said, sending herself up. 'I'm trying to make a difference.'

'You did make a difference today. You're the only one

here who could have talked to that boy and got anything out of him except four-letter words.'

She shrugged and smiled again. 'Thanks for saying it.'

They found themselves looking at each other in silence, both searching for something else to say. Grace felt the kick inside, the unexpected jag of attraction, and wished she hadn't; it was the last thing she needed just now.

'You're on the TV, Boss. You too, Gracie,' Ian called out.

They turned and separated by an unspoken agreement, and then gathered around the bar with everyone else. The barman turned up the sound on the early evening news. The team watched Matthew Liu, flanked by both Harrigan and Grace, make a plea for anyone to come forward with any information that would help them find the girl who had shot both his parents.

'You are so photogenic, Gracie. They're going to like that up top,' Trevor said, smiling at her indulgently as the clip ended.

Grace thought she might say that it was just the bad lighting and then decided to leave it where it was.

'Okay, folks, I think that's it,' Harrigan called out, breaking up the party. 'Back to it.' He ignored the groans as he led the way back to work.

Back at the office, he found that the time out had not refreshed any of them; there was a sense of languor throughout the room. Harrigan glanced at Grace as she worked her way through Greg Smith's files, considering her scruples as he did so. He thought about his own son. He felt the compulsion to go and see him and make sure that he was safe. The office was acquiring an unusual sense of enclosure, he wasn't sure he could breathe in here for much longer. He reached for the phone to call Cotswold House, but did not pick up the handset. Finally, when the day shift was going home and the graveyard shift was settling in, he got to his feet and went in search of Trevor.

'I'm taking an hour, Trev,' he said quietly. 'I'm going to see my boy. I'll be back as soon as I can.'

'Okay, Boss. I'll call you if anything happens.'

Harrigan collected his jacket and found himself at the lift at the same time as Grace. Caught a little awkwardly, he stopped and let her get in first.

'Did you see that?' Ian asked. 'Are they going out together somewhere?'

'He likes her and she likes him,' Louise said, breathing out gin. 'All they did in the pub for an hour was talk to each other.'

'Gracie's going home, people,' Trevor announced. 'I told her to piss off because she's done everything she can today. And he's going to see his boy. He told me so in case I need to know where to find him. He's coming back.'

'You want to make a bet?' Jeffo was grinning. He too was heading for the door. 'How much time do you waste on a spastic kid? She'd know where her bread is buttered. Fifty bucks says he gets it into her.'

Ian and Louise turned away as he spoke.

'Jesus, mate,' Trevor said, riled. 'You know sweet fuck-all about her and you say that. Why don't you keep your dirty mouth shut for once?'

Trev might divert the talk to other subjects but he knew that no matter what he tried to say now, there was no hope for it. Soon the gossip would be away in a pack with the dogs.

Down in the car park, Harrigan glanced around to see Grace a few cars away from his own, unlocking her own door. They had hardly spoken to each other as they came down in the lift. He waved to her self-consciously across the short distance and saw the gesture returned in a similar fashion. Then they both went their separate ways out into the winter night.

In her car, Grace determinedly watched the road ahead, resisting the urge to check in her rear-view mirror which way he had gone. In his own car, Harrigan was concentrating his thoughts on his son.

14

On her way back up to the house in the early evening dusk, Lucy saw that the dog was once again chained up in her kennel. Dora had disappeared some time during the afternoon and she'd wondered what had happened to her. As soon as Lucy walked into the kitchen, where Melanie was preparing dinner, her sister turned to her.

'You let the dog off her chain.'

'Yeah, I did. I don't see why she has to be chained up like that.'

Melanie leaned on the bench, her face taut. Every muscle in her body was rigid with tension.

'She's chained up because Dad wants her to be. So you have to leave her like that or he gets upset. And when he gets upset, he takes it out on me. He can still do that, even if he's only whispering at me. The things he says — they are just so gross. Would you not take her for a walk like that again? Please. It's too hard, Luce.'

Lucy turned away, shaking her head against rising furies.

'Do you want some tea?' her sister called out to her but Lucy did not reply.

She walked slowly down the hallway to the lounge room, drawn towards the sound of the television. Yellow light shone through the door onto the carpet in the hallway, a contoured and gleaming polyester blue. As Lucy drew closer, she began to chew on her thumbnail. Through the door she could see the television was turned on to an evening game show, 'Wheel of Fortune', the volume turned up high. Then her mother, sitting on the lounge watching the show, and her father, stretched out in his reclining chair, apparently asleep, the tray of medications Melanie had prepared earlier sitting near him on a coffee table. She stopped at the door. The room was filled with an odour of sickness, like rotting flowers. Seeing her, her mother pulled herself upright, dragging her cardigan down past her waist. She tried to speak but could not, looked from her daughter to her sick husband, whose eyes remained closed.

'Hi, Mum,' Lucy said, going inside.

Her mother nodded in silent response. Her husband opened his eyes and looked at his daughter.

'Hi, Luce,' he said. 'We heard you were home. How are you?'

Her father's face had become an under-face, the kind you arrive at after sickness has stripped everything else to the bone. Illness had drawn pain to the surface of George Hurst's face, it was almost the only thing that still existed of him. Lucy could not speak. She almost cried.

'Come home to see your old man at last,' he said against the racket of the television show. 'Come and give him a kiss, hey? I know I'm not too pretty to look at these days.'

She did not. She sat in an armchair opposite them both.

'Stevie asked me to come home,' she said slowly, looking from her father to her mother, who was still playing with the ends of her cardigan. She had not changed at all, she was a round-faced woman, a little pudgy, with flat hair brushed back behind her ears.

'How are you, Lucy?' she said, now that her husband had spoken. 'Are you keeping well?'

Above the noise of the television, the air seemed to simmer with a thousand jangling and unheard sounds.

'Yeah,' Lucy replied.

'I've been worried about you,' her mother said, her attention drifting back to the television set.

'What have you been up to out there?' her father asked.

'Don't you know?' Lucy said, poker-faced.

'Stevie told us you were living with some friends. You had a job in a shop. He said you were doing well,' her mother said.

'I'm glad you've come, Luce,' her father said. 'I wanted to see you. I haven't got that much time now. I want you to know your mother and me have always really cared about you. Always.'

'Always,' her mother said, looking away from the television screen and back to her daughter. 'I always did what I had to do for you, Lucy. I made sure I looked after you. I did the best I could, I couldn't do any more than that. I hope you know that.'

'We've been worried sick about you since you left.' Her father moved his chair a little more upright. 'I thought, my little girl out there all on her own. Who's going to look after her? And we never heard anything from you, except through Stevie. Not even at Christmas.'

'You could have sent us a card,' her mother added. 'We wanted to hear from you.'

'Why didn't you come looking for me?' Lucy asked.

'We couldn't, Luce. We didn't know where to find you,' her father said.

'You could have asked Stevie.'

'He said you didn't want to see us,' her mother said, her face slightly red.

'It's hard for a man, worrying about his daughter like that. My little girl, I thought, and I don't know where she is. And she won't tell me. She won't even tell me.'

The TV show host invaded the lounge room noisily and Lucy saw her mother's attention once again drift back towards the screen. She got to her feet and turned it off. Her mother blinked a little, but did not speak. Her father stared at her with eyes that were large and bright in his worn face. She sat down again, staring at him, unable to turn away even though she didn't want to look. It was horrible to see him like this.

'I'm a sick man, Luce,' he said, reading her thoughts. 'I can't hide it. Sometimes I think I can't bear the pain any more. I want it finished. When it's finished, I'm going to be happy.'

Lucy, watching and listening to him, had no thoughts. Her feelings were thin, her mind was blank, flat like a sheet of unpainted plasterboard.

'You have to understand that me and your mother love you. More than anything.'

Lucy did not answer, she sat there waiting. Her gaze shifted from her father to her mother and back again. Her mother kept glancing at the blank television set but she said nothing. Lucy felt weightless, with her feelings slipping towards chaos, the quiet sounds in her head buzzing like insects.

'Luce, I'm dying, but your life will go on and you'll do what you want to do with it. You'll get married and you'll be happy. And I'm glad for you, I'm glad. Because all that's ever mattered to me is how much I've cared about you. All I ever did was care about you. It's a normal thing for a father to do.'

In the midst of his illness, there was a flash of her father of old. She knew that look so well. On Saturday mornings, from her place at the cash register, she would watch him as he sold old or fatty or tough meat to his customers. He had always had that same look. Are they going to take it?

'Did you worry about me?' she asked.

'Yes, Luce. I did.'

'Did you lie awake at night worrying about me?'

'All the time.'

Lucy waited, again chewing her thumbnail. She imagined how her father would look if she shot him in the chest now, and then looked at her mother, working through the same fantasy, bringing both images together powerfully in her mind. Under her bulky sweatshirt, her gun pressed against her midriff.

'Did you ever lie awake and wish you hadn't done what you did to me?' she said.

'Look at me, Luce,' he replied almost immediately. 'I'm dying and I'm dying too soon. I want us to be friends before I go. You're home now. This is your home. There's always a place for you here. And in my will. I've remembered you in my will, Lucy, I've remembered you especially. You can think about me one day when I'm gone and thank me for that. You can say to yourself, my old man was very generous to me in his will, he did that for me, it's made my life easier now. Your mother and me have broken our hearts worrying about you these last few years. I've broken my heart worrying about you. But I'm not accusing you for that. There's no point in accusing people for things. Life's a matter of give and take. Let's be friends. Come on. Be friends with me, Lucy, before I die. Please.'

She waited in what seemed to be an endless silence, looking from one to the other expectantly, but neither of them spoke. She sat with her arms folded, pressing her gun hard into her waist.

'You really don't want to say anything else to me?' she asked.

Neither replied.

'You only have to say it once. You have to mean it, but you only have to say it once. You just have to say you wish you'd never done that to me. That's all you have to say.'

Again there was silence. Her mother picked at her cardigan. Lucy spoke in desperation. 'It's not just me! There's Mel too. What about her? Don't you want to say ...'

Her voice dried up.

'Luce,' her father said, 'I only want us to be friends. This is our last chance. I'm dying. You don't want to put things in the way of it. Let's just be friends.'

Lucy leaned forward in her chair and wept for some moments. She looked up, meaning to say something else and saw her father watching her, his expression still unchanged. If anything, there was a ghost of satisfaction in his eyes. She could not bear to be watched by him like this.

'I'm going back to my room now,' she said, 'but you — you can't — You're going to talk to me again, Dad. You are. You are going to say —'

She stopped and stood up to leave the room, still weeping. At the door, she almost walked into Melanie.

'Don't you want your tea? It's on the table,' her sister asked.

'Fucking later,' she said.

'Language!' she heard her father say, with the remembrance of a usual reprimand in his voice.

Lucy stopped still in the doorway and spoke without turning around. 'Don't you say that to me.'

Then she did turn and went towards him. Her hand moved instinctively towards her waistband before she remembered to stop herself. For the first time, he seemed confused. She stood over him.

'Don't you ever tell me what to say again.'

Anger had made her voice almost unrecognisable. He did not speak, there was sweat on his cheeks. Everyone in the room was silent.

'You won't, will you? Ever again.'

He shook his head.

'You say it, Dad. Go on, say it.'

'No, I won't,' he eventually whispered.

They looked at each other.

'I'm going to come and talk to you again, Dad,' she said. 'Because you owe me something. You know you do. And you are going to give it to me.'

He stared at her, showing anger and fear without any sense of disguise, and then rolled away from her, turning his back on her, refusing to speak.

Lucy left at once, moving quickly and hearing behind her as she climbed the stairs a sudden ruckus in the lounge room. The noise of her father calling out hoarsely for Melanie and the sound of the television set being turned on again.

* * *

In her room, she emptied her pack out onto her bed, scrabbling for her notebook computer, clumsy as she hurried, wiping away tears with the back of her hand. Lucy was going out on the Net to find consolation, someone to talk to, to get the buzzing out of her head. She set up her computer on her old desk, illuminated it with her desk lamp, plugged in the phone charger and then turned on her mobile telephone, intending to connect to her ISP. She took the gun out of her waistband and placed it next to the notebook. As she did, the mobile phone rang. She let it ring until it stopped. Then, as she was about to pick it up, it rang again. She looked at it for a few moments then answered it.

'Yeah,' she said. As she had expected, she heard the preacher's honey voice in reply.

'Lucy? Is that you? You sound very different.'

'Hi, Graeme,' she said in an unconcerned tone. 'Do I? I don't know why, I'm just the same as I was yesterday.'

'I'm glad to hear it. I was wondering how you were. I've been thinking about you every single moment since I found you gone.'

'I bet you have. But everybody always worries about me so there's no reason why you shouldn't as well. I'm fine. Great, you know,' she replied. There was a moment of silence. 'What do you want? I guess you want something. That's why you're calling me.'

'Yes, Lucy, I do want something. I want very much to see you. I've been trying to ring you all day but your phone's been switched off. I don't think you should have done that.'

'Don't you? Gee, it's too bad I forgot to turn it on.'

Lucy sat on the bed among the scattered goods that she had emptied out of her pack. She dragged her sleeping bag across her knees in the cold room.

'Do you know Greg is in custody?' he asked.

'Yeah, I heard.'

There was a pause.

'You have good information. You obviously know who to ask. And where to find things.'

'Yeah, I'm good at that,' she said.

'I'm going to get him bailed into my care, Lucy.'

'Are you? I don't think you'll be able to do that. They won't want to let him go this time.'

'I can certainly try. I have contacts too. In fact, I think I've got a very good chance of doing just that.'

Lucy bit her lip.

'What do you want, Graeme?'

'I want to see you. I really think you should come and meet with me.'

She did not answer. 'I don't think you can get him bailed,' she said instead.

'We'll see. Ria has told me he is likely to be charged with being an accessory to murder.'

'Did she ring you?'

'She left a message on my answering machine. The sort of message Ria Allard usually leaves on my answering machine. But fortunately, I won't have to hear from her again.'

'Greg doesn't know anything about it,' Lucy said, dismissively.

'You said he did, Lucy.'

'Yeah, but not like that, I mean. He wasn't involved or anything.'

'I don't think that will make any difference to the police. I think you'll find that being an accessory is exactly what he is. Apparently they have assigned a policewoman to deal with him. She will be interviewing him regularly from now on. We'll see what happens, won't we? Whether or not he lives up to your expectations and really does keep his mouth shut.'

'It's not murder anyway, Graeme. You said it was a cleansing.'

'I'm talking about how the police will see it,' he replied, speaking sharply. Lucy smiled to hear the irritation in his voice.

'What do you want?' she asked.

'Lucy, I've already told you. I want to see you. Soon. Somewhere private.'

There was a knock on Lucy's door. She reached for her gun and slipped it out of sight under the sleeping bag.

'There's someone here, I've got to go. Even if you can get Greg bailed, he won't go with you. So it doesn't matter.'

'He won't have any choice. None whatsoever. The police will hand him over directly to me. He'll pass from one sort of custody into another. After all, the only way he can avoid that is to tell them about you. Isn't that so?'

The preacher's voice had dropped to a strange, low whisper heard as a rustle within the inner ear. Lucy was silent for some time.

'Are you still there?' he asked.

'Yeah, I'm here.'

'Good. Because if you are so concerned about him, you should be very careful what you do from now on. And very careful who you talk to and what you say to them. Because I don't think Greg could be stopped if he decided to do something foolish while he's in my care.

Do you? And I can't be held responsible for a suicide or an accidental death, can I? I'll ring you tomorrow, Lucy. Leave your phone on.'

'You can't make me do anything, Graeme,' she said, and hung up, tossing the phone on the bed. She opened the door and saw Stephen standing there, carrying a small two-bar heater.

'I've got a heater for you. I thought it'd be cold in here,' he said.

'Yeah, it is pretty fucking cold, Stevie,' she replied. 'Thanks.'

He stood hesitantly in the doorway as she plugged it in.

'Were you talking on your phone just now?' he asked.

'Yeah. But it's no one worth talking about.'

'Want your tea?'

'Yeah.'

He went outside and picked up a plate of food from a sideboard in the hallway.

'What's Dad doing now?' she asked as he handed it to her.

'Mel's given him his shot for the night so he's pretty out of it. Please don't ask about anything now, Luce. Wait till tomorrow when you've both calmed down a bit. I'll have a talk to him and see if I can't sort something out. You told me you wouldn't argue with him.'

'Did you tell them I was working in a shop?' she asked.

'What?'

'Did you tell Mum and Dad I was working in a shop?'

'Lucy, I don't know what you're talking about. Not now, okay? Look, I'm not going back to work until this is over. I'm going to be home tomorrow and you can talk to me then if you want to. But I'm too tired now,' he said, and was gone.

Lucy shut the door and pushed her bedside table

against it. She turned off the overhead light and sat at her desk next to the heater, which filled the room with the odour of burning dust as the bars glowed with red heat. Liar, liars, liars, she said to herself as she logged on, thumping the keys. Everyone lies, don't they? Fucking, fucking bastards, that's all any of them are. Why do that to me, Dad? Did I ever do anything to you?

Between mouthfuls of Melanie's food, she went out on the Net, in search of Turtle, moving into their own particular space where she usually met him.

Turtle, are you out there? It's me, Firewall.

Are u there at last????? I've been here all day Where have u been?

You don't want to know.

Don't joke I do

No, you don't. Because I'm right down here in the dirt now. Right here in the shit. We don't ever treat each other like this. It's like we've always said — we always talk to who we really are, don't we? No lies, nothing like that.

Yes we do Heart 2 heart Mind 2 mind That's wot we always do It's wot we're always going to do

You talk turtle to me, don't you? You never lie to me?

No Firewall I dont lie 2 u I never have

I trust you, Turtle, I do. Have you told anyone about this?

No

Well, you can. If you want. You don't have to carry this by yourself. You can tell whoever you want.

Yeah? Well u tell me first Wot do we do????? Before I tell anyone about u why don't u tell me?? Wot now??? Because that has got 2 come from u No one else can decide that

In her room, Lucy lit a cigarette.

I've got to sort out a few things first.

Are u going 2 tell me wot?

Family things, mainly. A few things for myself with my dad.

Why? Firewall don't do that 2 yourself Don't waste your time Your dad = 1 big fat 000000 He is not worth ruining your life 4 That's your revenge on him My dad says that U dont let them hurt u Otherwise all u do is hurt yourself

It's not just him. I've got a friend I've got to think about too. I've got to make sure he's okay before I do anything else. But the thing is I don't know how. I've got my gun but I'm stuck back home again and I don't how I can use it to help him. You know, I feel so ... Do you still think I should go to the police?

Yes I do I do. Because maybe they can help your friend

Sitting at her desk, Lucy laughed aloud.

I don't think so. They're the last people to do that. But I am going to go public, Turtle, one way or the other. Whether I go to the police or the media, I don't know yet.

Why media????

So everyone will know why I did what I did. I've got to explain it to them.

U really think they care Firewall? Really think they care??????? They won't understand where u are coming from U have to see that It won't change how they think about u

They can't ignore me. Not after this. I wasn't killing for the sake of killing someone. That's what she does, she kills. I'm protecting people. So no one has to go through what I went through.

Not your job

If it's not mine, then whose is it? Don't say the police again because all they ever do is bash you up. And don't say they don't. I know they do, because I've seen them do it.

Lucy waited.

Turtle, are you there? Have I lost you?

I'm still here Firewall u can't think like that U don't kill people U know wot people say about me? They come up 2 my dad and they ask him why didn't he let me die when I was a baby They say it in front of me They don't think I can hear them Wot's the fucking difference??? Killing me and killing her?

She was evil. You're not.

Bullshit Bullshit Bullshit & I don't believe u think like that U tell me what u think 4 real U tell me that

Do you really want to know? I wish I'd never shot either of them, Turtle. I really do. Maybe I could've lived with just shooting her. I don't know. But shooting that man, I wish, I just wish I'd never done that. It's as simple as that. I told you it was simple from the start. It's just that there's nothing I can do about it now.

You got 2 go 2 the police Go now!!!! Just call them

I can't. Not now, not yet. I just can't ...

Before Lucy could type any more, Turtle stopped her. *End firewall,* their emergency close-down signal, flashed across her screen. She backed out quickly and found herself on his home page. It was a dazzling place: seas of high glass-blue Japanese waves with the wind blowing the foam back, seagulls swirling about the sky, and a small boat with transparent sails, sailing into the bright red sun. A figure in the boat waved and smiled out of the screen. 'Hi, I'm the Turtle,' the figure said as he sailed against a bright sky. Then the image dissolved into a photograph of a boy in a wheelchair with the written words: *Hi, I'm Toby Harrigan. I call myself the Turtle, because I'm like a turtle on its back when I'm out of my wheelchair. I can't move at all then except to shake my hand in the air, but out on the Net I can do what I want. I can sail, fly, do anything. Come and talk turtle to me because inside I'm just like anybody else.* The buttons, Meet Me, Meet My Family, Life at Cotswold House, Why I am the way I am, flickered into being one after the other but Lucy had other places to go. She wanted to work on her own site and slipped away out of cyberspace, taking the precaution of working offline on her own machine where no one could disturb her.

The kaleidoscope of her interior world opened out and she immersed herself in its electronic images, unwinding the tension in her neck, assuaging some of her grief and reducing the world outside to a succession of shadows. As she worked, she passed quickly over her representations of Dr Agnes Liu. Lucy was looking only for consolation.

15

'What's all this?'

Toby felt his father's hands on his shoulders, the familiar light pressure of the heel of his father's palm on the muscle, it was their greeting. He knew his father's individual odour, a tinge of sweat mingled with his familiar aftershave. His father's presence, the sound of his voice, and the touch of his hands soothing the twisted muscle down Toby's spine, were his first memories. His good hand flickered over his custom-made keyboard with its built-in mouse but it was too late to close the window. His father was reading aloud from the screen.

'She was evil. You're not. Bullshit, bullshit, bullshit. And I don't believe you think like that. You tell me what you think. For real. You tell me that. Do you really want to know? I wish I'd never shot either of them, Turtle. I really do. Maybe I could've lived with just shooting her. I don't know. But shooting that man,

I wish, I just wish I'd never done that. It's as simple as that. I told you it was simple from the start. It's just that there's nothing I can do about it now.'

Harrigan repeated the final words and then stood there in silence. His spoken greetings, his apology for arriving unannounced like this, were lost.

'What is this, Toby? Is it a joke? Are you and a friend doing a bit of role-playing over the Net? Is that it? Or are you going to tell me this is real?'

Toby had a file in which he kept his one-way conversations with his father, a silent recording without a playback option, a series of responses which begged the other side of the conversation. He opened it to a smaller window. He reached out to type, *Yes just a joke dad*, and stopped. His father pulled up a chair beside him, they sat in their common silence. Harrigan, who had never really heard his son speak more than a few disjointed words, always listened in his mind to the voice that he imagined Toby might have had.

'Do you want to tell me?' he eventually asked.

If I do, Dad, will you cut me out of this? If I could have just one more talk to her, then I could get her to give herself up to you. I could have said to her, you call my dad. He'll come and get you, he'll make sure they won't hurt you.

Words which Toby did not type, which instead, like so much of his speech, found no way into the atmosphere, living and dying like small moths in the hermetic seal of his thoughts.

If I tell u — then u have 2 let me talk 2 her when I want 2

'Talk to who, Toby?'

U have 2 promise

'I can't stop you doing anything on this machine.

We've been down that road before. That's your world in there, not mine. I know that.'

How come you're here anyway???

'You're prickly tonight. What is it?'

You are asking me & I am asking u Ok???

'Do you wish I wasn't here? Do you want me to leave? I can go if you want.'

No dad I'm just asking have U got a reason yeah??? U always do

Harrigan reflected that his son was better at reading his thoughts than anyone else had ever been.

'I haven't been able to concentrate, mate. I was worried about you. Something was on your mind this morning and I didn't know what it was. I wanted to see if you were okay.'

Toby did not type anything for a few moments.

U haven't promised dad

'I said I'm not going to stop you doing anything on this machine.'

That's not the same thing I was going 2 tell u anyway U just had 2 wait But u asked so I'll tell u It's no joke It's 4 real I wish it wasn't Dad I am telling u this because she's my friend I know wot she's done But u have to remember she's my friend Now u watch Tell u something u didn't know

In Toby's room at Cotswold House the screen flickered into life with the warning: *You are in Armageddon. The time starts now.* A clock was ticking down, second by second. A dark-haired figure in a short black coat and jeans appeared on the screen, she was in a long dark corridor of a house filled with rubbish. 'I am the Firewall. Stay with me, I'll keep you safe,' the figure said and stretched out her hand. Seven small glittering stars appeared, balanced in a diamond shape over her outstretched hand. The figure spoke again: 'We are in the darkness, you and I. Come with me and I'll show you the way to the light.' She reached out to Turtle in his wheelchair and drew him to his feet. They hugged each other and he walked with her down the corridor.

Toby tapped out words for his father. *She wants me 2 walk Said she'd give her life for that I said no one can do that 4 me So she did this instead*

Reduced back to his professional role as a watcher, Harrigan found himself excluded from the electronic scenario. This hurt him much more than he could have expected. He wondered how images as crude as these and voices so tinny had this kind of power.

'She can't want you to walk any more than I do, Toby,' he said in his neutral voice.

Within the confines of the monitor, Lucy led Toby past dirty rooms towards a distant doorway. A man and a woman followed them, grinning, carrying knives dripping with lurid fake blood. The corridor was truncated and the door opened. The Firewall stepped out into the open sky with Toby and together they went soaring among the glittering stars while the house burst into flames below them.

She only ever takes me this far She said it was too dangerous 4 me 2 go any further I said 2 her this isn't real She said it was And it is 2 her I say to her that's OK I can talk to u where u are I didn't think she'd do more than this I thought it was just the website and nothing else

The scene dissolved. Harrigan saw the sky split open and the four horsemen of the apocalypse raged across the screen. The scene switched to a back alley of terraces and warehouses where the Firewall appeared on the street, armed. A woman in a white coat walked out of a building and the sight of an end of a gun filled the screen. Light exploded within the barrel. The scene turned side on and bullets punched through the air. The woman was shot dead and the Firewall held a smoking gun. The buildings and the streets around them both were consumed by nuclear fire.

'Can you stop it?' Harrigan asked. 'Can you roll it back so I can see that again?'

Wait dad

As the whole city descended into devastation, an angel in gun-blue armour came to the Firewall and handed her a book. Its pages had been cut out and, instead of words, a gun was stored between the covers. The angel gave her the weapon and said to her, 'Knowledge is bitter.'

'I know that now,' Lucy said aloud, alone in her room, immersed in her images. 'I know what they mean now, when they say knowledge is bitter. Turtle, you don't understand — I did have to do what I did. I just have to be strong enough to live with it. You have to forgive me for it.'

On the screen, humans became monsters prowling the earth, murdering the living, eating corpses. The Firewall roamed amongst them, shooting them down. As they died, they evaporated into particles of light. In the end, there was nothing left other than an empty wasteland and the quiet sound of the wind, moaning like the voices of young children, fading into silence.

In her room, Lucy was working. She was building a new city in the middle of this empty place, a vision of towers, fountains and trees. A garden, rows of terraces with rhododendrons and camellias, azaleas and gardenias, sloping down to the edge of a eucalyptus forest. Out of the commands of computer language she was fabricating a place to be safe and happy, somewhere that was home.

In Toby's room, the screen was frozen on the image of Dr Agnes Liu dying in a backstreet. Harrigan sat staring at it for some moments.

'How long have you known about this website?' he asked.

A while A few months

'Has that picture been there all that time?'

Yes

'You didn't tell anyone?'

Tell them wot??? I never believed she would do it

'Do you know anything about this person at all? Her name, where she lives, anything?'

No she won't tell me She's just the Firewall She says she's got no home We talk dad, we talk all the time She said she knows what its like 2 be treated like she's just a thing and she does We talk turtle dad Just like u & me

'Like you and me? You know what she's done and you say that. She's a murderer, Toby.'

No she's my friend

'Someone like this comes to you from out of nowhere on the Net and you trust her with everything about you. She knows how to get under your skin, doesn't she? How do you know she really did this?'

She told me the morning she did it Before it was on the news or anywhere else

'She told you. She told you and you didn't tell me and you didn't tell anyone else?'

No I couldn't She hadn't told me I could yet

'Does she know who I am?'

No

'How do you know that? You've got my picture all over your website with 'my dad' written underneath it. I've been on TV tonight, and the night before. I'm just as likely to end up in the newspapers or on the Net tomorrow. She's going to see me one of these days if she hasn't already. How's she going to react to you then?'

She won't care She's my friend She understands U have 2 let me talk 2 her If I do that I can make her give herself up She will if I talk 2 her I can do that Because I understand her I can fix this

'No, you won't, mate. What you'll do is stay out of this. This is police business, not some game. You can talk to her if you want but we'll be watching everything you say to her. And why? Because I have to do that. I have to authorise people I'd prefer to know nothing about my private life to come and crawl all over your computer and talk to you. I've got to prove that you weren't an accessory after the fact and that I don't have a conflict of interest. Why didn't you tell me as soon as you knew about this?'

Why are u going 2 watch us What are u going 2 do?

'What am I going to do? I am going to trace her, Toby. And when I do, I'm going to put her away in gaol for the next thirty years or so for what she's done.'

U can't trace her She uses a mobile & she's my friend & its not a game dad So why don't u just go away

Harrigan stood up.

'She's not your friend. She's a murderer. She's used you, Toby, and you've let her.'

Toby turned off his computer; the room became silent as the sound of the machine died. There was a shudder through Toby's body, he uttered a strange sound. Toby was crying. Harrigan's son never cried.

'Don't do that to yourself, Toby. You don't need to do that.'

'My friend.' Toby spoke the words aloud.

He began to strike his desk with his hand. Harrigan hit the emergency call button and then tried to take Toby's hand but his son pushed him back. He moved Toby out of his wheelchair and set him on the bed, and then tried to cradle him there. Toby rolled away from him, gasping for breath. His body went into spasm as Tim Masson opened the door and came into the room. The nurse injected Toby with a muscle relaxant and they sat him upright so he could breathe. Harrigan held his son until his body had stopped shuddering. Masson handed him a towel soaked in warm water and he cleaned Toby's face. Toby shook his head to stop him.

'You need some sleep,' Harrigan said.

Toby signalled 'no'. They waited.

'Didn't use me. My friend,' he said at length.

Harrigan could not remember when he had last heard his son speak so many words at once.

'Yes, she is your friend. Whatever else she is, she is that. And she didn't use you. I was wrong to say that. I'm sorry. Just take that from me. I am sorry.'

Eventually Toby flickered 'yes' with his hand. Harrigan touched his son's hair, bright dark hair, just like his own, letting his hand stay there for some few short moments.

I always leave you in the end, I walk away and I leave you. Just you and what's in your head.

'You sleep now. I'll come and see you tomorrow. I'm sorry, okay?'

Toby closed his eyes, his nurse adjusted his pillows. He was slipping away into unconsciousness.

'I'll sit with him,' Masson said.

'Okay,' Harrigan replied.

'Okay,' he said again, as he walked down the corridor outside, wrung out. He stopped to stand on the back deck to the building, looking out over Cockatoo Island. 'I'm sorry,' he said to the night air, holding every muscle tensed.

Alcohol was not allowed on the premises of Cotswold House. Susie, dressed down at the end of the day, provided Harrigan with strong coffee in her office instead. She listened to him, occasionally blinking with tiredness.

'He's got us all on display, Susie, everyone. Me, Ronnie, Carolyn, all their kids, the whole family. He's my son, he's the closest thing to me. To me, this is about as private as it gets, but he's got me up there on the Net with everyone else.'

He was referring to what a former long-term lover had once called the Harrigan tribe: his two sisters with their extended and conjoint families, a gathering of people that could, when collected, fill a hall. On such occasions, Harrigan spent most of his time avoiding relatives who wanted favours from him. Photographs of them all, Harrigan included, filled Toby's website. Toby had not told the world that his father was a policeman, it was almost the only detail he had left out. Harrigan had refused to let him include it, saying that if he did, he could expect to find abuse, pleas for help, or outrageous flattery in every email he opened.

'He's not thinking about what it means to you, Paul,' Susie replied. 'He's thinking about what it means to him. His body keeps him constrained every second of his life. He's an adolescent boy. He needs to tell the world who he is.'

'Yeah. And you let him talk to a murderer. And you didn't even know it.'

Susie rocked a little in her seat with the force of the accusation, her cheeks tinged with red.

'I can't stop him talking to people on the Net. I don't think we should even want to try and do that,' she said. 'He never talks to girls anywhere else. He's a boy. What do you think he's going to do? And how could anyone have known who this girl was?'

Harrigan sat with his head in his hands, staring at Susie's desk.

'He trusted her, you know. Why? Why let someone like that hurt him so much? I —'

Harrigan stopped, obliged in common honesty to admit that he was the person who had most hurt his son that night. There was a hint of toughness in Susie's voice as she replied.

'What are you going to do? Are you going to lock him away so he can't talk to anyone again?'

'No, of course I'm not. I don't understand it myself, I like to see who I'm talking to.'

He knew that not everyone out there wanted to look at his son, that sometimes people turned away at the sight, repulsed. There was silence again. A little of the tension faded from the air.

'Toby is a very strong-willed person, Paul. He's the strongest person I know. He'll get through this.'

'Yeah, he will. I know he will. I have to go, Susie. I've got to go back to work. I've got to tell them about this. I'll come by tomorrow but I'm not sure when. Whenever I can get the time.'

'Don't worry about Toby tonight. We'll look after him, he'll be fine. Good night. Take care.'

She spoke in her professional voice but still managed to sound as tired as he felt.

'Thanks, Susie. Good night,' he said.

Harrigan walked out into the cold night air. His son's tears and his mucus were streaked down his shirt and jacket. This was love; it was the strangest thing in the world to feel, as fundamental and difficult as it was. He could not imagine existing without his connection to his son.

How he got through the next few hours he did not quite know. In the Gents, he sponged the stains off his jacket and shirt. Out in the office, he watched himself work, thorough, quietly spoken, controlled. Before he left that night, the information had been recorded, the responsibility for its investigation allocated and the team advised. He moved through it all somehow numbed against the pain but knowing that it was there waiting for him as soon as this anaesthetic wore off. By the time he reached home, the rain was pouring down; it was a relief to watch the city dissolve in the streaks of water down the windows. Tonight, he was exhausted enough to sleep as soon as he lay down.

In the Temple, the preacher was also at work. He sat at his desk, staring at the telephone, thinking of Lucy, of her particular insolence, considering that it was not a good thing for anyone to be quite so insolent. In the artificial light, he appeared aged beyond recognition. In the luxury of solitude, he let all his masks slip.

'Do you think I can't make you come to me, Lucy?' he said aloud, with no more emotion than if he was reflecting on the state of the weather. 'I think you'll see that I can if I want to. I think you'll see that it's really just a matter of timing.'

Lucy aside, the timing of events had become one of urgency. Thinking of this, he made a phone call.

'Yes? Yvonne Lindley speaking.'

It was an old woman's voice, creaky and sounding puzzled.

'Yvonne. It's Graeme. I hope I'm not calling you too late in the evening.'

'No, not at all. I never sleep at night these days. I should have realised it was you, Graeme. For one fleeting moment there I hoped it might have been a son or a daughter of mine but of course it's not. Nice to hear from you all the same. How can I help?'

'It's refuge business again, I'm afraid.'

'Always a good cause. You know, John would have been very interested in the work you do, he would have seen the value of it. What's the problem?'

'One of my charges, he was out on conditional release. He's a wild boy and I'm afraid he's gone and got himself locked up again. Which is a pity because we were making very good progress.'

'What did he do?'

'He was caught joyriding in a stolen car. I might add he was a passenger, not the instigator. He foolishly went out with some old acquaintances, one of whom turned up in this car, and they all went for a ride. He's only fifteen so he certainly wasn't driving.'

'When you're young, you're mad, aren't you? We certainly used to do things we weren't supposed to do. We had fun though, John and I. Do you know those were his last words to me? It's been fun, Evie, I've had a ball. Fifteen, you say? That's very young, isn't it?'

'Yes. He's quite young in the head as well, which of course is how he let himself be talked into this in the first place. The thing is, if I had him here at the refuge, I could keep up the good work, but as soon as he's back in the boys' home, he'll just slip into his old ways again.'

'We can't have that happen, can we? You leave this to me. I think we can get this sorted out without too much fuss.'

'You may find the police are not very keen to cooperate. Their only solution is to lock him away. And what's worse, Yvonne, and I have to tell you this, they are trying to pin some extraordinary charge on him. This is despite the fact that I know he had absolutely nothing to do with these events. They seem convinced that what is pure coincidence is actual guilt.'

'You just leave things to me, Graeme. I'll take care of this. We'll show them there's life in the old girl yet. I'll make them sit up and take notice. There should be a pen and paper here somewhere — won't be a moment — ah, here we are. Now, this boy's name is — what?'

'One that's very easy to remember, Yvonne. Greg Smith.'

Patiently he spelled out the details until she had all the information she needed and he was able to hang up, relieved of her presence even at the distance of a telephone call.

Now that business was out of the way, he had a task to attend to which he had been avoiding throughout the day. He went up to his bedroom and hesitated for a few moments in the doorway, an expression of aversion on his face. The windows were open and heavy rain had been blown into the room, soaking the floor. This pleased him: the force of the weather had cleared the room of its human odours and any sense of a physical presence. He walked inside and pulled the blankets from his bed, throwing them on the floor. He stripped the bloodstained sheets, the pillow, everything, tied them into a loose bundle and threw them down the stairs. He did not feel quite the same nausea that had gripped him last night when he had walked in here and put his hand onto the sheets when they were still warm and damp with Lucy's blood. He pulled the mattress from the bed and upended it down the stairs after the bedding. In the pouring rain, he dragged both the mattress and the bedding over the uneven ground to the edge of the demolition site, to a blue industrial waste bin which he knew would be emptied within a few days. He threw the bloodstained items into the bin and slammed the lid closed, a sound that echoed down the empty street.

He stood in the rain, letting it soak him, relieved that he had managed to do this alone, that he had not had to ask Bronwyn, a woman from his congregation who did his cleaning, to do it for him. He walked quickly back to his office, into the tiny kitchen, and dried himself, scrubbing his hands to remove the last touch of any stain. He wondered where he would sleep tonight; he could sleep almost anywhere if necessary. Physical comfort was something for which he had never felt much need. In the end, he decided not to stay in the Temple. It would be too easy for the police to find him here and he wasn't ready to talk to them quite yet. He needed time to think before Greg was delivered into his care.

He took the refuge van and went to take shelter with some like-minded people, acquaintances he knew he could rely on. He drove through the empty streets in the rain, his thoughts buzzing with possibilities for the future.

16

'Is there anyone in this picture that you recognise?'

Grace and Matthew Liu sat at a white table in the centre of the large room, close to the desk where the nurses came and went. Pale blue curtains surrounded the individual beds of the intensive care ward. Grace spoke quietly, the cushioned floors softened all extraneous sounds. In a glass room at the furthermost end of the ward, Agnes Liu slept on in shadows which had the quality of dark water. On a monitor, lighted graphs sketched the pattern of her breathing and her heartbeat in pencil-thin lines.

'Yeah,' Matthew said, 'that one. That's her. For sure.'

'Why are you so sure?' Grace asked.

Matthew Liu put the photograph back down on the table where it lay under his hands. The fine bones of his fingers splayed over its glossy surface. It was a photograph of a small group of homeless boys in Belmore Park, taken at an angle to increase the sense of distance. One of the boys stood to the side, talking to another figure seen only from the back, the slender female outline of a figure wearing a black jacket and jeans and with short curly hair. She seemed to have her arms folded in front of her, drawing her clothes tightly around the curve of her outline.

'The way she's holding her shoulders. That's how she looked when she walked away. She's like a cut-out in the air. You know who someone is when they do something like that to you. They're in your head, you can't get them out.'

He spoke angrily.

'Okay.' Grace slipped the photograph back into the file. 'How are you going today? Do you want me to stay and talk to you, or just stay? I've got all the time in the world if you want it.'

He shrugged. He had shaved his thick black hair in deliberate mourning and his cheeks looked hollowed out. He had taken on age, something laid roughcast over his features. He was dressed in worn black clothing. He had not cried once in her presence since she had sat with him in the street the morning that it had happened. He refused to talk, to her, to anyone. Sometimes when she visited, he only wanted her to sit with him in silence while he sat next to his mother, waiting.

'You don't have to stay, I'm all right. Mum's not going to die now, you know that. I don't want to talk. I'm going to go and sit with her.'

'You know where I am if you do want to call me any time.'

He shook his head and walked away. Everything he did broadcast grief and anger in equal proportions, both immense.

At the entrance to the ward, Grace found Agnes Liu's doctor waiting for her.

'Some of your time?' he said. 'I'm going to have to let her talk to you. She's not going to rest easy until she does and I can't persuade her that it really isn't wise. I think it's best to have this done with as soon as we can. I'll be in touch when I think she's able to talk for any length of time. Probably tomorrow afternoon at the earliest.'

'If you call me, I can arrange to be here then. Only me?'

'If you do bring anyone else, they'll have to stay outside. I don't want two people standing over her. One of you is bad enough. No offence,' he added as an afterthought before frowning and walking away.

Grace left St Vincent's mired in an old, familiar feeling: stasis, the sense of her heart becoming stagnate, her blood stopped. Numb to the end of each limb, each fingertip, she was gripped by emotional hypothermia. She sat with this weight on her, stranded at the lights on Oxford Street, watching the crowds pass by in the remains of the wet weather. It was her old habit of feeling either too much or too little, when all she wanted was balance. She had thought she was cured.

She arrived just in time for the morning's meeting in the incident room, something which usually happened earlier. Today's meeting had been shifted back and the room was filled with people hanging around, impatient. Harrigan, the buzz went, was trapped in his office, caught up with a telephone call from the Tooth demanding detailed explanations for the funds expended on the investigation and (as he said) the reasons for its lack of progress to date. The case had become stalled in a slow trickle of information, most of it leading them nowhere; they hadn't even managed to locate the preacher yet, he might as well have evaporated from the city. People said you could almost see Harrigan chafing as he worked.

Grace waited with everyone else. Carrying Greg Smith's file under her arm, she slowly walked the length of the Firewall's turbulent pictures, considering each in turn. The disconnected images unwound like bobbin threads along the corkboard, a glossy snakeskin depicting huge and random destruction. As she moved from sheet to sheet, she asked herself: if this is your game plan, what's your starting point? How do you get there?

Ian appeared at her elbow, startling her a little.

'What are you going to do for the end of the world, Gracie?' he said to her, smiling.

'I don't know. What do you have to do to get to the pearly gates? Scrub your teeth with bath cleaner? I'd like to look my best, I guess.'

'You wouldn't need to do that to look your best,' he replied. 'I'd sink a few golden ambers first. There's no beer in the afterlife.'

Grace watched over his shoulder as Jeffo slipped another photograph into the array of pictures. Several people standing nearby glanced at it and then at each other, raising their eyebrows. She held her breath. They did not look in her direction and they did not laugh. She relaxed and smiled at Ian.

'You don't know, it could be flowing in the streets up there. It's got to have something going for it,' she said.

'I wish,' he said.

'If you two really want to know,' Harrigan grumbled, passing them by, 'why don't you ask our woman up there on the board. She can tell you. She's already made it to the afterlife. The only thing flowing for her is her own blood.'

'Good morning to you too,' Grace said, softly.

'What's up with him this morning?' Ian said.

They looked at each other, and then at the corkboard. Louise had pinned up a second reproduction of the picture of the unknown woman lying dead across a set of steps with the words 'You can run but you can't hide' scrawled across her. This time, the reproduction came from an Internet news service and carried the headline: AVENGING ANGELS' DEADLY STRIKE. POLICE FAIL TO MAKE ARREST AFTER DOCTOR SHOT BY EXTREME ANTI-ABORTION GROUP.

Harrigan's arrival called them all to silence. He settled his papers on the table, taking a few seconds to dispel his irritation. Whenever the Tooth tormented him like this, some other scheme was usually in progress elsewhere, and for Harrigan the true questions were twofold. Were all their backs, his included, protected? And where were the real land mines buried? Time was ticking on, like the clock on his murdering girl's website. Not so many days had passed since he had first located the website but the pressures for a result were growing more intense by the hour. The Firewall was still out there, his superiors were still leaning on him, the politicians were leaning on them, and the media was baying for blood. He glanced briefly at the mosaic of diverse pictures on the corkboard without taking them in. They shone in the reflection of the overhead lights, the images lost in the glitter.

'We know who this is now.' Louise's voice was already coarsened by alcohol even though it was only late morning. She was tapping the picture of the dead woman with a slightly shaking hand. 'Dr Laura Di-Cuollo, obstetrician, Long Beach, California. She was shot dead on her own front doorstep sixteen months ago. That case is still open. The people who shot her call themselves the Avenging Angels. They took this piccie as soon as they'd done it and then they sent it out to every news service that wanted to print it. That's who they are. They don't believe in hiding what they do.'

'But our colleagues in the US of A do,' Harrigan said. 'We've been trying to open up the lines of communication with them on this but all we get is the cold shoulder. They hang up the phone on me as soon as they can; we email or fax them urgently and they lose the message. We're going to keep trying but we have to chase this our end as well if we're going to get anywhere with it. So — what we know about our killer. She's armed and dangerous. She's prepared to use her gun again. She's unpredictable. She's "stuck back home" wherever that is. What we don't know. Is our girl one of these Avenging Angels, so-called? People involved with this kind of organisation are inclined to firebomb clinics as well as shooting the staff. There are five Whole Life Health Centre clinics in the Sydney metropolitan area. I am trying to get a watch on them all but Marvin...' Harrigan paused, weighing his words '...is still considering the options, so he's told me. He'll let me know once he's checked over our budget. So consider this in your deliberations: are we dealing with a single killer? Or a member of an organisation which has its own resources to draw on, possibly from more than one country?'

'Why don't you tell us that yourself, mate? Maybe your boy knows. Why don't you ask him instead of us?' Jeffo muttered poisonously.

How far the words were intended to carry, Grace could not be sure. She was standing in the orbit of his voice and several other people close to her had smiled. Jeffo was giving voice to certain exclusions that had rankled badly with some. Toby Harrigan's relationship with the Firewall, all that side of the investigation, had been siphoned off to a small team working to Louise, with instructions to talk to no one other than Harrigan concerning anything they found. Grace had heard the sour rumblings of gossip. How the boss was favouring a burnt-out alcoholic, compromising the possibility of their results. A whispered heresy — 'Harrigan's losing it, he should take himself off the job' — had started to do the rounds.

'I'm going to ask each of you to exercise your mind on those questions,' Harrigan said, looking around at them all, speaking with an acerbic edge that implied he had picked up on the undercurrents. 'Every one of you, because there are no answers yet and it's time we had some. But right now we've got a picture of her, Grace tells me. Why don't you show us?'

'A picture of sorts,' Grace replied, taking the photograph out of her file and walking forward. 'This came out of Greg Smith's file at Juvenile Justice. It's a magazine photograph published about a year ago when someone was doing an exposé on what happens to state wards. It's too bad their research didn't go much past this picture.'

There was limited space left on the board, occupied as it was by the Firewall's website. Searching for room, Grace found herself looking at Toby Harrigan in his wheelchair, the photograph that welcomed viewers once they had surfed into his website. No other pictures of Harrigan's son had made it to the board, he had not allowed it. His son existed there only as part of the Firewall's ferocious world. Harrigan, standing close by, saw it at the same moment that she did. They glanced at each other but neither reacted. Harrigan, turning, searched through the assembled team until he located Jeffo and eyeballed him. The man looked away at once.

'Matthew Liu is certain this is her. He was sure from the moment I showed it to him and I believe him,' Grace said, taking the only available space, next to Harrigan's son. 'She's the right height, 156 centimetres. Tiny, in other words. She's thin and she could get into the clothes the shooter wore. You put her beside the website and there are similarities with the Firewall as well. It's not much to go on, but it is something to connect her to Greg Smith.'

'That's useful, isn't it?' Jeffo said, this time meaning to be heard. 'We can all go round checking the backs of people's heads.'

There was some laughter. Grace did not waste her time even glancing in Jeffo's direction.

'I look forward to you doing better, mate,' Harrigan snapped, with just enough venom to make sure everyone knew what his feelings towards Jeffo were. He spoke to Trevor, 'It's enough for a description. Get it written up and get it circulated, the photo as well. Yeah, what is it, Dea?'

His administrative assistant, a small and tough-looking woman with dyed blonde hair, had appeared in the doorway.

'Marvin's on the phone again,' she announced.

Oh joy, Harrigan thought irritably. He nodded to Trevor to take over and left the room. Trevor was cynically cheerful as he handed out the jobs for the day.

'You finally get to go and chat up young Greggie this

arvo, Gracie. The shrink says it's okay. They're expecting you at three thirty,' he said to her. 'Tough luck, mate. It's a dirty job but someone's got to do it.'

'I'll cope,' she said, faking a blithe indifference.

Dirty jobs done dirt cheap a speciality, Trev, Grace improvised from a well-known song, reflecting on her present conditions of employment.

It surprised Grace to find that Toby Harrigan was still on the board when she came in after a brief lunch, presumably because Harrigan had been locked in his office since the meeting, kept there by constant demands from the Tooth. She looked at the boy and thought that he had Harrigan's face, twenty or so years back. Harrigan was not the only one with someone he loved in a wheelchair, she had someone there herself. Someone who was both a one-time lover and a friend, who found himself confined to the same means of transportation by fate, bad luck, call it what you like, a disease in the genes he had grown into without knowing it. Grace thought of the clock running backwards for her friend as his nerve strings were cut one by one, bringing him to a common meeting point with Harrigan's son.

At the age of not quite thirty, Grace had acquired a lasting sense of uncertainty, she lived every day with the anticipation of insecurity. At any time, something might happen that would blow you out of the water and you would never know it. In her imaginings, the Bondi Pavilion could easily have doubled as the deserted cantina from some spaghetti western where the roofs were open to the skies, drifts of sand massed in the corners of deserted rooms and bird shit painted the walls. One day, those same white walls might crumble into the sea, leaving behind broken archways in silhouette against a hot blue Sydney sky. Wistful dreams compared to the visions on the Firewall's website, imaginings of annihilation which reduced Grace's own to a production which (she had to admit) was strictly amateur night.

She stopped to look at the Firewall and Toby Harrigan in their imagined embrace in the hallway of what looked like a prison, a space which gave the impression of airlessness. Briefly, she touched the two figures. You can't see her but you love her. She knows who you are and she loves you. You're both down there together in her eyes. That's why she wants to get you to your feet and save you. Save you and save herself.

'Who do you love?' Grace sang softly to herself.

'Are you curious about my boy, Grace? Do you want to know something about him? I can give you all the textbooks you like. They have open days where he lives if you're interested. Come along and have a look one day, you don't have to be shy.'

Harrigan appeared beside her and removed the photograph of his son from the board, sliding it into a folder.

'No, that's not why I'm here,' she said at once. 'I came in here to think, it's the only place where it's quiet enough to. He looks like you, that's all that was in my head.'

He shrugged, apparently embarrassed by what he had said. There were lines of strain around his eyes.

'Yeah, you could say that. Same face if you like. Poor kid.'

He spoke more quietly.

'I was really thinking about her,' she said, changing the subject, glancing at the anonymous figure in the photograph. 'I'm trying to work her out. She didn't go out looking for blood. She wasn't doing it for kicks.'

'I almost wish she had been, I'd find her easier to understand. I don't cotton on to killing people for fantasies like this.'

'This is so extreme, I almost don't know where to start with it,' Grace said, glancing along the board. 'You look at it and there are no holds barred at all. Where do you have to come from to see the world this way?'

'Nowhere we want to go. I don't care what makes her what she is, Grace. I want her off the streets before she does something to someone else. You put a gun in the hands of someone who thinks like this and they will use it, it goes with the territory. Why are you asking yourself that question?'

'It's one way of getting her off the streets, isn't it? Working out who she is, what she might do next.'

He glanced along the corkboard. 'You look at this and you say to yourself, this is who she is,' he said. 'And the answer is, so what? Some people have no problem killing, they like to do it for fun or profit. Other people do it because they're away with the pixies. We know that. The rest is just work.'

'Don't we have to out-think them?' Grace replied, looking at the slender and unknown girl in the photograph talking to Greg Smith. 'Isn't that the point? Apart from anything you might feel for the people they've damaged. Doesn't that make you want to ask those questions?'

She said this last not as an argument, but as an expression of something felt.

'Yeah, the people involved do matter,' he said. 'As it happens, Grace, I ask myself those questions all the time. I read all the books as well. Every time a new one comes out, I get hold of it and I think, maybe this one is going to tell me something. What I'm saying is, I don't see that it amounts to very much in the end to know what makes her what she is. It won't be a blinding insight into anything.'

Unconsciously, Grace flicked a stray strand of her long brown hair back from her face, an unexpectedly elegant gesture to Harrigan's observation.

'You have to be one step ahead of them whatever you do,' she said, unwillingly seeing in her mind the man who had raped her and whose body was still imprinted on her own however much she wanted to scour it away. 'People can play all kinds of games with you at a distance. You can't let them do that.'

Harrigan, looking at her, did not reply for a few moments.

'That's a good way of seeing things if you want to do this job,' he said. 'Are you taking that picture with you when you go to see that boy?'

They both glanced at the photograph taken in Belmore Park.

'Yeah, I've got it already. I'd better go, it'll take me a while to get there.'

'Why don't you come and see me when you get back? I'd like to hear what he's got to say before you write it up. And don't forget to ring me if you get any spectacular information.'

'Sure,' she said.

She smiled at him and left the room. He walked out after her. Come and see me and then we'll go out and eat together somewhere. No, let's not do that, that really will give everyone something to talk about. There were enough whispers doing the rounds at the moment without adding something like that to them.

At that moment, Harrigan was called back into his office to take yet another phone call from the Tooth's personal assistant, a woman who possessed the perfect up-your-arse voice, demanding yet more information on what they'd spent, what they'd achieved. Trapped at his desk, he watched Grace readying to leave. She wouldn't want to spend her time with him anyway. Would she? As the idiot woman rabbited on in his ear, he watched Grace walk out of the office — a nice light movement, full of ease — and wondered.

As soon as Harrigan had escaped from his telephone call, he quietly shredded the photograph of his son. Jeffo was going to regret his little joke. All the signs were there: Harrigan was being undermined from both the outside and the inside, and if he wanted to survive he'd have to watch every step he took. It was the worst possible time to think of something so scandalous and stupidly suicidal as sleeping with his most junior officer. He had much better keep his eye focused on things that were likely to have more reliable benefits. Such as hanging onto his career and making sure that too many knives didn't go thud between his shoulderblades.

Out on the road, Grace drove nimbly through the traffic, pleased with her freedom. She sang to herself as she drove, hits on the airwaves and remnants from songs she had sung during her own short career. She felt restless, something which usually ended in her dusting off her shiny clothes and high-heeled shoes and going out to party. She was good at living it up, Sydney people generally were, they knew how to party. There was Bondi with its tarted-up strip on the edge of the beach and the shining sea, and the city itself, bright in a sunlight with an ancient, hard clarity to it. It was a city lazy in the sun, casual and brash with its eye on the good times, thorough in the execution of its corruption, the way it went about everything that mattered. She never wanted to live anywhere else.

She overtook the slower cars on the expressway, approaching the river, speeding down the descent towards Brooklyn and the Hawkesbury River Bridge. Almost fourteen years ago she had travelled this same distance in the reverse direction, at that time by train, leaving home to work in the city, with a sense of freedom she had never again felt with such intensity. The railway line had twisted (still did) along the backwaters of the Hawkesbury River, past disused oyster beds and decaying blue and green fibro houses isolated in the midst of the eucalyptus forest on the water's edge. The train had picked up speed as it climbed through the tunnels approaching the river crossing and had then come roaring out of the dark onto the bridge. She had felt that the sky had opened out around her, that she was flying. To the east of the railway she had seen the grey pylons of the old bridge, the green river between the tree-covered hills as it flowed to the sea, and the town on the south bank beneath her, a pastiche of white buildings and red roofs, with cars glinting in the sunlight. In the mid afternoon on a working day, as she crossed by the road bridge, racing a commuter train in the distance and beginning her ascent towards the Central Coast, the river was still a boundary line. Travelling across it had always had a peculiar bitter-sweetness for her. Today, she felt a shiver of anticipation, of energy, down her spine.

This energy lasted as long as it took her to reach Kariong, to be shown into the office and meet a man who wanted to spend as little time as possible speaking to her. Sooner than expected, she was back out in the car park ringing the boss.

'Harrigan.'

'It's Grace here.'

'Yeah?'

'I'm afraid I've got some not very good information. I'm at Kariong but Greg Smith isn't. He's been bailed.'

'You're joking. Who bailed him? When?'

'Preacher Graeme Fredericksen. He bailed Greg from the Children's Court at Parramatta early this afternoon while I was still on my way up here.'

'He's finally surfaced, has he? So why didn't anyone tell us? Why weren't we involved in this?'

'They don't seem to want to include us in this at all. They didn't get any warning themselves, or so they're telling me. Two departmental officers arrived in a government car at lunch time and picked him up. The paperwork came down from the department with some very senior signatures on it.'

'Is he with the preacher now? Have they gone back to his refuge or whatever it is?'

'That's who Greg left the court with. But I can't reach anyone at the refuge and I can't raise the preacher. No matter what number you ring, you only get through to the voice mail. They're shut down to the world. I can tell you they left the court in the refuge van at about 2:45, but that's all the information I've got.'

'Get back in here as soon as you can. I'll take it from here.'

It had been a pointless journey. Driving back out onto the expressway Grace looked down the Gosford road, thinking of home, knowing it was just a short drive to her father's house at Point Frederick on the Broadwater and wondering what he was doing now. He could be in his study, caught up in his work, writing research papers and speeches, or standing in his back garden on the edge of the water, wondering why things had worked out the way they had. She hadn't the time to go and see him now, however much she might want to. She had work to do.

Grace sped up over Mooney-Mooney Bridge, heading back to the city. From about fourteen onwards, she could have found herself in a stolen car being driven too fast along this same freeway; the pleasure she had taken in the speed was with her as she drove now. Back then, the acceleration had been in her own head, she had wanted to get inside the sense of the speed itself, to let go completely, shouting at the driver (some other kid, completely spooked by her) go faster, let's smash through something. They never had smashed anything — their car or another or the sandstone embankment — all they had done was to come very close. She had to admit it, she had wanted to save that lost boy's life. Now all she could do was draw the line Harrigan had talked about.

When she reached the office, neither the preacher nor the boy had been found and every available person was out searching for them. She stopped in the doorway to Harrigan's office, hesitating. He was on the phone and gestured to her to wait. As he hung up, he looked at her expectantly.

'I've got the paperwork from Kariong for you if you want to see it,' she said, feeling cold as she spoke. 'It looks like they used the psychiatric assessment as a lever to get him out.'

'Yeah.' He was distant, unreadable. 'Leave it with me, would you, Grace? I don't have time to talk now. Okay?'

'Sure,' she said.

She went back to her desk, hiding behind her make-up and scrubbing out a sharply felt disappointment.

Not long after, Louise knocked discreetly on Harrigan's door and put a message on his desk. It was the transcript of an email they had retrieved from the trash file on Toby's computer.

Firewall, u have 2 be so careful now, the police know about your web site and they are watching everything u say and do. U remember I love u, Firewall, love u always.

Harrigan nodded as he read it.

'Keep me posted,' he said, and buried his head in his paperwork, working at a murderous pace, driving all other thoughts out of his head.

17

In the afternoon, Lucy woke from her electronic dreams to a curious sense of lassitude. It was the sixth day since the shooting. The thought 'I am here' was voiced in her mind as an acknowledgement that she was as good as imprisoned there. Events had slipped into suspension. Elsewhere in the house, her father slept his narcotic sleep. After they had spoken to each other, he had withdrawn into his bedroom, shutting the door against her, holding her at bay. Out in the rest of the world, everything existed in an uneasy stability. She had the sense that neither she nor the preacher could move without initiating violence. She felt the threat of it in the same way that she might have listened to the sound of someone she feared approaching her from a distance.

She left her room to go and wash. At her door, she stopped and looked down the corridor at the closed door to her father's bedroom. She only had to walk in there and say, 'I'm here, Dad. I just told you, you owe me. Can't you give a bit, the smallest bit?' Words that became a craving as she thought them. He had nothing to give her, that door was closed against her, she could not expect to find any mercy in there. If she walked into his room with those words, he would turn his back to her and wrap himself in impenetrable silence and deafness. He sent whispered messages through Melanie, asking her not to leave, saying he still wanted to see her but only if she was kind to him, because he was a dying man. Come and be my friend before I die, he whispered to her through her sister, there's no point in accusations. She could not use her gun against that whispered voice.

In the bathroom, she washed herself carefully. Her bleeding had stopped by now but she still washed herself several times a day, polishing her unfamiliar skin and body as a child might. She sat on the edge of the bathtub, carefully drying the soft skin of her vagina, then dressed herself, thinking that no one could touch her now. She traced the edge of her face as she looked at herself in the mirror, unnerved by the awareness that this mask and no other was her face. She felt she was inhabiting herself the way a ghost might take possession of someone else's body.

As she came downstairs into the hallway, she heard the television in the lounge room. From the kitchen she heard softer voices, Melanie and Stephen speaking to each other, words that were partly indistinct but which seemed to be about everyday things. She stopped at the open door, to see Stephen smoking as he sat at the table reading the day's paper, while Melanie stood at the bench slicing potatoes. He looked up and smiled at her.

'Hi, Luce,' he said.

'Hi.'

This single syllable filled the air like a breath finally expelled and the past overlaid the present, going back years. It was late at night. She had left her room immediately after her father had and was going to the bathroom to wash herself. When she came out, she saw her father walking downstairs and then Stephen standing in the hallway watching them both. He was staring at her with his mouth open and his face white. He did not speak to her, he turned and went downstairs to the kitchen after their father. She stood at the top of the stairs, too frightened to move, listening. She heard the sound of Stephen's quieter voice but she could not make out the words. In the cold and silent house, she heard her father shouting with that sudden anger he had, and then the sound of someone at first being hit and then crashing to the floor. She ran downstairs to find Stephen with his knee cracked on the laundry floor, rolling about in pain. She could say nothing; he gripped on to her while he refused to make a sound. Her father was eating a slice of bread, something. He finished, brushed himself down and then called an ambulance. As the ambulance arrived in the driveway, her mother came down to the kitchen for the first time.

'You okay, Luce?'

Stevie was talking to her. Both he and Mel were staring at her. She shook her head to bring herself back to the present.

'Yeah, I'm okay,' she said.

'You want something to eat?' Mel asked.

'No, I'll just have some coffee.'

'Whatever you like.'

Lucy looked up from making instant coffee to find Stephen watching her, the expression on his face a mixture of concern and fear.

'Where's Dad?' she asked.

'He's still in his room. I don't think he's coming out again.' Melanie answered the question for her brother, tossing her knife down and turning and standing with her arms folded. She spoke without energy. 'Do you know, he spent the whole time I was in there this morning whispering in my ear about how much he loves you. I can't deal with that, Luce. I can hardly even deal with the sound of his voice.'

Melanie waited for her to reply but Lucy said nothing. Her sister shook her head.

'You two are just so alike,' she said, 'you won't let go of anything. He's never going to say what you want him to say, Luce, never. He's just going to keep getting at me and at Stevie until you say to him that it doesn't matter what he did to you. If you're going to stay around, just give him what he wants. It doesn't matter now anyway, it's too fucking late.'

Again Lucy did not answer. She had no voice; everything she had to say was stuck in her throat.

'Mum's in the lounge, is she?' was all she managed in the end.

'What do you think?' Melanie said, turning away again.

Stephen said nothing, only lit another cigarette from the end of the one he was already smoking.

Lucy took her mug of coffee and went outside to sit next to Dora and scratch the old dog's head. As the dog nuzzled closer to her, she thought she would let her off the chain, and then go and tell her father how evil she thought he was. She did not move: thoughts of her father had caused her to become paralysed. She did not know what she wanted, whether she should stay or go. What was the point of staying here other than that it was somewhere to hide. She shook her head against the confusion. The sound of her phone, stashed in the pocket of her jacket, interrupted her thoughts.

'Yeah?' she said, knowing who it would be.

'Lucy,' the preacher replied. 'How are you today?'

'I'm good, Graeme. I've never felt better in my life. What do you want?'

'I've got someone here I want you to talk to.'

Lucy felt cold as she listened to him pass the phone to someone.

'Luce?'

'Hi, Greg. He got you out, did he? He said he would.'

'Yeah, he did. Those fucking pigs put me straight in the van. Look, I . . . What are you going to do?'

Lucy put her hand on her waistband and felt her firearm, hidden under her baggy clothes. She did not leave her room without carrying her gun.

'Whatever he wants, Greg. Did you get my message? The one I asked Ria to give you?'

'Yeah, I did. I can't talk, you know, I — '

'Then you know you have to be as careful as you can. You watch everything he does. I'm going to do what he wants. Everything I have to. You remember that. I'm still out here. I haven't forgotten you.'

'Yeah, I will. You okay, Luce?'

'Yeah, I'm okay. What about you? Did they shave your hair off, take away your beanie like they always do?'

'Yeah, I got no hair any more but I hung onto my beanie this time. It's all I got left, everything else has been ripped off me. Look, I got to go, he wants the phone.'

'I'm here. You remember that.'

Lucy listened to the sound of traffic down the line as

she waited for Graeme. She glanced across the national park towards the vicinity of the northbound expressway, wondering where they could be. All she saw was the curve of the sky and the clouds massed on the horizon.

'You see, it's just the way I told you, Lucy,' the preacher said. 'I have my contacts too. You should remember that.'

'I hadn't forgotten. But I don't mind coming to see you, Graeme. Because I've got my insurance.'

'Do you think you'll use it?'

'Why wouldn't I? If you've used one of these things once, you can always do it again. Because you really know how to then. It's not like shooting at a tree any more.'

There was silence.

'Graeme?'

'I was just thinking that's not quite how you talked about it the last time we spoke. Are you changing your mind? Do you feel a little easier with it all now?'

Lucy felt frightened down into the pit of her stomach.

'I just do what I have to, Graeme.'

'I see. Well, why don't we all get together this evening? I thought we could meet at the garage.'

'Not this evening,' Lucy snapped back. 'I haven't got any way to get there. And anyway, I don't want to go there. I don't like it there. Last time I was there I ... there are ghosts in there, Graeme, I heard those kids' voices last time. I'm never going back there again. No, I want to say where and when we meet. Okay? Me. I say.'

'Just as you like, Lucy. You set the terms.'

'I'll meet you out the back of Central there. In that warehouse.'

'Isn't that a little too public?'

'No one sees you in a crowd, Graeme. If you're in a big enough crowd, you just disappear.'

'Yes, that's true. So. When?'

'I don't know. I've got to get a car.'

'Where are you? Perhaps I can help.'

'I'm nowhere, Graeme, so I wouldn't worry about that. I'll ring you back. And when I do, I want to talk to Greg. Okay? Every time I ring you or you ring me, I want to talk to him.'

'You will. I promise you, you will. And I promise you, he'll be with me when you and I meet.'

Lucy did not speak. There was an implication in his tone that she could not puzzle out, and if she asked him what he really meant, she knew he would only play more word games with her.

'I'm hanging up now,' she said.

'I'll wait for your call.'

'Graeme ...'

'Yes.'

'Don't do anything I won't like.'

The connection went dead.

'What am I going to do, girl?' she said aloud to the bitch.

The dog only nuzzled closer, drinking in the attention, the closeness of another presence.

Lucy went back to her room, logged on and went out onto the Net.

Turtle, are you there?

Firewall I told u We are being watched

I don't care. I've got to ask you something.

Wotzup

I've got a friend in bad, bad trouble and I don't know how to help him out without getting in deeper myself. Is that possible? Can I get in deeper than I already am?

Yes u can Easy Wot do u want me 2 do U just have 2 ask

I just need to know what you think.
Firewall I already said U've got 2 go 2 the police
What can they do? They can't help my friend.
Why can't they??
For one thing, they don't know where to find him.
Do u know???
There are some places I know about where they might take him. But I think what they'll probably do is move him around. I'm not really sure.
They???
Oh, yeah. There's more than one person out there, Turtle.
Go 2 police Do it now
Why are you so sure that's the right thing to do?
There's nothing else u can do Because they are not going 2 stop till they find u Firewall I know they won't U go 2 them & u won't get hurt I promise u I do
You don't know that. Anyway, I'm not frightened of them, I don't care what they do to me. That's not what I'm thinking about. I could go looking for my friend myself if I had a car. Maybe that's what I should do. I need a car. I could —
U could do wot????
I could take my gun and go and see the people who've got him. Say to them I've got a gun, they've got to do what I want or I'll use it on them this time. But for all I know, they might be waiting for me to do that. I'm not the only one with a gun. Maybe I'll just end up getting shot myself. That's what I'm expecting to happen really, when I think about it.
No don't do it U just get in more trouble The more u do things like that the worse it gets Don't Firewall U stop now
What am I going to do, Turtle?

Ring the police & wot about the people u shot Have u forgotten????

No, I haven't forgotten them. I don't think I ever will. It's like they're always there, it doesn't matter what I do. They're with me all the time. I wake up in the morning and it's like, 'Oh, hi, guys, it's you again.' They never go away. I am going to see those people and hear those shots for the rest of my life. I've got to go and think now. I'll be back, okay? Talk to you later. Love you, Turtle, love you always.

Firewall u go 2 the police NOW ok???? U have 2

I'll think, Turtle.

U wait don't go U got 2 believe me I'm your friend I am 4 ever I love u always 2 U go 2 the police before something really bad happens

Turtle, I've got to think. Okay? I'll be back.

She closed down and then, feeling the enclosure of the room, opened the door. As she sat on the bed looking out into the hallway, she saw Melanie go past in the direction of her father's room, carrying a tray of medications. A little afterwards, she saw Stephen come back the other way, limping on his bad leg.

'Stevie,' she called.

'Yeah. What do you want, Luce?'

'How's Dad?'

'He's as sick as a dog. Why? Are you going to go and see him? He was just asking if you were still here and I said you were.'

Lucy stood in the doorway, glanced down towards the closed door of her father's room.

'What does Mel do in there?' she asked.

'What do you think she does? She washes him. She feeds him. She gives him his pills and his shots. Listens to him whenever he's raving on about something. I don't know how she does it.'

'What about you?' she asked, suddenly sharper. 'How are you? How's your knee? Do you still get that pain the way you used to?'

'Don't worry about my knee, Luce. I can deal with it.'

'Oh, yeah. You can deal with it. We can all fucking deal with it.'

'He's in real pain. You haven't seen it.'

'Good,' she said.

'No, it's not good. You haven't seen what it means. It's horrible, it doesn't matter if it is him,' he replied, angrily.

'No, he deserves it,' she snapped back. 'Why are you doing this anyway?'

'I'm doing it for Mel. And because it's going to be over and done with soon. And after that I'm going to clear everything I can out of this place. We're going to clean it from top to bottom, I'm going to paint it and it's going to be like new. And that'll be the end of it. They're the only reasons I've got. I don't want to talk about it any more. Can you give it a rest for the moment?'

'Stevie, I've got to ask you about a —'

'Not now!'

He walked away.

She went back into her room and then thought she could not stay in there. She went downstairs and followed the sound of the television to the lounge. Her mother was in there as usual. Lucy stood in the doorway, her mother looked up at her and did not speak. She pulled her cardigan close about her and turned her attention back to the television. Wrapped up in her old windcheater, Lucy went and stood out on the back lawn, walked to the edge of her grandmother's garden and looked across the national park. It was late in the afternoon, not long before dark. In the distance, she saw the house lights that marked the edge of the suburban sprawl begin to appear. The sky was overcast and the contours of the tree tops in the distance were the colour of fresh-cut coal.

Hugging herself in the growing dusk on the edge of the woodland, she shook her head against the furies rising in her mind, the sounds in her head. 'Don't,' she said, 'don't,' as the familiar cries of her own personal ghosts came back to haunt her. She sat down on the damp grass, holding her head in her hands.

When she came back to herself, she heard the dog's chain clinking as Dora moved around. 'Fuck you, Dad,' she said, looking up at the ragged sky, and went and let the dog off her chain. With a strength drawn out of anger, she ripped the chain away — it came easily away from the rotten wood of the kennel — and threw it out into the tangle of the garden. She pulled her windcheater off and stood out there in the bitter cold, letting the chill freeze her body. She felt the gun pressed into her waist grow cold against her skin and did not care if anyone saw that she had it. She waited until ice seemed to take hold of her and she felt nothing.

She needed a car. Even if she went to the police, she would still need a car. She would ask Stevie in the morning if he could help her. She rang the preacher's mobile telephone number but only reached the answering machine. 'Graeme,' she said into the mechanical emptiness, 'it's Lucy. I'm going to call you tomorrow in the morning. I should know if I've got a car by then. Okay? You had better be there, Graeme. And remember what I said to you about when we're on the phone. It's not just you I want to talk to. So don't call me, I'll call you. You make sure you wait for me to call.'

She went back inside the house, to her room. She had stopped in the hallway to look at the door to her father's room when the door opened and Melanie appeared, carrying a tray of dirty dishes and utensils. The tray was heavily laden and she walked awkwardly. She stopped near her sister's room and leaned the tray on the railing at the top of the stairs.

'Do you want me to help you or something?' Lucy asked, feeling powerless.

For a few moments, Melanie stood with her eyes closed out of tiredness.

'No, it doesn't matter,' she said, shaking her head, and then, 'Well, yeah. If you do want to help? Go in there and tell him you don't care, you don't give a shit what he did to you. Because he's still punishing me for what you said to him the other day. Me and Stevie together. You want to make it easier, you can do that for us.'

'Tomorrow,' Lucy said with steel in her voice, and shut her door.

She logged back on to her computer, asking herself again, what would Turtle say she should do? He wasn't out there. She logged off again, disappointed. Driven by hunger, she went down to the kitchen to find something to eat, before going back to her room and working on her creation of the celestial city, the only place she knew where she did not feel like a stranger.

18

The morning's newspaper was just one of a number of things on Harrigan's desk which convinced him that today was going to be an even better day than yesterday. The *Daily Telegraph*'s headline, MEET THE FIREWALL — MURDERER'S WEBSITE REVEALED, would give his murdering girl all the publicity she had ever dreamed about, something he was obliged to admit was necessary however much he disliked the idea. There were pages on the story, it included every picture and description they'd ever released. Some fool in the publicity department had thoughtfully sent out the latest photograph of him while at the same time announcing that he was in charge of the investigation. Information which the paper had then printed with a breathless biography he would not otherwise have recognised as his own. The only thing he read which cheered him was the announcement of a reward of $25,000 for any information leading to the arrest of the killer. He should feel happier about it. In all the fuss, no one was yet publicly reviling them for managing to lose their sole witness.

He looked at his other papers, including Louise's print-out of Toby's latest communication with the Firewall. *Love you, Turtle, love you always,* he read. This miasma of declared personal love, as he saw it, reverberated angrily in Harrigan's mind. She can come and wash and feed you if she really loves you, Toby. She can massage your back. She can clean you. I'll supervise her. And is she still going to feel that way about you when she reads the newspaper? *U got 2 believe me I'm your friend I am 4 ever I love u always 2 U go 2 the police before something really bad happens*, Toby had written in reply. This particular time bomb was due to go off sometime today, it had to. Toby, why have you done this to yourself?

Without giving himself the chance for a second thought, Harrigan sent out an email to his son. *Check the paper today, Toby, I'm in there and she has to see it sometime. I don't want this to rebound on you. Get in touch with me if you want me. I'm here.* He could deal with any rebuff or accusation from Toby better than the memory of neglect.

He did not need this convergence of his work into his personal sphere; it asked too much of him, it made it too delicate to balance. He felt this all the more as he flicked open an urgent memo from the Tooth. Under current staffing levels, insufficient police personnel were available to guard Whole Life Women's Health Centre clinics on a twenty-four-hour basis. The application of risk management principles indicated that the clinics would be better off employing a private security firm, to which end Marvin recommended a highly reliable agency.

While Harrigan mused over the possible financial incentives the Tooth might have for this recommendation (personal investment, favours owed, the promise of a future directorship), he thought of the warnings he might send out to the extensive crew of health workers now left unprotected. Be alert for strange individuals approaching your door carrying timed incendiary devices — they may not be there to discuss their personal medical problems. Yes, be alert, the country needs lerts like never before and so do I. He rubbed his eyes. The absurdity gelled nicely with a telephone call he then received from the duty sergeant at the front desk. A Preacher Graeme Fredericksen had asked to see him, did he want them to show him up? The man was insistent on seeing him and him only. Harrigan did not say that he'd had every available officer out searching for the man for some eighteen hours or so now, and a fair few others for quite some time before that.

When the man appeared, he made what could only be described as a smooth entrance. Somehow he managed to slip into the room unnoticed, his uniformed escort notwithstanding. Harrigan was collecting a small folder of papers when the preacher was suddenly there at the desk talking to Dea. Not a tall man. Clothes which were nondescript and looked like they had possibly been slept in. A young–old face, squarish features, frank and open-looking, dark hair without any grey tint. Once, he would have been very good-looking. Not any more; that beauty was damaged and fading away.

'It's okay, Dea,' Harrigan said. 'Preacher Graeme Fredericksen? You wanted to see me — Paul Harrigan. How do you do?'

Harrigan offered his hand; the preacher shook it without any apparent trace of self-consciousness. He had a weak and sliding touch. He looked directly at Harrigan with an unembarrassed gaze. He had clear eyes and gave the disturbing impression that he did not blink.

'Paul,' he said, as though meeting an old friend, 'it's most kind of you to give me your time. I saw your picture in the paper today and I thought, yes, you will be the best person for me to approach. I hope that you will be able to help me. I am afraid I'm very much in need of your help at this time.'

'Yes, you can call me Paul, Graeme,' Harrigan replied after a slight pause, assuming his usual neutrality of tone. 'We don't stand on ceremony here. There's a room down here where we'll be comfortable. Dea, a couple of coffees?'

'No, please, don't take the trouble. I know time is important to you, Paul. I will try to use as little of it as possible.'

If the clothes were nondescript, the voice was not. It was pleasant to hear and invited familiarity. It seemed to assure you that he was your friend, that he had known you for years. People would listen to him and be comforted because they would know from his voice that they could surely rely on his goodwill.

'We're here to help, Graeme. Let's see what we can do for you. Just in here — this is one of our interview rooms. The decor's nothing to write home about, I'm afraid.'

In the drab and perfunctory room, he pulled back a chair for the preacher. He placed the manila folder on the table and saw the man glance at it as he seated himself opposite.

'Now, I'm sure you're aware that we've been trying to get hold of you for some time now, and particularly since last night. What can we do for each other?'

'No, I must assure you, I wasn't aware that you were. My work takes me out into the community so often that there are times when I simply cannot be reached.'

He spoke without giving the slightest sense that he was lying.

'Take it from me, we have been,' Harrigan replied. 'We need to talk to a boy who's in your care. Greg Smith.'

'But he's exactly who I've come to see you about.'

The man rested his hands on the table. His fingertips brushed at the edge of the folder Harrigan had brought with him, and he fought the urge to move the papers out of Fredericksen's reach. The preacher appeared wholly unconcerned by his surroundings; the sight of the blank window, the tape recorders and the lockable door did not seem to affect him.

'This is fortuitous. I had some hesitation whether I should approach you or not, but now I am most relieved that I have come here. Can you tell me why you are looking for him?' The preacher smiled as he asked the question.

'Why don't you tell me why you've come here first, Graeme? Then I'll be only too happy to answer your question.'

Let the man talk. Who knew what he might say.

'Of course. Obviously, you know that Greg is in my care. Of course you do — there is the matter of this unfortunate business in which he seems to have been implicated, I am very certain, quite wrongly. Besides that, you know that I'm a preacher? That I have a church in Camperdown, a congregation. That I run a refuge.'

Harrigan nodded.

'Then you know my concern is for the dispossessed. Addicts, alcoholics, thieves, dealers, the destitute, the violent, those without hope. All those souls that no one else in this world wants. To them, my door is never locked. I am always there to take them in. You see, I have all the strength I need for my vocation from God. Nothing can prevent you from doing what the Lord expects of you. And of course, I am fortunate in that he has given me the benefactors to help me along.'

'I see. Perhaps you'd like to tell me who they are,' Harrigan replied.

'Mrs Yvonne Lindley. Do you know of her? She's endowed my refuge very generously this last year. She's actually my mother's half-sister. I've known the family all my life, of course. I was an only child; her children were my true brothers and sisters, we played together when we were small. I went to school with Geoffrey but, as you can see, we've gone very different ways. He's quite senior in the Premier's Department now. I'm not sure if Elizabeth approves of me any more. She calls me God's anarchist. They are my only earthly family, Paul, my mother and father died some years ago. We are a support to each other.'

There was a useful family connection if ever there was one; it explained Fredericksen's ability to open doors at the Family Services Commission. Yvonne Lindley was the aged widow of John Lindley, lover of horseflesh, sometime state politician and a cabinet minister for every portfolio going, including the police. He had died not long ago, leaving his family independently wealthy. Always a renowned political operator, Yvonne Lindley still had strings to pull. The preacher sat waiting but Harrigan did not speak.

'You must understand, Paul,' he continued eventually, 'my refuge is of great importance to me. The children who come my way — they have no one. I offer them the only home they may ever have had. Greg is the perfect example. He has no one in this world, no one at all. He needs the most loving care or we will lose him. He is addicted to self-harm. He is on the edge. You must remember that. Because when you find him, you will have to approach him with great care. Anything could happen. Anything at all.'

'Is that what you came here to tell me?' Harrigan replied after a short pause. 'That we need to find him? And we should be careful when we do?'

'Yes. I would have come here sooner but I've been out searching the streets for him all night. I know the places he goes and I thought, arrogantly, that if anyone could find him, I could. By first light this morning, I understood that I cannot do this alone, I must accept help. Greg's welfare is paramount to me, Paul. I am very afraid for him.'

He spoke passionately while his face remained oddly blank of any expression of emotion.

'Where did you lose him?' Harrigan asked.

'Very close to the refuge, within sight of safety. I'd just turned off Parramatta Road. I think he was waiting until then because it's easy for him to get into the city from there. It was dark, so it would have been a little after six perhaps? I stopped at an intersection and he was out of the van and away before I could stop him. But the point here is Greg. He needs every care. All last night as I walked the streets looking for him, I thought, I have failed him. I have failed him and I cannot permit that failure to be continued by others.'

There was another silence.

'Six o'clock, you say?' Harrigan asked.

'Yes.'

'You'd bailed him by a quarter to three. What were you doing in the meantime? It doesn't take that long to drive from Parramatta to Camperdown.'

Harrigan's fingers tapped the manila folder on the table, which held a transcript stating that at 4:09 p.m. the Firewall had chatted online to Toby, to say that she had a friend in bad trouble and she did not know how to help him without getting herself in any deeper than she already was.

'In many ways, Greg behaves like a normal adolescent boy, Paul, despite his unfortunate history. I took him to McDonald's, then we went to an entertainment arcade, at his request, where he played video games. It was the release of a pressure valve for him, a time in which to think.'

'Where were you at about four o'clock?'

'I'm not really sure...' The preacher paused, his fingers brushed against the folder once again. 'I think the van was on the road between McDonald's and the video parlour at that time. I was too busy thinking about Greg to notice the clock.'

'I see,' Harrigan replied. 'Last night — did you go looking for him in the refuge van?'

'No, someone else needed to use it. I had another car, one belonging to a member of my congregation.'

'Yes, we had a bulletin out for your van last night but it seemed to be off the road. Why should you think Greg's come to harm? He could just be out and about. He's used to that sort of life, after all.'

'Greg is a very wild young man. He takes appalling risks, his life is one of terrible recklessness. I have watched him often with my heart in my mouth. I have to say I am very afraid for him. Particularly if he is faced with a return to custody.'

The preacher's insistence had been without emphasis. Harrigan sat in silence for a few moments, looking at him, unconsciously tapping his fingers on the table top.

'You say you don't think he's involved in the shooting we're making inquiries about?'

'I am sure that will be revealed to be a mistake. I should be very surprised to discover that he was.'

'Right.' Harrigan put a light emphasis on the word. 'Does the name "the Firewall" mean anything to you?'

'Yes, I've read about her — I understand she's female? — in the paper today.'

'Do you know anyone who uses that name?'

'Know in what sense, Paul?'

'Know of, Graeme. Or know personally. Take your pick.' Harrigan sat back in his chair, apparently relaxing for the duration.

'I find that in my line of work people often have more than one name. I know of no one who has introduced themselves to me by that name.'

'Let me ask you, is there anyone in this picture that you recognise?'

He took a photograph out of the folder and placed it on the table. The preacher looked at the homeless boys in Belmore Park.

'This was in the paper today but I have already seen it before in any case,' he said. 'It was taken some time before Greg came into my care. I was quite angry that they chose to characterise him as they did. Other than that, I can tell you nothing about it.'

'Is there anyone else you recognise? Someone familiar to you?'

'Other than Greg? I don't think so.'

'What about her?'

Harrigan pointed to the female figure shown only from the back.

'It's difficult to recognise someone from the back of the head, Paul. Why do you think this is your killer?

Because she's talking to Greg? On first glance, that could be described as discrimination. Unless, of course, you have some other information — which I would hope you would pass on to us. If not to Greg, then at least to me as his guardian. He does have legal rights.'

The man spoke with a neutrality equal to Harrigan's own, his eyes so pale as to seem sightless.

'Just an inquiry, Graeme. You know of any friends of his who might be this girl?' Harrigan asked.

'Girls are the last thing Greg would talk to me about, Paul. You can't force information out of your charges.'

'No, that's true,' Harrigan said, returning the photograph to the folder and waiting a few moments. 'You have something of an American accent there, Graeme. You've spent time in the States, I take it?'

The man's composure was unruffled by the change of questioning.

'My voice gives me away, doesn't it? I have indeed, more than half my lifetime. I've come back only recently. I recommend that you visit there one day, if you never have. It is genuinely a land of great opportunity. Why do you ask?'

'I'm just trying to place you. What brought you back?'

'The realisation that this is home after all? It certainly had that feel about it when I was walking through the Sydney Terminal.'

'You've always been something of a traveller perhaps?'

'Yes, I have. I travel for God, I go where I am called. I feel that I am most useful where I can reach as many people as possible. There is no more wonderful sight in the world than the dawn as you watch it by the side of the road and you know there is another town a little further on where they need you. It's like being in the new world to see the sun rise at those times. People open their hearts to me, Paul, I understand them. I understand them better than they understand themselves. I am someone who can reveal to them who they truly are, who can lead them to act in a way that is closest to their true wishes. They trust me and I always reward their trust.'

Harrigan had the rare sensation of a chill down his spine.

'I guess in your business you need to,' he said. 'It helps in mine as well from time to time. You're a people person, are you, Graeme? Does that describe your approach?'

He listened in what could only be described as detached astonishment to his own words. In the light of his feelings towards the man sitting in front of him, they were nothing less than a bad joke.

'Oh, yes. Very much so. I can say that I truly love people, that their fate is of the greatest concern to me. And I know them. I know their hearts but I also know their faces and their names. I never forget anyone. Whoever comes to my door, whoever I encounter in my work, I remember them. I have that gift.'

'I see.'

There was silence. In the small familiar room, Harrigan felt claustrophobia while the man in the other chair appeared unmoved.

'When you were in the States, where did you spend most of your time?' he asked.

The preacher smiled.

'Everywhere, Paul. Everywhere. If I may say so — I'm a little surprised by these questions. I wonder if you shouldn't be more concerned for Greg at this point. Shouldn't you be organising a search?'

'We're out there looking, Graeme. Every available officer I've got. I've already told you that. And from what you've just said to me, I'd have to judge there's probably no great urgency about it now.'

'But there is, Paul. There is great urgency. I must emphasise that. Why wouldn't there be?'

'Then let me thank you for your help in putting us on the track. Perhaps I can show you out.'

The preacher smiled again and got to his feet without waiting to be asked twice.

'Certainly. Thank you for your time. This meeting has been most valuable to me. I will remember it. I hope we meet again.'

'We will, Graeme. For one thing, we'll need to talk to you about Greg. Whether we find him or not. I will brief one of my officers on this and she'll be in touch with you pretty much as soon as is possible.'

'By all means. I'll wait to hear.'

At the elevator, Harrigan stood with the preacher waiting for his escort to arrive. Dea, at her desk, watched them between telephone calls.

'I understand your congregation in Camperdown is quite popular, Graeme,' he said, having heard no such thing, simply curious as to what response he might receive.

'It's thriving, Paul. I hope to take it out west in due time, I think there are many people out there who need me. I thought so yesterday when I was out there with Greg. But if you're interested, why don't you come to a prayer meeting one day? You would be most welcome. Several other policemen have been members of my congregation at various times in the past. Why don't you take my card?'

Harrigan took the offered card and looked at it. It gave the address of the New Life Ministries and the times of its prayer meetings, together with the text: *And behold I come quickly; and my reward is with me, to give every man according as his work shall be.*

'Thanks. I'll bear it in mind,' he said, pocketing it.

Just then the elevator doors opened but instead of the preacher's escort Grace appeared, returning from her daily visit to the hospital. She greeted Harrigan and glanced at the preacher before walking towards the office. Seeing her, Harrigan returned to the practicalities of work.

'Grace. Have you got a moment?' he called out.

'Sure,' she said, turning.

'This is someone you need to meet, Graeme. This is Grace Riordan. Grace, this is Preacher Graeme Fredericksen. Grace is the officer I've assigned to Greg. She'll be dealing with him, should we find him. If you have any information you think will be useful to us, you need to tell her. You two need to make some time to talk.'

'I'm pleased to meet you,' Grace said with her professional smile, offering her hand. 'If you've got the time, I can talk to you now.'

'Now will not be possible,' he replied.

He had not accepted her handshake and was staring at her. Grace, finding her hand ignored, reached into her shoulder bag instead.

'Would you like my card? You can call me,' she said.

'Thank you,' he said automatically, taking it without so much as glancing at it. He said nothing else, his gaze still fixed on her. Across his face there appeared like the most transient of skinscapes an expression of loathing, gone in the lightning flash of less than a second. For that passing second, he became completely aged.

'Do you have a card yourself?' she asked into the vacuum of his response. 'If we need to be in touch —'

He stepped back from her but was still staring.

'That won't be necessary,' he replied.

The elevator doors opened again and the preacher's uniformed escort appeared.

'We'll see each other again, Graeme,' Harrigan said, having watched the whole scene with fascination.

'Yes, I'm sure we will,' the preacher replied with a smile and was gone.

When the doors had closed, Grace turned to Dea.

'I must have forgotten to put my deodorant on this morning. I can't get by without my Mum,' she added, with exaggerated sarcasm.

'Not you, darl,' Dea replied with a guttural laugh. 'That was his problem. I was wondering when I was talking to him, the way he was looking at me. He doesn't like women. You can feel it.'

'We found him?' Grace said to Harrigan.

'No,' he replied, 'he found us. And an unpleasant little rendezvous it was too. I need caffeine.'

'There's some fresh brewed coffee in the tea room. Why don't you both go and get some?' Dea said, glancing from Harrigan to Grace and back again.

The tea room smelled of stale milk and over-brewed coffee, the bins jammed with takeaway food containers, a sign of the pressurised work put in by Harrigan's team. It was a place where they pinned bad jokes and cartoons up on the noticeboard next to cheese-cake calendars, although these days the porn had mostly gone. Grace poured herself coffee before passing the jug to Harrigan.

'Maybe we can get someone else to talk to him. If talking to me is such a disgusting thing to have to do,' she said.

'I don't think you have to worry about that, Grace. That man came in here to tell me — he couldn't just pick up the phone, he couldn't talk to Trev, he had to see me in person — to tell me he's lost that boy, that he's spent the night pounding the streets looking for him and now he's deeply concerned for his welfare. And why? Because, he says, the boy is inclined to do himself harm. If that kid isn't dead by now, he will be. If we ever find him again, he'll be dead from an overdose or he'll have fallen into the harbour while he was under the influence. Something we can't possibly prove wasn't suicide or an accidental death.'

Grace stirred milk into her coffee, staring at the grubby wall. He sipped his black, standing beside her.

'I was two hours too late for him yesterday. Probably the story of Greg's life,' she said, shaking her head, sending a shiver running down her spine. 'You'd really need more than a hide to come here and do something like that, wouldn't you? If you had killed him, I mean. You'd have to get a real charge out of knowing what you'd done. Watch me while I push my luck and see what I can get away with.'

'I'll tell you one thing, he was having a high old time while he was here. I don't think I fathom our preacher just yet. I walked out of there thinking, nothing would touch this joker.'

'What about Matthew Liu?'

'I doubt it.'

'Speaking of that,' she said, 'it's sometime this afternoon for Agnes Liu. They'll call me. They've said they'll give me about an hour's notice. So I should have the transcript and the recording back here by this evening.'

'No, I don't want to wait for that. Knock on my door when you're ready to go. I'll come with you. I want to listen in.'

'Are you sure?' she replied, with some hesitation. 'They're only going to let me in.'

'No, I want to be there, I want to hear what she's got to say. We can fix you up with a listening device. I'd like to catch up with Matthew too, particularly after this morning.'

'Okay. When they call me.'

Jeffo came in and looked at the two of them standing side by side.

'Hi, Boss. Hiya, Gracie,' he said.

He sat down at the table over some takeaway lunch, grinning at her. Grace replied with a glance that would have reduced most other people to ash.

'I've got to go and do this morning's write-up,' she said and left the room at once, coffee in hand. Harrigan, who had things to do himself, walked out after her.

Once back in his office, he looked at Grace working at her desk before again studying his photograph in the paper. It was quite an array: his own picture, Greg Smith's, the vague image of the Firewall in the park, lurid shots from her website, together with the obligatory appeal for information. He hoped that out of the wells of fantasy and posturing these appeals always tapped into, someone would actually have something useful to tell them. She was still out there; the transcripts of her chats with his son were like baits dangled in front of him. That direct connection to a few bits of light on a screen would take them directly to her, if only they could track it down. In an unexpected change of mood, he took on patience with the sense of a trap quietly being set. Whatever he might feel, it could only be a matter of time, and whoever she might be, she could have no way out.

19

On the other side of the city and in the clear liquid light of midday, Lucy prowled the ruined garden with her old dog. Dark red camellia blossom had fallen onto the muddy paths, detached petals fanned out in small heaps on the dirt. For Lucy, the glitter of the leaves in a pale sun and the transparency of the sky had the interior light of electricity. There was no depth to her perception of them, they could have been reflected on the surface of a shallow pool of water. Her balance and her thoughts were poised within this shallowness, she was chasing possibilities in her mind. If she had a car. If she could track Greg down. If she could get to Graeme. Getting into the Temple wasn't easy when the door was locked against you and you had no key. The question remained: what then? This is my gun to your head, Graeme. No, this is your gun to your head. What are you going to do about it? Twist words. Play games. What was she going to do about it? Could she fire a gun a second time?

She sat on the edge of the escarpment near the sleep-out and took out her gun, aimed it at a tree and pretended to fire, making soft sounds to imitate the crack of shots. *Ka-chung, ka-chung.* As she sat there, she was caught unawares by a memory. In a clear vision in her mind, Dr Agnes Liu looked her in the face in the immediate second before she pulled the trigger that morning in the Chippendale alley. Lucy swallowed as she revisited the almost ordinary, surprised expression on Agnes Liu's face when she looked up from seeing the gun and then directly into Lucy's eyes. You didn't know who I was, Lucy said to herself. You couldn't see who I was because Graeme had said, don't let them see you. So I didn't. I covered my face. I shouldn't have. I should have let you see who I was. Then you could have known why. Not to make it worse for you, but so that you at least knew why it was happening. And I should never have fired the second shot at that man. Never.

The word faded in her mind as she rested her gun in her lap. Every feeling she had ran out of her, leaving her empty, without will. I wish it wasn't like this.

'I'm sorry,' she said, out of this thought, 'I am so sorry I did it.' There's nothing I can do now. I've just got to keep moving.

Stephen had gone to Hornsby first thing that morning, to shop, to pick up medications and to see the doctor who came daily to visit his father and who was due to call at the house early that afternoon, to talk over privately how things were. As Lucy climbed the hill, she saw Stevie's car parked in the driveway. She found him in the kitchen unpacking white plastic bags. Several packets of cigarettes lay on top of the morning paper on the kitchen table.

'I bought you some cigarettes. I thought you might need them,' he said. He spoke quickly, without looking at her.

'Yeah. Thanks.' She was puzzled by the way he was speaking to her. She picked up the cigarettes and saw the newspaper underneath. She put the packets down and stared at it.

'Shit,' she said softly.

DO YOU KNOW THIS GIRL? On the front page, she saw the picture — of her back — taken in Belmore Park almost a year ago. She knew the picture well. Stephen knew it well, she had shown it to him herself. She looked up at him. His mouth was open a little, his round rimless glasses seemed to bring a refraction to the look of shock in his eyes. They understood each other as clearly as they ever had in this room. Their understanding remained unspoken. Just now, silence was the only kindness they had to offer each other.

'You have to go,' he began to say but she spoke over him.

'I'm going to leave soon anyway, Stevie, as soon as I can and I won't come back. But I've got to talk to Dad first. Whenever I can. I've got to talk to him. I've got to say something to him. I've got to finish it, I can't go without finishing it.'

'What do you think you want to say?' He sat down, reached for his own cigarettes, lit one. She sat opposite, he pushed the cigarettes across the table towards her and she lit one as well. 'Do you want to tell him — that this is all his fault? Is that what you want to say?'

He gestured to the paper as he spoke, an odd tight movement. Lucy smoked in silence. This was the closest Stephen would ever get to acknowledging what had happened.

'No, Stevie, I'm not going to say that. Everything I do is what I do. It's not him, it's me. I just want him to say that he shouldn't have done what he did to me, that he's sorry, anything like that ...'

'Luce, I don't know why you ever thought he was going to do that.'

'It's a craving you get. You want it really badly. Why wouldn't I want it? Once you get it, it doesn't want to go away. No, I know it's no good now,' she said. 'He owes me. He owes me from here up to the sky for the rest of my life but, like Mel says, maybe it is too fucking late. Maybe I don't care any more. I've got to see it finished before I go. That's all I can do now. Fucking finish it. There's nothing else. I've got to do that for me. Before I deal with anything else.'

They spoke to each other like two people who have agreed to finish their marriage, neither of them wishing to do so but both knowing they have no choice. Both trying to avoid saying what cannot be retracted, or doing anything that will make matters worse.

'If you're going to talk to him, just don't make it harder for us.'

'No, I won't do that. I don't want to hurt you and Mel. You tell him from me it's okay. I've got nothing to forgive him for but I just want to talk to him. And I'm not going to hurt him or accuse him. Or anything.'

She laughed. 'I'm not going to hurt him,' she repeated. 'What a joke.'

'It doesn't matter any more,' Stephen said very softly.

'It does matter. It's just that there's nothing I can do about it. I've got a favour to ask you. Have you got a car I can borrow?'

'Yeah. You can have the old Datsun, I've just had it fixed up. Take it when you go if you want. I can give you all the papers. I'll get some petrol for you this afternoon. Is that okay? It's all I can do, Luce. It should take you some way away from here. I don't know how far.'

'No, that's good. Don't worry.'

'I'll talk to Mel about Dad for you,' he said.

They did not seem to know what else to say to each other. As they sat in silence, there was a knock on the back door.

'That's the quacktor,' Stevie said, 'he said he'd be early.'

'Can I take the paper?'

'Yeah, take it with you when you go,' he said, not looking at her.

'Yeah, I will,' she said, 'I'll get rid of it for you.'

Stephen ushered the doctor, a man of about thirty-five, into the kitchen just as Lucy was gathering up her packets of cigarettes.

'Good morning,' he said, glancing at them. 'They're very bad for you, you know. You don't want to end up like your father.'

Who gives a shit, Lucy thought, looking at him in disbelief. She did not bother to reply and walked out.

In her room, Lucy turned the newspaper pages, looking over the reproductions of her website, photographs of Greg, pictures of the scene of the shooting. She read paragraphs which described her in ways she did not recognise as herself. She was not cruel, she felt this deeply. What were the magic words that would make the newspaper people and the radio announcers understand what she had really tried to do? These thoughts occupied her until she came across a photograph in the paper, not of herself or Greg, but of someone she nonetheless recognised. A face that she knew well but from a different place. She sat looking at it for some moments before opening up her computer, logging on and going out onto the Net. After she found what she was looking for, she felt what was almost a sense of relief, a final letting go of everything. As Greg had said to her often enough, nothing matters.

Are you out there, Turtle?

I'm here Firewall I've been waiting 4 u

Why is that?

I just am

Lucy did not type anything for a few moments.

Are u there?

I'm here, I'm always here for you. Or I was. Turtle, you said that you never lied to me. That you never have and you never will.

Never have never U believe me Its true I have never lied 2 u

No? Are you sure about that?

No I never have

I saw a picture in the paper today. It's the policeman who's looking for me. And I thought, I know who that is. That's your father, isn't it? I know who he is because I've looked at his picture, all your family's pictures. I used to look at them for hours and think, Gee, I wish they were mine. You said he really looked after you. You said he loved you. And I thought, wouldn't that be nice. People who did that. And then I read the paper today and there he is. You never said that's what he did. You never said he was a pig.

He is not that He told me not 2 tell any1 He said people would keep on at me if I did I didn't tell u It didn't matter It had nothing 2 do with u & me

So when you're telling me that I should go to the police, you're saying that because it's good for him. He gets what he wants. And you're doing that for him.

I don't know if it's any good for me, but it's good for him.

I didn't say it because of that I am not my father U should know that better than anyone U are not your parents r u??? Everything between us is u & me Nothing else Its never been anything else U can't say it is

I don't believe you. You tell lies like everyone else. People tell you lies and then they laugh at you behind your back. And you're a liar, Turtle. You lie like everyone else does. You just lie. Lie like a dog.

No

Do you know what they're saying about me in the paper? That I'm a really cruel person. I like killing people. I like seeing blood. They had this poll — they asked people what they thought should happen to me and all these people said I ought to be shot too. Every day I think about what I did. I didn't do it for fun. I did it because I had to. Is that what your father thinks I am?

There was a brief hesitation.

Yes he does but I told him no I said u are not like that I said he mustn't see u like that

What difference does that make? You've been telling me one thing, and maybe you've been telling him something else as well, and all the time you've got some other reason for what you're saying to both of us.

U have 2 listen I care about u I don't talk 2 anyone else the way I talk 2 u U don't have a choice Firewall U have nowhere 2 go That's the only reason I said u should go 2 the police Because if u don't I don't know wots going 2 happen 2 u If u do this my dad can help u I can make him help u

No. Where I go and what I do, that's my choice. And

if I end up dead, so what? No one's going to care. You're deciding things for me and you can't do that.

Wot do u want??

Nothing that's possible, but that doesn't matter. I wanted to say goodbye, that's all.

U never listen U never listen 2 anyone

I almost listened to you. But you were lying to me.

She was gone, closing down, logging out. She was floating in space, there was nothing to anchor her, only the next step, the next action. She picked up the phone and rang Graeme. As she did, she thought that he had no power over her any more, the next action was just whatever game the two of them were playing at the time. He answered his phone almost immediately.

'Hi, Graeme,' she said. 'Are you okay to talk?'

'Lucy. Yes, I am. Where have you been? You've kept me waiting. I've been here with Greg for hours.'

'We're all waiting for something. Last time I talked to you, you were waiting for the end of the world, weren't you? How are you?'

'I am fine, Lucy. I am very well indeed and I'm very glad to hear you are in such good spirits. I've got someone here you want to talk to. Just as you've asked.'

There was shuffling as the phone was passed over.

'Hi, Luce.'

'Hi there, Greg. How are you?'

'I'm okay.'

'Are you?'

'Yeah, I am, Luce,' he said. 'It's sort of okay at the moment.'

'Where are you?'

'I can't tell you.'

'Why not? You said it was sort of okay.'

'Yeah. But only sort of. I've got to go now.'

'No. I —'

The preacher came back on. Lucy listened to his voice with irritation. 'It's time we got together,' he said.

'Yeah, I've got a car but there's a couple of things I've got to do here. Tomorrow at the latest. Tomorrow night. Okay?'

'Why do we have to wait till then?'

'Because I have things I've got to do here, Graeme. And they're important.'

'What time?'

'I'll just be there, Graeme. From about ten. You can come by whenever you want to. But we'll all be there, the three of us, won't we?'

'Of course. We have an arrangement then?'

'Yeah, yeah,' she replied impatiently. 'You want to put Greg back on again?'

'All right,' he replied, after a pause.

'Before you go,' she said, 'like I told you, don't ring me. I'll call you.'

There was no need for this. She just wanted to make him dance a little.

'As you wish,' he said.

'I just wanted to say we'll see each other,' she said, once Greg was back.

'Yeah, we will sometime, Luce. Look — you make sure you're okay, all right. And don't worry about me. Because everything's going to be all right. You just remember that. You don't think about me any more. You've just got to think about yourself,' he replied, and then the phone went dead.

Lucy went out into the fresh air again, to a clearer if colder day than yesterday. This time she did not take her gun with her, she left it behind, pleased not to feel its pressure against her skin. The doctor had gone, ages ago probably. She stood on the edge of the slope looking down to the escarpment. The dog was not in her kennel, although the remains of some bones were scattered by her dish. No one had replaced the chain. Wherever she was, Dora was living in freedom.

Stephen appeared, coasting the old Datsun he had promised her down the driveway, parking it behind his car. He got out and walked towards her. He stopped at a short distance.

'I got you a full tank, Luce,' he said. 'Do you want some money as well? I can give you a few hundred dollars if you need it.'

'Yeah, if you could,' she replied. 'How's Dad?'

'The quack's given him a shot so he'll be out to it for quite a while. Mel said she'd give you a call when he wakes up but that could be pretty late tonight. You might not be able to talk to him until tomorrow.'

'That's all right. I'll just wait. I've got the time.'

Because this is the endpoint, this will be goodbye for ever. It was the last piece of time left to her.

She watched him walk into the house. It seemed to crowd forward to the edge of the slope, a squat redbrick dwelling. Her choice would have been to burn it, not to paint it over. When she left here this time, she would not be able to come back. She accepted this as final before she turned to walk back inside and go up to her room. It was growing late in the afternoon but perhaps it would be as much as another day before she could leave. I'm waiting for you again, Dad. It's what I always seem to do.

20

A short time after the Firewall had stopped talking to Turtle, Louise placed a transcript of their conversation on Harrigan's desk. He read it over and said he would keep it. Once Louise had left, he rang Susie and asked her how Toby was.

'Tim's with him at the moment,' she said, 'I'll check.'

Eventually she was back on the line.

'He's okay, Paul. He is upset but he doesn't want to talk to anyone about it.'

'I'm coming over to see him now,' he said.

'No, don't.' She spoke quickly. 'He said you would do that and he doesn't want you to. I have to tell you that.'

There was a brief silence in which Harrigan did not trust himself to reply.

'Paul — if you can just accept this. We can look after him from our end. He's not going into spasm or anything like that. But he needs his own space. You have to give him his space.'

'You tell him from me, I'll be there tomorrow morning no matter what. Unless he wants to get in touch with me beforehand and ask me to come earlier. But I'll be there tomorrow regardless.'

'I'll tell him that, that's not a problem.'

'Good.'

He hung up and sat reading over the transcript.

I am not my father. Did I ever say you were, Toby? I've only ever wanted you to be yourself. I must have told you that.

The only cure for this investigation was to pass it to someone else — which he would not do because there was no one he trusted — or to solve it as soon as he could. In his experience, the emotions were usually deadened by fatigue, and constant work almost always resulted in lasting fatigue. On this thought he went back to work, reviewing, checking, reporting, requesting follow-ups, driving his team the way he drove himself.

He was relieved when the phone call from the hospital came through to Grace later that afternoon. She appeared in his doorway to say that she was on her way and they went in their separate cars. Out on the streets, peak hour was in full flow, the traffic edged along. The Firewall's website had infected him, it muscled in on his sensibilities at the end of the day. He had the sense that the roads were crowded with people fleeing the city. He joined in with them, feeling as much at a loose end as anyone else.

At St Vincent's, the bright corridors and the murmur of noise gave some sense of activity to this end-of-world feel on a chill winter's day. Grace was waiting for him. When Harrigan appeared, she thought the lights had over-painted his face with a sheen curiously like the stage make-up she used to wear. Why not? To her observation, he spent a fair amount of his time performing for others. Together they went upstairs to the intensive care ward, where Matthew was waiting for them in the ante-chamber.

Harrigan, seeing him for the first time since the shooting, took in the shorn hair and the black mourning.

'Hello, Matthew. How are you?' he said.

'You said you'd catch her,' Matthew replied, his arms folded.

'We will. That's a promise.'

'You haven't yet. But if you don't, I will. And then she'll pay, she'll really pay. That's a real promise, that's not just a wank.'

'You won't have to do that because we will find her. But right now we're here to see your mother. Every bit helps. Every step's a step along the way.' Harrigan had no other reply.

'If I were you, I wouldn't have the nerve to tell people that sort of shit. I'd be too fucking embarrassed,' Matthew said, and walked away.

Harrigan watched him go, expressionless.

'Bear with me while I remember your reports,' he said to Grace. 'Is he like that towards you?'

'He's not that aggressive with me but it's the same thing. He lashes out at everyone and he won't let anyone reach him. He can't last, one day he has to break.'

Harrigan thought that when that happened he did not want to see it.

In the glass room, Dr Agnes Liu lay in her high hospital bed on a mass of pillows which her nurse was rearranging carefully.

'Whatever Agnes thinks,' her doctor was saying to Grace, 'she's not up to any marathon sessions. If I have to, I'm going to close it down. I'm warning you in advance.'

'I'll take it very gently,' she replied.

Harrigan stood a little out of range of Agnes Liu's vision, waiting and watching.

Inside the room the nurse nodded to Grace and then sat to the side. A human odour, of injury and sickness, and another, of antiseptic, filled the room. Grace sat beside Agnes Liu, the speaker to her miniature cassette recorder affixed to her lapel.

'How are you, Agnes?' she said.

'I think that everybody worries too much,' the woman replied. 'But I'm not used to being the patient.'

She took Grace's hand as she spoke and Grace leaned forward. Shock had worn Agnes Liu's face, a fine mix of Anglo-Australian and Chinese descent, to its constitutive bones. She was in her early forties. Her eyes were dark, her skin ivory-pale. Her black hair had been lately washed and brushed out to display silver-grey lights curling back from her forehead.

'Where's Matthew? He's very angry with me for talking to you. I told him it has to be done.'

'He's outside. I spoke to him just now.'

'How is he?'

'He's all right. He's coping. He's a very strong boy.'

Agnes spoke each phrase as something short and measured, the careful apportioning of a limited strength. 'Yes, he is. But he doesn't know how to hide things yet. You have to realise, I was taught never to let inconvenience make me lose my composure. My mother met my father at university. She fell in love and they married. In 1955. She was eighteen. It was a scandal, her family didn't speak to her again for decades. My grandmother, my father's mother, she was as bad. She refused to welcome her. We always had to keep up appearances no matter how we felt. Matthew doesn't know how to do that yet. When I'm better, I'll talk to him.'

She stopped.

'Do you know what I remember most about the morning I was shot? That girl. How we looked at each other. I turned and she was there on the street. Just there. Just in front of me. With a gun. I remember thinking, oh, that's so small. And I looked at her. We were looking each other in the eyes. And I knew she was going to kill me. I knew it so naturally. Oh, here's someone for an appointment, I thought it like that. I was looking her in the eyes when she fired. I thought, I know you.

'I've been lying here thinking it over ever since. Thinking, how can you know who someone is when all you can see of them is their eyes? But I remembered other things as well and I thought, yes, it's her. About four months ago, someone called. My home number. I don't give that to anyone. None of us do. But this person had it. She said, do you know who I am? I said, no. How could I? She was just a voice. She said, I am the butcher's daughter. Did I remember now? No, I didn't, not then. She said I was a murderer and one day I would die for what I had done. She was crying. I hung up at once. We got a new phone number. I put it out of my mind. I have to put that sort of thing out of my mind.'

She paused, everything became still.

'I can't remember every detail. There are gaps. But I can remember this. One day — when Matthew was nine, I think, around then — one very hot day, I remember everyone saying how hot it was. The air conditioning could barely cope. This woman brought her daughter into one of the clinics. It was late morning.

They didn't have an appointment. This child, she looked so ill, and so young. I said I would see her right away. And then she miscarried, almost immediately, right there in the reception. There was so much blood, I ... There were women there, they had brought their children in for check-ups, older women, they saw it all. We called an ambulance. I said to this woman — do you want to drive your own car? Or do you want to go in the ambulance? They didn't have a car. They'd come by train, and bus. Some extraordinary distance. I said to this woman, I don't know how your daughter survived the trip. Couldn't you see how sick she was? Why did you come here? It's so far away. Someone told me about you, she said. I didn't know what else to do. But if the only way to get to hospital was to go in the ambulance, then she would go in the ambulance. We were all shocked. She was so unmoved. In the end one of my staff drove her. I thought, that poor child.'

Again there was a pause. Grace glanced up at the nurse.

'I want to keep talking,' Agnes Liu said, and they waited.

'Agnes,' Grace spoke quietly, 'can you remember where they lived? Just the suburb?'

'I've tried to but I can't — I have a blank.'

'The clinic?'

'No. I travel, you see. I go from clinic to clinic. I want to make sure things are being done in the right way. I can't picture where I was. I know these things happened but I can't picture any of it.'

Include five possibilities out of five clinics, Harrigan thought, standing outside.

'I rang the hospital that evening to see how she was. She was already home, they said. Her father had come to get her. I was furious with them. I said, she needed care. Oh, they were so busy. There was no staff, no one had realised. They had no address for her. Or not one that made any sense. There was nothing I could do. But I was distressed. I thought, why was any of that necessary? Then one day — quite a few months later, I'm not sure how long — this woman, she came to the clinic again. They had an appointment with me but I didn't know the name. I think it was a different name, I can't remember what it was. She wanted to see me.

'I spoke to her in my office. The first thing she said was, we have a car this time. I didn't quite know what to say. Her daughter was pregnant again, she said. She wanted an abortion, she was waiting outside in the car now. Would I do it? I was flabbergasted. I said, why have you come to see me again? Oh, she said, I didn't know where else to go. I said, what does your daughter want? Oh, this is what she wants. And then the woman said — I didn't know if she was being deliberately stupid — my daughter's uncontrollable. My husband wants her to go on the pill so this doesn't happen again. He doesn't like it.

'There are times when I'm talking to people, when I'm watching their faces. I looked at this woman and I wondered, is this stupidity or cunning? I don't know. But it's evil, whatever it is. I said I wasn't prepared to do that. Her daughter was young, I think she was only fifteen. It's not good to go on the pill at that age. I asked her to bring the girl in. I spoke to her privately, I insisted. I asked her about her boyfriend. She gaped at me. I asked her about her father. She didn't seem to know what I meant. She said he was a butcher. Yes, I thought. I asked was this what she wanted? She said, yes. What else could she say? The mother was waiting outside my office. And she looked at me. I can only say

I knew — I was certain from the look on her face — that this child's father was the father of her child. I thought, yes, this is cunning. You want to implicate me. This is your way of shifting the blame. If I know, it's not your fault, is it? It's mine. I felt ill.

'What should I have done? Call the police? Throw them out? I thought, I have an obligation. I have to protect this child from injury. I can perform this abortion and then I know it will be done properly, not some bungled thing. I wouldn't have trusted the woman not to do something dreadful. I said to her that I needed family details, would she fill out a form? She did. I performed the abortion. And when it was over, the child began to cry. I thought she would never stop. I didn't wait. I went and I called the police. But when I was on the phone, I saw the woman dragging her daughter out of the recovery room. I didn't know what to do.

'I put the phone down and I went after them. Out to the car park. I stopped them leaving. The girl was in the back seat, curled up. Still crying, I think. The car door was locked. I said to the woman through the window, she can't have sexual relations with anyone for at least a fortnight. They had to know that. It was all I could do for the girl. This woman just drove away. She almost knocked me down. I rang the police. Then I found out from them — every detail this woman had given me was false. Of course. I was so naïve to think otherwise. I still don't know if I did the right thing.' She stopped, closing her eyes. 'I think, that girl crying in the back seat — was she someone who hated me for what I did? I don't know.'

There was a pause.

'Could you describe her to us, Agnes? Would that be possible?'

'I don't know. I'm not sure — her face is there but I don't know how to ... She was so young ... '

Standing outside, the doctor signalled to the nurse.

'That's it. You're putting too much pressure on her,' he said to Harrigan. 'We're finished.'

The nurse touched Grace on the shoulder. Grace nodded. She began to disengage her hand.

'I'll leave it there, Agnes. Don't feel you have to think about it any more. Thank you for giving us that. That information's very important.'

'Wait,' Agnes said, in a voice that was too soft to be heard by anyone else, 'come closer.'

Grace bent down, the woman whispered in her ear.

'I know you. You came to a clinic. This mad woman was bothering us. You threw her out.'

'Yes, that's right.'

'You look better. Much better than you did.'

Her hand slipped away and Grace found herself outside the room with Harrigan, watching the doctor and nurse bend over the bed.

'Excuse me,' she said to Harrigan and took refuge in the Ladies, holding tissues under her eyes to stop the tears from brimming down her cheeks. Mascara flickered fine black speckles onto the white paper. Holding herself in grip, she repaired her make-up and then went outside to find Harrigan waiting for her in the corridor.

'The doc's okay,' he said, studying her face. 'She's out to it but she's okay. We've been told we can go home now. How are you?'

'I'm fine.'

'Do you want me to buy you a cup of coffee? Since you don't drink.'

'A cigarette is what I really need,' Grace replied, letting a chink of her feelings out.

'Why don't we try for both?' he said. 'Let's take half an hour off. We can spare each other that much time.'

In a coffee shop nearby, where you could sit in an individual booth unwatched by the crowd, Harrigan ordered at great expense a short black and a strong flat white from a silver-studded waiter. Grace lit a cigarette and inhaled the poisonous smoke with gratitude. She forced a shiver down her spine, releasing tension, and came back to the present to find Harrigan watching her from the other side of the table.

'That was a nasty story,' she said.

There was no sympathy for the Firewall in Harrigan at that moment. 'You can say that,' he replied. 'I can tell you I've heard worse. It's not a new story.'

What could be worse? Grace found herself unexpectedly shaken by this reply.

'No,' she said and then was silent, staring at the tablecloth, drawing on her cigarette. When she looked up, Harrigan saw an expression of extraordinary sadness cross her face.

'We don't even know it's her, do we? The doc could be talking about someone else who's got nothing to do with this,' she said.

'She could be, that's possible. I don't think it's very likely but it's possible.'

'Well, if it is her, then why? Why take it out on the doc? Why not just go and shoot your own rubbish father if he's done something like that to you? Or your idiot mother. Now, that would be justifiable homicide. I wouldn't convict her.'

She drew down more smoke, an angry glint in her eye. Harrigan found himself laughing dryly.

'Good question. We can assume she's been manipulated in some way. But I wouldn't say that explained her.'

The waiter brought their coffees. After a few seconds' hesitation, Harrigan ordered a neat whisky. He looked at Grace to see if she wanted anything else as well but she shook her head.

'If you look at everything about her,' she said, 'she's such a wild card. How far can you manipulate someone like that?'

'I think our friendly neighbourhood preacher would consider it a challenge,' Harrigan said. 'Now there's someone who wouldn't like some upstart girl getting up his nose if she wasn't doing what he wanted.'

He was tapping his fingers on the table top as he spoke.

'He'd get a kick out of doing that? Putting a gun in her hand and saying, go out and use it?' Grace asked.

'He'd love it.' Harrigan was musing. 'Take a good look at him the next time he comes in. I don't think I've met many people more cold-blooded than he is.'

'No? Haven't you dealt with some really choice characters — serial killers, people like that?'

'No one worth talking about. People like that are nothing, Grace. They're an empty space. Their only quality is how dangerous they are. Someone like that is strictly business. You run them to earth, you put them away, you forget their existence. They're not worth one second of your time.'

The waiter placed a shot glass containing a thimbleful of whisky on the table. He amended the bill before returning to drape himself decoratively over the bar. Harrigan glanced at the sum charged and wondered if he should not have taken out a mortgage on his house before deciding he needed an evening heart-starter.

'Then she's not like the preacher,' Grace said. 'If that's what he is, she isn't like that.'

'How do you know she's not?'

Grace ashed out her cigarette and wanted to light another but did not.

'She was raped,' she said to Harrigan, looking at him directly, preventing her voice from shaking. 'I'm not saying it justifies anything, but it does give her a reason for what she did.'

'A reason? Her reason for shooting down two bystanders is that she was raped?'

Grace's back was immediately bathed in a cold sweat. 'You don't think that matters?'

'No, that's not what I said. And it's not what I think either.'

'You heard the story,' she said, with forced detachment. 'It wasn't exactly straightforward. Not that I think it's ever straightforward. Why wouldn't it be a reason?'

'Do you think reason is the word you want to use?'

Grace folded her arms and leaned a little forward, resting on the table.

'Maybe it is. It's a reason to her even if it's not for us. Compulsion, if you think that's a better word. Maybe I do want to get into her head so I know why she does what she does.'

'You want to be her?'

'For a little while maybe. Just to get the insight.'

'Grace, could you shoot down two people in cold blood?'

'I don't think she did act in cold blood. But no, if you're asking me. I hope I couldn't.'

She gave in and lit another cigarette.

'Then you can't be her. For the exact same reason you say you want to. She's got no insight into what she's doing, she can't have. And you do.'

'I want to know that she's human. I want to treat her like she is.'

'Why does someone like you want to get down in the dirt with someone like her?' he asked.

Why does your son? To have asked him this question would have been unforgivable.

'Is it dirt?'

'Yes.'

'Well, if that's what it is, we're all down in it, aren't we? One way or another. It's all just people doing what they do to each other all the time. Lovely, lovely people.'

'No,' he said, 'I don't see myself down there. And there's no way I'd ever see you down there. Not for one second.'

'I can't see it as hard and fast as that,' she said. 'It's like a spectrum, we slide up and down it.'

'Maybe. But some people like it down there, Grace, they like being in the dirt. They do things, they leave devastation behind them, and they walk away like it's never happened. They don't care. They'll give you any excuse why they don't have to think about what they've done. I don't believe either of us is like that.'

You don't know who or what I am, Paul, she thought in reply. There was a brief silence in which they looked at each other.

'You're tired,' he said, thinking aloud.

'Aren't we all? So are you,' she replied, crushing out her cigarette.

He did not answer.

'That session got to me,' she said. 'More than I thought it would.'

'That's going to happen, it's better to admit it upfront. Do you have something you do when you want to unwind?' he asked.

'I go and sink myself in music. I can get lost in it for hours. I might do that when I get home.'

'Probably a good idea.'

Silence.

'Do you have anything you do?' she asked.

'If it's bad, I go and see my son. He always makes me feel like I'm a human being again. If I want a real break, I go fishing down the coast. I like to hear the sound of the sea. Nothing very exciting.'

Once more, they sat in silence. Why are we sitting talking like this, he thought? Why don't you let me ask you home? I've got a sound system of my own even if the last time I bought a CD was a year ago and I can't remember what it was. I've got a comfortable bed upstairs in my bedroom. I would love to see you sitting naked on my bed with your hair out on your shoulders, your mind as far away from work as it can get. He shook the thoughts out of his head.

'What is it?' she asked.

'I was just thinking about the work I've got to do,' he said, slightly embarrassed, glad she could not see into his mind.

'Yeah,' she said, looking at him with that same sadness, 'I won't hold you up any longer.'

'I wasn't rushing you, Grace. Please don't think I was.'

'It doesn't matter, I've got to go anyway. I've got work to do as well. What do I owe you for the coffee?'

She was already on her feet, putting on her coat.

'This is on me, I told you that. Why don't you go home if you're feeling low. Give me the tape and I'll get it written up.'

'Yeah, okay. Thanks.'

She set the tape on the table without looking at him and walked out, leaving him with his own company, an unfinished coffee and a half-drunk whisky, asking himself what it had all meant. If it had meant anything at all. He watched her through the window of the coffee shop as she crossed the street, thinking that he had made her a gift of his time when he had none to spare and she had not noticed.

He finished his whisky, left a note on the table to pay and walked out as well, going back to work.

Out on Oxford Street in the bright lights and the moving traffic Grace felt savage, emotional pain, just as she had in the hospital; the cold air woke her to its rawness. Whatever you want, Harrigan, I don't want you to waste your time with me. I don't need to feel anything for you that's just going to go nowhere.

This was an old grief, wasted emotion, possibilities that die at birth. She worked to put him out of her mind as she stood at the traffic lights. She might keep Harrigan out of her head but the Firewall stayed on, hooked into her. Grace crossed the wide road with everyone else, pinned between the bright lights of the cars. Your father did rape you, didn't he? And your mother stood by and she let him. And then they cleaned you up when they needed to without even talking to you. I know how you feel, I've been there once upon a time myself. *But it wasn't your father.* This quiet whisper of fact in Grace's mind nonetheless held the implication of its reverse: that other fathers did, something scarcely comprehensible to her in terms of her own experience. In terms of her work, it was a simple fact, like a piece of rock which for some reason had a particular shape. It was just the way it was.

At home, she stripped, washed, changed, shook out her hair, brushing it until it shone, but even so, in her tiny lounge room the walls closed in. She switched off the main lights and sat on her couch, looking out at the streets below, to the small scrape of beach in the near distance. On her lap, she held a red silk box fastened with an ivory catch. After a while, she opened the box and set out its contents on the coffee table. Saucers, miniature cups with elegant handles, an ornamental teapot, a sugar bowl, all removed from their pockets of faintly yellowing white silk. A tea set, her grandfather's gift to her when she was nine, something pretty and delicate, bought in Hong Kong when he was twenty. The very first time she had taken these pieces out to look at them, she had cracked the fragile bowl. Her grandfather had comforted her as she cried. 'Don't worry, Gracie,' he said, laughing at her softly, cuddling her, 'nothing is for ever.'

Even in the soft light, this faintest of hairline cracks threw a shadow on the fine china, an indelible discoloration of age. If she turned the bowl towards a certain fall of the light, she could not see the crack, only a courtesan's face and dark hair in a soft surrounding cloud. The bowl sat in Grace's hands as she might have held a tiny living child, a child whose watching eyes looked out at the world from a perspective no one else could reach, but who could not speak. This was her own thought child, the child Grace chose not to have. Its brief existence lived on in her as an only twin might carry somewhere in her body the partially formed foetus of her brother or sister, knowing it is there, curled and sleeping, that it could have grown and separated but has not done so. A ghost fixed as a part its mother's being, as something not quite living and not quite dead.

I am not sorry, she thought. I cried then and I think about it now but I am not sorry. All I felt when it was over was relief. That's all I feel now.

Nothing is for ever. She set the pieces of china out in a pattern on the coffee table. Moonlight and streetlight streamed in through the windows. In this light, the fine white china was almost radiant, its delicate shapes formed into a pattern of partial shadows fitted against a pale transparency. Grace's mind was making images, of a mother and daughter sitting side by side on a train or a bus, both of them silent, both of them looking straight ahead at nothing perhaps, the young girl uncertain of their destination and left wondering if she was going to live long enough to reach it. What would they say to each other, sitting side by side like that? Nothing. Nothing at all.

She could not stay in this room, it was too small. Grace phoned her old lover and asked him for sanctuary.

'Come on around, sweetheart. You're always welcome. I'll put some music on. I'll even indulge you in some Elvis Costello. Christ!' he said.

Grace laughed.

'I'm hungry,' she said. 'Will I pick up some takeaway for us?'

'Yeah, do that. You can help me eat it.'

'Okay. We can share it with some apple juice.'

She heard him laugh on the other end of the line.

'Not what we used to do,' he said.

'No. See you soon anyway.'

Grace binned her cigarettes and then dropped her beeper into her bag but made sure that her mobile phone was turned off for the duration. She stopped at a takeaway place, a glass window on the street that sold experimental mixtures of cuisine, and bought solace for herself and her old lover with the plastic containers. In her first months of abstinence from alcohol, the world had settled into a dry balance. Her mind had taken on something resembling clarity and she had rediscovered appetite and taste, qualities she had thought were lost for ever. Her brother, Nicholas, was a cook, an unexpected occupation for an army officer's son. He had taught her how to eat in those first days, practising his cooking on her while they had shared a house together, where she had recovered and he had learned his art.

Now, if we were ever to have sex, Paul, I'd cook for us first, or I'd want us to eat somewhere nice, because food's important. She and Harrigan would never do so, so the possibilities did not matter.

She drove up the coastline to the northern beaches, to Whale Beach. The stars were distant out over the sea, made pale and small by the reflection of the city's lights. She sang 'Time after Time' softly to herself as she drove.

By the time she arrived and could hear the sound of the waves breaking on the beach, she felt she could be herself. The outside light was on and the door was open and waiting for her. She didn't come here often enough any more, not the way she'd used to. Another life was taking her over, pushing the old one to the side.

'Hi, Frankie. How are you?' she called out, walking in the door.

'Hi there, Grace. Pretty good tonight.'

He was waiting for her in a wheelchair in the centre of a wide white room with polished floorboards and windows that looked out over the sea. A big man, even in his chair, with thick black curly hair and a bright red shirt covering his broad chest. He glided towards her. She put her collection of plastic tubs down on a table.

'You look good,' she said, leaning down to kiss his cheek, hugging him from where she stood.

'How are you, more to the point?' he said, looking at her shrewdly.

'I could be better. I need a break from work, it's getting to me. I need to get back into the real world for a little while.'

'What do you do that fucking awful job for? Why don't you do something civilised with your life? Somewhere where you'd meet people with minds? You know. Cleaning railway station toilets or something like that.'

'You know me, Frankie. I have to know. I have to keep pushing to see what's next. Why else?'

He laughed. He had turned on the music; she went to the kitchen to put the food in the microwave, to get forks and spoons, a drinking cup that did not spill its contents when the drinker's hands shook.

'Where's Phyllis tonight? Did you give her the night off?' she asked when she reappeared with a tray, wondering where Frankie's live-in nurse had got to.

'Yeah, I gave her a break. I thought she might like some time to herself.'

'Yeah. She probably would. We can have some to ourselves now as well.'

Tonight, Grace and her old life and her old lover would be just comfort enough for each other. Nothing much else was necessary.

21

Grace left Whale Beach as the waves were crashing in on the headlands and the wash was spreading out across the sand. The swell rolled in, its faint streaks of white water glimmering in the pre-dawn darkness. She was heading home, in her mind choosing the day's outfit. She phoned in to check if there were any messages on her answering machine and because of what she heard recorded there did not go home but drove straight to work instead. In the office sleepy people, the first arrivals, were setting polystyrene cups of steaming coffee on their desks. She knocked on Harrigan's door where he was sitting working out the day's business with Trevor and Ian. He looked up, unable to prevent himself from taking in the full sight of her without make-up and in casual dress finished off with a worn leather jacket. She was wearing the midriff and navel look, as he called it. He tried not to look at the bare skin between her too short T-shirt and the line of her jeans.

'I'm sorry to interrupt,' she said to him.

'You're dressed for work, are you? What is it?'

He was frowning. He himself was casually dressed, which meant that he was without his garrotte for the day, a tie.

'I haven't been home yet to get dressed,' she replied. 'This was on my answering machine when I rang in this morning to check.'

As he took her phone, Harrigan had the pleasure of watching Ian ogle Grace and grin salaciously behind her back. He listened to the message before passing it on to Trevor and Ian in turn. The first sounds of the recording were of silence, and then of someone moving, and then of a voice, slurred and slow.

'Is that that woman, Grace? The one who talked to me? It's Greggie. I'm ringing to tell you that I'm flying at the moment. And I'm flying because I want to. I don't think I've ever felt this good in my life. Because I'm on my way out and no one can do anything to stop me and I'm free now. And I've never felt happier in my life. I just feel that I'm going to sleep. He won't like that because I'm fucking it up for him, serve him fucking right. I just wanted to say — you've got to understand her. The Firewall, that is. She wouldn't want me saying who she is. I rang her but she's got her phone off so I can't say goodbye. Will you do that for me? If you do give a shit like you say you do. Just say I wanted to say goodbye to her. She's got her reasons, you need to talk her round, just talk to her. She's not like him, you remember that.'

There was a faint clink as the phone was turned off. After a short break a mechanical voice read out: 'Tuesday, 18 July, 3:59 a.m.'

'That was our witness,' Harrigan said. 'Goodbye, Greggie. Poor bloody kid.'

He sat there expressionless, tapping at the desk, otherwise unmoving. He radiated sufficient tension to render everyone else in the room momentarily silent.

'He. Him. Who's that?' Ian asked, giving the phone back to Grace.

'Who do you think? Our friendly neighbourhood everyone's-my-mate community refuge preacher from the New Life Ministries. I'll lay you odds,' Harrigan replied.

'"I'm fucking it up for him",' Trevor repeated. 'He didn't want him dead.'

'Just not yet, is all that means.'

'That was loyalty, wasn't it?' Grace said. 'He wasn't going to tell us who she is, not even then.'

Harrigan looked at her from across his desk.

'You didn't hear that message when it came through? Why didn't you answer your phone? Why wait till now to share it with us?'

'It's like I said. I've only just heard it.' There was a brief silence. Harrigan was still waiting. 'I'd turned my mobile off. It couldn't ring through,' she said.

'You weren't home, you turned your mobile off. You weren't contactable.' He felt the back of his neck burn.

'I had my beeper with me.'

'That's not good enough. No, it's worse than that, it's bloody useless. You knew that boy had your number, you gave it to him yourself. If you'd had your phone on, you could have talked to him. You could have asked him where he was, maybe we could have done something for him, we could have traced the call. If everyone else can manage it, I don't see why you can't.'

She looked back at him stony-faced; he turned to Ian. 'Get on to that and check out where that call came from. See what you can trace.'

Ian got to his feet. 'Can I get Jeffo on to that? Because if I do it, I won't have time to —'

'Jeffo doesn't know his fig from his date.' Harrigan's voice was short to say the least. 'You do it.'

'I'll do it,' Grace said, angrily. 'I can do that.'

'Then get on with it.' Harrigan knew his face was blood red. 'And some time today, get changed!'

She gave him one more glance and then walked out of his office, Ian following her.

'Take it easy, mate,' Trevor said quietly to Harrigan after they had both gone. 'Watch your blood pressure. We need you to protect us from Marvin.'

Harrigan did not immediately reply. He was watching Grace pull her long brown hair into a ponytail as she stood by her desk talking to Ian, and wondering who she had been making herself available to at four in the morning. She hadn't been interested in his company.

'Don't worry about it. All I need is some fresh air and a change of scenery,' he said and collecting his coat went in search of both.

How are u dad?

Harrigan should have expected his son to take the initiative. He looked at the computer screen.

'How are you, more to the point?' he asked.

I'm okay dad I'm still here I don't know that I want 2 talk 2 much about wot happened yesterday U didn't tell me how u were

'I'm fine.'

U don't look it

Harrigan sat down beside his son. He almost smiled. He did not quite know what to say. He hadn't come here to talk about women in general, only one in particular. A population of one that did not include Grace. He looked from the screen to his son.

'You love her.' It was something he felt he had to say.

She knows what I look like She says she loves me I believe her Still think she does

Harrigan waited.

Thought she'd understand but she didn't She didn't listen I don't know Maybe she'll come back and talk 2 me again

'She owes it to you, Toby. You've given her more than anyone else has.'

His son flickered his good hand, that 'oh yeah' gesture.

'Why her, Toby? I know you don't want to talk about it. But do you want to tell me that much, so I understand?'

Why do u think??? Because She talked 2 me I can't do anything dad Like I tell everyone I'm a turtle on its back That's me Girls don't talk 2 me They don't even want 2 look at me Why would they want 2 She did She knew what I looked like & she didn't care I said 2 her we're both fucking cripples She said yes we are & we are 2 dad That's why

'You aren't like her, Toby. You couldn't even think about doing something like that.'

I might U don't know I'm locked in this chair She's locked in her head That's why she did wot she did Don't know wot I'd do if I wasn't in a chair

'You live in the real world. She doesn't.'

I live in my head dad I live in a screen Nowhere else I can go without someone helping me

'You don't just live through a screen. You've got me for the rest of my life. You've got Ronnie, you've got Carolyn, there's your cousins. They love you, mate. You can't say we haven't shown that.'

Not the point, is it, dad? Wot girl wants 2 have sex with me????

Harrigan sat there silent.

'There are alternatives,' he said finally.

Are there?

'Yeah.'

Pay someone u mean??? Is that what u did?

'No, it wasn't,' he said eventually.

Wot did u do?

'I had a girlfriend. First time we did it, we were on the back seat of her brother's car. In the garage. He was a petrol-head too, I don't know if he ever found out what happened to the upholstery. God, it was uncomfortable.'

Better than 0

In retrospect, not so very much. Things had improved after his girlfriend, through some obscure arrangement, had borrowed the keys to the flat her university student sister shared with a moving company of friends.

'It's whatever you want, Toby. You just have to ask me and I will organise what you want. That's all you have to do.'

Not someone who cares about me

'Toby, if you just ask me, I will do the very best I can for you. There are people out there who are better than others. I can find them for you.'

Toby flickered 'oh, yeah' with his good hand once again. Harrigan stood up.

'I have to go back to work now,' he said. 'I have to be somewhere. If you want anything, you just ask me. You tell me what you want.'

U know what I'm going 2 do??? I'm going out looking for her Maybe she'll talk 2 me again

'Maybe she will. In the meantime, you remember — I'm here if you want anything.'

Yeah okay dad Don't worry so much

If it was what Toby wanted, the possibility of paying someone for sex had crossed Harrigan's mind on several occasions before. It was not something he viewed with any great satisfaction. The idea that there would be a negotiated price to pay filled him with distaste; the idea had always left him with that feeling. People smiled at you when they took your money, they manipulated you whether you paid them or they paid you. Either way they bought you out. It was just that for Toby, it was either do that or leave him to pictures on the Net, that was just the way things were. You don't want to worry about it too much, Toby. Decent women are like hen's teeth and if the two of you just want to unwind, who gives a shit what they do with their lives? What does it matter? Just think about it like that.

Harrigan walked out into the bright morning feeling a strong sense of bleakness and the need for solitude. It wasn't something he had the time to indulge in just now. He had places to go.

Harrigan parked near the New Life Ministries Temple as the first prayer meeting for the day was about to start. A small crowd had gathered in the street outside, waiting for the doors to open, just as they might have done when films were shown here. Once the picture theatre had closed, it might have become a suburban boxing ring, the kind his father had taken him to when he was a boy. Later still, they might have held dog or cock fights here. He thought of the soiled bank notes passing from hand to hand among the watchers as the animals were set against each other in the pit.

The preacher, wearing a cheap dark suit and tie, opened the doors to the church and welcomed the crowd in. 'I am so pleased you could come,' he said to each of the newcomers. 'Good to see you again,' to the regulars. He knew each one of them by name, and if he did not, he made sure they told him who they were. Harrigan was the last to present himself.

'Paul. This is a surprise. Good morning. Are you here to tell me you've found Greg?'

'No, Graeme, I'm afraid I have to say we haven't. But we're still out there looking for him. I guess he hasn't come back here or you would have let us know. You haven't seen him at all? Talked to him?'

What do you know, Harrigan thought as he watched him.

'No, he hasn't come home, unfortunately,' the man replied, words Harrigan could read any way he wished. 'I always live in hope but so far I am without that singular reward. So you are here for our prayer meeting?'

'I thought I'd like to come along since you were generous enough to invite me. You don't mind if I sit in?'

'I'm sure we'll be very happy to have you amongst us, Paul. There's no reason why we should not. You won't mind if I ask you to participate? It's something I ask of everyone who comes here. My door is open to everyone provided they come with an equally open heart.'

It could hardly be worse than his monthly management meetings at Area Command with the Tooth.

'Happy to,' he replied.

'Please, come in.'

He followed the preacher through double glass doors into a tiny foyer and then into the auditorium where the sound of his footsteps echoed and the room was bright with unshaded lights. The preacher locked the glass doors to the street and then closed and locked two thick wooden fire doors between the foyer and the auditorium. Harrigan noticed this with some surprise.

'Don't you let your latecomers in, Graeme?'

'There is only a very narrow opening for us in this world, Paul. People must come on time or they will be shut out.'

Abandon all hope, Harrigan thought ironically, glancing at the solid barrier the doors formed against the outside world. His backup would have a hard time getting in here. He hoped he wouldn't need them.

The congregation sat in chairs arranged in wide concentric circles like the white stubby petals of a plastic flower. There was a song sheet on each chair. Harrigan took a seat at the back, near the door, watching. There were more people at this gathering than he would have expected, they had filled the rows to brimming. Families, men with their wives and children, people he assumed were unemployed since it was a work day. Older couples in cheap clothes. Individuals, a man in his late twenties, his features sharp and protruding, his skin the colour of ageing milk, twisting his long hands together. An older woman with grey square-cut hair, in a sombre suit and a pink blouse buttoned to the neck. A drab woman of about forty-five with large glasses and wearing a blue tracksuit. People you would barely notice in any crowd. Perhaps he should have sent Trevor down there after all; he knew that his 2IC went to mass regularly with his partner, a fact which had surprised Harrigan when he had first found it out. Perhaps Trev would have understood these people better, whoever they were.

Harrigan had always gone to church in the company of women: his beautiful mother, his hard-faced aunt and, until they had rebelled, his two sisters, with himself in the middle, the loved child. His father's absence had been pure defiance against the church and, Harrigan thought now at a distance of years, this all-enclosing regiment of women and, as Jim Harrigan saw it, their dotage on his son. Like his father, Harrigan had lost faith a long time ago. When he was a small boy, it had a magic for him. He remembered walking up the hill to church on Sunday morning and looking up at the high steeple of St Augustine's climbing into the sky. He thought it was beautiful. In the church, he had been fascinated by the statues of Mary and Jesus on either side of the white wedding-cake altar, imagining them coming to life, Jesus reaching out his hand, Mary smiling. Visions of Bible stories had filled his head, brightly coloured images that he had taken from the picture books he used to read. Visions which had strangely and paradoxically died — over time, it had taken time — in the rigours of his adolescent education at St Ignatius. The thoroughgoing arguments he worked through diligently in class had turned the words to ash on the page; words were all they were. After this he had gone through the motions, had become a stranger in that particular world. Someone perfectly in disguise but in reality a double agent, something he had been ever since. Any residual belief had been erased by his mother's death. Almost. When you live with images for that long, they are burned onto the skin from the inside out. They still hold on to you, if only in memory, like everything that comes out of the past.

In this cold and ugly hall, the people were subdued, waiting. There was no need for the preacher to call for quiet. He stood at the centre of the inner circle, at the centre of the seated crowd.

'Friends,' he said into the silence, 'today we are fortunate enough to have some new companions among us. People who, like yourselves, want to find the way to redemption and truth, to a lasting peace of mind. So I would like to ask our new companions to stand up and introduce themselves and tell us why they have come today. Perhaps we could start with you, Martin. You say your wife left you. Do you want to tell us about it?'

Following this initial invitation, people stood one after another to tell stories of intimate and scarifying detail to a room filled with strangers. Harrigan himself listened and waited. He spent his working days with people who were either professional liars or wanted to strip themselves naked like this. On the whole, he preferred the liars. Their agenda were easier to detect.

'I'm Paul Harrigan,' he said, when his turn came. 'I'm here as someone who worries about the fate of our young people. I wanted to see what you might have to offer them, Graeme. Whether it's some way of life which might give them more hope for the future than many of them seem to have today. I meet a lot of them in my work. I was listening to one of them talk about that just this morning. I wonder what his fate will be.'

'That's very admirable, Paul. Yes, our present world destroys all hope, does it not? Do you have children of your own?'

'I'd like to keep that to myself. This is about me, not anyone else.'

There was a rustle of surprise. The preacher smiled.

'Normally we have no secrets in this room, Paul. It's a condition of entry here, as I thought I had told you. But if that is how you see it. Would you like to tell us what you do for a living?'

'I'm a law enforcement officer.'

One way of announcing you're a fucking walloper, as his father had always put it.

'Thank you, Paul. I don't think we have any other policemen here today, although we have had in the past. We'll begin now. Bronwyn?'

In a wholly unexpected move, the woman in the blue tracksuit walked to the back of the auditorium and extinguished the lights. Harrigan found himself sitting in complete blackness. He became still, listening and waiting, a prickle of apprehension at the back of his neck. There was the collective noise of those in the room breathing, and then a shuffling, scraping noise, the sound of someone who had become disorientated and had dropped something. In the darkness, there was the suspension of any sense of place. Then a woman's ghostly and untrained voice was heard, singing:

Praise you the Lord in the heavens,
Praise him in the heights,
Praise him all his angels,
Praise him all you stars of light,
Praise him all who live in darkness,
Praise him all who dwell in day,
Let them praise the name of the Lord.

There was silence. Then Harrigan heard the preacher's voice, disembodied and echoing against the high ceilings of the hall: 'We are in the darkness, you and I. Come with me and I will show you the way to the light.'

As he spoke an image began to take shape slowly on the screen at the back of the hall: a figure in a long white robe, seven small glittering stars balanced over his outstretched hands. The preacher stood in silhouette against this image, his shadowed face edged with light. Pale wall lights appeared around the auditorium, illuminating the faces of the watching congregation.

'Welcome to you all, my blood brothers and sisters in Christ. Please stand and link hands,' he said. There was a rustle as each person took the other's hand. Harrigan grasped the hand of an elderly man on one side and a woman of indeterminate age with vague blue eyes on the other. 'As we stand here on the edge of eternity, I ask you to remember this, my brothers and sisters. You and I are one flesh, one body. Yes, and we love each other, as parent and child, brother and sister, so we love. Close your eyes. Think on this. We are as one. Repeat after me. We are as one.'

'We are as one.' The response came strongly, fully voiced.

'We are as one,' the preacher said again.

'We are as one,' the crowd responded.

'We are as one.'

'We are as one!'

In the shadow and light, a sense of anticipation continued to grow. Harrigan, perhaps the sole person in the room who had not closed his eyes as requested, glanced from one person to the next, and then to the preacher. The preacher was also open-eyed and watching, looking at him directly or so it seemed. He gave the impression that everyone in the room was within his sight.

'Please be seated,' he said.

There was another rustle as the participants let go of each other's hands and sat down again. The preacher began to speak without emphasis, almost without emotion, moving from one person to the next in the circles of chairs. Those present turned their heads to watch him, straining towards him. His voice took on the quality of a chant, unremitting and at an even tempo.

'We know, do we not, that Jesus loves us, even beyond death. His blood is the blood of life, one drop of it has the power to redeem us. To wash us all clean of the grievous weight of life. That is the depth of his love. But do we return that love?'

He stopped in front of the man who spoken about the breakdown of his marriage. 'I ask you this, Martin. Do you cry aloud in the night for God's love? No?'

The preacher leaned towards the man and spoke softly, although his voice was heard throughout the hall. 'You must. You must hunger beyond life for the love that God can give you. Until that hunger consumes you, you will never be satisfied. No one ...' He paused and stood upright, then continued moving. The silence was intense. '... no one can deny God and live. Do, and in your heart there will be only death. And then? Oh, my friends, I only tell you this, these are the end-times and Jesus will come for you now on any day, at any hour. He will come with terrible speed and there will be no time for you to say, Oh, I must do that before I go. When we push open these doors to the streets, will the storms that presage the end of the world be raging outside? How do we know they will not? In the next day, the next hour, will it be you who stands on the bridge to all eternity with the abyss of Hell beneath you? Will there be a way across for you? Then the fear of God will come to you, and oh, yes, it will raise up the hairs on your head and a cold black wind will drive you down to Hell for all eternity, to a world without end.'

As he listened, Harrigan had the strange sensation of feeling cold down his spine. That needle along his backbone was genuine fear. It was the second time the preacher had had this effect on him. He glanced at others around him, some of whom sat with open mouths, waiting on every word.

'But fear not,' the preacher became soft and soothing. 'No, fear not, my brothers and sisters. Because *you* will stand before God and say: *I* fought against the unnatural and the perverse. *I* stood between the murderer and the unborn. Satan walked abroad in the world but *I* defied him. Remember the words of Saint John of the Revelation. Be you faithful unto death and I will give you a crown of life. Now, I know you will reach into your hearts and each of you will find in there the love that is God and the strength to go out and to do His work.'

He returned to stand in the centre of the circle and there was a release of breath, a communal sigh.

'I ask of you now — tell us all, my brothers and sisters, what is it that you will do that will bring you forward as Christ's witness, that will place you in the company of the saved at the end of time? Paul. You are new to us today. What will you do?'

Curiously Harrigan heard his name called almost with relief. As he stood up the crowd turned to look at him, their faces still partially shadowed in the half dark like the preacher's. Others among them would have preferred to have been chosen. They were hungry to speak, he could see it in their faces.

'Like you say, I'm here for the first time. Why don't you tell me what you think I should do?'

'Go and close down an abortion mill today. That's what the police should be doing,' the man with creamy skin said, seated near the centre of the circle and smiling aggressively. His face was almost silver in the light.

'Fight against those things which are an abomination in God's sight,' the preacher replied without hesitation, ignoring the man who had spoken. 'You, Paul, are privileged, you have the force of the state behind you. We do not. We stand here as a lone voice. We exercise no earthly power. And if you come here, Paul, as you say you do, seeking hope, why have you not done more with the powers vested in you already? Are you afraid to? Or will you not answer me?'

'I work within the law, Graeme. I have to.'

He sat down.

'Abortion is against the law.' The man with creamy skin spoke again.

'Indeed it is. But no one wants the law enforced, so people flout it without fear,' the preacher said. 'So we protest. But unlike you, Paul, none of us need fear anything from anyone. Even if protest is all we have. With our protest, we have God's backing. Nothing can stand against that.'

'I have done that. I have protested,' said the woman in the dark suit, louder than everyone else among the shouted responses. 'Every day I know the Minister for Health is going to be out in public somewhere, I'm waiting for her. Wherever she goes, I'm behind her. As long as she allows the unborn children of this state to be murdered, I'll be there. I've told her what she is.'

'I write to the politicians,' the man with creamy skin said. 'I tell them that what's happening in Australia is a sin against God. I say to them, there's no such thing as a gay lifestyle, it's a deathstyle, it corrupts everything it touches. But what do they do about it? Nothing. They don't even write back to me.'

Harrigan considered it was just as well that he hadn't sent Trevor down here.

'None of that is enough,' said the woman who had sung, Bronwyn. She had been standing at the back of the hall throughout proceedings, not far from where Harrigan sat, next to a small table on which stood a projector. 'We have to give everything we have.'

'What does that mean — giving everything you have?' Harrigan asked. 'How far do you have to go?'

She looked at him a little startled, a plumpish figure with long slightly curling hair and wearing a silver medal of a baby's tiny feet around her neck.

'We must go as far as it's possible to go,' she replied quietly. 'Here, we have nothing to lose. Those who stand against us only make us stronger. Because we have no ties, no obligations other than to God, there is nothing anyone can take from us. The only obligation you can ever have is the one you have to Him and you have to do anything that is necessary to fulfil that.'

'I'll tell you what it means,' the pale man said. 'The way things are today, you have to make a choice. You have to fight back. And if people get jack of it so much that they start to use force, then the only people who'll be surprised are the ones who never listened in the first place.'

'But you have to understand, we wouldn't do that because we wanted to. We accept the role given to us by God. We're not about death. We're about life. We're not the killers,' Bronwyn said. 'But the doctors in the family planning clinics are. And that's what being homosexual means. They infect everything, they're diseased, they're destroyers. We offer life. But we keep being attacked because we're the only ones brave enough to stand up and say so.'

There was a waiting silence as she spoke. She moved forward into the circle, her voice carrying throughout the auditorium in the colourless light. 'I am Alpha and

Omega, the beginning and the end, the first and the last. Everyone here believes that. The only law we are obliged to obey is God's. And we must obey that law, no matter what we face. Graeme taught us that.'

'Bronwyn,' the preacher said, 'it's time to move on. If you could change the slide?'

The figure with seven stars above his outstretched hand disappeared; the image of a simple white-robed figure, which Harrigan assumed to be a depiction of Christ, took its place. It bore no relationship to the complex images he had studied and lived with throughout his boyhood.

'Perhaps we should return to ourselves and to the present now, and speak of the peace that can be found from faith in God. You, Martin,' the preacher spoke to the divorced man, 'remember that while you are here, you are among your family. Speak to us now about what is in your heart.'

Harrigan sat for another hour while those around him detailed and wept over their personal heartbreaks, until the preacher said at last, 'Bronwyn, would you open the doors, please.'

The main lights flickered on, the doors were opened. Glancing out onto the inner city street, Harrigan's first sight of the outside light gave him a sense of disorientation, it appeared as something momentarily less real than the shadows in the dark room. The congregation filed out, the preacher said goodbye to each one and shook their hands as they went. Fredericksen, Harrigan noted with some surprise, did not ask his congregation for any money. He watched as the preacher shook the divorced man's hand and said he looked forward to seeing him again.

'You've given me heart,' the man replied.

Harrigan was the last one out of the hall. The

preacher offered him his hand and he shook it against his wishes, feeling that same weak, sliding grip.

'Paul,' the preacher said, 'thank you for joining in the way you did today. I hope you didn't find our approach to things here too confronting. But there is so much in the world these days against which we need to speak out. I speak from the heart, I'm afraid; it's got me into trouble before today. I do hope we'll see you here again.'

Harrigan wondered if he should question whether there was a point to the invitation, if the world was likely to end in the very near future.

'It was no problem, me being here, Graeme. Thank you for the insight. I notice you didn't take up a collection.'

'No. No one who comes here has any money. I don't take what little my people have. Why? Would you like to make a contribution? We'd certainly be most grateful.'

'I wanted to thank you for your generosity. It's unusual these days. Just as a matter of interest — are these people your people? Is that how they see themselves?'

'Yes, they are. They come to me because I am the only one who takes the trouble to care about them. I show them the way to peace of heart. The way Christ did. He went out to the lepers, the sick, the outcast and he offered them life. You must try and understand me, Paul. I have said to you that I love people and that is true. I am someone who is very sensitive to the needs of others. I can see into the heart. These people — they're ordinary people, lost people, looking for hope. Like you. You're not a happy man, Paul. I can see that. If you came here to me and genuinely opened your heart, I would find you happiness. I would give you hope.'

'You know, Graeme, even if that was true, I'd have to say that was my problem, not yours, and I don't think I'd care to share it with you. I'll see you again. When I find Greg. Because I do intend to find him. That's a promise.'

'I don't doubt that. I hope indeed you find him very soon,' the preacher replied, smiling.

Sydney air had never smelled quite so sweet to Harrigan as when he stepped out onto the street. As he drove away, he turned off his recording device and called Trevor.

'How'd it go?' Trevor asked.

'They owe me more money after that, Trev,' Harrigan replied. 'I'm on my way back in now.'

'See you when you get here. We'll be ready to go for this afternoon. We're just waiting for the film.'

'All right. I'll be there shortly.'

Harrigan drove through the slow traffic considering what he had just seen. He could call it cheap theatrics, ask whether — for the preacher — it was a case of stamina or addiction, and question who fed off who, but it would make no difference. The preacher's congregation believed in the man; the man believed in himself. Some of those people were capable of being dangerous, but how dangerous? Nuisances and harassers rather than arsonists and murderers. How much was just talk? The preacher had let his congregation put themselves on display and they had willingly done so. He had not displayed himself, he had made no threats, barely offered an opinion that you could not hear any day from the shock jocks on the radio.

Harrigan drove back into the city, deep in thought. In the houses across the street from the Temple, the backup officers collected their belongings and left by the back way. The photographers and surveillance teams remained in place, watching everyone who came and went, twenty-four hours a day.

22

Lucy sat out on the back doorstep smoking, wrapped in her old coat, thinking that nothing existed except this time and this place. She would just take each minute as it was now, give it no other meaning than the sight of the light in the sky, each breath she took, each beat of her heart.

She was waiting to see her father. As the time came closer, she wondered why she wanted something quite so much as this. Her memory of him clung to her with the strength of a baby's grip. She wanted to cut him loose and then just to live, in each instant, without any connection to the past or the future, without weight. Just to exist in pure, unending light. When her phone rang, she thought, someone is chasing me. Why? I haven't anything to give them. I have nothing. All I do is exist.

'Lucy,' the preacher said in an angry voice. 'How are you?'

'I told you not to call me, Graeme,' she replied, uninterested. 'I said I'd call you.'

'I had to call you, Lucy,' he said, 'I have some very bad news for you.'

'What?' She was suddenly frightened.

'I can't get there tonight. You will have to wait until tomorrow when I can put other arrangements in place.'

'Why?'

'Because I am being watched by the police.'

'How do they know about you?' she asked.

'Through Greg, Lucy. How else? You had to tell him what you'd done. And because of that, they are at my door. They believe I'm involved. Which is all they need to think to make themselves troublesome.'

'Well, you are involved, aren't you, Graeme? So they're not wrong there,' Lucy replied with a grin. 'Anyway, how do you know they're watching you?'

'Because one of them came down here today. He sat in the congregation, he insulted everyone, he was so much better than the rest of us. He thinks he is so clever. He will find out that he is not. He has no power, whatever he thinks. You go and find yesterday's paper, Lucy. You'll see him in there. Swollen with arrogance like the sons of Belial.'

Lucy's hands were shaking, she swallowed fear.

'In the paper,' she said, mechanically.

'Yes. You look at that face and you'll see the son of the devil.'

'You don't know that. He could be anyone. He could be someone's father for all you know.'

'It doesn't matter who this person is, Lucy, he is still our enemy. He is someone who does not deserve to live. You know who people are when you see who they consort with. Now you listen to me, I am telling you this.' Lucy was silenced by the fury that came across the line. 'I have seen who they are. I have been there. I have walked into their den, I have sat and talked with them. I have seen who works there. I met one and I knew her. I knew her face, I knew that name. Because I know who these people are, I make it my business to know. And when I got back to the Temple I searched our catalogue of witches and yes, there she was. That is who we are dealing with, Lucy. With the —'

'I don't care about any of that just now, Graeme.'

She cut him off ruthlessly.

'There's only one thing I care about now and that's Greg. I've got a car now and some money and I just want to get hold of Greg and go north, go away, wherever. So you don't have to worry about anything, because I am just going to go away and forget about you all. And you had better let me do that. Because I really don't care what happens to me. But I bet you care what happens to you. I'll see you tomorrow night. You be there. You can do it.'

'Lucy, there are certain things you should think about first.' The preacher's voice had become calm. 'Wherever you go, the police will find you. And what are you going to do then?'

'How are they going to find me? They don't know who I am. They can't prove anything. No one's going to tell them about me. You won't. Greg won't.'

Neither would Stephen, he would just pretend that he had never known in the first place. Despite this, Lucy's confidence was shaken.

'No,' the preacher replied in his usual voice, 'that's very true. Greg will not betray you, Lucy, now or ever. I'll see you tomorrow night in that case. I'm sure we have a great deal to talk about. Goodbye.'

He was gone more quickly than she expected. She was sitting there wondering why he had cut the line so abruptly when Melanie touched her on her shoulder.

'Do you want to see Dad now?' she asked. 'He's awake and he's looking rested at the moment.'

'Yeah, okay. I'll just get myself together first.'

'That's all right. I'll tell him you'll be a couple of minutes.'

This early July afternoon, the door to her father's room was open to her. As Lucy approached, she smelled the coldness and cleanliness of the outside air. The windows had been opened, the smell of sickness was being cleaned out, if only temporarily. The room looked out over the national park, Lucy could see the high white clouds in the wide curve of a pale sky and the sea of trees reaching to the horizon.

Her father sat up against his pillows, his arms resting on floral sheets. As she stood hesitantly in the doorway, he spoke to her.

'My little girl,' he said.

She did not reply. She looked around. Melanie was sitting in a chair near the window.

'Come on in. Come and talk to your old man. Come and give me a kiss,' he said.

She stood at the end of the bed. It was old-fashioned with a slatted wooden bedhead and she rested her hands on it, looking at him. She was seeing him in x-ray, every impurity had been burned away by sickness, only a faint pale fire remained inside him which was consuming itself. The man she had known four years ago no longer existed. Only the voice was the same, that cajoling voice persuading you to what he wanted, to believe what he said. Seeing him, she realised she did not have to tell him that she had nothing to forgive him for. There was no compulsion on her to do so. She could walk out of here now and it would all be over soon in any case; Melanie and Stephen would be released.

'Don't just stand there, Lucy. Come and give your old man a kiss.'

She realised with a faint shock that she could do this. She went up to him and kissed him on the forehead and, for a short moment, felt the dry texture of his skin, something she had known well, something she had tried to scrub away, sometimes ferociously. She found herself shrugging the memory away as something finally used up, a cicada's shell, brittle and transparent.

'We've got nothing to blame each other for, have we? You're going to tell me that, aren't you, Luce?'

'I used to have, Dad,' she said, speaking at last. 'But I don't any more. You say you don't blame me for leaving you and Mum and not telling you where I was going. And now I don't care about what's happened between us. I can't hurt you any more and you can't hurt me. You can't do anything to me ever again. So I am just going to walk away from you all.'

'Luce ...'

Melanie spoke fearfully, leaning forward in her chair, her body tensed, but their father was not quite listening.

'You don't have anything to hold against me,' he said. 'You said that.'

She opened her mouth to say that she did and he should know that; it was just that she was finishing with him. But she did not speak it. She looked at him. The man lying in bed before her had been reduced to the fragility of a broken spider's web.

'No, I don't, Dad. You can sleep on that.'

It was as much as she could say to him but it was enough.

'I knew that's what you thought in your heart of hearts. I knew you understood me. Everything between us, it didn't matter. It was normal, you know that. I knew you'd get over the blame game one day,' he said.

'Yeah, okay, Dad. It is all over. I'll go now,' she said, needing to be out of there.

He nodded, his eyes were closing. At the door Melanie caught her by the hand briefly.

'Thanks for doing that,' she said.

Lucy smiled without meaning it and was gone. She went downstairs, out of the back door and found the dog sitting in her kennel. 'Come on, girl,' she said and the dog followed her, down into the garden, to the escarpment.

Lucy stopped part of the way down to look at a camellia bush: the blossoms were a pale pink and damp with the night's rain, the leaves shining in the sun. It had been one of her grandmother's favourites for the colour and the shape of the flower. Lucy looked at it without any words in her head to describe it; it became an image fixed permanently in her mind as something solely visual. She had lost the power of speech, of thought based on the use of words. The impressions in her mind were of images, of what was felt and seen only, her knowledge of language had been washed out of her. She stood there for some moments before walking down through the garden and then into the bushland. Eventually, she stopped to sit at the edge of the stream and, in this space, to forget the world existed until she went out into it again. She would sleep at the house tonight and then, in the very early dawn, she would be gone.

23

I don't doubt that. I hope indeed you find him very soon.

The preacher's voice was touched with rhetoric even in conversation. The tape of the prayer meeting finished and the incident room became quiet.

'That must have been a fun two hours for you, Boss,' Trevor commented, as the assembled team began to shift and stretch in the relieved silence.

'You are not joking. Don't cry on my shoulder today, I'll have rheumatism for the rest of my life after sitting through that,' Harrigan replied.

'We are in the darkness, you and I. Come with me and I'll show you the way to the light,' Grace said in her own clear voice. 'He can really project, he goes out after you. He could probably sing pretty well if he wanted to. It's such a pure voice.'

There was an edge to her words. Harrigan looked at her. Sometime during the morning while he had been out, she had disappeared back into her regulation dress and make-up. She was watching with the others as Ian pinned to the corkboard pictures of the photographer and the gadfly who had ambushed her outside the Whole Life Health Centre clinic a little over eight months ago. Both had been photographed as they left the prayer meeting that morning and now were being posted to the board for display, observation, dissection.

'Can you tell that just by listening to him, Gracie?' Ian asked.

'It's one of the things that makes him so easy on the ear. If you can forget the garbage he's talking at you.'

'I'm glad you said that, Gracie. The shit those people were talking would turn your stomach,' Trevor said.

'Okay, Ian. What can you tell us about these two acolytes?' Harrigan asked, stymieing any possible discussion on the nature of opinions which, to his knowledge, were not so very far removed from those of some people in the room.

'Enough to know they've missed their calling — they should be on this job,' he replied. 'They're regular protesters outside the Whole Life Health Centre clinics, they travel from clinic to clinic. How do they track the clients down? They buy confidential information from government sources and we're pretty sure we know who their contact is. They get an ID first and they chase it up. Sometimes they follow the women back to their cars and get their registration numbers, sometimes they do it some other way. There have been break-ins at the clinics and some medical records have been stolen. They work at it, it gives them something to do with their lives.'

'That lump of lard isn't the Firewall,' Louise grumbled,

staring at the picture of the woman Bronwyn. There's no sign of a mind in that face. It takes a mind to put the Firewall's website together, twisted or not.'

'Well, we know she's not,' Ian replied, 'but she'd send the doc her hate mail and like doing it. These two, they do what they're told. For them, it's how high do I jump, where's the cliff?'

'What about the preacher?' Harrigan said, moving things along. 'What do we know?'

Trevor walked forward and laid down a folder of papers on the metal table, then smoothed down his short black hair with one hand, collecting his thoughts.

'It wasn't that easy to track him down. We started with the resumé he gave Family Services and, give him his due, he's what he says he is, a travelling preacher. He says he studied theology at the Freedom World Theological College, Illinois. That's a joke, folks. Freedom World is a trailer park out of Chicago. Send money and the postbox will send you the piece of paper. They'll even fax it to you if you've got a tight deadline the way we did and don't mind paying for it. We got one for Ian for his birthday. Happy Birthday, mate, you've got a whole new life in front of you. Congratulations.'

There was laughter throughout the room as Trevor pinned an ornate degree awarded in Ian's name onto the corkboard next to a photograph of the preacher. He stood with his hands on his hips.

'Okay. You're skint and you're cooling your heels at Mascot for the first time in twenty-five years. Who are you going to call? Auntie Yvonne Lindley. She puts you up. Why not? She's sitting at home all alone in that mausoleum of hers out at north St Ives. Glad to have the company. Want a recommendation to the Family

Services Commissioner for your community care refuge? Auntie Yvonne will get you one written on the Minister's letterhead. She even lets you have a couple of her buildings rent-free, courtesy of the Lindley Family Property Trust.'

'She's eighty plus, isn't she?' Ian said. 'She must be past it by now.'

'Sharp as the day she was born, Ian,' Louise croaked, 'and with about as much sense.'

'Careful what you say,' Trevor continued, 'the family will have you round signing forms to have her carted away. Word is she wants to write her kiddies out of her will and write the preacher in. This is where you get told to stop pushing the envelope and fuck off, mate. Geoff Lindley tells you to butt out or he will close you down. Result? Mother bars son from house. Check. Elizabeth Lindley lets everyone know that poor dear old Mum's lost it, it is just so sad, folks, maybe it's time to call in the family doctor and get her declared mentally unfit. Checkmate. End of the current state of play. Life is not as rosy as it was in the land of Lindley.'

'Does he have any money of his own?' Harrigan interrupted. 'He must have some somewhere, surely.'

'Nothing that we can find and, believe me, we've looked,' Trevor said. 'So if the supply gets cut here, what does he fall back on? We don't know.'

'It'd be good to cut the supply and find out. Make him sweat,' Ian said.

'If he can sweat. Maybe he can't,' Louise reflected.

'Let's go over to the States,' Trevor said. 'Why go there in the first place? There's no answer to that one. Your parents are dead. You spend a little time here studying to be a minister but you don't finish it. Nothing to keep you round here. But why the States?

Because it meant not being here? Because there you can buy yourself a piece of paper and it makes you a preacher? He's the only one who can tell us that. Meanwhile ...'

He pinned up onto the corkboard a photograph of a group of ordinary-looking people with humourless faces and dressed in shabby clothes.

'Oh, God, look at them. Meet the Addams Family,' Grace said.

There was some laughter at this, including from Harrigan.

'No, Gracie, this is the Life Support Group.' Trevor was grinning. 'These are the people who stalked Agnes Liu when she was in California. They are way out on the far side of the pro-life movement. Ask them about abortion and they will tell you it's Satanic sacrifice. Women get pregnant so they can go and have abortions and then become witches and work for Satan. That's where these people connect to the world.'

'Nothing like being in touch with reality,' Louise muttered.

'You said it, Lou. These people are classic urban terrorists. Clinic bombings, threats, harassment, it's all in a day's work for them. One of them is in gaol for arson as we speak. You can look her up on the Net. She's got her own website, she's a prisoner of God. Is there a connection between these people and the preacher? We could not get one scrap of information out of our American cousins on this bunch, they wouldn't talk to us. So we did what everybody does when they're stuck — we went and found our very own Deep Throat. And that's the journalist who wrote that story.'

There were howls of derision as Trevor pointed to the print-out from the Internet news service that carried the headline: AVENGING ANGELS' DEADLY STRIKE. POLICE FAIL TO MAKE ARREST AFTER DOCTOR SHOT BY EXTREME ANTI-ABORTION GROUP.

Trevor brushed the commotion away with an airy wave of his hand. 'Laugh as much as you want. But when we got in contact with her, she gave us information. Pages of it. This for starters.'

He pinned up the photocopy of an article from a Californian weekend magazine which had the lead line: IN THE DARK MIND OF EXTREMITY: THE BLOODY CONSEQUENCES OF MILLENARIAN BELIEF IN THE ANTI-ABORTION MOVEMENT. STORY BY JANE MONAHAN.

'What's all that crap about?' Jeffo asked.

'All you need to know, mate, is that you're looking at this woman, Jane Monahan's, life. Writing exposés like this one. That's all she does. It seems she was a good friend of Laura Di-Cuollo. When that investigation went nowhere, she picked it up in the press. When we got in touch with her, she didn't want to stop talking. She knows a lot about the Angels: according to her they've got more than one shooting behind them. Trouble for us is, how much of her info can we use? Most of it would get thrown out by any half-decent lawyer. But it fits. She knows Fredericksen, he's mentioned in her latest article but just in passing. He was living in the vicinity of Berkeley at the same time the doc was there and had a set-up very similar to the one he's got here now: rich benefactor, political connections, a private church. Except he wasn't the main man, he was more of a sidekick. People active within the Life Support Group were connected to his church. This woman's talked to people who've moved away from that group and some of them knew our man. The "nice talker" one of them called him, the man who sets things up. And she knows about the gun that shot her friend. She says she got the ballistics information out of the police forensic lab by paying for it — would you believe, she actually told me that — and if it's true, I can tell you that the same type of gun — not the *same* gun, but the same type — that shot Di-Cuollo also shot our doc. It's a modified pistol and Monahan tells me it's a calling card for the Angels. The preacher left the States not long after that shooting. Everything was a bit too warm for him. He's connected, but we've got nothing except our journalist friend to help us prove it.'

'But is the Firewall one of them?' Grace asked.

'That doesn't matter just at the moment,' Harrigan said, speaking to her again for the first time since that morning. 'We know he's connected. What she is is something we ask her when we find her.'

A short silence followed.

'It's a game then,' Grace said eventually. 'He likes playing with other people's lives. It's a blood sport for him, it gives him a high. It's not money. It's the rush.'

'Yeah, whatever, Gracie,' Trevor said.

Harrigan found himself looking at her again.

'Okay,' he said, 'that's good, that's all good. That's taken us a lot further along the road. Keep digging. And while we do that, we watch the preacher's every move and we see what happens. We've got to turn up something soon.'

'Like a body maybe?' Trevor asked him as they all left the room. 'Say, like poor old Greggie's?'

'If I'm going to be honest about it, Trev, I think hell will freeze over before we find that kid,' Harrigan said.

Grace, moving past him, glanced at him as he said this. Before he could speak to her she was gone into the crowd.

* * *

Cafeteria coffee was not Harrigan's favourite beverage but as he needed both caffeine and a break from the team it was his best choice. He had sat down to drink it when he saw Grace out on the terrace, leaning against the railing and looking out at the cityscape as she smoked a cigarette. After some moments' thought, he went out to join her. She looked up in surprise as he appeared. She greeted him and then again looked out at the jumble of roofs and high-rise.

'How are you?' he asked.

'Fine.'

Yes, he could see that.

'I'm sorry I ripped into you this morning,' he said. 'It was out of order for me to say that to you in front of everyone. You're doing a good job, Grace. I'm not trying to make your life more difficult.'

She stood upright and shrugged, ever so slightly.

'Thanks. But I wish I had left my phone on. I wish I had taken that call,' she said.

'What could you have done? We would have known a bit sooner and that's about all. Don't take it on.'

'It's more that it's all of a piece. That kid sends his last message out to the world and I wasn't even there to hear it.'

'Where were you?' he asked, a question he knew he had no business asking.

'Sleeping on an old friend's couch,' she answered lightly, with a slight touch of steel and a sharp glance at him. 'Somewhere I go when I'm feeling stretched.'

They stood in awkward silence while Harrigan tried to think of something intelligent to say in reply.

'I wasn't trying to be *abrupt* when I left last night,'

she said before he had the chance. 'I'm sorry if it came over like that. I think I was feeling a bit worn.'

You take so much on, Grace. Why do you think any of these people are worth it from you?

'Don't worry about it,' he said, 'it doesn't matter. We all get worn. We've all got too much work to do.'

'Yeah. I'll just finish my cigarette.'

'No, it's okay, Grace. I'm not rushing you. Take your time. I'll see you later.'

'Yeah, sure,' she said, embarrassed by her hypersensitivity.

He walked back to his office, a little lighter in spirit than he had felt all day. The watchers inside the cafeteria had no idea that they had just witnessed the unprecedented event of Harrigan apologising to a member of his team.

24

Less than an hour after he had spoken to her in the cafeteria, Harrigan startled Grace by appearing without warning at her desk, with his tie loose and his sleeves rolled up. He handed her a file and leaned on the desk with both hands.

'She's just a little prostitute,' he said. 'I've told her I'm offering her immunity if her story checks out, but so far she's being very cagey with the details and I don't know why. I want you to talk to her on your own. You have to put her at her ease. You can do that, I've seen you do it before. Read that file and think about it. Bring your cigarettes with you when you're ready. She's asked if she can smoke and I've told her she can. She's smoking like the proverbial at the moment.'

He disappeared in the direction of the interview room. Grace drew breath and opened the file, and thought, you're on, girl, better tune up the vocal chords. The head shot showed an olive-skinned girl, her shoulder-length dark hair dyed with blonde streaks. Gina Farrugia, aged twenty-two, resident of Potts Point. One conviction for possessing a trafficable amount of heroin. Released into the detox program seven months ago. Known associates: one lover, Mike Sullivan, ex-boxer, sometime bouncer, small-time dealer, occasional police informer, addict. That was all. A thin file. When she reached the interview room, Trevor was waiting with Harrigan.

'You ready, Gracie?' he asked her.

'Sure.'

'Keep it gentle and take your time. I've told her who you are. You remember — I want this information,' Harrigan said.

How could she forget?

Grace opened the door expecting to feel ordinary tensions filling the air, zigzags of apprehension and defensiveness. The atmosphere in the grey box this afternoon had another quality to it. The young woman looking up at her exuded an animal smell, fear, something as palpable as a small rustling creature curled up tightly into a corner of the room, head pressed to the wall. The air was heavy with cigarette smoke, the ashtray filled with ash and stubs. An empty cigarette packet lay beside it.

'Hi, Gina,' Grace said to a barely perceptible nod. 'How are you?'

There was no direct reply. As she sat down, she saw Gina's gaze shift past her to the blank eye in the wall.

'Who's watching us?' the girl asked.

'You don't have to worry about that. You're just talking to me. Do you want my card?'

The girl glanced at the card and pocketed it.

'Don't I have to worry about that?' she said to Grace. 'You know something I don't, do you?'

'No. There's just nothing for you to worry about. No one here's going to do anything to you. Do you want a cigarette?'

'Yeah.'

Grace lit both their cigarettes and put the packet and her lighter in the middle of the table.

'Help yourself,' she said.

The girl nodded. She sat there, smoking quickly, and then spoke too quickly.

'If you want to know why I didn't come in before — I couldn't get here. That's the truth. I just couldn't get here. I would have come in sooner if I could have.'

'That's not an issue for me, Gina. As far as I'm concerned, you're here now and that's all that matters. The only question for me is what you've got to tell me.'

'That's something else, isn't it? There's a reward, isn't there? $25,000? I need to know. Would I get that?'

'You certainly could. If you've got information, then you should get at least a part of it. Maybe all of it. It would depend on what you've got to tell us. Is that very important to you?'

'I just need to know, that's all. When would I get it?'

'You need it soon, do you?'

'Yeah, I do.'

'Probably as soon as you want it, in that case. But it all does depend on what you've got to say. Why don't you just relax for a bit and think about what you've got to tell me? We've got plenty of time if you need it.'

There was a brief pause. Gina was tapping ash into the ashtray, frowning. She glanced up at Grace and then at the blank window again. Grace saw panic in the girl's face, a split in the fabric, control briefly lost and then regained. She ashed her cigarette and picked up the packet, turning it over and over in her hands before taking out another cigarette and lighting it.

'What if I want something else? I mean, what if I want something besides the money?'

'What else do you want?'

'Couple of hours? Of your time. Would you do that for me? Just a couple of hours.' Her hands were shaking as she looked at Grace. 'That's all I want. And the money. When I get it.'

'Why do you want my time?' Grace asked.

'I just do. You don't have to worry, nothing's going to happen. I promise. And I do promise.'

'You want two hours of my time? What do you want to do?'

'What do I want to do?' The girl bit her lip. 'Nothing really. I just want the company. You know all that junk food, chips and that? It's my favourite food, I love it. Do you want to have a hamburger with me? One with everything? We could do that.'

'I don't mind,' Grace replied equably. 'I like junk food when I'm in the mood. You want me to go and have a hamburger with you? We can do that. What else do you want to do?'

'Just sit somewhere and talk. That's all. That really is all I want.'

'That's all?'

'Yeah.'

Grace was silent for a moment. The girl crushed out her half-smoked cigarette and waited.

'Why do you want that, Gina?' Grace asked.

'I just want the company, that's all.'

'Have another cigarette,' she said and waited while the girl lit it up.

'There isn't anyone else you want to be with for two hours?' she asked.

The girl shook her head without speaking.

'Gina,' Grace said, 'what happens after two hours?'

'You just go home.'

'But what do you do?'

'I go to work.'

'You're still working?'

'Yeah. It keeps the money coming in. I just don't want to be alone this evening.'

'You could stay here.'

'No,' she looked around at the ugly room, 'I don't want to stay here. I want to be out there. It's just that my boyfriend's not around and I don't know where he is right now. I get worried about him. I didn't want to be alone out there just thinking about him.'

'Okay,' Grace said after a pause, 'I think I can do that. That shouldn't be a problem.'

'Have you got some coffee? Some really strong coffee. I really would like a coffee,' the girl said, almost desperately.

'Yeah, I'll get you some coffee.'

At that moment, Harrigan knocked on the door and asked Grace to step outside.

'What do you think you're doing?' He sounded outraged. 'You don't know what she's planning. You could be walking into anything.'

'I don't think she's planning anything. She's genuine.'

'Genuine is not the point.' Harrigan could have been talking to a slow child. 'It's what's waiting for you when you get out there with her.'

'She's just a girl. I can deal with it,' Grace said, keeping her reciprocal outrage under wraps as best she could.

'Boss,' Trevor intervened, 'why don't we wait and see

what she's got for us? If Gracie's out with her she's got to be careful, but she should be able to handle it. That's what she's paid to do. We'll have backup out there for her.'

Harrigan glanced at him angrily before looking through the one-way glass once again.

'The air in there — how can you breathe it?' he said to Grace, who did not reply.

Both of them watched him calm down. On the other side of the one-way eye, the girl watched without seeing them, her face expressionless, like a rabbit sitting blankly in a set of car lights. Grace looked once and looked away.

'Get her some coffee and let's get on with it,' Harrigan finally said.

The coffee was sent for. Gina sipped it and lit yet another cigarette.

'Has your boss made up his mind? Or are you going to back out on me?'

'No, we've still got a bargain, Gina,' Grace said. 'And you've still got things to tell us. It could be worth a lot of money to you.'

Gina grinned in reply, a thin and bitter smile.

'Yeah. I guess. Something to look forward to, isn't it? But this has got to be worth something. Because we were there. The morning that shooting happened. In that little shop? It's just a place people go, we'd been there all night. Me and Mike in that shitty little room. It was so fucking cold. He'd had a hit and he got sick, but I guess you noticed that when you went in there.' She sipped more coffee and drew on her cigarette. 'It was getting light and I wanted us to get out of there but I couldn't shift him. Then I heard someone coming in the back way and down that hallway. And I thought, we're getting out of here now if there's someone else around. I got Mike on his feet and out the back somehow, I don't know how, and I sort of had him leaning in this doorway at the back of the warehouse there. I saw there was this car there and I thought, good, we're going to take that. Then I heard these shots. These really loud cracks, you know, one after the other. I couldn't believe it, I was so shit scared. It was like Mike just woke up, right then. We were standing in this little doorway staring at each other. And she came out the back. Running. She had this gun. I was just staring. Then she tripped, you know? She fell and this gun, she dropped it and it went skidding somewhere, I don't know where. I didn't see where it ended up. I thought it went in a drain or something. And then she got up and she got in the car. Like she hadn't even noticed she'd fallen down. She had this thing around her face but in the car she was pulling it off. Just kind of ripping it away like she couldn't breathe. She drove right past us really fast. I don't know how she didn't see us. I don't know what she was looking at. We didn't wait around, we just got out of there. We got a taxi out on Broadway. Some drivers don't care, you just have to wave your money around and they'll pick you up anyway. Doesn't matter what you look like.'

There was silence. Grace could sense Harrigan leaning on the glass outside the room, waiting.

'Did you see her face, Gina? Can you give us any kind of a description?' she asked.

Gina smiled to herself and took another cigarette, lighting it from the end of the one she was smoking.

'You going to keep your word?' she asked.

The thin and fixed smile was still on her face. Grace felt a small shock as she watched the girl's expression.

'Have you got a name for us, Gina?' she asked.

'Yeah, I do. But I have to know if you're going to keep your word first.'

'I'll keep my word.'

'I knew her. That was the thing. I knew who she was. She was a friend of mine once.' The girl rubbed her forehead, her face haggard. 'Lucy Hurst. Yeah, Lucy. I liked her, you know. I never thought I'd do this to her.'

On the other side of the glass, Harrigan stood upright. 'Yes!' he said. 'Got you!'

'Do you have an address?' Grace asked.

'No, I don't know where she came from. She used to hang around near where I worked. She used to buy from me sometimes, if you really want to know. That's how we got to know each other.'

'She was an addict?'

'Sort of. She moved in and out a bit, she was someone who could do that. She'd binge sometimes. I used to think she was playing some kind of funny game of her own, I don't know what. Lucy could be really strange.'

'She didn't work herself?'

'Oh, no. No way. No one got within cooee of Luce. I'm not saying she didn't get jumped on while she was out there, she did. That happens, you just can't do anything about that. But she never got involved with anyone. She used to hang with this kid called Greg. But they were just friends, you know, they never did it or anything like that. And she had this brother who used to come around looking for her sometimes. His name was Stevie.'

'Can you do an identikit for me?' Grace asked.

'Yeah, I'm good with faces. I've got to remember the ones I don't want to see again.'

'One more question, Gina.'

'Yeah?'

'Why did you take so long to come in here with that information?'

The girl drew a circle on the edge of the ashtray with her cigarette. She stared up at Grace with a look that seemed to be waiting for some kind of blow, violence of some kind, as if she had withdrawn into herself before this expectation. It was a look that said she had never grown used to it.

'I really couldn't get here before. I couldn't.'

'But now you can. Because you want the money?'

'How much of it am I going to get?'

Grace glanced at the blank window before she spoke.

'Quite a lot of it on that information. All of it, probably,' she replied.

'I've got to have it,' the girl said very softly, almost a whisper. 'I just have to.'

'It's okay, Gina. We can fix it up,' Grace said. 'Let's go and do the identikit.'

Outside the interview room, Trevor was waiting by himself.

'Harrigan wants to see you before you leave with her, mate,' he said quietly.

'Sure,' she replied, not without some anxiety.

Later, Grace placed the identikit, together with a statement, on Harrigan's desk. He picked up the slightly surreal picture: a robotic, not quite cartoon-like reproduction of a young woman's face. A face with high cheekbones, a wide forehead and short reddish-brown hair.

'Not a bad-looking face,' he said. 'Do you think this is reliable?'

'Yes, I do. She was very clear about it. No hesitation, didn't change her mind once.'

He put it back down on the desk. Outside in the main office, small groups of people had gathered to look at the picture as another copy did the rounds. There was a buzz of activity as his officers rang contacts, searched databases and checked lists for any addresses and possibilities.

'Where are you going?' he asked.

'The Cross.'

'How did I know that? Stay in contact. The last thing I want is anyone hurt.'

Or dead, but superstition prevented him from saying that aloud.

'I'd like to ring Matthew and let him know. Is that okay with you?' he asked.

'No, that's no problem,' she said. 'Don't let him find it out on the news.'

'Grace,' he said, as she stood up to go, 'this has got a very nasty smell to it. You have thought about that?'

'Yes, I've thought about that. I've thought about it quite a lot. What are we going to do about it? Go after Gina? Is that what we do now?'

'I'd like to. I'd like to charge her with withholding information. I'd like to throw the book at her for sitting on that name for all this time. But no, we don't do that. I'll tell someone else about her and maybe they'll go and look into whatever is going on. If they've got the time and the money. In the meantime, watch your back. Make sure you ring in when you're finished. You'd better get going.'

He went back to his papers, she walked out. Neither of them looked at each other, until the last moment when he looked up to see her walk out the door, just in time to see her glance back at him. Once she had gone, he rang the media unit, advising them he had an identikit on its way over to them to be released for saturation coverage. Then he rang the hospital and asked to speak to Matthew Liu.

25

'Where do you want to go first, Gina?' Grace asked as she eased out into the evening traffic.

It had clouded over and begun to rain, just lightly. Gina was lighting one more of Grace's cigarettes and looking at her side on. She leaned forward, bracing one hand on the dashboard. Her nails were bitten to the quick, her cigarette smoke curled up against the windscreen.

'Do you want to go to Maccas? I can show you where you can park.'

'Okay.'

Grace cruised up Liverpool Street. The bright lights of the traffic flowed around her.

The girl hummed a tune which Grace recognised. She sang along quietly.

'*Corinna, Corinna, where you been so long?/Corinna, Corinna where you been so long?/Got no home, baby, since you've been gone.*'

'You know it?'

'Yeah. I used to sing it once. I used to be a singer. That was a while ago now.'

'It couldn't have been that long ago. What did you give it away for?'

'Got sick of it. I wanted to do something else for a change.'

'It's my working name,' the girl said, 'Corinna. Because I like the song.'

'Yeah, I do too,' Grace replied.

'You've got a nice voice,' Gina said after a little while. 'I wouldn't have given it away if I could sing like you. I would have kept going.'

'Well, I didn't. I still don't want to. It wasn't that much fun after a while. It was just everyone wanting a piece of you.'

'Everything's like that, it doesn't matter what you do,' Gina replied. 'What you do now must be like that.'

Grace smiled. 'Maybe a bit. No, it's not the same,' she said. 'You're clean now, aren't you, Gina?'

'Yeah. I got my mind back. Weird.'

'How'd you do it?'

'It was that or gaol, wasn't it? I don't really know how, to tell you the truth. Just did, I suppose. I was helping Mike out. I thought maybe he could do something for himself. Stupid. He was never going to do that.'

'Attached to him, are you?' Grace said sympathetically.

'Yeah. You do get attached. People start to mean something to you.'

'They do. They get to you after a while.'

They get under your skin whether you want them to or not. Even if you're not sure what to make of them. Or what they think of you.

Gina found Grace a parking spot down towards Rushcutters Bay, near a large run-down terrace, its exterior painted in bright colours. A man sat on a nearby step, his arms tensed, rocking backwards and forwards in the light rain, lost in the drug. Grace looked at him and notched his existence into her mind, an imprint of the outside world. They walked past him up a narrow, dog-legged road. They went to McDonald's on Darlinghurst Road where they had hamburgers with everything, fries and hot apple pies.

'How well did you know Lucy, Gina? Do you want to tell me something more about her?' Grace asked, ploughing her way through the food.

'She used to come in here.'

Grace looked up more sharply at this answer. Gina had wiped her mouth clean and was looking around. Her gaze did not seem to have a focus as she stared at the people near her, most of whom looked away, some of them laughing. Her mouth was moving but she did not speak. Grace followed her stare.

'What is it?' she asked.

'Nothing.' Gina regained a toughness as she spoke. 'It's just that we all used to come in here. We'd sit and we'd talk and that. Just over there in the corner.' Grace looked at a large table, with seating for about six people. 'We'd sit in here all afternoon and we'd just laugh.'

'She really was your friend?'

'Yeah, she was. For a little while.'

'What happened?'

'Nothing really. Just time. You don't see people any more for all sorts of reasons. She can't be my friend now. She's going to gaol for ever because of me. And I don't know what's going to happen to me.'

'What do you think might happen to you?'

'I was just saying that. Anything can happen to anyone. You never know what's going to happen, you could walk under a truck tomorrow. But we used to come in here. We used to have fun. I wanted to have a look at it again because of that. Because they were good times. She'd say these things, she'd make you laugh. She wasn't frightened of anything.'

Grace glanced around at the plastic fittings, the bright lights against the light-coloured walls and mirrors.

'And she liked a hamburger as well?'

'She did. And a chocolate thickshake. That was her favourite meal.' Gina was shredding her used napkin into small soft snowflakes of paper. 'Do you want to go somewhere else and have some coffee? I want to get out of here now. I know a place where they have really nice baklava, they make it themselves. We can smoke in there. I need a cigarette.'

'That's fine with me. I could use a smoke too.'

They walked out into the damp, crowded night-time street, full of light and movement. Gina looked around, her mouth moving silently as it had in the restaurant.

'I used to work back down there a bit. You can get really tired by the end of the night. But I don't care about that, you know. I love it here. I do. There just isn't anywhere else for me.'

'Does there have to be anywhere else for you? If this is what you want,' Grace asked.

'I'm just saying it. It's really nice to be here right now.' She stretched her backbone, her mouth a little open, drinking in the soiled air. The rain touched her face, she laughed. 'It's just being here. That's all I want. Just for this little while.'

'I've got more time than a couple of hours if you want it, Gina,' Grace said. 'If you want help, I can try to help.'

'No, I've got to be somewhere. Let's go, okay?'

Inside the café near the other end of Crown Street the air was blue with cigarette smoke. They sat at a table at the back and were served thick sweet coffee and small diamonds of baklava dripping with honey.

'You know Lucy,' Gina said unprompted, 'she did things no one else would do. She could steal anything that wasn't tied down. She used to take orders.' The girl laughed. 'She got me clothes, all my make-up once. She never wanted any money for them, nothing. If she wanted any stuff for herself, she'd just go and take it. But then other times she just gave things away. She used to rip things off just to give them away. Anything. It was a game, that's what she was doing all the time. She used to say the whole world is crap so what does it matter what I do. That was her way of letting everyone know it. I don't really want to see things that way. You don't have to think like that. You've got to hope sometimes. Don't you think?'

'I do think that,' Grace said. 'Sometimes you just have to hang in there till things get better. Sometimes it's the only thing you can do.'

'Yeah, that's right. That is the way it is. That's how I see it.'

'What are you hoping for now, Gina?'

'That things will work out. What else would I want?'

The conversation faltered. The girl looked at her over her cigarette, a challenge in her eye.

'Did you ever do any sex work?' she asked. 'While you were singing maybe? You could have done. You could have made a lot of money.'

Grace shook her head, mindful that everything they said was being listened to and recorded.

'No, Gina, I've never sold sex. Just my voice,' she replied quietly.

Yes, her voice, that was all she had ever sold of herself. It had still been her though, up there on display on the stage. No, Gina, I don't sell sex, I never have, I never will. I give it away and sometimes I go out looking for it. That's my choice. Just so long as I can choose who and when and how, it's okay.

Gina was still talking.

'It's a good way to get money if you need it. But if you work the way I do, you've got to be careful about your customers. They could be anybody.'

So can the people you sleep with for nothing, for love or the passing need. It's all on the finest balance between love and hate and you never know what the man you're with might do next, no matter how close you get to him or how naked you both are.

There was silence.

'Are you armed? Have you got a gun?' the girl asked suddenly, aggressively.

Grace, whose firearm was nestled against her ribcage under her armpit, did not answer.

'You are, aren't you?' Gina said.

'Why do you want to know?'

'Well, if you really want to help me out, you can give it to me.'

Grace shook her head.

'If you want help, why don't you just come in, Gina? Talk to someone. Talk to me,' she said.

The girl laughed softly at her, shaking her head.

'What time is it?' she asked.

Grace looked at her watch. 'It's still early. Half past nine.'

They sat in silence for a little while longer. Grace watched Gina look down into the coffee cup, checking the thick black leavings, and then look up again. The girl's blank stare meant terror, nothing simpler. She shook back her hair.

'Time to go. I can't wait around any more,' she said but did not immediately move. 'Thanks for the talk. And the smokes.'

'Gina, ring me if you've got any more to tell me. You can get me on the numbers on that card any time. You remember that. Any time.'

'Yeah. Why not?'

They went out into the street. It had begun to rain heavily. The roadway was greasy in the wet, shining with the lights of passing cars.

'Do you want a lift somewhere?' Grace asked.

'Nup.'

Standing in the rain, the girl spread out her arms like a dancer about to spin out of a spotlight. She laughed aloud.

'See you sometime maybe, Gracie.'

'Gina . . .'

'What?'

'Remember you can call me.'

The girl laughed once again and then she was gone, half-walking, half-running along the empty street until she disappeared from sight.

Grace called in to say she was on her way back, and then sat in her car where it was parked off the road in another spot that Gina had found for her. She thought, I won't see that girl alive again. She sat quietening her breathing, letting her hands lie loose in her lap. You have to draw a line. You have to do that now.

She drove away, unable to follow the girl on the one-way street that channelled her car in the opposite direction. So where was Gina going now? Don't even think about it, because there's nothing you can do.

Once Grace had called in for the night, Harrigan collected his things and left. Trevor had already gone, leaving the graveyard shift ticking over ready for the next day. Harrigan left instructions for them to call him as soon as they had an address, an identification, anything at all. Lucy Hurst's picture was already appearing on late-night news broadcasts and Internet news services.

He did not go straight home but snatched another half hour and went via Cotswold House. Toby was still out of bed, waiting for him. As he entered the room, Toby signalled to him with his good hand.

'Hi, Toby,' Harrigan said, and looked over his shoulder at a website dedicated to mountain climbing in Peru.

Look dad See how steep it is? Do u know these mountains are really high Next highest after the Himalayas?

'No, I didn't know that,' he said. 'How are you?'

I'm ok I guess Wot about u??

'I'm okay, bit tired maybe. Toby, I've got something I've got to talk to you about.'

Wot????

Harrigan had sat down.

'Mate — I shouldn't be doing this, okay? I've got to ask you this. Are you going to warn her? If I tell you this.'

U know who she is??

'Yeah.'

Toby turned his wheelchair in a small circle to look at his father. His good hand rested on the keyboard.

U said u would find her Wots her name?

'Are you going to warn her?'

She's not talking 2 me dad I can't warn her

'You're out there looking for her.'

It's 2 late for u 2 ask me that now anyway dad I can just send her an email Firewall they know who u are be careful

'Will you?'

Why are u doing this?? Wot do you really want to know dad? Who I love more? Her or U?

'No, mate. It's not like that.' He hunted for an explanation. 'This way you know where we are. I don't know what's going to happen from now on in. I don't know what she's going to do, or even if she's going to walk away from this.'

Are u going 2 shoot her??? Is that wot u want 2 do??

'I don't use guns until I have to. That depends on what she does. If I can avoid it, I will.'

Why shouldn't I warn her then??? She's out there Maybe u're going to shoot her and if u don't, u're going to lock her away She's never been locked away before That's going to be horrible 4 her

'And if I don't reel her in, Toby? What's she going to do then? Kill someone else.'

Toby sat tapping his good hand on his desk. Harrigan watched his own gesture reflected back at him.

Sometimes I think she might I don't know what to do then

'You don't take that on, Toby. You call me, I keep doing what I can.'

They sat in silence for a little longer.

Can't save her Wish I could Who is she??

'Lucy Hurst, Toby. She's the Firewall. This is what she looks like.'

Toby manoeuvred the identikit to the centre of his desk with his good hand.

It looks funny

'Yeah. No one looks human in these pictures.'

I thought she would look a bit like that
'Why do you say that?'
I dont know It just looks right somehow She's sort of pretty don't u think?? I do It's not a bad face dad She doesn't look evil

'It's going out on every outlet in the city at the moment, Toby. We have to find her soon. Someone is going to tell us where she is.'

When u do will u ask her if she wants 2 talk 2 me? Coz I want 2 talk 2 her

'If that's what you want, yes, I will.'

They sat without speaking.

'Why do you want that, Toby? She told you to go away. Why ask her back?'

We're connected dad We understand each other I'm going to be here for her

'You and her?'

Yes her & me

How can you be connected to her?

'Whatever you want, Toby.'

U dont mind???

'No. It's whatever you want. Look, I'm going to go now, Toby. I've got to get some sleep while I can. I'm going to try and get back to see you but I don't know when that will be now. You email me if you need anything. Okay?'

Can I keep this??

'That's for you. I brought it for you.'

U & me are different dad She doesn't stop us from being who we are

She does that to me, Toby, even if you don't know that.

Even so, when he left Cotswold he felt a lessening of the pressures. It had to be finished with soon.

26

When Harrigan arrived home, he found Menzies curled up on the kitchen window ledge, snoring happily, shedding fur with the rise and fall of his rib cage and radiating the indefinable odour of old cat. He decided he would try his luck at sleeping as well and went to bed with some journalist's much hyped exposé of a well-known Sydney racing identity. The book was more entertaining for what it had wrong than any other feature and he could have written a fairly acidic, laugh-a-minute review along those lines if the information had not been so dangerous. Perhaps it did relax him. When, sometime before dawn, he was woken out of a deep sleep by the sound of the telephone, his bedside lamp was still on and the book was lying dropped on the coverlet. His first thought was for Toby; his second was for Lucy Hurst.

'Harrigan.'

'It's Grace here. I'm sorry to wake you up so early.'

She was the last person he was expecting to call him at this or any other hour. He sat up, the book falling to the floor with a light thud.

'What is it?' he asked.

'I've just had a call. From someone on the job I've never heard of before. They've found Gina. And her boyfriend.' She stopped and seemed to be gathering breath. 'They're both dead. They're in Surry Hills just off Foveaux. I've been asked to go down there. But I've been asked to go alone and without telling anyone I work with. He said just come by yourself and we'll work out the rest later. I don't see why it has to happen like that.'

'Who is this?'

'Jerry Freeman. Do you know the name?'

Shit! Harrigan thought.

'Yes, I do happen to know Jerry. Why did he call you?'

'Gina had my card in her pocket. He said it made him curious.'

'Where are you now?'

'I'm still in my flat.'

'Give me twenty minutes. I'll meet you there. Don't get there before me. Okay?'

'Yeah, okay. But who is this person?'

'Ask me that question later, Grace.'

If Freeman was up to his old tricks, then this slotted in under the heading of Murphy's law at work and the unpleasant odour Harrigan had detected last night had just got a lot nastier. As he showered and dressed, he wondered if his old sparring partner had even bothered to call in the pathologist or the crime scene people. He drove through Birchgrove up to Darling Street in the strange quiet between sleeping and waking. It was still raining, the roads were slippery with oil. He approached the city, the lights of the tower blocks were distant in the darkness of the early morning, slurred with the rain.

When he reached Foveaux, his car lights illuminated an inner city landscape of factory outlets selling cheap clothing and dark shop windows barred up against the street. Racks of clothes, ranged like the outlines of people, disappeared into the shadows. Bright lights surrounded a small crowd of police cars and people near the entrance to a short dog-legged alley several blocks up from Central Station. A few bystanders, derelicts and alcoholics were watching from a distance, dark figures gathered on the edge of the light. At least there were other people on the scene and it wasn't only Freeman leaning against a car, waiting for Grace to show up. Harrigan parked his car and then introduced himself to the sergeant in charge. From a distance, he looked briefly at the bodies on the other side of the ribbons, before standing aside to wait, having no desire to be involved. Freeman, a big man who was fifty plus, overweight and balding, appeared from out of the crowd.

'Good morning, mate,' he said, 'haven't seen you for a while. Thought you'd still be in bed. I was looking for your girl. She must be the careful type if she went and called you up. Unless you were there when I rang. What happened? You get lucky, did you?'

He guffawed and slapped Harrigan on the arm.

'No, mate, I was home alone,' Harrigan replied, shaking the man off. 'But good morning, Jerry, it's nice to see you too. What do you want her for?'

'Just a couple of questions, my friend, nothing else. Easy as pie for her. Why not? I hear she's a good-looking woman. I'm looking forward to meeting her.'

'I might have a few questions of my own first. What did this girl have to do with you?' Harrigan asked.

'Let's just say her and her boyfriend have been helping us out with our inquiries on a range of matters lately, but they're not going to be doing that any more, are they? What was she doing for you?'

'She was our witness. Just by chance. She happened to be in the wrong place at the wrong time. For her that is, not for us.'

'Not for that chinkie who got shot? She won't be singing for you now, mate. Bit of bad luck for you.'

Someone called out to Freeman before Harrigan could reply and he took the opportunity to walk away while the man was distracted. Grace was later arriving than he had expected. Then a taxi came to a halt on a nearby corner and she got out.

'What happened to your car?' he asked, walking up to her.

She was dressed for work, with her hair braided over one shoulder, but her face was clear of its usual pancake.

'The alternator's gone, I think. It's going to be one of those days.' She glanced towards the flashing blue lights where the incident team was going about its work. 'That's where they are — over there?'

'Yeah. Neither of them look very nice. Are you up to dealing with it?'

'Yes, I can deal with that. I'll follow you.'

Under the flicker of the ultraviolet lights and the more distant glare of the street lamps, Gina Farrugia sat against a mossy brick wall on the corner of an alleyway, side by side with her boyfriend and leaning against his shoulder. Patches of bright and dark red covered his yellow T-shirt. Kenneth McMichael had finished his examination and was packing his bag. Harrigan watched the incident team gather like circling sharks while Grace hunched down and looked into Gina Farrugia's face. Her head drooped forward like a stone carving of wilted flowers, tied about the stem with red string.

'Don't quote me just yet but not much more than a few hours at the most for the both of them.' McMichael was adjusting his dirty coat like a flasher. 'She was raped beforehand, I'd say, very likely more than once. That looks like ordinary plastic rope to me, the kind you can buy in any supermarket. So I would say her first, then him. I think that was probably the point. He got to watch. There is a question of how long it took. Let's hope it was quicker than it seems. It's all over now anyway.'

Harrigan watched him shamble away into the dark, his brown polyester trousers flapping at half mast, and felt a powerful sense of relief that he had not been found like this ten years ago.

'Dumped, were they?' he asked a young officer with close-cropped hair and a face like a choir boy.

'Looks that way. It didn't happen here and they didn't walk here afterwards.' Freeman reappeared, elbowing the choir boy out of the way. 'This your girl, is it, mate? Aren't you going to introduce me?'

'Don't call me a girl,' Grace said.

'No need to be like that. I just want to have a friendly chat. Put a face to the name. Nothing for you to get upset about.' Freeman studied Grace's face at his leisure while he got out his notebook. 'If you want to give me a few details. Where and when you last saw her. What you talked about. That sort of thing.'

'Jerry,' Harrigan intervened, 'we've got a tape of all that. You can have a transcript if you want.'

'What about the tape?'

'You don't need that. A transcript's just as good.'

'Just let me talk to your girl, mate. Let's not have any fuss, okay? Just let me get this out of the way.'

'Do you mind?' Harrigan asked Grace.

'I don't care. I don't think we said anything to each other that couldn't be in the paper today if someone wanted to print it.'

Freeman only grinned.

Harrigan stood by and listened irritably as Freeman tried on Grace all the tricks, traps and travesties of truth that he would have tried if he had been interviewing her. There was no joy in having it known that he had sent one of his people into a minefield where Jerry Freeman was also tramping around. If nothing else, the story made him look a fool in the telling. Finally the man closed his notebook and strolled off, grinning again as he said goodbye. By then, Gina and her boyfriend had been lifted away and the incident team had packed up their wares. All that remained were the patches of slightly darker stains on the wet bitumen and police ribbons flapping in the wind. Grace stood silent for a few moments, looking at the wall and the dark stains. Out on Foveaux, the small group of watchers stood by for a few moments longer before disappearing into the streetscape.

'Do you want a coffee?' Harrigan asked.

'Where can we get a decent one at this hour? Yes, I would. And a cigarette. I think I must have smoked more in the last week than I usually do in a month.'

'This isn't relaxation, Grace, it's work. We've got a few things to talk about. I know a place that makes the best coffee in Sydney and it never closes. You can smoke in there as well. I'll drive. It's not far.'

Harrigan was feeling guilty. It was a rare emotion. Protecting his officers' backs was one thing; concerning himself with their personal feelings was another.

It was an older-style café, like a milk bar, long and thin, the air stale, with cardboard boxes stacked beside the back exit. The man behind the counter had his silver and black hair tied back in a ponytail and greeted Harrigan by his first name. He drew on his own cigarette before he put saucers on the counter top.

'Mind if we use the room?' Harrigan asked.

'Sure, mate. I just cleaned it up. Go on through.'

'Why are we in here?' Grace asked, leaving her coat on against the cold, looking around at a wood-panelled room hung with photographs of soccer teams. Ashtrays on individual stands had been placed around a small and rickety card table. She sat down. Harrigan turned on a heater and the smell of burning dust competed with the faint sharpish smell of old cigarette smoke. He took off his jacket and sat opposite her.

'We need the privacy,' he replied as the coffee arrived. The counterman looked Grace over as he left the room. Harrigan waited while she lit a cigarette and she looked at him expectantly, a little wary.

'How do you know about this place?' she asked.

'I come here and play cards from time to time. When I can afford to lose the money. I've got to ask you this. Was that the whole truth, like they say? Or were you being economical when you were talking to Jerry?'

'No. That's what happened. Why would I lie about it? It's all on the tape.'

'Because I have to be sure. When you get back in, you write this up. Exactly what you told him. Give it to me and I'll sign it. You get a transcript of the tape to go with it. You get one copy hand-delivered to Freeman, you put one on file, you give one to me, and you keep one in your bottom drawer. When you've done that, you don't talk about this to anyone unless you have to. You keep it to yourself and then you forget about it. Whatever else you do, Grace, you do not take this on.'

Grace blew smoke into the air.

'Why?' she asked. 'Or do I get to work that one out for myself?'

'You get to work it out for yourself. That's all I want to say about it.'

She was silent for a few moments.

'Why don't we just give him a copy of the tape?' she asked.

'Because I want it to stay pristine. I don't want any imaginative recreations floating around out there where they might do us all damage.'

She put her cigarette down and looked at him for a few moments.

'What about that girl? If this is what you're saying it is, then what happens about her?'

'She's someone else's problem now. You let them worry about her. You don't want to know, Grace. Believe me. You do not want to know how or why that girl and her boyfriend ended up dead.'

'Why don't I want to know? It might matter to me.'

'My advice to you is that it doesn't. We leave it where it is. And we didn't talk about this. I don't want this conversation to go any further.'

Grace's mouth was set in a thin, angry line, a momentary disfiguration.

'So probably no one's ever going to know how or why they got killed? And we just forget about something like that.'

'From where we sit now, we don't have any choice. If someone else wants to chase this, it's up to them.'

'She matters as little as that? Just a little prostitute?'

'I don't like this either. I don't like seeing dead girls or anyone else in an alleyway like that. But there is only so much you can do. Do more and you end up history yourself. It's as simple as that.'

She shook her head with disbelief.

'No, Grace,' he said, before she could speak again, 'you leave it. End of story.'

Watching him, she asked herself why this was so urgent for him and wondered how much of it might be his own piece of history.

'She knew this was going to happen,' she eventually replied, with an intense and competitive cynicism. 'Do you know what she was doing when I was out with her last night? She was going through her last rites. A hamburger and coffee and home-made baklava and cigarettes and a walk through the Cross and a bit of company. That was all she wanted.'

'You did her a favour then, didn't you? You were there to give them to her. No one else was going to do that for her.'

'But she couldn't have known they were going to do that to her. You couldn't walk into something like that if you knew that's what they were going to do.'

'She was trying to buy their way out of whatever it was they'd got themselves into,' Harrigan said. '$25,000. It wasn't enough.'

'Is Jerry greedy, is he?' Grace asked innocently.

'I've never asked.'

His reply was quiet. Grace's cigarette had gone out. She picked up her cup and took a sip. 'The coffee's cold,' she said, more to the air than to him, a neutral comment not a complaint. Harrigan hit a button on the wall behind his chair. Shortly afterwards the counterman reappeared.

'Could we get a refill, Con? Thanks.'

'Do we have the time?' Grace asked as the door closed again.

'Why shouldn't we? We can take some time off the job. Anyone can find me if they want to call.'

She leaned forward with her chin on her hands. Her face was drawn and tired.

'I don't want to do that,' she said. 'I don't want to leave it just like that.'

'Grace, just listen to me. Let it go. Protect yourself.'

The door opened and the counterman came in with two fresh coffees. He glanced at them both and walked out again. They sat in silence for a few moments, drinking.

'Days like this I almost wish I'd stayed a singer and that's saying something,' she said.

No, you're not cut out for this shit job, Harrigan thought. You shouldn't be doing it. You're not cold-blooded enough. You think too much, you feel too much. 'What made you stop?' he asked.

'It sucks you dry. Performing, I mean. With singing, it's so personal. It's you all alone up there on the stage and the audience just wants to eat you alive. There's nothing left of you by the time you're finished. That's how I felt anyway.'

'This job's not like that for you?'

'No, it's different. I can do this. It doesn't drain me like that.'

'Boxing is like that,' he said, after a pause, 'the way you described singing. It's personal like that.'

'Do you box?'

'I used to. I made my living at it for a while. Not a very good one, I've got to admit. That was when I was young. Nineteen, twenty. It was good for me, it got me through a bad time.'

'When did you start?'

'When I was about eleven. My father took me up to the police boys club, as they called it back then.'

'Isn't that really young?'

'No. You can't do yourself any damage at that age, you don't hit each other hard enough.' He grinned. 'That happens later.'

'But you didn't stay with it,' she said. 'Why not?'

'They don't say "float like a butterfly" for nothing. You have to know how to dance. I wasn't as light on my feet as I needed to be. But I liked it. There's a lot more to it than people think there is. People don't understand what's involved in a fight. In the ring, it's just the two of you. Until the bell rings. It's just you and personal survival.'

'You liked that?'

'Yes, I did.'

'You still go to fights?'

'When I get the chance. Haven't you ever been to a fight?' he asked.

'No, I've never wanted to. Do you ever go to concerts? Listen to music?'

'No,' he replied. 'What I know about music could be written on the back of a postage stamp.'

'How can you live without music?' she asked, smiling.

'I don't know. I do.'

No music. Maybe you could be persuaded to want it in your life. Grace had not noticed that her hand was soothing down the scar on her neck. He watched her begin to stroke that faint line, unaware, he thought, of what she was doing.

'That scar,' he asked, 'is that the reason you taught yourself to shoot?'

She stopped touching it at once.

'No. It's got nothing to do with it.'

'Why do you shoot? Do you mind me asking you?'

'No, I don't mind. It's a fact about me, I don't pretend it's not there. I used to be an alcoholic. My hands used to shake a lot.' Her hands were carefully manicured and without jewellery. She might have been telling him she used to be a girl guide. 'I took up shooting because it taught me how to focus again. My father suggested it — he knows how to shoot, he used to be in the army. He said it was one way of getting my hand–eye coordination back. It worked too.' She smiled with a faint mockery. 'I don't do it that much any more. I don't think I ever really liked it. Shooting holes in a target is pretty boring when you get down to it. Why do you want to know?'

'I don't like guns very much.'

'But you use them in your job, you have to.'

'When I have to. I avoid them if I can.'

The room was quiet as they looked at each other.

Your father was in the army. But he wasn't a nobody, was he? Mine ended up a petty crim. 'You stopped drinking,' he said, 'just like that.'

After I woke up in hospital one day, in detox, with cuts all over my legs and couldn't remember how I'd got there or what my name was, yes, I stopped. 'I didn't have much choice,' she replied.

'No one would ever know it, Grace, looking at you now.'

She smiled in reply, with that odd, sad smile she had.

'What is it?' she asked.

'It's you. You look so different without your make-up.'

'No mask,' she replied. 'I haven't put it on yet. I can be myself for a little while.'

'Let me touch your face,' he said.

'That's stepping way over the line, Paul.'

'Well, let's do that, then.'

He stroked her cheek with the backs of his fingers, bringing his hand to rest lightly under her chin, touching her neck before tracing up into her hair and stroking the loose strands at the edge of her plait. She leaned into his hand and then reached up and took hold of it. He wound his fingers into hers, stroking her skin. They were leaning across the rickety table towards each other when, with the perfect timing he had come to expect in his work, Harrigan's phone rang, bringing them both back into working hours. They let go, drawing back. He answered his phone and then took hold of her hand again, massaging it slowly.

'Harrigan. Good morning, Trev. No, mate, I was just waiting for the call. Where? Have you got the patrol on to it? I'll meet you there, I'm on my way. I'll see you.'

They separated, he cut the connection. Grace had already stashed away her cigarettes, he reached for his jacket.

'We've got an address. Let's go,' he said.

'How much for the coffee?'

'Nothing. It's on the house.'

She looked at him.

'They don't charge me, Grace, they never have. They owe it to me for the money I lose here on the cards. Don't worry about it.

'Thanks, Con,' he said as they passed the counter.

'No worries, Paul,' said the man, looking after Grace as they went out into the street.

Dawn had begun to light the steep, narrow hill down to Central Station in a pale wash, touching on the litter in the gutters.

'Can I drive?' Grace asked.

'Go for it.' He threw her the car keys.

'How'd they get the address?' she asked as they got in.

'A Doctor Andrew Matheson from Hornsby rang the hot line. He says he's sure he saw her at a house in Berowra Heights yesterday afternoon. He's treating a man there for terminal cancer. The man's name is Hurst and he used to be a butcher,' Harrigan said.

'Berowra Heights. That's a long way from the city.'

'We could have her. We could have her in half an hour.'

She glanced at him. He was punching his fist lightly into his other hand. Take it easy, Paul. Don't let's assume too much just now. Meanwhile, she would have to deal with the speculation that would be rife after she was seen arriving at work in Harrigan's car first thing in the morning.

27

In the hour before dawn, Lucy was woken by the sound of footsteps and whispered voices in the hallway outside her room. She got out of bed, put on her old dressing gown and opened the door. The door to her father's room was open and the room was lit by a soft light. Melanie appeared, hurrying.

'It's Dad,' she said, 'I think he's dying. I'm calling the ambulance.'

She had tears in her eyes as she turned to go down the stairs.

'Can I go in there?' Lucy called out to her.

'If you want. But I don't know if he can hear you. I think it's too late.'

Gathering courage, Lucy walked towards their father's room. Inside, Stephen was sitting beside him, holding his hand. There was almost no sound in the room. Stephen looked up and saw her. He shook his head.

'He's dead,' he said quietly, in disbelief. 'He's gone. It's all over.'

Lucy could hear the sound of rain on the window. The window was open a little, the curtain moving in the cold wind. The pale fire she had seen in her father the day before had gone, his body was just what it was called: remains. His face had no connection to the face she had known as her father's. It was less than a mask, something completely used up. As she stood there, she shivered. She felt a sense of claustrophobia, a stifling airlessness. She was convinced that he was still here in shadow, caught in this room. She pushed the window open wide and let the strong wind into the enclosed space. It burst in with unexpected force, knocking the bedside lamp to its side. The room seemed to flash from positive into negative and back again within an instant and she felt that now he had gone, it was empty.

Stephen, startled out of his thoughts, let go of their father's hand. He stared at his sister.

'It's all finished,' she said to him. She was shocked at the depth and the painfulness of her relief. Her heart was racing, her breathing so deep she could have been intensely frightened by something.

Stevie stood up and shut the window, righted the lamp.

'I'm sorry,' she said. 'It was like he was still in here, I had to let him out.'

'It's okay, Luce. Don't worry about it. Let me just sit quiet for a moment.'

He went back to their father. Lucy looked out of the window and saw in the distance a few scattered lights on the edge of the park. The reflection in the dark glass superimposed the image of her father's body over the scene. She turned back to the room to see Stephen pulling the floral bedsheet over the body's face. As he did so, her father was reduced to an outline.

'We don't have to wait in here,' Stevie said. 'Let's go downstairs. We don't have to look at him.'

He left the light on in the room behind them. Just before he closed the door, Lucy looked at the covered figure one last time.

'I'll see you down there, Stevie,' she replied. 'I'm going to get dressed. I'm leaving.'

'Are you sure?' he asked.

'Oh, yeah. I'm sure.'

Yes, she was cut loose completely. There was nothing here to hold her.

Lucy went back into her room and dressed slowly. She had packed her backpack the night before. Her gun was concealed in an outside pocket, where she could reach it. She sat on her bed for a few moments before standing up and walking out into the hallway again, and then glancing one last time at the closed door to her father's room.

On her way downstairs she heard the familiar sound of the television set in the lounge room and saw that the light was on. In the kitchen, she found Stephen and Melanie sitting at the table, drinking instant coffee. Melanie was crying softly. Stephen was smoking.

'Does Mum know?' Lucy asked.

'You heard her, did you?' Stephen blew smoke out. 'Yeah, she knows. Mel got her out of bed. It doesn't matter, Luce. Whatever she does now, it doesn't matter. She can watch TV for the rest of her fucking life.'

'Yeah,' she said. 'I'm going now. You don't need me. I'll just be in the way.'

'Why do you have to go?' Melanie asked. 'You don't have to leave now.'

'Oh, yes, I do,' Lucy said.

'I've got this for you. I meant to give it to you last night,' Stephen said.

Melanie stared as he handed Lucy several hundred dollars and a set of car keys.

'It's out the front,' he said, and she nodded.

'Thanks.'

'I don't get it,' Melanie said.

'There's nothing to get, Mel. Don't worry about it,' Lucy replied.

The three of them walked through to the front of the house, towards the noise of the television set. Lucy stopped at the lounge room door, wondering what she could say, if there was anything to say. Her mother stood up and stared at her. She gaped at her daughter and then pointed at her. Her mouth was open like a fish blowing bubbles but no sound came out. Lucy guessed at once what had happened and walked into the room to see her face in identikit on the television screen, with a request from the announcer that anyone knowing the whereabouts of Lucy Hurst should ring Crime Stoppers immediately.

Looking at her mother, Lucy suddenly laughed out loud.

'Let me leave you something to remember me by, Mum,' she said, and putting down her backpack she drew her gun out of its pocket. She aimed it directly at her mother.

Her mother screamed, Stephen shouted, 'No, Lucy, don't!'

Lucy turned the gun from her mother to the television set and shot it to pieces. The screen cracked, smashed and went dead; a stray bullet shattered the window behind.

There was utter silence and then the sound of crying. Her mother had fallen back onto the couch and was weeping. Melanie was bent over, holding her ears, crying and shaking where she stood. Stephen simply stared at his sister as she put the gun away and hoisted her backpack onto her shoulder.

'Goodbye,' she said and walked out the door into the pre-dawn light and drove away in Stevie's old Datsun towards the city.

Thirty minutes later the police cars from the Hornsby patrol came screaming into the driveway, immediately behind an ambulance which had been proceeding to the same destination at a much slower pace.

28

Why did the air in the house smell like this? A faint and secondary odour under the cold, something in the skin of the walls, an invasive rottenness that Harrigan noticed as soon as he walked in the door. He looked at the incandescent lights burning in competition with the growing daylight outside, the shattered television set and a window broken in the spray of bullets, a young girl he did not know rocking herself on the sofa with her arms folded around her body, weeping. Nothing out of the ordinary. Domestic rubbish left behind by a night-time explosion of violence, shock spreading in the aftertaste of the morning hangover. Lucy Hurst's earlier presence was printed on the air; her absence was a shadow in every room.

Harrigan was in role: considering the information he had to hand, deploying his people, speaking quietly. Genuinely untouched by what he saw, he set about playing the watcher. Seeing if anything could be salvaged from what was otherwise a wasted exercise; something he had realised as soon as he had walked down the driveway, past the patrol cars and the ambulance and seen the expressions on the faces of the waiting officers. He sent Grace to comfort Melanie Hurst and talk to the mother, Trevor and Ian to talk to the brother. They met Stephen Hurst in the hallway, just as he came down the stairs.

'My father's up there. He hasn't been dead for more than an hour. Can't this wait? Can't I see to him first?'

'You have called your doctor, Mr Hurst?' Harrigan asked.

'Of course I called him. He's up there now. I just spoke to him.'

'Then may I go up there? I need to speak with him before your father is removed.'

'I don't believe this. I didn't believe it when she took that gun out and I still don't believe it. If you want to, go up. There's nothing to see. Just my father.' Stephen Hurst shook his head.

Harrigan nodded and walked upstairs, listening as Trevor asked if Mr Hurst would like to go through with them into his own kitchen for just a few questions. He glanced back down and saw that the young man walked with a noticeable limp.

Upstairs, he stopped to look into an empty room which someone had already cordoned off, into which, once they arrived, he would send the forensic team to comb for any human trace. On the floor, the sheets, anywhere. Hair, body fluids, blood. He thought dispassionately of Lucy Hurst's electronic voice reaching out to his son from this ordinary, shabby, adolescent room and moved on. The door to the main bedroom was open. The doctor was drawing the sheets up over the head of the dead man. He and Harrigan introduced themselves at the foot of the bed, shaking hands in front of the mute form lying under pink cotton flowers.

'I will be signing the death certificate,' the doctor said, slightly pompous. 'This is a wholly natural death, I have been waiting for it. It's a good thing for him it's over.'

'Yes,' Harrigan replied laconically, without a trace of irony.

'I understand the family don't know I was the one who called in?'

He was waiting. Harrigan nodded.

'I'd appreciate it if it could stay that way,' the doctor said.

'At the moment, I think they're probably waiting to hear from you what you've just told me,' Harrigan replied, with a perfunctory smile.

The doctor left.

The odour of human sickness Harrigan had detected throughout the house was no stronger here, but in a room which was both cold and seemed airless it had an extra bite. He looked at the figure in the bed. Unmoved by the dead man's presence, he peeled back the sheet to look at the death mask. The features had already shrunk back onto the skull. As wasted as it was, the corpse had the presence of a familiar spirit, malevolent if impotent. Harrigan considered that wherever he had so far set foot in this house with its narrow corridors and packed boxy rooms, it had left its imprint. This particular demon had played itself out. What it had loosed was somewhere out there in the city, out of his reach and, for all he knew, was only just beginning its own campaign. He replaced the sheet and walked to the window to look out over the national park. Rain clouds were building on the dawn horizon and he could see the wind moving through the tree tops, hear it worrying at the glass. He left the window closed and touching nothing else went downstairs.

The kitchen was a dark room with no external window, the only outside light would come through the back door into the adjacent laundry. This door was now closed against the weather, he could see it shaking in the wind like the window upstairs. At the present moment, the room was lit by a single fluorescent tube flat against the ceiling. Harrigan appeared silently and stood leaning against the kitchen bench where he could watch Stephen Hurst. The boy had a candid face, presently shadowed in the spread of the white light. Ordinary things had been placed at random on a green laminex table: cigarettes, plastic lighters, ashtrays, chipped coffee cups which were half filled with instant coffee. Stephen, wearing a dark red and blue check flannelette shirt, leaned on his elbows, a numbed expression on his face. He was smoking, the air thick with the smell of it. Harrigan watched him, assessing the variables of fact, emotion and agenda in each of the answers he gave.

'She's got some money, your car and a full tank of petrol. A brown 1977 120Y Datsun?' Trevor said, without so much as a grin.

'Yeah.'

Harrigan wondered how he might explain to the waiting media that their home-grown terrorist had escaped New South Wales's finest by trundling away in an infamous, shit-brown 120Y.

'She can't be travelling very fast, I guess,' Ian commented. 'Do you think your sister would steal a car if she needed to?'

'She probably already has,' Stephen replied, exhausted.

'She's good at that, is she?' Ian continued.

Stephen did not reply.

'You say you don't know where she's gone,' Trevor said. 'Do you know of a Preacher Graeme Fredericksen?'

'I don't think she's gone to see him.'

'You do know him then?' Trevor asked.

'Yeah, I've met him. Sleazy creepy little bastard.'

A pity your sister didn't see him that way, Harrigan thought.

'Why do you say she won't be there?' Ian asked.

'Because I went looking for her there once. The day those people got shot. That afternoon,' Stephen replied. 'He said she wasn't there but he was lying, I'm sure he was. I went back and found her later that night. She was a mess, she looked so sick. I don't know what happened but I think ....' He stopped and swallowed. 'I know it seems like a mad thing to say but I wouldn't be surprised if he hadn't tried to kill her or something. She doesn't trust him now. I've heard her talking to him on the phone sometimes —'

'She's phoned him?'

'Yeah, quite a few times. Or he's phoned her. At least I think it's him. Graeme. Who else would it be? I don't know what's going on. That's the honest truth.'

'Do you mind if I ask a question — Ian, Trevor? Do you mind, Mr Hurst?' Harrigan asked, quietly neutral as usual, pulling back a chair.

'No,' Stephen said, shaking his head, reaching for another cigarette.

'Your sister was a mess, you say, when you found her that night. Did you ask her why she was in such a mess?'

'No.'

'You didn't ask her any questions?'

'I never ask Lucy questions. I haven't for years.'

'Your family ask a lot from you, Mr Hurst. Money. A car. All night out on the streets looking for your sister.'

'It's not only me. Ask Mel, they drink her blood too. Used to anyway, not any more.'

'I notice you walk with a limp, Mr Hurst.'

'I broke my kneecap when I was fifteen. It never healed properly.'

'Did your father do that to you?' Harrigan asked out of pure guesswork.

Stephen did not reply.

'When did you realise your sister was a murderer?'

'I didn't know. You wouldn't think that sort of thing about your sister. I didn't know till this morning when she was leaving.'

'Then why give her money and a car? Did you see something in yesterday's newspaper that alerted you perhaps?'

'I didn't know.'

'You did know. Why didn't you do something?'

Stephen Hurst leaned his face on his hands, pushing his glasses awry. His cigarette dangled from his fingers. When he looked up, Harrigan saw that the edge of one side of his glasses had impressed a mark under his eye. The boy smiled bitterly.

'I didn't know. All I'm trying to do is keep things turning over here so Mel and me can walk away from this in one piece. I don't know what else I'm supposed to do. What do you want from me? I don't see what I can give you.'

'I want to find your sister before anyone else gets added to the list of the injured and the dead, Mr Hurst. At the moment, I have more people on that list than I care for.'

'I don't know where she is. If I knew I would have told you that first thing.'

He drew on his cigarette again. Harrigan was pushing back his chair, standing up.

'My officers will take your statement now. Thank you.'

'You do that, do you? Come around and ask people those kinds of questions and then go away again,' Stephen Hurst said, almost to himself, grinding out his cigarette.

'No, Mr Hurst. I'm the one who has to cover all the angles regardless, because if I don't, then I can't do my job,' Harrigan replied.

He walked out into the hallway in time to see Grace leaving a room, closing the door softly behind her. He smiled at her, she smiled back.

'How did you go with the mother?' he asked.

'Listen to this,' she replied quietly.

He listened at the door and heard the sound of a television set.

'She's got a portable in there,' Grace said. 'That's what she wanted. Tea, toast and the television set. Talking to her is like talking to nothing, she stares back at you like she's a baby chicken. I think she made sure she had no idea what was going on.'

'What about the girl?'

'She's out of it, the doctor's given her a shot. She's exhausted. I don't think she would have had the time to know what was happening. Neither of them can tell us anything.'

'Par for the course,' he said, 'no one here can. She's given me the slip, Grace, by thirty minutes.'

'What do you want me to do now?'

'I don't think there is much more you can do here. Do you want to take a cigarette break? Catch up with me a little later.'

'Okay.'

Grace went and stood out on the edge of the ruined garden but did not light a cigarette, letting the cold air shift the odour of the house out of her nostrils. She braced her hands behind her head and felt the strength of the gathering wind. It was strong and icy and pushed her back as she turned from side to side, loosening the muscles in her neck and spine. A bank of black cloud was continuing to build on the horizon. On its patch of ground above the trees the house stood exposed before the full force of the weather.

The garden on the slope just below had already been searched and was not cordoned off. Grace walked down into the green shade, picking her way along the muddy paths. Dead flowers littered the ground, old rhododendron trees and camellias were massed together. At the base of the slope, an ancient and decaying sleep-out stood near the edge of an escarpment. The door was open like a mouth. Grace looked inside but did not go in. The room was dark and smelled like a cave of moist earth and the windows were covered with cobwebs.

Are you in there? There could be no one in there, the area had been searched. The waiting quietness of the shadows felt like a trap about to close. Grace turned away to look out over the native forest in the national park and then heard a soft growl behind her. She looked and saw an ancient dog in the doorway to the sleep-out, snarling at her from the shadows.

'You horrible mongrel,' she said softly, 'you don't have to protect her now, she's gone. I wouldn't go in there anyway.'

The dog growled more loudly, more savagely. It moved forward, herding her towards the escarpment.

'Go away. You don't frighten me.'

The dog stood its ground, grinning yellow teeth. It moved forward again. Grace stood still where she was and then took a step to the side, towards the path to the house, staring it in the eyes.

'You stay there, you just stay there.'

It was braced on its claws but as she moved slowly away it stayed still, watching her off. When she gained the pathway, she saw it relax its stance and then disappear back into the sleep-out. Grace walked back up the hill quickly, thinking that this was no place to be, it was dangerous, full of trapdoors and tripwires. No one would want to live here.

She found Harrigan in the hallway near the door to the lounge room, talking to Ian and Trevor. He signalled to her to join them, the others looked at her speculatively. Avoiding their joint gaze, she glanced through to the lounge room where a forensic team was working on the ruined television set.

'There you are,' he said, following her line of vision and then looking back at her again. 'We've been tossing a few ideas around. We're shadow boxing with her so I'm going to make her dance for us a little. Do you want to talk to her?'

'Out there in cyberspace, you mean? Is she still out there?'

'Why don't we find out? Why don't you send her an email — give her Greggie's last message. Quote it word for word. That's what he wanted you to do.'

'Who am I talking to? Lucy Hurst or the Firewall?' she asked.

'What do you think?'

'I think I should talk to the girl who's protecting the world.'

'Yeah. Go out looking for the Firewall. Okay, I'm staying on here for a little while longer but you can all go now. These two will take you back,' Harrigan said, glancing at them. 'I told them not to go without you.'

He walked away. Grace found herself watching him go.

'Okay, Gracie,' Ian said with a faint touch of sarcasm, 'do you want to hop in the back?'

'Would you mind if I drove?'

'Careful, mate,' Trevor said, 'Gracie's a speed queen.'

'No, that's okay,' Ian said, handing her the keys and grinning at Trevor. 'You can ride in the back. No smoking.'

'Sure,' she replied.

Driving was a relief. She reached the Pacific Highway quickly and zipped along through the traffic, letting the speed work the tensions out of her head. For a short time, they were silent.

'That was a horrible place,' Grace said after a while. 'Why doesn't she burn that place down while she's about it? It needs it.'

Trevor laughed in the back.

'Don't give her any ideas, Gracie. You really think you want to talk to her?'

'Yeah. Why not?'

He shrugged. 'I don't know if that's the right way to go. I don't know how dangerous it might be.'

'Yeah, that's right. Who's she going to kill next? You don't want to be anywhere near the firing line,' Ian said.

'We don't know that yet,' Grace replied, a little bleakly.

'She will, Gracie,' Ian said to her, almost gently. 'I hate to say it, but she will now she's got started.'

'What does Harrigan want you to do?' she asked them.

'Go and pick up the preacher. He wants the three of us to talk to him, whatever we're going to get out of that,' Trev replied.

They were silent again.

'Okay, Graciekins,' Trevor said suddenly, 'enough of this pissing around. Where did you spend last night? You weren't at Harrigan's place, were you?'

'What kind of a question is that? No, I wasn't. I was in my flat. In my own bed. By myself. You are such suspicious-minded, nosy people.'

'It's what we do for a living,' Ian said, helpfully. 'You're supposed to think that way too.'

'I am not sleeping with Harrigan!'

'I'm just saying what everyone else is saying.' Trevor sounded defensive. 'If you do want to fuck him, you might as well go ahead and do it now because everyone thinks you are.'

'Trev, you are so *crass*!'

'I'm just telling it like it is,' he said, taken aback by her degree of anger.

Ian had been laughing but he stopped himself.

'We believe you, Gracie,' he said, wiping his eyes, 'but I don't know if anybody else will.'

She shook her head but did not reply. She sped up, driving too fast, feeling an unfocused sense of urgency. 'Take it easy, mate,' she heard Ian say after a little while and she did slow down, taking it quieter. Why is life like this? she thought to herself. Outside, the sky held the threat of a deluge not quite delivered.

29

Lucy dumped the Datsun off the road near a station not far from Hornsby and stole another car from a commuter who would not find out until he had disembarked from his evening train. The best she could do for disguise was to pull the hood of her jacket over her head and hope that no one looked at her too closely. Circumstances favoured her: it was early, barely light, and the weather was bad, dark and cold. She drove carefully in a thin stream of traffic towards the towers of the city, on her way to the only place she knew where she could hide both her car and herself. There was no other choice.

The garage at Randwick was as anonymous as the first time she had driven in there after the shooting. There was a new padlock on the door but she cracked this open with a screwdriver she carried for this purpose. She drove inside, into a hermetically sealed sanctuary, an island of concrete within four brick walls hiding her from everyone's sight.

She parked beside the pit, stood once again in the centre of the deserted building and considered that she was back where she had started. It was as dark in this place as it had been before. She took her pack out of the car and stowed it in the office, moving uneasily in the shadows, wondering if the ghosts she had encountered here earlier were still waiting for her. She walked out into the main part of the garage again.

What do I do now?

She did not have to go to the police to give herself up. She only had to call them and they would come for her. They would fill the street outside and, once they had her in custody, she would never have to decide to do anything again. She would be moved from place to place as the system needed her to be moved, she would only have to make sure that she was ready to go when they wanted her to and that she talked to whoever she was told to talk to. That she did what she was told to do and kept herself clean and fed. If she did not do this, they would force it on her. No, she wasn't going to call them, not yet.

She had the whole day to fill, the conundrum of how to meet Graeme that evening to solve, the future of her life to decide. At present, her ghosts were quiet and she felt oddly that she had no power of emotion left. The memory of the people she had shot was not troubling her just now, those thoughts had faded since she had shot out her mother's television set. She smiled as she thought of this.

She began to prowl the perimeter of the garage, kicking at bits of rubbish. Unseen until she stood over it, she came across a worn, dark red beanie tossed to the side out of the way. She picked it up and whirled it around on the end of her hand, staring at it. The almost abstract thought that her father had died that morning came into her head. She felt nothing for him and did not pretend to; it was more that something which had pressed down on a nerve was gone. As she stared at the beanie, another thought joined with this; the meaning of a difference in the look of the garage registered with her for the first time.

For some moments she felt too frightened to move, but told herself she could face anything, she already had. She walked to the pit on the other side of the car. It had been covered over with heavy wooden boards. She looked at the boards and decided she would not move them. She did not want to see someone she loved turned into the same thing that her father had become.

An interior stillness took hold of her, an emptiness unlike the gossamer lightness she had felt the last time she was here or the quietness which usually preceded the rustling sounds of her children's voices. She had no blood. She was made of layers of rustling, dry parchment, an accumulated skin only. Her articulated thoughts had a curious density, like sounds not quite heard, muffled by a wall of thick, discoloured glass. With this odd and echoing interior voice she thought, quite calmly, that all that mattered was the next action, the next step. And then, after that, nothing would matter, because it would all be finished.

She walked around to the other side of the car and leaned against it. Unbidden and unwanted, the ghosts in her mind were returning in force, a jangling mess breaking furiously through a curtain of silence. She screamed at them in her head to stop. They fell silent immediately, they had somehow melted into the air. An intensity of anger took their place. A hushed sound, burning as it made its way through her bloodstream, hummed in her head, obscuring her vision.

'I don't have to be frightened of anyone, do I? Not you, Graeme, not anyone. I've been there,' she said aloud.

Anger flipped to coldness, white toxicity became planetary iciness, powerful in its capacity to plan. This detachment was an anaesthetic, it was useful. She could be possessed by grief or rage and still act. She had things to do. Important things to do.

Lucy started her car and moved it so that it straddled the pit. She needed to have a barrier between her and whatever might be in there. She went into the office and taking her phone out of her pack rang Graeme. The battery would need to be recharged soon but there was nothing she could do about it. He answered at once.

'New Life Ministries. Preacher Graeme Fredericksen speaking.'

'It's only me, Graeme. You don't have to go on with that sort of shit,' Lucy said.

'I'm sorry, but I don't quite understand you. I don't think I know who you are. Is there someone in particular you wanted to talk to?'

'Someone gave me your name. And your number. I thought you'd know me,' Lucy said, assuming from this reply that Graeme was expecting someone else to be listening in on their conversation. 'You see, I'm looking for someone. Someone who matters to me a lot. And they said you might be able to help. So don't hang up.'

'Tell me what you want,' came the reply. 'I'm always here to help those who need it.'

'Yes or no is all I want. Will I find who I'm looking for ...' She paused, thinking. 'You know, there are places where I was afraid to go. Because I thought if I did I'd meet all my old ghosts back there and I'd be frightened of them. But I had to go back there because I had nowhere else to go, and I can tell you now, I'm not afraid of anything any more. Am I going to find who I'm looking for here? I look around this place and I can see that something's changed, it's all boarded up. You know what's different, don't you? Now you had better be honest with me. You really had.'

'Yes, I think you're right. You probably need to know that. You probably also need to know that the person you seek is there because they chose to be. They sleep where they sleep now through their own actions. If they sleep in the cradle of death's river, it's because they chose to be there.'

'Do you know the thing that hurts me most, Graeme? It's when people let me down. I really hope that's not going to happen any more. I'll be waiting to find out. I'll be where I said I would be and I hope everyone else will be there too.'

'Though you may have to wait longer than you expect, I'm sure you won't be disappointed.'

Lucy cut the connection. Time was no longer on her hands, she had things to do. Things to work on, things to build.

She cleaned her gun, reloaded it and left it sitting on the table, ready to use. In the cupboard she found switches and devices, explosive materials that Graeme had stored there. He had taught her about these things as well but she had not been quite so interested in them at the time. Now they could be useful. She fossicked around until she found in a drawer a stapled document titled, *Ka-boom: Ways to stop abortion that work.*

I'm going to give you a memorial, Greggie, the only type that anyone will ever take any fucking notice of where you're concerned. I'm going to take something out for you in return for what they did to you. You'll see.

She went to work, believing herself to be simply working and not sitting with every muscle tensed, concentrating ferociously on each connection built, obsessed by what she was doing. When she had finished, she was exhausted and terribly hungry. She tossed her sleeping bag on the pallet and lay down on it, holding her gun, aiming it at the ceiling, making pretend shots at the shadows. You be there tonight, Graeme. Then you can explain to me a few of the things you've done lately, can't you? I'll be waiting for you. Despite her hunger, after some little time she slept, as deeply as she would have done if she had been drugged.

30

Harrigan wanted to make Lucy Hurst dance for him but the truth was that he could not move. Once the options were laid on the table they came down to a single possibility: watch and wait. Exert pressure, push people a little and see what will break, then pick up the pieces.

He had put in place all the resources he had: surveillance teams, street patrols, saturation coverage in the media, his own people monitoring every scrap of information that was fed to them, waiting for the break. Other than that, he was fixed in the small square of space that made up his office.

Outside his window, the weather seemed to be engaged in the same kind of phoney war. The wind was chasing rubbish through the air, using it as a punching bag for unseen fists. The ground was dry, there was as yet no rain, only an anticipation. He was detached and sealed away in this building, watching for an outcome through his wide glass window, an unwilling spectator at some organised gladiatorial event where the pleasure for most of the other spectators is that the outcomes are real.

His people had brought the preacher in and Harrigan had decided to keep him waiting, although he doubted that this tactic would have much effect on the man. He laid his photographs out on the table one by one and asked himself what he could achieve by placing these images in front of someone he had already decided was unreachable. The preacher was still human. Most people are accessible through fear and others can't resist a game. He gathered the photographs into a folder and walked out of his office.

In the interview room, the preacher sat waiting with Trevor and Ian. Harrigan greeted him with his professional smile. Ian moved his chair back to sit against the wall, Trevor to the side out of the way. Harrigan had asked for space while he talked with the preacher.

'Thanks for coming in, Graeme. We appreciate it,' he said, taking his seat.

'Paul, I am happy to assist you in any way I can. I hope I will have something of value to tell you.'

'Good.' Harrigan's tone was perfunctory. 'Just a point to get clear to begin with. You know Lucy Hurst?'

'I do indeed. She is a member of my congregation, a very troubled young woman. She was, or is, in desperate need of help. However,' the preacher forestalled him, 'I am afraid I am unable to repeat any of the conversations we may have had together. They are strictly confidential. I'm afraid that confidence is inviolable.'

'That wasn't my question, Graeme. Let me tell you what I do want to know. You're a man of God. That's what you say you are.'

'That is what I am.'

'What makes you that?'

The preacher sat upright, his hands clasped in front of him, resting on the table.

'You don't need to ask me that question. You know the answer. You've heard me preach. You know I reach into the heart. It is not my voice that speaks through me but the voice of eternal love, no, of primal love, the first of all loves that speaks through me. I speak an eternal truth to those who will hear it.'

'Then why do you need this? Your resumé with the Family Services Commission says you have a Master of Theology from Freedom World University. Our information says that's a postbox in a trailer park in South Chicago. Why bother? If you have all those skills without this piece of paper?'

The preacher glanced at the ornately decorated degree that Harrigan had slid across the table towards him.

'Ian Enright,' he said, reading the name of the recipient. He looked at Ian. 'That's you. Again you have the answer to your question, Paul. You have already identified the true worth of these pieces of paper.'

'My question was, why did you bother?'

'People need the reassurance these things offer.'

'Why not get a real one?'

'I have no need of it.'

'You don't need a real degree but you do need a fake one?'

'It's a crutch for others, Paul. I don't have the time to devote myself to that sort of study. I have the world out there to concern myself with. No one asked Christ if he had a degree.'

'You don't have a problem presenting yourself fraudulently to others?'

'I am not presenting myself fraudulently. I am exactly what I say I am. That piece of paper allows others who may doubt me to cast aside their doubts and see me for what I truly am.'

Harrigan looked at the preacher for a few seconds. Then he gave a short, offensive laugh.

'I couldn't agree with you more, mate,' he said. 'I think it says exactly what you are.'

The lines of the preacher's face hardened into expressionless anger. The atmosphere tightened, the ante was upped slightly. Harrigan retrieved the imitation degree and returned it to his folder.

'I have a list here I want you to read aloud, please, Graeme.' His tone was brusque. 'You were associated with the New Life Ministries in Berkeley, California. These are the members of the Life Support Group who were also associated with that church. Tell me the ones you know.'

The preacher smiled and rested his fingers on the list without looking at it.

'I meet so many people in my work, Paul.'

'But you never forget anyone. You told me that yourself. When I was at your prayer meeting you even knew who the children were. You have to be able to glad-hand people in your line of work, don't you? You want to control them so they jump when you say jump? Then you have to know who they are, don't you? Read those names and tell me the ones you know.'

'I am not obliged to do that.'

Fredericksen pushed the paper back across the table.

'Trev?' Harrigan asked. They listened as Trevor read each name aloud.

'Recognise any of those names, Graeme?'

'They're just names to me, Paul.'

'Are you a member of a group called the Avenging Angels?'

'What are they?'

'You know what they are. You tell me.'

Fredericksen replied with unshakable self-possession.

'I am my own man, Paul. I do only what I am called to do. Where people are concerned, I am just myself, nothing else.'

'Do you know this woman?'

He placed on the table the picture of the woman shot dead on her front doorstep with the words 'You can run but you can't hide' written across the image.

'Again you ask me to identify someone from the back of the head.'

'This woman's face was shot away so it wouldn't help you much. Let me introduce you anyway: Dr Laura Di-Cuollo, obstetrician, Long Beach, California. She used to carry out abortions at a local women's health clinic.'

Fredericksen glanced briefly at the photograph. He drew his head up in what appeared a gesture of fastidious distaste. Then the swiftest of expressions, joy, crossed his face.

'Does this picture appeal to you? Does it please you?'

The preacher did not speak. Harrigan continued.

'It's a cruel picture, Graeme. Don't you feel grief, sorrow, anything, when you look at it?'

'This woman dealt in death. Why should anyone, herself, her fellow travellers, be surprised if one day death catches up with her?'

'You're saying she deserved to die?'

'No, not at all. Only that those who deal in death should not be surprised if one day their partner in life comes to claim them.'

In the room, briefly, there was a sense of extraordinary cold.

'I see,' Harrigan said eventually. 'What about this?'

He placed in front of the preacher the picture of Professor Henry Liu lying dead in a Chippendale street.

'None of this has anything to do with me. Why are you showing me these things?'

'What about this one?'

A picture of the professor in the same street with the blue handkerchief Harrigan himself had dropped across his face. He set the two photographs side by side.

'You show me pictures, Paul, but you don't tell me why.'

'The morning this shooting happened, and we got the call to go down there, we found one dead body and one living one. And one teenager with his life shot to pieces. I dropped that handkerchief over the dead man's face because of the way he looked.' There was a pause. 'Don't you find that sickening to look at?'

Harrigan's voice was quiet. He watched the preacher look from one picture to the next without blinking or registering any change to his expression.

'Do you know what this man did for a living? He taught music. I'm asking you, Graeme: should he have expected to be shot dead like that?'

As he spoke, Harrigan very briefly felt the memory of his conversation with Grace that morning, an impression gone in a second. There was silence. The preacher stared at Harrigan, his hands resting on the photographs.

'I have no idea,' he replied calmly.

'Do you feel any grief for him? His son? His wife? You know who she is, Graeme. Your mates from your congregation spend half their lives outside her clinics buzzing around her clients.'

'She dealt in death. Her son should be accusing her. So should the ghost of her husband. Perhaps in the afterlife he will, when the scales have fallen from his eyes. Perhaps he will accuse her while he watches her fall into her place in Hell.'

Again there was a sense of profound cold in the room. Harrigan saw how the attention of everyone, himself, his two officers, was fixed on this man who drank it in, unafraid.

'There's only God's law for you, Graeme.'

'There is only God's law for every one of us, Paul.'

'Does this represent God's law to you?'

He tapped the pictures, avoiding any physical contact with the preacher. Fredericksen smiled at him with a slightly taunting expression.

'You are the law enforcer here, Paul. Tell me how you see it.'

'I see it as cold-blooded murder.'

Silence. Fredericksen continued to smile.

'Then we wait for the answer to your question. We wait until the day that we are called to account before God. On that day, the true representatives of the law will be revealed to us. We will see whose blood is innocent and whose is not.'

'You want to talk about blood guilt?' Harrigan said. 'The Lius were shot by the same type of gun that shot Laura Di-Cuollo. They're not all that common in this country in the hands of nineteen-year-old street kids. Did you give Lucy Hurst that gun?'

'How can I have given her a gun? I have no gun. I can't answer that question.'

'You can't answer my question?'

'No.'

'Because to answer the question would be to lie to me directly.'

'I don't lie, Paul. I tell people the truth in their hearts.'

'Did you give Lucy Hurst a gun and tell her to go out and do this?'

There was a fraction of a hesitation.

'No, I did not say that to her,' he replied.

'She killed the wrong person. She didn't even know how to control the gun. Why pick someone so young? No one else have the nerve? Including you? Enforcing God's law is fine provided *you* don't have to do the dirty work.'

Harrigan laughed in the preacher's face.

'Her actions have nothing to do with me,' the man replied.

'You mean the fact that she made such a dog's breakfast of it?'

'None of this has anything to do with me.'

'You don't kill people. You get other people to do it for you.'

'That is untrue.'

'You mean you kill people as well?'

The preacher's face was not so much white as colourless. He sat completely still.

'I am not an agent of death. Others are the agents of death. Why don't you harass them?'

'Your agents. Would you kill Lucy Hurst if she was a danger to you?'

'I am not an agent of death. I am a preserver of life.'

'Haven't you ever wanted to kill someone? Wouldn't you like to have a go at me now?'

The preacher drew himself up with the same fastidious movement, and the same brief expression of savage joy crossed his face.

'You are not my concern, Paul. Your fate will be decided by a force far stronger than you, or me for that matter. I may be its agent. But I am not an agent of death. I offer eternal life.'

'Careful what rubbish you say there, mate.' Trevor spoke very softly and very angrily, words that had been forced out of him.

The tension snapped like a piece of fine and brittle glass. The preacher jumped from his seat. *'How dare you talk to me!'* he roared.

Harrigan was on his feet and in the preacher's face before anyone else could move.

'You will not talk to my officers like that!'

The force of his words pushed the preacher back into his seat. There was silence. The preacher's face had been transformed by fury. He sat there shaking.

'Am I under arrest?' he asked.

Harrigan shook his head.

'I wish to leave now in that case or I will bring a complaint of unlawful detention.'

'You agreed to come down of your own accord, Graeme. But you can go anyway. I'm finished here. But I'm sure we'll talk to each other again soon.'

This time the man did not speak or smile. He stood up, the doors were opened and the four of them walked to the lifts. At a nod from Harrigan, Dea phoned for an escort to see the preacher out. No one spoke. The escort took his time.

While they stood there, they heard the sound of female voices: Louise and Grace returning from some girls' only coffee break. They appeared in the foyer on their way back to work. Harrigan and Grace looked at each other without intending to. Then he saw her look at the preacher with that steel in her expression she sometimes had. Fredericksen watched her go, his face impassive. The lift doors opened and the escort arrived.

'Do you know, Paul,' the preacher said, turning to him, 'it's never wise to be arrogant. Pride does go before a fall.'

Harrigan placed himself between the preacher and everyone else and spoke quietly and affably. He was smiling.

'Who are you threatening, Graeme? Me or one of my people? Because that would be a very stupid thing for you to do.'

'I am not threatening anyone, Paul. I never do. Everything is in the hands of God. Does that worry you? Would that make you step outside your own limits?'

'This man will organise you a lift home,' Harrigan replied. 'Thanks for coming in.'

They looked at each other and then the preacher turned away. 'Good day to you,' he said to no one in particular.

He was gone and they all breathed.

'Fuck me,' Ian and Trevor said, simultaneously.

'Snap,' Trevor said. 'Sorry, Dea.'

'That's okay,' she said, with an unconcerned wave of her hand.

'He's a first for me, I've got to say that,' Harrigan said, damping down the fact the interview, and Fredericksen, had disturbed him much more than was usual.

'Why did he scream at you like that, mate?' Ian asked.

'Who gives a shit?' Trevor shrugged.

'Why did you say that to him?' Harrigan asked.

'Because of all the crap he was going on with. What would he know? I need a smoke.'

'Take a break and then come and see me in my office, the both of you,' Harrigan said.

He went back into the main part of the office and saw Grace about to disappear into the computer room. He walked up to her.

'My office,' he said, 'now.'

'What is it?' she asked, surprised.

'Work.' The comment was overhead by Jeffo who, Grace noticed, grinned at them both and made a face behind Harrigan's back.

'What is it?' she asked as she sat down on the other side of his desk.

'I need to know — would the preacher or anyone connected with him have any reason to know anything about you?'

'Why are you asking me that?'

'Because if they do, I would have to say you are in considerable personal danger as of now. I'm going to ask you again. Do they know anything about you? Your address, anything. Anything you tell me is confidential, Grace.'

Grace pictured herself sitting in this chair telling him how she had had an abortion eight months ago, or even confining her information simply to describing how the preacher's hangers-on had tracked her down and leaving it to him to fill in the gaps. She could not bring herself to say any of this, the confession stuck in her throat. What would it matter if she did say nothing? What could she tell him that he didn't already know? He would finish the investigation soon, within days at the most. She shook her head without speaking.

'Are you sure?'

She shook her head again. He tapped the desk with his fingertips.

'Have you sent out an email to the Firewall?' he asked.

'Yeah. I haven't got anything back yet.'

He was silent for a little longer.

'I'm going to take you at your word, Grace,' he said. 'You're responsible for what you do in here —'

'I've never seen it any other way.'

'I'm not saying anything different. We were talking about murderers the other night. You just saw the genuine article standing in the foyer. He gets a kick out of it. Think about that. Let me know as soon as you get anything back online.'

'Okay,' she said and left, meeting Trev and Ian at the door.

'Hi, guys,' she said and headed back to the computer room.

'Did we interrupt anything?' Ian asked disingenuously.

'No, mate, there's nothing to interrupt,' Harrigan growled. 'Let's get on with it.'

In the computer room, Grace sat in front of the monitor waiting to see if the Firewall would come online, asking herself, what could Harrigan do to protect her anyway? Take her off the job, lock her away? She concentrated on her work. Work was her only possible relief at the moment. She decided that even tedium could have its uses when you needed it enough.

31

Hunger woke Lucy. She lay considering that she had hours to wait before her next action and nothing to do between then and now. She went to the sink and drank water to ease her appetite and then looked at her computer and mobile phone, wondering how long either of them could last now that she had no means to recharge their batteries. In the garage, there was a suicidally dangerous and illegal electrical connection which ran the lights but no usable outlet. Even so, she logged on and went out onto the Net.

Various messages were waiting for her. From Turtle: *Are u out there Firewall Come & talk 2 me please*. She ignored the tug of feeling that said, yes, talk to him, there is nothing you need more. She deleted his message. Then there was an email from someone she did not know, with the subject line: *Message from Greg*. She opened it at once.

This is to the Firewall. You don't know me but my name is Grace. I'm going to tell you straightaway that I'm with the police. But I have a message for you from Greg. What I am telling you is word for word what he said to me. I talked to him once just before they took him up to Kariong and then later he rang me and he left me this message on my answering machine. It's for you. I have the tape if you want it. If we can find a way to get it to you, we'll do that so you'll know that what I'm telling you is true. Once you've read it, if you want to get back to me, you can email me or you can chat to me. Whichever way you want to do it. But if you do want to talk to me, I'm here to talk to you. Just come and find me. Grace.

Lucy read both messages several times before going out in search of the sender.

Are you out there, Grace. Are you real? Whoever you are. It's the Firewall here. Why do you want to talk to me?

Firewall? Is this really you?

Yeah.

How do I know it's you?

How do I know who you are?

I sent you Greg's message.

I can tell you something in return. I already know that Greggie's dead. I've got his beanie and it's sitting on the table right beside me now. I know where he is too and I can tell you that. And I will. But first I want to know why you want to talk to me. Why should you? What do you want?

On the other side of the city, Louise appeared in the doorway of Harrigan's office to tell him Grace had the Firewall online.

'Yes,' he said, and was on his feet. In the computer room he leaned over Grace to read the words on the screen, his closeness to her crowding her space. A small group gathered behind them.

'I've just got her,' she said to him.

'Keep her talking.'

In the garage, Lucy waited for Grace's reply.

I want to know if you're okay. Where you are now. And what you're planning on doing next. We're both caught in a loop, Firewall. We need to find a way out.

There is no way out for me. You know that. I bet you want to know where I am but that doesn't mean I'm going to tell you. Who told you who I am? It wasn't Greggie?

No, it wasn't. He wouldn't tell me anything about you. He never stopped being loyal to you, Firewall.

I said he wouldn't, no matter what. I told people we didn't have to worry about Greggie.

Who did you say that to?

I'm not telling you that. Not just yet. What's your last name?

In the computer room, Harrigan shook his head. 'No,' he said.

I'm not going to tell you that just yet either, Firewall.

Don't you trust me?

Can I trust you?

I don't care if you don't really. I only care if I can trust you. What do you want? I'm not going to hand myself over to you right now so what else do you want?

I wanted to talk to you. It's better if we talk than if we don't.

People say that kind of thing all the time. And then they just walk away and leave you to die. How do I know you're not just a liar like everyone else?

I'm not lying to you, Firewall. Why don't you want to try and trust me just a little?

Because even people you love and think you can trust for ever turn out to be liars sometimes. Make me trust you. Tell me who told you who I am.

Grace looked up at Harrigan.

'Tell her,' he said.

Someone you used to know saw you that morning when you were driving away. She came and told us who you were.

Who?

Gina.

Gina? Corinna, you mean? She didn't.

She was pretty desperate, Firewall. She needed protection.

She could have come to me, I would have looked after her. Where is she now?

She's dead.

She is not. You're lying.

I am not lying. I wish I didn't have to tell you that but it's true.

That's why I'm out here, Grace. You listen to what I'm saying to you. We were all in a group once, me, Greggie and Corinna, and now there's just me left. Just me. And they're dead. And that's why I have to be out here. No one else is out here for us. That's why I don't trust anyone, Grace, including you. Because, in the end, everyone stabs you in the back. And they like doing it. People laugh at you while they're hurting you. Is that what you want to do?

No. I've told you the real reason I'm talking to you. You know who I am and what I want. I'm not hiding anything from you. I wish I hadn't had to write that Gina was dead. I mean that.

Do you? I wish I knew what to think. I talk to people and it's like I don't know where I am.

I feel like that sometimes. I used to sing and I started to write a song about that once. It went something like: Sometimes when I'm talking/It feels like I'm walking/In the dark/Don't where I'm going/Don't know where I've been. That was the chorus. That's how I felt too. That was about as far as the song got, I think.

It is like that. It is like I'm in the dark all the time. What do you want me to do? Everyone who talks to me tells me what they think I should do. What do you think?

I'd like you to tell us where you are so we can come and get you. That way, no one else gets hurt.

What good is that going to do me? Lots of people are already hurt. How is that going to help them?

It will mean that no one else is going to get hurt. I'm sure you want the chance to do something for Greg.

What do you think I can do for him now?

You don't want to leave him where he is. You want to do the right thing by him.

Of course I do. But I'm not going to tell you how to find him until it's the right time.

When will that be?

I don't know yet.

Do you have something else you need to do first?

Yes, I do. I've got people I need to talk to for one thing. I have to sort things out with them. I'll tell you what, Grace, I'll talk to you again and see what I want to tell you then.

'She's meeting the preacher,' Harrigan said. 'Get a time.'

When will you talk to me again?

Later on tonight. Because I do have to talk to other people first. Then I'll talk to you. It might be pretty late. Maybe sometime after midnight?

You can't tell me more exactly than that? Just so I can make sure I'm here.

No, I can't. Does that mean you're not going to do what you said you would?

No, I'll be here.

So you're telling me I can depend on that? For you to be there?

If I'm not, it's only because I've just left my desk for a little while and I've gone to get something to eat or something like that. And if that happens, you just say that you want to talk to me and then I'll come back and I'll talk to you as soon as I can.

There are other people there?

Yes, there are.

Are they watching us talk?

Yes, they are.

You didn't say that. But I can trust you, can I?

Yes, you can. You can trust me to be honest with you.

No, Grace. Can I trust you full stop?

You can trust me full stop. But will you do that, Firewall? Will you come in? Will you tell us where you are?

Not yet. Everything's not yet at the moment.

As these words appeared Lucy's computer seemed to freeze. The battery on her mobile phone had died.

On the other end of the line Grace waited.

'Something's happened,' she said. 'The connection's gone. We've lost her.'

'Try again,' Harrigan said.

Firewall are you out there? Have I lost you?

There was nothing.

'She's gone. Maybe she's just dropped out,' Grace said.

'It's a start,' Harrigan said, standing upright. 'We keep talking to her. We keep talking to her and we keep watching him. Sooner or later they're going to meet up. We just have to be patient.'

Grace leaned on her elbows looking at the screen.

'She's just a kid. She talks just like a kid,' she said.

'Yeah. A dangerous one,' he replied.

Grace kept looking at the screen, shaking her head. The rest of the crowd dispersed.

'Keep me posted,' he said, resisting the urge to touch her on the shoulder, and went back to his office.

He looked out of the window wondering, if the Firewall and the preacher did meet, who was going to kill who? At the moment, he had his money on the preacher. Outside, there was no rain. The clouds were almost black and although it was supposedly still day it was dark enough to be night. He waited, it was all he could do. He was waiting for his turn to make a move.

Lucy picked up her dead phone and shrugged. She threw it into a heap of rubbish in a corner then went outside into the main part of the garage. She sat on the concrete floor and leaned against the wall near the office door, looking towards where her car straddled the pit. She drew her knees up and leaned her forehead on them. She began to think of death as a combination of presence and absence, where the body is there only to remind you that you can never talk to someone again. She chased this idea around in her mind, drawing circles in the dust on the floor, shaking her head. Absence compounded on absence; she had no power to cry for anyone. She was dry, used up.

'I've got nothing to lose, have I?' she said to her silent ghosts. 'No one can tell me I do. Not Grace, whoever she is. Even if she is walking in the dark just like me. I don't feel anything.'

She lit a cigarette and threw the match, still burning, onto the concrete floor. It burned for a short time longer, then went out.

Turtle would say that she still had things to lose. He would know, better than anyone. How are you, Turtle? Does your father still come and rub that pain out of your back, the way you said he does? If I could, I would come and see you, I would sit with you and I'd feed you, the way you say he does. I would take you out if you wanted to go out and I wouldn't care what anyone thought about either of us. You say that sometimes people won't look at you. You say that they stand right beside you and say that you don't have a brain or any feelings. If anyone said anything about you like that and I was with you, I'd make sure they never said anything hurtful to you again. I'd tell them what they could do.

She felt an intense need to talk to him, to go online and say, will you forgive me? I forgive you. I want to talk to you so much. She had no means to reach him and no way of acquiring those means. All she had was time, hours in which to wait. She leaned her head against the wall. This was endgame. One more sleep and it would all be over. If she ever slept again.

32

The waiting ground on, like slow wheels. Harrigan had put in place the graveyard shift and sent some of his other people home, but by late in the evening they felt as worn as he was, the enclosure was getting to them. They manned the phones, checked the information they received constantly from the public and found that almost all of it was either old or useless. Opposite the Temple in Camperdown, the surveillance teams sat rubbing their eyes as they waited outside a silent, almost dark building. The sheer boredom ate at everyone. Harrigan told his people to catnap whenever they could and sent them out on breaks to give them some fresh air, to get them to move.

A little after nine, he took a phone call from the surveillance team telling him the preacher had just left the Temple.

'He's been picked up by a very nice Jaguar,' a female voice said, 'chauffeur driven. Our registration check says it's owned by a Mrs Yvonne Lindley, north St Ives. Looks like he's going out to a late dinner. There he goes. He's heading off to the Harbour Bridge by the looks of it. Going north.'

Half his luck.

'Keep on him,' Harrigan said. 'Don't let him get away from you.'

'We'll do our best.'

'No,' Harrigan replied, 'you won't lose him, is what you'll do.'

In an excess of self-protection as much as anything else, he had earlier rung the security firm charged with guarding the Whole Life Health Centre clinics. They had assured him that the clinics were under twenty-four-hour protection. He asked for that in writing and then logged the time and date of his call. He emailed Marvin, copying the message to everyone he needed to if he was going to protect his back, expressing concern that at least one of these clinics just might go up tonight, only to receive in reply a phone call from the Tooth's personal assistant saying that they had every confidence in present arrangements. 'Send me that in writing,' he said to her, knowing that she would not. Harrigan was snookered, he had no people he could send to fill the gap. He was reduced to making sure the street patrols had been alerted and having the staff at the clinics warned personally by his own people.

As the time ground on, he took another call from the surveillance team.

'We're sitting outside Yvonne Lindley's pile on the north shore. And a very nice pile it is too. He's inside,' the female voice said.

'Call me if anything happens.'

'And the rain comes down at last. We'll be back to you as soon as he's on the move.'

The storm which had threatened all day had finally broken; the rain began to pour in sheets down his window. It was a relief. He went out into the main office to see who was there and who was out. He saw Grace disappearing into the tea room, presumably in search of coffee; a small group in a corner with Jeffo, Ian sitting nearby. Trev was out in search of fast food. Grace reappeared on her way back to the computer room. Engrossed in whatever it was they were looking at, the small group around Jeffo had not seen him. He had turned to go back to his office when he heard laughter, some quiet, almost whispered comments, louder laughter and then Ian speaking, not quietly.

'Fuck off, mate. I wouldn't show that around here if I was you.'

Harrigan turned again in time to see Grace stop nearby, putting a mug of coffee down on a desk.

'What's that?' she said.

Jeffo said something to her, Harrigan could not hear what. He was waving a picture from side to side in front of her, moving his body with it and laughing. She walked up to him. The crowd around him parted a little.

'Give me that,' she said.

'No way, José,' Jeffo replied, passing it out of her reach to someone else.

She hit him hard across the face with an open hand, the sound like a whiplash throughout the open office. He jerked back in shock and touched blood on his mouth. There was a collective gasp and, in the background, muted cheers from a few other watchers. Jeffo stood up slowly, moving around towards her. She stood her ground.

'Gracie, you back off now,' Ian said urgently, on his feet as well and circling them. 'Jeffo, why don't you sit down and just shut up for once.'

'You bitch. I bit my lip,' Jeffo said, moving dangerously close to her.

'You give me that,' she said again, not moving, facing him.

Harrigan was between them, outraged.

'What do you think you're doing?' he said to Grace. 'You never do that. You never, never hit anyone you work with. Don't you ever do that again. Not while you work for me.'

Grace stepped back, pushing her hair out of the way, smudging her makeshift make-up. She looked sideways and then back at him and barely nodded. Jeffo had also stepped back, muttering a single word to her as he did so. He was grinning as he took repossession of the photograph but no one else was smiling. Harrigan turned to him just as he was slipping it out of sight into his top drawer.

'What's that, mate? Let me have a look,' Harrigan said.

'It's just a joke. Nothing.'

'If it's a joke, let's share it. We can all have a laugh, we need one. Come on. Let's see it. Give it here.'

There was silence as Harrigan found himself looking at a picture of a younger Grace on a stage somewhere, holding a microphone and wearing high heels but otherwise naked to the waist and barely clothed at all.

'That is not me,' she said angrily. 'That is airbrushed rubbish. It's got nothing to do with me. I don't even look like that.'

Harrigan felt sick to his stomach. He eyeballed Jeffo while he tore the photograph into four pieces and shouted for Dea. The tiny woman appeared at once.

'Shred it,' Harrigan said. 'Flush it down the toilet with the rest of the shit. Got any more of those to go with it, mate?'

'No, it's just the one.'

'Don't tell me that. You've always got something up your sleeve. Let's have a look in your desk.'

Harrigan pulled out an envelope containing several more pictures. He tore those up as well. They stood in silence listening to the shredder mince them to pieces.

'So where did these come from?' Harrigan asked, looking at the envelope. 'Old Roger. Straight out of Marvin's office, in other words. Wouldn't you know it? Nice to know they've got nothing better to do with their time down there. Or their money, for that matter. Unlike the rest of us.'

He smiled. The room remained completely quiet.

'You love this, don't you, mate,' he said to Jeffo, still smiling, 'little jokes like this. You just love them.'

'It is just a fucking joke, Boss. I'm not the only one that's got them. It's nothing. What does it matter?'

'Oh, but you love it. Sticking a knife in there, bad-mouthing someone here, playing little games, pinning nice little pictures up on the wall. You've always got something for everyone else to laugh at. You get a charge out of it, don't you? You're someone everyone here can rely on when they really need to, aren't you? You know what loyalty means. You're here, waiting to stick it to them when they need you most.'

'It was just a fucking joke. There was nothing to it. Why worry? Everyone knows —'

He stopped.

'Everyone knows what?' Harrigan asked.

'Nothing.'

'No, come on, tell me. Everyone knows something

that I don't. I don't think Grace knows it either. What is it? You want to say it?'

Jeffo was silent. He looked at Grace, who had moved to sit down at a spare desk. She looked away, meeting no one's eye.

'Okay,' Harrigan said, 'no one knows anything. Except this. Clear your desk and get out. You can go home now.'

'You can't do that.'

'I can. Get out. Now. While I watch you. And don't waste your time doing it.'

Harrigan stood by as Jeffo cleared his desk and went towards the exit. At the door, he stopped.

'Why don't you piss her off instead of me?' he called as a parting shot. 'Wouldn't be a problem then. But we all know the answer to that one, don't we?'

'Get out,' Harrigan almost shouted, unexpectedly stung to real anger.

Jeffo was gone, into the lift. Harrigan turned to look at everyone else. Grace was watching him but it was impossible know what she was thinking. She looked down at the desk, rubbing her forehead. He did not speak to her, there was nothing he could say publicly. The air jangled with the contrarieties of tension, relief and tiredness, a sense of chafing, human irritation pushing at the edges.

'Everyone who's got work to do, do it,' he said. 'Everyone who can take a break now, take it. Get some fresh air and something to eat. Forget about the last twenty minutes. We have to keep our minds on this. Take your pagers with you.'

One or two people did leave after he had spoken, friends of Jeffo, but there was nothing he could do about that. Others went back to work.

'Boss.'

Louise's slow and gravelly voice interrupted him. She was standing beside him, breathing whisky.

'What is it, Lou?'

'Something you should see. I came out to see you earlier but you were preoccupied.' She smiled a slow, sardonic, alcoholic smile as she glanced around at the room. 'Thought I'd better wait. You need to know about this. You might like to get some other people in here as well. Gracie, you need to look at this too. This is a different sort of picture,' she added very quietly.

They gathered around the monitor. Grace sat in her chair, back a little and staying out of the way. She felt a tap on her shoulder and looked up to see Ian handing her a fresh cup of coffee.

'Don't worry about it, Gracie,' he said quietly, 'Jeffo's just a shit.'

She smiled at him out of pure relief.

Harrigan noticed the small communication and briefly wondered about everything and nothing that might exist between the two of them, before turning his attention to the screen.

'I went looking for the Avenging Angels,' Louise said a little creakily. 'I thought, they'll be there somewhere. If people enjoy sending out photographs like the one they sent out, they'll be on the web somewhere, showing off. And sure enough, there they were. This site moves around. You'll see why. It's amateurish, I've got to say, you could do better. There's no talent here. The Firewall would do a better job, she's got some imagination. But you'll see. Here we go.'

The site opened to the tinny sound of a drum beating and the words 'Avenging Angels: Abortionists made to face God' appeared on the screen. A set of doors opened and the sound of gunshots rang out in the background. An angel with ammunition belts slung around its hips pointed with a handgun to a poster on a brick wall in an alleyway. 'Bounty Hunters Wanted,' the poster said, 'Generous rewards offered for the destruction of persons performing abortions, those who authorise child-killing, and the buildings that house these Hellholes. Whether you work for God or the Devil (and let the Devil's own kill each other, we say) the Avenging Angels are prepared to pay good money for the bringing of these mass murderers and the witches who serve them before the ultimate court, God's tribunal. Be a hero. Save a child. Guarantee of payment on receipt of positive proof of destruction, death or disabling.'

'This is serious?' Harrigan asked.

'That's what I asked myself. I thought, someone's playing a bad joke on me and I didn't come down in the last shower. No, it's serious. Here's the proof,' Louise replied.

A gallery of eight pictures titled 'The Damned' appeared on the screen while the background noise became one of children crying.

'Here we go. One more time.'

Louise clicked on a picture of Agnes Liu marked with a red slash. She was standing in a supermarket car park at a location presumably somewhere in California, with her sunglasses in her hand and a bag over her shoulder. The words 'Bounty Paid' appeared underneath.

'For your information, that bounty isn't small. Whoever shot the doc got $20,000 US for it. Which is even better in Australian money. And here's the piccie our friends sent the doc the morning Hurst shot her.'

The image of Dr Laura Di-Cuollo expanded to cover the screen. The words 'Bounty Paid' were also stamped underneath it.

'There's a whole file of names and addresses and photographs in there of people who've got prices on their heads and where you can find them if you want to.'

'Is there anyone else we know in there?' Harrigan asked in his neutral voice.

'No. These lucky people are all Americans and Canadians. I guess they just picked on the doc because she was in California for that little while. They thought she was fair game.'

'Where is this site?'

'Don't know. I've got a trace out on it but I can't give you a location just yet and they might shut me out any minute.'

'Who are these people?' he said.

'Oh, no, Boss,' Louise was grinning, 'they don't go around telling people who they are. They just put everybody else's name out there.'

It wasn't quite what he had meant.

'Who got $20,000 US for shooting the doc?' he asked.

'The preacher,' Grace replied. 'Lucy Hurst doesn't have it.'

'Neither does he, Gracie.' Trev, swallowing a mouthful of hamburger, had appeared later than everyone else and stood in the background. 'We've checked Fredericksen's finances backwards. That money's not there.' He moved forward. 'So is Hurst working for them? With them?'

'Maybe they're using her,' Grace said.

'Might be she's using them,' Louise replied.

'Hurst hasn't been back online?' Harrigan asked Grace.

'No. Her mobile's dead, I think. If that's the only means of connection she's got, we won't hear from her again until she can steal another one.'

Harrigan looked at his watch.

'All right. We pick that information up and we follow it. Meantime, we still wait. We watch the preacher. We take the phone calls. We keep monitoring. As soon as anything moves, we're onto it.'

The crowd dispersed, Louise leaving the room with them. Grace turned her chair back to her computer screen and buried her hands in her long hair, then looked up to see Harrigan standing at her elbow.

'Yeah?' she said.

'Come and talk to me while I've got a little time, Grace,' he said very quietly. 'Come and enlighten me on a few matters. You owe me an explanation. More than one.'

Grace looked at the screen.

'What if she comes back on?'

'If she does, Louise will be here, she can get you back in. I'm going to my little Greek café around the corner for an ouzo and water and to remind myself there's another world out there. You can join me there if you want to.'

Not long after he'd left the room, Louise returned. She might as well have been listening to them talk.

'Take a break, Gracie,' she said, 'go and get a cigarette. I'll keep an eye on things for you.'

'Will you?'

'Yeah, don't worry, I'll call you,' the older woman replied. 'Go have a fag. Indulge yourself. Life's too short. Too short for anything.'

'Thanks, Lou.'

Grace smiled and left, in desperate need of nicotine. In the women's toilets, she washed away her smudged make-up, feeling too worn to replace it. The cold water on her face revived her. Returning to the office she saw that several other people had also left to get some fresh air. She slipped out. Those remaining noticed that she was gone, checked that the boss was also out, and drew their own conclusions.

Outside, the lights of the tower office blocks burned spangled gold in the rain, a chequerboard of light and dark. The streets were empty, more as a consequence of the weather than the lateness of the hour. Debris littered the footpaths but the rain was reduced simply to a storm, the strength of the wind had dropped. Grace parked illegally, working on the belief that no one would be delivering goods or handing out parking tickets on a night like tonight. The café was empty. Yellow lights gleamed on dull wood and polished grey linoleum. The man with the silver and black hair tied back in a ponytail stood behind the counter, looking a little more crumpled than he had that morning. He recognised her as she walked in.

'He's out the back,' he said. 'Do you want anything?'

'Coffee. Do you have anything to eat?'

'Yeah, I can get you something. Go and sit down.'

The room smelled the same as it had early that morning. Harrigan sat at the table in his shirtsleeves, drinking an ouzo and water and eating a bowl of some sort of meat stew. His pager and mobile sat on the table where he could see them. He smiled at her.

'You did come,' he said. 'I didn't know if you would.'

She smiled and put her cigarettes on the table.

'Light up if you want.'

'No, I'm not going to do that,' she said. Coffee and a simple meal arrived on the table in front of her. 'What's the food like here?' she asked after the counterman had left.

'Basic,' he replied. 'It's just fuel. It'll keep you going.'

She started to eat just as he finished.

'Talk to me, Grace,' he said. 'Tell me why I threw Jeffo off the team just now.'

'Are you sorry he's gone?'

'That's not the point. And you know that. You can tell me. Is there anything else out wide that I need to know about right now?'

Grace ate in silence for a few moments.

'It's not Marvin,' she said. 'It's Baby Tooth. I was at the Academy with him.'

'Lucky you,' Harrigan said with genuine sympathy, forbearing to ask if she'd had the pleasure of knocking back the attentions of Tooth junior, who was noted for going after anything that could wear a skirt.

'It's like father, like son with them, isn't it? It was our last night. We were having a party and he got legless. Me and a friend took him back to his room so he could sleep it off. And guess what? He had these exam papers on his desk. They had "Embargo" all over them, he'd got them from head office. He cheated at every exam and he still didn't do that well.'

'Grace, I thought you had a brain. Tell me you didn't.'

'I didn't, it was my friend. He was so mad, he went and dragged the principal out of bed. That was Sweet Freddie, wasn't it? He didn't want anything upsetting his retirement. He sent it up the line to head office. Nothing happened. Until graduation, when the Tooth walks up to me smiling from ear to ear and tells me ever so quietly I might as well quit now and not waste my time because if I don't I'm going to be really sorry. He's spent the last eight months proving it. I've seen that picture stuck up on a lot of walls. And I know it's still out there.'

'What happened to your friend?'

'He already had another job. In London. I didn't know that. He's a forensic accountant. He's making a fortune over there.'

She tried to laugh it off. Come to London with me, Gracie, but I don't want anything like babies. She could hear him saying it. Everything between them had died there and then.

Harrigan watched her as she ate in silence for a little while longer and then pushed the plate to the side, the food not quite finished.

He walked out on you, didn't he? Dropped you right in it and walked away. I'd treat you better than that.

'That wasn't too bad,' she said.

'You don't have to be polite.' He watched her light a cigarette. 'That's a nasty story.'

'It's just a story.'

'The Tooth can't do anything to you while you work for me. But don't ever do that again, Grace. You never hit anyone. It doesn't matter how much they provoke you.'

'Well, I did,' she said. 'Maybe I'm only human. Maybe I got pushed too far.'

He wanted to say, you can't be human and do this job; you're too human, that's your problem. In the brief silence, his mobile rang. It was his surveillance team.

'He's on the move,' the voice said. 'It's bucketing down out here and the visibility is very bad. This is not going to be easy.'

'You don't lose him,' Harrigan said. 'It doesn't matter what happens.'

Grace was looking at him expectantly.

'The preacher's on the move,' he told her.

'We should get back in.'

'In a moment. You still haven't been straight with me, Grace.'

'Yes, I have.'

'Not completely. Don't tell me you have.' He had finished his drink and sat leaning his elbows on the table. 'Marvin's dangerous but the most he can do is run you out of your job. Don't think I don't know what that means. But the people we're dealing with right now will do a lot more than that. You tell me. Do they know you? Just give me an honest answer. I need to know.'

Grace ground out her cigarette and was faced with a fundamental inability to lie.

'Yes, they know who I am. I don't know if they've made the connection yet.'

She sat back, feeling cold, her heart beating strongly. She was afraid and her hands were shaking badly. She refused to look at him.

Harrigan leaned his chin on his knuckles.

'Fredericksen has,' he said. 'From the moment he laid eyes on you. He recognised you again today and he threatened you to me. He knows exactly who you are.'

'He can only have seen my picture. I don't know how he could know who I am just from that.'

'You've got a face that's very easy to remember.'

'It's just a face,' she said. 'Anyway. They took my picture. One day when I was on my way into the city clinic. They hassled me, I showed them my warrant card and I sent them on their way. I shouldn't have, should I? They remembered my name. They sent me one of their lovely letters saying they knew where to find me.'

'They had your address and you didn't tell me that?'

'You didn't need to know.'

He was silent, staring at her. He could not quite believe what he was hearing.

'When did this happen?'

'Just before Christmas,' she said, again not looking at him.

He did the mathematics while Grace lit another cigarette. She was still not looking at him.

'You could do that, could you?' he said, very quietly.

As soon as he said it, he wished he hadn't. Unexpectedly, he had felt the nudge of the prohibitions he had been taught during his boyhood, an unexpected repugnance that she could have had an abortion. He didn't want to feel that.

She looked at him, drawing on her cigarette. 'Yes, Paul. I could do that.'

Her tone was icy. There was silence.

'I don't need this,' he said.

'That's all that matters, is it?'

'It does when I'm holding everything together.'

'This is not your business,' she said angrily. 'It won't stop you wrapping this up.'

'If something happens to you, who goes to see your family? I do. These lunatics shoot people they think deserve to die. Do you think I want to knock on your family's door and have to tell them something like that? You don't get paid to take risks like this.'

Grace shook her head. 'Isn't it my life? Don't I make that decision?'

'Not while you work for me.'

'No? Do you know you don't give people much space, Paul? You like to organise them too much. You think you know how they ought to feel and what they ought to do. Maybe you don't.'

Harrigan felt heat rise at the back of his neck.

'You're getting very personal there, Grace. Anyone else but you and you'd be gone.'

'This is personal. Because we are personal, aren't we?

Everything we do is personal. I know we were for about twenty minutes in here this morning. I don't think I was imagining it. You asked me.'

Harrigan watched her hand smooth the scar on her neck. He had wanted to ask her if she would sleep with him, he had thought she would. He did not know what he wanted to ask of her now. He did not know how to describe her any more.

'Do we have anything else to say to each other? Do you need to know anything else?' she said into his silence, taking it to mean that their original twenty minutes was finished. 'I should get back to work.'

Before he could reply, his mobile rang again.

'We're on the Pacific Highway,' the voice said. 'I'm sorry but I've got to tell you that we've lost him.'

'You haven't.'

'We have. He gave us the slip, he had it planned. He got out of the car at an intersection and disappeared down a lane and into someone's garden, we think. We don't know where he went after that. We stopped the Jag and we've spoken to the driver. The target had asked him to stop and let him out. We've got a search on but I think we've lost him for the night.'

'Then keep searching. And tomorrow morning you can come in here and you can explain yourselves to me.'

'They've lost him,' he said to Grace in disbelief. 'What do they do for brains? They're supposed to be the best. *Fuck!*'

She was shocked to see how much the exhaustion and strain had changed his face. 'Excuse me,' he said, strangely polite, and walked out of the room.

She waited for a few moments then ashed out her cigarette. She collected their joint goods, coats, phones, her shoulder bag, his wallet which he had left on the table. She stopped at the counter on her way out.

'What do I owe you?' she said.

The man shook his head. He looked out through the doors at Harrigan who was standing under the shelter of the entrance way, staring at the weather.

'He works too hard,' he said.

'Yes,' she replied. Don't we all.

'Thanks,' she said and left, appearing beside Harrigan in the doorway to hand him his coat. He accepted it without speaking, together with his pager, his phone and his wallet, the sight of which made him raise his eyebrows in some surprise.

Grace felt the warmth of Harrigan's physicality in the fabric of his jacket, the cotton of his white shirt, with all the closeness of aftershave and ordinary human odour. Crossing the line to connect to the body beneath the fabric had slipped past the bounds of possibility. All the sexual need she still felt for him had led her into grief, not much else, but this was usual. It was better to ask why she might want to put herself into the poisonous situation of having an affair with her boss.

He looked at the empty street, waiting for Lucy Hurst to appear any moment out of the dark. A degree of control had returned to his face.

'You should have told me all of that sooner than now, Grace,' he said. 'None of the things you've done tonight have been very professional.'

She did not know how to interpret the disappointment in his voice.

'I'm just starting out. I'll toughen up in time, the way I'm supposed to,' she said, without looking at him. 'I'll see you back there.'

She left him standing in the doorway of the café and ran through the rain to her car.

'Yeah. Probably you will. You've probably got that in you somewhere,' he said quietly to himself, watching her go.

Grace breathed in solitude as freedom. No one need know she was letting herself slide badly enough to cry as she drove back to the office, the tears grudgingly squeezing out for her. Out on the streets it was still pouring rain. Lightning strikes split the sky.

33

The lightning crashed down over the bell curve of the sky and, for an instant, illuminated Lucy in her car, driving away from the Whole Life Health Centre at Randwick. She knew this building from her own experience: she had been taken there twice without wanting to go there, and then had passed it by when she went to and from the garage. Mostly, however, like the others in its chain, it had been studied for some months by the others in Graeme's inner circle. It had been photographed, notes taken of its interior layout, and its possible destruction discussed at the Temple. Discussed, as most of these things were between Graeme and Bronwyn and the select few. As something wanted desperately, the way people she knew out on the streets talked about who they had last fucked or how much money they would get once they had done this one job, this single deal. Destruction was a fantasy never achieved by any of them. Lucy was here for another reason; she had her own point to make.

'Alarms ring back at base', the signs on the building said. Lucy treated them with scepticism and, with practised skill, entered through a narrow back window into a toilet, out of weather that was harsh enough to keep anyone inside. Not that she cared, she was happy to let the rain chill her to the bone. She had kept the device she had made dry by wrapping it in plastic around her body, and delivered it whole to the building, placing it next to the electrical circuits, unconcerned for the danger she was putting herself in. She only needed enough charge and accelerant to start a fire that would gut the inside of the building and she knew how that could be done. She was the only one in the darkened building, so what did it matter if it did go up and she went with it? As she left, she considered that if the alarms had rung back at the base, then no one had bothered to answer them. They must all be watching TV and saying how bad the weather was.

She dumped her car on the other side of Central Station, leaving it to be cannibalised. She had come to her final place of sanctuary, a former garment factory in Surry Hills marked for redevelopment, the owners now bankrupt, the ground-floor windows broken and boarded up. Inside, scraps of material, broken sewing needles, clothing racks and parts of discarded dressmaker's dummies covered the floors. The space had been appropriated by the needy and the homeless, and accommodated another community, a shifting body of artists who wanted the light that came through the wide windows overlooking the street on the second floor. The upper storey room was filled with their leftover works. Soft sculpture and collage, paintings and unfinished objects were spread across the open space amidst the pink, plastic limbs of the dummies.

Lucy trod quietly through these plastic things and sidestepped the prone figure of someone sleeping in the midst of the debris. She went up to the top floor, to a small dog's leg of a room opposite a filthy bathroom. She had barricaded this room against invasion by others with her own locks. It had a narrow bed, a limited view and a curtainless window where the rain had covered the glass like a crystal frosting. There was a very weak light in the room, something to push back the shadows a little. She dumped her backpack against the wall and took out her gun, which she left on the bed. She dried herself as well as she could and then sat on the bed with the gun in her hands and waited. She looked at the dial on her watch, luminous in the darkling room. Just on midnight. Time was ticking down.

The same storm caught the preacher as he crossed a deserted suburban park somewhere on the upper north shore, a lightning flash briefly revealing the isolated figure in the darkness. He hurried through the sparse trees, huddled in his coat, head down, intent on where he was going. He pulled his hood further over his face as he ran towards a waiting car on the far corner of the park, near a house where an outside light was burning. He got in, greeting the driver, and the car pulled away from the kerb. Some minutes afterwards, the outside lights of the nearby house were extinguished.

The rain had been hammering down but as they drove it began to cease gradually. They travelled the backstreets towards North Sydney. Here the preacher left the first car to claim another which had been left waiting for him in a twenty-four-hour car park. He drove into the city between the tower blocks that surrounded the approach to the steel coat hanger and then over the curve of the bridge misty in the lighter rain.

It was just after midnight. In the near distance, the office towers of the city appeared as hazy pillars of electric light. The preacher saw them as hollow structures floating in profound darkness, a prelude to the day when time would stop and there would be only light everlasting. On that day, he hoped to satisfy his own hunger as a collector of souls. His hunger never let him rest; it pushed him now to meet with someone he was quite sure would be waiting to greet him with a loaded gun.

He parked not far from the garment factory in Surry Hills and went inside. By now the rain had almost stopped. As he approached the room on the third floor, he wondered whether she had yet arrived but when the unlocked door opened to him he knew that she was there to meet him. He stepped inside and, in the half-shadows, saw Lucy sitting on the bed aiming a gun at him. She said in her familiar voice, 'Stop right there, Graeme. Don't move. Just sit on the floor.'

The preacher closed the door and sat with his back against it.

'Lucy,' he said, 'it's nice to see you again.'

'Yeah, right,' she said, smiling.

'It is. You should believe me. I have been looking forward to this meeting very much. We have a great deal to talk about.'

Lucy laughed.

'There are times when I don't believe you. You could walk into anything. You don't even look worried.'

'Why should I be? If God puts his cloak around you, why should you be afraid? God has his cloak around you at the moment, Lucy. You should realise you don't have a reason to be frightened of anything.'

He spoke smoothly. She shook her head, trying to shield herself from the immediate hypnotism of his voice.

'Fuck you, Graeme. I didn't come here to listen to you talk shit to me. I want you to tell me about Greggie. I want to know what you did.'

'I did nothing. Greg overdosed and he overdosed because Bronwyn is too stupid to lock a cupboard door properly. You should talk to her. The woman's a fool. I sometimes wonder what dimension she really inhabits.'

Lucy rested her gun on her knees and laughed again.

'You did nothing. You never fucking do, do you? Not because you didn't want to. In case you've forgotten, I was there when you were talking about helping both me and him to the afterlife.'

'Those were only words, Lucy. The afterlife is all around us but we don't realise it. Now listen to me. What do you think you're going to do now?'

She thought how easily he changed the conversation. Nothing fazed him. She glanced at her watch. 'Don't know,' she replied.

'I can help you —'

'To Paradise? Yeah.'

'I can. I can get you out of this building. I can give you money. Do you want to go to California? You can go to California. It costs money but the money is there and it can be done. If I think it's worth it.'

'If you think it's worth it? Graeme, I'm the one who's holding the gun.'

'But I'm the one who has the means. You have to ask yourself: what do you want?'

She smiled pure steel. 'I ask myself that all the time. At the moment there's nothing for me to want. I'll tell you something. You know the clinic on Anzac Parade?' He nodded. 'It's going up in a little while.'

He was not quite laughing as he replied. 'You never joke about these things, do you?'

'No, I do what I say I'm going to do. I'm the only one who does. It's for Greggie. Nothing else is going to make anyone take any notice of him. And then maybe I'll just ring the pigs and say, hi, here I am. Blow me away if you want. I don't care.'

'You're going to put yourself in the hands of the police?' He sounded contemptuous.

'What does it matter if I do? They can beat the shit out of me. You take it if you have to. How can things be worse than they are now?'

His face had an odd look, not quite triumph, not quite joy.

'You'll find out in gaol, won't you, Lucy? You'll have the rest of your life in there to think about it. And for you, that's a very long time indeed.'

'I'd be careful, Graeme.' Her voice was shaking. 'I might blow *you* away for saying that.'

'But you won't. Because you once told me you wished you never fired the gun in the first place. Isn't that how you feel?'

'I can use this on you if I have to, Graeme. Don't worry about that.' The threat was unconvincing even to her. 'But, yeah. I do wish I'd never shot that woman and that man. But that's different to now, it's way different.'

He laughed.

'Oh, yes. It's very different, Lucy. Think about it. The woman you shot brought death to thousands, including you, ultimately brought death to her husband and ruined her son's life. But you blame yourself. She should be accused, not you.'

'Graeme, I pulled that trigger. It was me, not her.'

'Do you know what you're doing when you say that? You're taking this woman's guilt on yourself. You're inviting her to injure you for a second time.'

You don't know! Lucy screamed the words in her head. She stared at him.

'And for this,' he continued, 'you want to give yourself up to the police. You don't even know who the police are. I want you to look at this. It's all right, I don't have a gun in here.'

He reached into an inside pocket and took out a photograph which he skidded across the floor to her. Lucy put her gun on the bed. She reached down and picked it up.

'Her name is on the back,' he said. 'She's with the police but that's not all she is.'

Turning it over, Lucy looked at a card that had been stapled onto the back, peering at it in the half light.

'Grace,' she said. She looked at Graeme watching her. The sight of his face made her pick up her gun again.

'That woman is a torturer, Lucy. She's the woman they sent to persecute Greg.' His voice became a quiet rustling whisper that ate into the intimacy of her thoughts. She pulled back from his gaze but could not escape his words. 'I'm sure he feared her. I'm sure when she had him in a cell she tormented him beyond endurance. I don't find it at all surprising that he should be driven to take his own life. She would put that seed into his head herself. Think of her saying to him: You are nothing. Why not die now? She's a torturer and a witch. We took that picture of her when she was on her way into an abortuary. Bronwyn stopped her. She said, think of that innocent child you're about to kill. She laughed in Bronwyn's face. She assaulted her. Get out of my way, she said. Watch me while I kill. That woman walks blood through the streets. Can you imagine what will happen to you when you put yourself in her hands? She will know how to hurt you. Do you want to be tortured the way you were in your own family? Because this time you will be in gaol for ever and there will be no way out. No streets to escape to.'

His voice had become a sound in her own mind. She felt surprised when it became silent. The gun hung loosely in her hands. She did not speak.

'Now there is someone who deserves to die, don't you think?'

Lucy swallowed. 'I couldn't get near her.'

'Finding her wouldn't be hard. We have her address. But you wouldn't have to go to her. In her arrogance, she would come to you. And you would be waiting for her. Then the police would know what they really are. That this war does not work just one way. They can be defeated, they can suffer humiliation as much as anyone else.'

'Maybe I don't want to kill anyone. Maybe I've done enough of that.'

'You have a building that's about to burn. People could die as a result of that if that's what worries you.'

'No, they won't. I'm not hurting anyone. There's no one in there.'

'Fires spread. The rain has stopped, there's nothing to prevent it now. That building is a Hellhole, it will burn fiercely. Others around it may also burn. I don't say it will happen. I won't be concerned if it does. That building has to be expunged from the face of the earth and if that's the price to be paid, so be it. But I do say to you, you have the courage others lack. I can help you. I can get you out of here.'

'How can you get me out of here?'

'I can get a car sent here to pick you up. You stay and lock yourself in. I'll have them come for you tomorrow evening. No one will notice anything. Then there will be a nice house for you to rest in until we can send you away to safety.'

'Yeah. And along the way I end up dead.'

'No, Lucy. You will have nothing to be afraid of because I will know that I can rely on you. You will prove it to me. That woman is a murderer. But you will expunge her evil. And you know that it'll take only a few seconds because you've done it before. We'll help you. Believe me, we will. You are someone very special.'

Lucy sat with the gun lying loosely in her lap. She thought: my throat is full of broken bones.

'What will you do?' he asked.

'I have to think.'

'There's no time.'

She sat for a few moments in silence. 'You trust me, do you, Graeme? If you think I'm someone special?'

'Would I ask you to do this if I didn't trust you absolutely?'

'Then I want some things from you. I need a phone. My phone's dead. Have you got one?'

'I can let you have the one I've got with me. Why do you need it?'

'I just need it, okay? Don't ask questions. Don't worry, it hasn't got anything to do with you.'

After a moment's silence, he took his mobile phone out of his pocket and passed it over to her. She looked at it, then dropped it on the bed.

'You have to be careful who you call. You don't know who is listening these days,' he said.

'There's something else I want.'

'What is it?'

'I want a key to the Temple.'

'You can't come anywhere near the Temple, Lucy. The police are watching it twenty-four hours a day. They're across the road in that offensive woman's house and they think I can't see them.'

'I want my key to the Temple back, Graeme. I want that more than anything.'

'There's no need. You can't use it.'

'You've just said I'm special. Prove it. I used to have a key and we both know why I don't have one any more. I know you, I've watched you. You ask people in and then you lock them out again whenever you feel like it. And you never tell them why. You're not doing that to me. People have been lying to me all my life. I have to know that you can't lock me out after this. Not with what you're asking me to do.'

After a moment's silence, he took his set of keys out of his pocket.

'The keys to the kingdom,' he said. 'You can have this one.'

'How do I know you're not lying to me?'

'You can see it's new. I'll show you.' He matched the two new keys to each other, the shiny brass finish gleamed faintly in the weak light. He slipped one of them off the key ring and handed it to her.

'It's nice to have you back, Lucy. Don't lose this. It's the only spare key I have and I won't be having another one cut.'

'I never lose anything I want to keep,' she said, slipping it into her jeans pocket.

'This brings you back to the heart of things. You won't leave it again now. You'll always be there.'

She did not answer this. She looked at her watch. He stood up. He was smiling and relaxed.

'Aren't you going to wait with me for that building to go up?'

'No, I think I should go now. Some sleep for us both would be in order. And a new day tomorrow, a new life.'

'Yeah, that's right,' she said.

She stood up also, leaving her gun and the phone on the bed. He opened the door, then stopped. She was quite close to him. He leaned forward and kissed her on the forehead.

'You are very brave,' he said.

She watched him leave, he did not look back.

In the room, she sat on the bed. I'm hungry, Graeme, you could have brought me something to eat. Her throat ached, she would not have been able to swallow anything. She had been hungry before; it was not unusual for her to go without food. She had gone hungry for longer than this when she was out on the streets. There was no sound in the room. Her own breathing, the movement of her blood, was reduced to a regular, silent beat in her ears. Her gun lay beside her on the bed. She looked at her watch. There wasn't much time.

34

Harrigan was taking a catnap when a sleepy-eyed Trevor shook him by the shoulder.

'The Firewall's online,' he said.

'Is she talking to Grace?' He said her name as just another of his officers.

'No. She's updating her website. Come and see.'

He followed Trevor into the computer room. The graveyard shift had already gathered there. Grace sat a little to the side, watching from where she was seated in front her own monitor. She did not seem to notice him.

'Lookee here,' Louise said, as he appeared, 'this is the promised land. It's so pretty. This girl has so much talent, it's a waste.'

The screen displayed a green slope of flowering trees leading down to a honey-coloured rock looking out over a wild forest. Small streams flowed down to become clear waterfalls over the rock, blue and white flowers grew in carpets underneath the trees. At the summit of the hill there was a small, glittering, turreted castle with wide doors and windows. Birds flew across the blue sky behind it.

'I know that place,' Grace said, 'but it doesn't look like that now.'

'Where is it?' Louise asked.

'It's her home,' Trevor replied for Grace. 'She's tarted it up.'

'It's endgame, Lou,' Grace added quietly.

Harrigan had pulled up a chair beside Louise. 'Where's she coming from?' he asked.

Louise shook her head. 'I've got a trace out but nothing so far. She's just downloaded this. I don't know what she's doing now.'

'She got a phone from somewhere,' Ian said.

'She's met with the preacher,' Harrigan replied. 'He's supplied her with one and who knows what else. At least she's still alive to tell the tale.'

'You put money on that, did you, Boss?' Trevor asked with a grin.

'No, mate, I didn't think it was a very good bet at the time.'

'She's online,' Grace said suddenly. She acknowledged Harrigan for the first time since he had come into the room: 'But she's not looking for me, she's looking for your son. Will he be online now?'

'I'm sure he is.'

He came and looked over her shoulder with everyone else.

Turtle, are you out there? Do you still want to talk to me? I'd like to talk to you.

Hi Lucy I'm here U are talking 2 me after all I've been waiting 2 hear from u I was hoping u would talk 2 me

You know who I am now. You don't have to call me the Firewall any more.

Want me 2????

No, I like you calling me Lucy. I'm still going to call you Turtle though. Do you mind? Will you forgive me for getting so angry with you? I'm sorry, Turtle, I felt so lost.

That's ok I just wanna talk 2 u Where are u? Don't tell me if u don't want 2 Are u ok???

I'm all right. I'm really, really hungry. I haven't eaten since yesterday.

That's no good U have 2 eat soon

I've gone hungry before, I know what it feels like. My father died yesterday morning, Turtle. I was there when it happened. I saw him die and I didn't feel a thing.

U don't have 2 feel for him

But that's it. I wish I could. I know what you'd feel if your father died.

That's different That's way different

I know that. That's what I want to ask you about. Didn't you tell me once he taught you how to talk?

'Mate,' Trevor spoke quietly to Harrigan, 'is this okay with you? We can do this more privately.'

'This is work, Trev,' Harrigan replied. 'Just keep watching.'

He didn't teach me 2 talk because I can't really talk. I learned what words were from him. He always kept talking 2 me when I was a baby and he kept the radio on. He took me to see Auntie Ronnie and Lyn all the time and they never do anything but talk. He just kept talking words at me so I'd know what they were

Why did he do that?

Coz they said I couldn't have a mind. Because of the way I was. He said, fuck u, I'll show u he does. He got people to teach me to read, there's special ways u can do that. Why?

Grace looked towards Harrigan, wondering how he could bear seeing this on the screen. He was watching her but it was impossible to know what was in his head. Her sense of loss was too strong for disguise. She turned away.

I just have to know, that's all. Do you ever meet anyone he works with?

Sometimes Why????

What are they like? Are they like everybody else?

Just people Why????

I missed you, Turtle.

Me 2

Nothing was typed. The computer room was silent as everyone waited.

Do you think your father is watching us talk?

Probably. He wants to find u, Lucy. He's going to do that. Why??? Wotzup?

I've done something else, Turtle. I have to tell people about it.

'Here we go,' Trevor said.

Lucy u haven't killed someone?? Please tell m u didn't

No. Not yet anyway. This is something else. In about twenty minutes, this building is going up in smoke. I was doing it because someone who mattered to me killed himself and I couldn't cry for him either. I wanted people to know what happened to him. But I didn't want anyone to get hurt. But someone said to me, what if the other buildings around it go up as well and people do get hurt? I don't want that to happen. All I want is for everything to be cleaned away so we can start again. Why can't I just make that happen, Turtle? What do I do now?

Where is it?? U tell me

'Yeah,' Harrigan said to the silent room, 'where is it? Tell me.'

Randwick.

Call the police Call them now

Harrigan pointed to Trev. 'Fire Brigade. Now. I'll call the top brass. Lou, email my son. Tell him we know. You stay here and keep me informed. The rest of you, go now.'

In the release of activity the office was cleared and, in a shorter time than Harrigan had hoped for, every available officer was heading in the same direction, speeding through the streets of Surry Hills on dangerously slippery roads. They came down Anzac Parade in convoy behind the fire engines and the emergency services, sirens sounding in a stretched linear movement. Close to one of Harrigan's most loved places on earth, Royal Randwick, Trevor was about to say, 'We're there,' when, near the corner of the block on the other side of the road, a white brick building began to produce in a manner almost surreal flickers of fire out of its roof and, smashing outwards through the windows, sheets of red and yellow flame.

'Fuck,' Harrigan said. Far away so close. For the second time in less than twenty-four hours, she had been one step ahead of him.

What do I do now, Turtle?
U call them
They know already. They were watching, I know they were. No, I meant about everything else. You have choices, don't you? Don't you think, Turtle?
Everyone can choose Lucy, wot do u mean???
It's just the choice I've got to make. What do I do now?

Whatever u do don't hurt anyone Including yourself

I've gone too far for that. I haven't got that sort of choice now. It's one way or the other, that's what I've got to pick.

Wot are u going 2 do??

I think I'm going to go away. Far, far away. I've got to say goodbye to everyone I care about first. That's almost just you now.

U don't have 2 say goodbye 2 me We can talk

If I went away, I would have to say goodbye to you.

I don't understand Wherever u go everything is the same U are still u I'm still me that doesn't change Wot u did won't change Wot about those people u shot Have u forgotten them??

No, I haven't forgotten them. I'm never going to forget them. You know what I think is one of the worse things?

Wot???

That woman couldn't see me when I shot her because I had my face covered. She didn't know who I was. She had a right to know. I should have had the courage to look her in the face. You shouldn't do what I did to her if you don't have the courage to look someone in the face.

Lucy No no no no no u don't do it simple I said 2 u its wrong

It's wrong if you don't face up to what you've done.

Wrong anyway It doesn't matter wot

Yeah. Love you, Turtle. See you sometime, I hope.

U aren't going 2 talk 2 me again??? Is that wot this means????

She cut the connection.

In another building not so far away, Louise took a mouthful of whisky from her silver hip flask in the luxury of solitude, and decided that whatever chaos the boss was surrounded by at the moment, he needed to know this. She called him.

In her room, Lucy sat on the bed holding the picture of the woman, Grace. She could not see the face clearly in the light. She checked her watch and thought, yes, the building's gone by now, and whatever else might have been burned because of it. They would be out there picking up the bits, all of them, including Turtle's father. Lucy left the picture on the bed, took the phone and her gun and went out, to Belmore Park.

She felt afraid of nothing as she walked through deserted streets flooded with sheets of water. She crossed the wide intersection on Elizabeth Street and walked through the underpass to Eddy Avenue. There was almost no traffic. At Central Station, yellow lights glowed under the colonnade where people slept like bundles of dirty clothing in alcoves and niches. No one looked at her. With her hood pulled over her head, she was as anonymous and ragged as anyone here. Further along the colonnade, a woman and two men began to fight. One man and the woman beat the other man and tore at his clothes. Their voices echoed harshly at a distance but she could not understand what was being said, all she heard were curses. Soon the police would come by to break them up. The possibility caused Lucy no concern. She felt that nothing could touch her, in her mind she walked through this place unseen, less than a ghost.

She crossed into Belmore Park and stood in the middle of the open space between the Moreton Bay fig trees where she had last seen Greg. The gazebo had a dull fluorescence in the city's partial darkness. She looked up and thought she saw a flying fox outlined against the sky. She waited with the world in balance, believing that in the next second, at the next turning of the earth's curvature, it might tip into nothing. Time might really end and there would be a way out of this without her having to do anything more. There seemed to be a cessation of all movement. There was only the sound of rain dripping from the trees, then quietness. The voices of the people on the other side of the road were silenced. Instinctively, she thought that it had happened, that this was the quiet that comes before the world is broken open and there is no more time. She waited, hardly breathing. She was light, floating.

Then the gap closed around her and time returned. A car driven too fast along Eddy Avenue came to a halt at the traffic lights at Pitt Street, skewed to one side. A night train rumbled past on the tracks which spanned the overhead bridge. Across the road under the colonnade she saw two police officers weighing into the fight she had seen start and heard the shouts and curses once again. She smiled sardonically. There was only this time and this place to be dealt with.

She walked out of the park and across the road, turning her back on the police almost within their sighting distance, and went back to her sanctuary. She looked at her watch. Soon it would be dawn and the start of that brand new day Graeme had promised her.

The blue and red lights of the fire engines flashed on the wet roads while firemen spread their hoses out around the white building, dousing the flames. The takeaway shop next door was flaming greasy fire and its window crashed outwards from the heat. The smoke had driven the residents from the block of flats on the other side of the clinic out into the street. Some had had to be evacuated, to their confusion. Huddles of dazed, damp people found themselves marooned on the wet streets, wrapped in blankets over their nightclothes while the media circled them like hungry dogs. They had got here at speed, as they always did; Harrigan wished his people could be as efficient. The television crews were unpacking their goods on the other side of the fire engines, their stand-up comics were getting ready for their routines in front of the cameras. The scene was a mess of umbrellas and damp people bumping against one another.

'Keep them out of the way. I don't want to have to worry about those clowns,' Harrigan grumbled to the uniformed officers before going in search of the senior sergeant in charge of the local patrol.

'Where were the security guards?' he asked her. 'My information was that this clinic was under twenty-four-hour surveillance.'

'So was mine. Don't know where they were, but they weren't here, that's for sure,' she replied sharply. She glanced across the road. 'Look at that mess, will you? They should put the scum who did that in gaol and throw away the key.'

'If we hadn't got here when we did, we'd have had deaths,' Harrigan said. 'You can tell them that at Area Command. You can tell them it came from me, personally.'

'I will. No probs.' She grinned with pleasure at the prospect and walked away.

On the other side of the road, all traffic was being diverted to the southbound lane and waved on its way by uniformed police. It was dawn, the morning snarl was beginning to build, already stretching towards the beach suburbs in the south and the city in the north. It grew light on a snake-like mess of fire hoses, burnt-out buildings still smouldering in the damp weather, and convoys of vehicles taking those left homeless to temporary shelter. Harrigan watched his team stop for takeaway coffee, saw Grace light a cigarette and roll her shoulders wearily. He wanted to speak to her but did not know what he could say. It was twenty-four hours since any of them had had any real sleep other than a stolen hour or two.

In the midst of this, he took a phone call from the surveillance team watching the Temple to hear that the preacher had arrived home on foot. He told them to leave the man alone and hung up, wondering what Fredericksen had done with his time between midnight and dawn, or what he might have been able to tell them about the scene surrounding him now. He was then surprised to take a phone call from the Commissioner's Office. When he had finished talking, he went looking for Trevor.

'I've got to take the car, mate. I've been summonsed by God, he wants to have breakfast with me. I'll see you all back in town.'

'Have fun, Boss. Don't forget to say g'day to the Commissioner for me while you're there. What does he want with us anyway?'

'Who knows? I've been told it might take a while. I don't know if that's good or bad.'

Why did they want him? Presumably to explain why he had permitted a firebombing to occur in the middle of a state election campaign, not a very clever thing to do. He got into the car with the premonition that events were about to become more complicated than they already were. As he drove away, he saw a dark blue van come to a slow stop on the other side of the road near the blue and white ribbons. *Acme Security. We're there for you.* He looked at the car's digital clock: seven forty-five a.m. Daylight hours. Welcome to the job, boys. Ask me for a reference one day.

35

Some time after Harrigan had been ushered into the Commissioner's office, Lucy stood in her room overlooking the alleyway that led from the street, methodically checking her watch. Finally, she put on her coat and slipped her gun into one pocket and her mobile telephone into another. She thought she was weighted to one side, dragged down like someone about to drown themselves. She pulled up her hood to hide her face and went out, leaving everything else behind, hurrying down the back stairs and exiting through a small loading dock. Standing back and out of sight, she looked into the narrow lane at the cold, steadying rain that came out of a steel grey sky. There was no one there to see her as it came down harder, blown into the loading dock by a strong, cold wind. It seeped through her coat but she felt no discomfort. Her body was impermeable, light and clean. Her throat no longer hurt. She felt a sense of loosening, an expectation of release.

She stepped forward a little and saw a car parked further along the narrow laneway near the back entrance to a discount clothing store. 'I want to die in the open air. I hope I do,' she said to herself. A young woman came sprinting through the rain towards the car. Lucy reached the woman just as she had unlocked the car door, she pressed her gun into the woman's ribs.

'Don't say anything,' she said. 'Don't call for help. Just take me where I want to go and you'll be fine.'

The woman looked at her, recognised her and did as she was told. They got into the car. Terrified, the woman drove where Lucy directed her: to the New Life Ministries at Camperdown. The sky turned from black to green and there was the sound of thunder. Hailstones the size of cricket balls began to crash down, reducing the visibility to almost nothing.

'My car,' the woman gasped when the hail smashed onto the bonnet and cracked the windshield.

'Keep driving,' Lucy said. 'Go faster. Now.'

They came skidding dangerously down the hill towards the Temple. Lucy told the woman to drive up off the road towards the back of the theatre until she was as close to the back door as possible. She already had her key in her hand. They bounced over the uneven ground of the demolition site and slewed to a stop almost at the door, the tyres torn and useless. Lucy did not speak as she left the car. She was inside the building almost before the woman realised she had gone. While she sat at the wheel, too shocked to move, her car was suddenly surrounded by people. The door opened.

'We're police,' someone said, 'come with us. Please don't be frightened.'

Dazed, the young woman was taken by the arm, pulled out of the car and hurried away. Two officers had raced towards the back door of the Temple after Lucy but they were too late. She had slammed the door and dead-locked it. They were all left outside in the weather while the hail continued to come down around them. Just as quickly, they ran for cover.

Harrigan walked into the office, feeling barely fed after having lost his appetite ten minutes into his meeting with (as it turned out) both the Commissioner and an Assistant Commissioner. He was wondering how to handle what he had to do next when, almost simultaneously, his mobile rang and he was stopped by Trevor. Around him, the office was full of racket and movement.

'We've got her. She's at the Temple. I think we've got a siege on our hands,' Trevor was saying.

Harrigan gestured him to quiet and took the call. It was his surveillance team at the Temple. He told them to cordon off the area and call in the local patrol. He then rang the Tooth immediately. He needed bodies down there, he said, and the place sealed off immediately. Marvin was amenable, but he had no choice.

'I'd better be able to rely on that, mate,' Harrigan said, in a dangerous tone.

'You can,' Marvin replied. They both hung up on each other.

'Everyone, quiet. We've got work to do,' Harrigan called to the room, desperately pleased to have a perfect excuse to avoid telling them what he otherwise had to say. 'We take this step by step. I need you all to stay on now, no one goes home. Ian and Trev, I'll want you in my office to work out what we need to — Whose phone is that? Grace. Make it quick.'

Grace went to her desk and answered her phone.

'Grace Riordan.'

'Is that you, Grace? Since you wouldn't tell me what your last name was yesterday. Is that who you are? Are you the woman who talked to me yesterday?'

'Yes, this is me. What would you like me to call you — Lucy or the Firewall? What do you like better?' Grace replied, turning on her speakerphone and broadcasting to the room. Harrigan walked towards her desk in the now silent office.

'You can call me Lucy. How are you, Grace?'

'I'm good, Lucy. Where are you now?'

'Don't you know that? I'm at the Temple. I thought you'd be the first people to find that out.'

'What are you doing there, Lucy? Did you want to see someone there?'

'I've come to see Graeme. You see, Graeme came and saw me last night and he told me I could have a whole new life. A whole new life. So I've come to talk to him about it. Haven't I, Graeme?'

In the bleak auditorium, Lucy looked at the preacher who sat, white-faced, angry and frightened both, in front of a small crowd of people pushed up against the side wall and huddling together on the floor. Bronwyn, a woman with her small son, an old man and his wife, some few others who had come out even in this terrible weather. The plastic seats had been upended and tossed aside. The hail, which had crashed so loudly on the old roof that it was hard to hear anyone speak, had ceased although the rain continued to come down.

'Yeah,' Lucy said, 'it's him and me and there are about seven other people here as well. We're all in her together. They can't get out because all the doors locked. And you can't get in for the same reason.

see, Graeme likes the doors locked. He always keeps them locked. But I thought we could let you in, if you wanted to come in. I thought you might like to come down here and talk to me.'

'Why do you want me to do that, Lucy?' Grace said, sitting down. Harrigan sat opposite, watching her as they all listened.

'I want to talk to you. I want to talk to you with everyone listening!'

Grace glanced at Harrigan who nodded.

'I can come down there and I can talk to you. That's no problem. If we come now, I can talk to you as soon as we get there.'

'No, let me tell you what I want, Grace. I want to see what you look like. I want to know who you are. I have to look at you, I have to talk to you face to face. So I want you in here looking at me. Looking at me and fixed up for sound.'

Harrigan was shaking his head.

'Okay, Lucy, we're coming down. You wait for us there.'

'No, Grace, you're not listening to me. I am sick of people fucking lying to me,' Lucy screamed across the office. 'When you come here, you're coming inside to see me and you are going to talk to me. I am telling you something. I have a gun with fifteen bullets in it. Now that's one for everybody here, one for me, and six left over. Now you *are* coming in here. Because I have put everything on the line to talk to you. You are coming in. And you're going to tell me that you are in ten seconds from now or I am going to start shooting people. You listen to me. I am counting as of now. One. Two. Three. Four. Five . . .'

Harrigan gave Grace the faintest of nods.

'I'll be there, Lucy. I'll come in and I'll talk to you.'
'You will?'
'Yes, I will.' Harrigan leaned his chin on his hands.
'But you have to promise me you won't shoot anyone. Will you do that?'

'As long as they don't move, or try and do anything silly, they'll be fine,' Lucy said. 'And is that a promise from you that you'll be here?'

'Yes, it's a promise from me,' Grace replied. 'So who is there with you, Lucy?'

'There's Bronwyn. And Graeme. He's really pleased to be here, I can see it in his face. There's this woman and her kid. Lucky kid. There's an old lady who doesn't know what day it is and her husband who looks after her and his sister who looks after him. And there's this other white-faced guy who's always here. That's all.'

'And you're not going to hurt them.'

'Not if they just sit there. But I'm waiting for you, Grace, so you'd better come.'

'Give me your number, Lucy, so I can call you and tell you where we are and what we're doing. So you don't think we're not coming.'

Lucy read out the number which Harrigan wrote down.

'Before we go, Lucy, how did you get my number here?'

'Graeme gave it to me. He knows all about you, Grace. He showed me your picture. I just want to see if that really is you. I'll see you soon.'

Grace hung up. The room stayed silent as people glanced at each other and waited for Harrigan to speak.

'We need a negotiator to talk to her. As well as you, don't we, Grace? The best we've got.' He looked her in the eye, the memory of earlier conversations between them in both their minds at that moment. 'We've got to try and talk you out of this if we can. We'd better hope we can. You'd better get ready to talk to her. Ian and Trev, in my office now. The rest of you, get yourselves ready to go.'

The crowd broke up.

'Where are you going, Gracie?' Ian asked, as Grace headed quickly for the exit.

'I'm going to wash my face and change my blouse,' she replied grimly. 'If I'm going to get shot, I want to be wearing clean clothes.'

Harrigan was suddenly in front of her. People stopped to stare.

'You do not say that, not for any reason, not even as a joke. Do you hear me? None of you are getting shot and that includes you. You take that back.'

'It wasn't a joke, Paul. But I didn't say it anyway,' she replied, shaken that he should be so angry about something which, for her, was just a way of coping with events way past the limit.

'Good.'

He walked away, thinking he was glad that she had listened to him for once; others simply noted that she had called the boss by his first name.

In his office, he asked Ian and Trevor to wait while he made his first phone call. He was putting the essentials in place before he did anything else. Negotiators were all very well but sometimes there was no substitute for a reliable marksman or two.

He also had another job to do before he left along with everyone else. He went to Louise, who he had instructed to stay behind, and asked her to email his son.

'Just tell him what's going on,' he said.

He didn't want Toby to find out by accident through an Internet browser that the girl he thought he loved had been shot dead by police on a rainy morning in Camperdown.

36

Lucy listened as the sirens began to grow louder outside. She smiled and aimed her gun more directly at the preacher.

'Listen to that, Graeme. And it's all because I've got this. Nothing else would make anyone waste their time on me like that.'

He tried to shift forward to speak to her.

'Don't move!' she snapped and he stopped where he was.

'Lucy, listen to me. There's nothing you can take out of this. If you put yourself in my hands, perhaps I can bargain for you. We can try and talk this through somehow.'

She smiled at him in reply.

'No, Graeme. No way. You just sit there. The only thing I want you to do is keep your mouth shut. It'll be nice not to hear you talk for a change.'

Briefly, the anger in the preacher's face was greater

than his fear. Suddenly afraid herself, Lucy tightened her hand around her gun.

'That's who you are, isn't it, Graeme,' she said, 'playing all those little games. No, not little games, all those big games. You want to know why I'm here? Because I'm going to deal with this in my own way from now on. I'm not hiding my face this time. You set this up. This time, you can just sit there and be part of it.'

'Do you want me to go to gaol with you, Lucy? Is that it?' he said, taking just enough courage to speak.

She laughed. 'I don't know what's going to happen yet. I really don't. It depends on all sorts of things. I'm not expecting that I'm going to walk out of here alive and I don't care if I don't. But you just sit there. Don't talk, don't say a word. Don't even think anything. That goes for the rest of you as well.'

The others remained huddled against the wall, too frightened to think of moving. Bronwyn cried silently. The child began to cry softly as well, leaning against his mother, his voice echoing beneath the now quieter sound of the rain on the tin roof. Briefly, Lucy closed her eyes.

'Keep him quiet,' she said dangerously, her voice shaking and her hands squeezing on the gun.

The child was hushed. Lucy met Graeme's eyes and thought, you don't really give a shit for anyone, do you? No one. You don't care about me. I don't know what you do care about, but it's no one here. She did not say it. She put her free hand on her phone and waited for the call.

There was no such silence in the street outside, it was filled with activity. In the midst of the multitude of requirements this operation had — including once again keeping the media at bay — Harrigan was fixed on two simpler items. The first was the line of leadlight windows in the upper storey of the hall that looked out along the laneway. The second was a small group of armed men wearing bulletproof vests over nondescript blue overalls who had finally arrived at the scene. When they drew up in their van, Harrigan resisted the urge to say, thanks for taking your time about it. They seemed to him to move with deliberate slowness. They carried their high-powered rifles with the ease of practice.

'Where do you want us? And what do you want us to do?' the chief overall-wearer asked.

'There's two places I need you,' Harrigan said. 'We have to negotiate one of them first. But I've already started on the other. Just around here.'

He led the man down the narrow laneway where he had two officers on temporary scaffolding, checking the dark blue windows near the back of the building.

'If we can get that window out without being noticed — which is a pretty big ask, I admit, but I'm going to see what we can do — I want one of you up there and ready to fire. The other place I want you is opposite the front door — in case I can get it open. You can deploy everyone else around the building. I want you to make sure the target does not use her gun. I want her neutralised. The last person who gets hurt is my officer. Is that clear enough?'

'We can do that,' came the slow reply. 'Nice to have a challenge. We'll get set up.'

You do that, Harrigan thought as he walked away, don't rush it too much now.

In the centre of a smaller crowd, Grace was having a sound device adjusted. She stood with the negotiator, a big woman with a little-girl blonde haircut and dressed in brightly coloured clothing too tight for her large frame. Grace spoke to Harrigan as soon as he appeared.

'I should call her. She'll be getting very edgy.'

He did not reply. He looked at his watch and then the negotiator.

'I think we are pushing it,' she said.

'You've briefed my officer?'

'I have.'

'Okay, Grace, you can call her,' Harrigan said.

Lucy answered the phone at once.

'You took your fucking time, Grace,' she said, angrily.

'I'm here now, Lucy, I'm outside. So what do you want to do now?'

'I want you to come inside.'

'How are we going to do that?'

'I open the door and you walk in.'

'You open the door?'

'Maybe not me. I'll get someone else to do it. I've got just the person,' Lucy said, looking at the child.

'Lucy, before we do anything, I need to talk to you. Just to sort a few things out.'

'There's nothing to sort out.'

'There is something, Lucy.'

'What?'

'Will you leave the doors open for me? Those wooden doors that open onto the foyer. Just so people out here can see me through those glass doors at the front and know what's going on.'

'Is that all? Is that so they can get a clear shot at me?'

'It's so the people out here can see what's happening.'

'Yeah, I don't care about that. I'll do something else as well. Once you're in here, I'll let everyone else but you and Graeme out. How's that?'

'That's a good thing to do. Will we organise that?'

'Yeah, let's do that. So — are you coming in now?'

'Lucy, will you let me ask you something first? Why do you want to see me? What are you going to do? I would like to know that.'

The negotiator was nodding her head.

'I told you. I want to look at you. I want to see what you really look like. I want to talk to you. I told you all that. There are seven people in here, Grace. Now I can just shoot three of them if I have to. And then maybe you'll come in.'

'Are you going to shoot me? Is that what you want to do?'

'That depends on you.'

'How does it depend on me?'

'You'd better come in and find out, hadn't you,' Lucy snapped. 'I am sick of talking to people. I've told you what I want. No more talking like this. Finish!'

Outside on the street, the negotiator shook her head.

'Okay, Lucy. I'll be in there very soon. We're just getting the sound right for you. I'll call you back as soon as I can. Just give me a little more time.'

'Don't you keep me waiting too long.'

'I won't.'

'Okay,' the negotiator said once the conversation had ended, 'when she says, don't keep her waiting, she means it. You have to keep her logic focused on not using that gun. She needs to be given a reason for not using it. You have to play a waiting game in there. Keep her talking. She does want to talk. Don't lie to her whatever you do. If she thinks you're lying to her, you're probably gone.'

The negotiator spoke in a voice at odds with both her appearance and her words, one that offered the listener a sense of immediate reassurance. Grace drank this reassurance down as a temporary relief for the impossible.

'That isn't enough,' Harrigan said. 'Keep her talking? What else can you tell me?'

'We have no leverage,' the negotiator replied. 'It's a matter of the choice you make. She's decided she's got nothing to lose. She's made her choice. She will kill people, I am sure.'

A sound technician from the nearby van appeared amongst them without any noticeable concern for what he might be interrupting.

'I need a sound check,' he said to Grace. 'Can you say something once I'm back in my van?'

Grace, who had lit a cigarette, smiled. On a signal from the man, she sang, *Hey, yeah, you with the sad face/Come up to my place and live it up/Hey, yeah, you beside the dance floor/Whattya cry for let's live it up*.

The technician laughed as he leaned out of the van door. 'Clear as a bell,' he called.

Harrigan found himself scratching his chin.

'Thanks,' he said to the negotiator, 'I need to talk to my officer now. I'll call you when we need you next.'

The woman disappeared into the crowd.

'It's just a song I like, Paul. My first boyfriend used to sing it to me,' Grace said with a smile before he could speak.

'You can't go in there if you can't see this through. You want to walk away? Now's your chance.'

'I know that,' she said, dropping ash on the wet road, 'I can do it.'

'You haven't put any make-up on,' he said.

Grace almost said that no, she hadn't had the energy for some reason but she had changed her knickers, that was something. She pushed down the desire to laugh out loud.

'No, and just when I need the protection too,' she said, looking away.

'Look at me,' he said, and she did. 'Just keep it calm. Do what the negotiator says — play for time. Call her now and talk some more. You don't go in there until I say you do.'

Again, Lucy answered the phone at once.

'Hi, Lucy. We're still out here. It won't be long now.'

'And you're still taking your fucking time, Grace. What are you up to?'

'We're about there with the sound, Lucy, and I'm having a cigarette before I come in. I need one.'

'You smoke? Why don't you bring them in with you?'

'Sure. We can both have one.'

Last cigarettes, Grace thought.

Lucy laughed in the gap of silence, she might have heard this thought on the airwaves.

'I'm telling you, Grace, don't think about it. I don't know what's going to happen. Everything could be just fine.'

'That's nice. I haven't always managed to have everything just fine in my life.'

'No, me neither. I'd like to stop fucking around. I'm sending someone to open the door in five minutes. You'd better be there. Or you're going to hear shooting. And then there's only going to be one person who'll walk away from this, and that'll be the person who opened the door.'

Grace hung up and dropped a second packet of cigarettes in her pocket. Harrigan contacted his ring-in carpenters.

'How are you going on that window?' he asked.

'The seal's very brittle so it's looking more hopeful than it did. We're doing our best. But it's going to take time.'

'Just do it,' Harrigan said.

'Wait here,' he told Grace and walked across to the house opposite to speak to the marksman. He was set up in a room where the heavy green lounge suite, the radio, carpet, even the ducks on the wall were loving recreations from the fifties and sixties. His rifle was trained through the open window, past an effigy of Elvis, onto the front doors of the Temple.

'We've got the door open. Remember, I want her neutralised.'

'No worries,' the man replied.

'I'll be outside the van. Make sure you communicate with me whenever you have to.'

He went back outside to speak to Grace, who was dropping yet another cigarette butt on the bitumen.

'You'll be fine,' he said to her. 'I'll buy you a lime and soda at the Maryborough when this is over with.'

'We can do better than that, Paul,' she said with a grin. 'We'll go upmarket, where they sell fresh lime. That'd be better.'

'Anything you want,' he replied.

He gave people their last-minute instructions, they took up their positions. Harrigan squatted down near the sound van where he could see inside the hall. If he discounted being almost shot dead in an inner city alleyway ten years ago, watching Grace walk across the open space towards the door of the Temple rated as the worst moment of his working life.

A dowdy-looking woman had opened the wooden doors between the foyer and the hall and stood waiting by the glass doors, but instead of running out as soon as Grace went inside, as he had expected, she turned and followed her back in. Very shortly afterwards a small group of people appeared in the tiny foyer and came running down the steps into the street, where they were met and spirited away by his waiting officers. There was no woman and child. Harrigan trained binoculars into the hall and saw Lucy sitting on the floor holding the child in her arms. The marksman contacted him at that moment.

'I can't get a clear aim at her. She's using the child as a shield,' he said.

'Yeah, I can see,' Harrigan replied. 'Just keep waiting.'

Inside the Temple, Grace watched the small group of lost souls disappear out of the building into the grey weather. Her footsteps were too loud on the bare floorboards, the air around her was icy cold; the atmosphere gave the extraordinary sense of the auditorium as a place without exits. Only the preacher, lying face down on the floor, and the woman who had guided her in remained. The woman was standing near the wall, her arms hanging loosely, an expression of appalling fear on her face. Lucy sat towards the back of the hall, holding the weeping child in her lap.

'You can sit down, Grace. Why don't you sit just there? Next to Graeme, where I can see you. You can sit up now, Graeme.'

The preacher rolled over with agility. He looked at Grace with revulsion but this did not touch her. They were almost side by side, a V shape with Lucy at the apex. Once they were in position, Lucy pushed the child towards his mother, who scooped him up and ran for the door. She was gone in an instant, the glass door clicking shut on its automatic lock behind her.

'It's just us now. Isn't that nice?' Lucy said. 'You're Grace?'

'Yes,' Grace said, looking at a small girl with a square and pretty, almost innocent, face and clear eyes. Her pale skin was delicate next to her reddish hair. She held her gun unselfconsciously, apparently unafraid of what it could do.

'Are you wired for sound?' she asked.

'Yes, I am. Everyone can hear.'

'Yeah, I want people to hear. I want them to know what I'm going to say. You know what I want you to do first? I want you to sit on your hands.'

'Why, Lucy?'

'I just do. I want to touch your face. Now you be careful. You just have to look at this gun and it goes off. Remember that, Graeme. Because if you move, it's Grace first and then you. And I'm faster than you.'

Grace leaned forward, hard on her hands, and felt the gun barrel pressed in her stomach as Lucy stroked first one cheek and then the other. Her touch was cold and smooth. They were eyeball to eyeball. Grace, chilled to the base of her spine, controlled panic by staring into the rage mirrored in Lucy's eyes. She told herself, meet it full on. That's the only way you can know what there is to fear.

Outside, the marksman contacted Harrigan.

'She's got them in a position where I have to shoot one of them to get to her. And if I did do that, I couldn't get her before she got your officer.'

'Wait your chance,' Harrigan replied.

'That is you, isn't it? That face, it's you,' Lucy was saying, her voice thin and metallic over the communication device.

She drew back, the gun ready to fire at a breath. Grace reconnected to the possibility of staying alive a little longer.

'Yes, this is me. Is it okay if I get off my hands now?'

'Yeah, you can do that. You've got a nice face.'

'Why is that important, Lucy?'

'Because it's who you are. I need to see who you are,' Lucy said. 'You see, when I shot that woman and that man, I got blood all across my forehead. Some of it got up into my hair. I don't even know whose it was. It just hit me. I can feel it all over me again now. And that man, he didn't have a face left. He wasn't anything any more. Nothing. I never should have shot him. But you know one of the things that really bothers me?'

'No, Lucy,' Grace replied. 'You tell me.'

'I didn't let that doctor see all *my* face. She had a right to know who I was. That's why I wanted to see you.'

'You want me to be looking at you when you do whatever you're going to do?'

Oh Christ, Harrigan thought.

'I don't want to hide from you the way I did from her,' Lucy said.

As Lucy spoke, Grace felt a movement beside her. She glanced at the preacher. He had leaned forward and was staring at Lucy with a hungry expression. Lucy looked at him at the same time.

'Don't you move, Graeme, and don't you talk. Not till I tell you to,' she said. 'Because if you do, I'll get you before you can do anything.'

He sat back, his expression unchanged.

'Do you think a lot about what happened that morning, Lucy? Is that what you're telling me, that it's always on your mind?' Grace asked.

'Yes, it is. But I don't know what to think about it.' She was shaking her head. 'I think about it and I get lost.'

'You're walking in the dark again,' Grace said. 'That's

what we're doing now. Walking around in the dark. But something else bothers you about that morning. You said that — that it was just one thing.'

'Yeah. Do you want to know what it is?'

'You tell me, Lucy.'

'I should never have done it at all.' She sounded like a small child. 'That's how I feel now. I should never have done it, it was such a bad thing to do. Really bad. But that's it, you see. How do I deal with that? I know that because I feel it. But what if it wasn't such a bad thing to do, the way Graeme says it wasn't? And then if shooting that doctor was the right thing to do, I should do what Graeme wants me to do right now. I should shoot you as well. And that's what I've got to know.'

'Why do you have to shoot me?'

'Because you killed your baby. Graeme knows that about you, everyone does. And he says that's what I should do.'

'You don't have to do any of this, Lucy,' Grace said. 'You can put your gun down and just walk out of here. And that's it. You can walk out of here with me and I'll make sure nothing happens to you. That's all you have to do. You don't have to do anything.'

'No, I do. That's the point. I killed someone. I'm stuck here. I am.'

'No, Lucy, you're not —'

'*I am!*'

'Don't argue with her,' the negotiator said quietly, close beside Harrigan. 'Whatever you do, don't argue with her.'

There was silence. Lucy's hand tightened on the gun and then relaxed a little again. Grace breathed.

'I am, Grace,' Lucy was saying. 'Now I've got to solve this. I've got to solve it.'

There was silence. Lucy sat gathering her breath, taking courage. She looked from Grace to the preacher.

'All right, Graeme. Talk. What do I do now?'

He seemed to subside with relief when she said this.

'Whatever your conscience tells you to do, Lucy,' he replied easily, as though he was sitting at his desk in a counselling session. 'You must know in your heart what's right.'

'What do you think is right?'

'I'm not the actor here,' he replied. 'I can't take the place of your own conscience.'

'But what would you do? You said that Grace here walks blood through the city streets. She deserves to die. You said that to me last night. You said to me: you can get rid of the evil she is, you can wash it clean. That's what you said. So what would you do? If you had to.'

You fucking bastard, Harrigan thought. You fucking, fucking bastard.

'I would leave her to answer to God,' the preacher said.

'Well, what does that mean? Does that mean it happens the way it did last time? I shoot her for you and you get to hear about it on the radio?'

'No, Lucy. It means we all have a role to play and mine is different to yours,' he said. 'If I am not here, how can anything be accomplished? It is my work to lead, to organise. There are a great many sacrifices in that.'

Lucy looked away from the preacher and back to Grace.

'You killed your baby. Why did you do that?' she asked her. 'You think what I did was wrong, don't you? You do, don't you?'

'Yes, I do,' Grace said.

'But how can what I did be wrong if you can go and do that? It's just as bad, isn't it?'

In the few short seconds before she replied, Grace thought she was gone.

'I don't know if there's any way I can tell it to you so you'd understand me, Lucy. I'm just going to say to you that that's what I chose to do, it's what I felt I had to do. I don't see it the way you do.'

'You chose to?' Lucy asked. 'You did? On your own?'

'Yes.'

Lucy raised her gun.

'I still think that's murder, Grace, whatever you want to say,' she said, and fired three times.

In moments during which the world turned white for her, three bullets crashed past Grace's head into the thick wooden door where it stood open behind her. She felt her body turn to water and then become solid again. Her eyes blinked as the scene around her faded, then came back to life. Outside, Harrigan contacted the marksmen and told them to take out Lucy Hurst as soon as they could.

'Did I frighten you, Grace? Well, look at Graeme,' Lucy was saying in a half-incredulous, half-laughing voice. 'Yeah, just look at you, Graeme. You really thought you were going to see blood this time, didn't you? You're hanging out for it.'

His expression was open-mouthed and ecstatic, frozen with a smile of pure joy.

'It wouldn't just be hers either, it'd be mine too, because the first thing that'd happen is I'd get blown away as well. Get up. You just fucking get up, Graeme. You are a liar. You don't care about anything. All you do is get off on killing people. That's all you do. You sit there and you talk rubbish to me and all the time, you just want to get off on it. And you just want to see me fucking do it for you.'

'You listen to me, Lucy. All you have seen is righteous joy —'

'You shut up!'

'Don't do that, Lucy,' Grace was saying as they scrambled to their feet, 'leave it. You know what you want to know now. Just leave it.'

'No, Grace. Don't you fucking listen? I killed someone. I've got to make up for that.'

'No, you have to leave it — '

The preacher suddenly screamed and ran at Lucy. She jumped backwards and shouted at him to stop where he was. They froze where they stood, staring at each other. In that instant, a pattern of bullets thudded between them into the floor where Lucy had just been standing. All three of them looked up to a square of grey light where a window above and behind them had been removed. Lucy laughed aloud, dancing back out of range.

'Too late. Too bad,' she said.

In that second, the preacher turned and ran for the door. She fired at him repeatedly as he ran, seemingly unaware of the recoil of the gun knocking her backwards. He fell to the floor. Grace cracked Lucy on the wrist with the side of her hand and the gun dropped, crashing onto the wooden floor. Grace kicked it aside as Lucy dived for it, stretching her hand out towards it. They wrestled on the floor, Grace fighting an unexpected strength in Lucy's thin and wiry body. She heard the glass doors being broken open behind them.

'Stupid!' she was shouting, 'it's stupid. Why waste your life?'

'Why do you care? I didn't want to have to shoot you.' She heard Lucy's voice, furious and breathless in her ear. 'Didn't you know that?'

Then Grace was bodily lifted up and away as armed police swarmed around them. They held Lucy face down on the floor and retrieved her gun. Grace was on her feet, looking at a hall filled with people and Harrigan standing in front of her.

'Are you all right?' he was asking her in his neutral voice.

'Yes, I'm okay,' she heard herself say.

'No injuries?'

He was looking closely at her face.

'No.'

'Good. Why don't you go outside with Trev and get yourself a cigarette? We'll clean up in here.'

'Yeah, Gracie.' Trevor was there behind Harrigan. 'Just come outside with me and get some fresh air for a moment.'

'I'm okay,' she said.

'Of course you are. Come on,' he said, in the voice that he always used to organise his friends.

She followed him out, passing the paramedics who had come in behind everyone else and were kneeling beside the preacher.

'No, he's gone. There's nothing we can do here,' she heard one of them say.

Then she walked out the door and down the steps into the open street.

'It's stopped raining,' she said. 'Oh, it's nice to be outside.'

'Yeah,' Trevor said, 'and the sun's coming out. Have a cigarette.'

She accepted it, shaking her head, light on her feet.

'I feel really strange, Trev. My head feels about four times the size it should be.'

'You're in shock, mate,' Trevor replied. 'Just stand there and smoke your cigarette. Don't do anything.'

'I'm still alive,' she said, drawing in a deep breath and laughing, with tears in her eyes.

'Oh, mate,' Trevor said, losing it. He shook his head and gave her a bear hug, destroying her unlit cigarette.

In the hall, Harrigan looked down at the preacher. He lay on his side staring up at the ceiling and his blood had spread out over the floor. Harrigan almost expected to see the man wink at him and hear his voice whispering quietly in his ear, 'Don't worry, Paul. Between you and me, this is just a ruse.' The thought was real enough to be disturbing.

He turned to look at Lucy Hurst where she was being held face down on the floor and motioned to his people to stand her up. This was the girl his son thought he loved, the one who had led him on a dance from one end of the city to the other. She hardly came up to his chin, was barely old enough to be his concern.

'Lucy Marilyn Hurst,' he said, 'I'm going to arrest and charge you with two counts of murder. Do you understand what I'm saying to you?'

She looked him directly in the eye, unafraid. Small particles of dust covered her reddish brown hair.

'Yeah, I understand,' she said, dismissively. 'I know all about that stuff.'

He began the ritual, noticing that as he spoke to her she did not once look in the direction of the preacher. She seemed to have erased the fact that he was there.

* * *

To Grace's surprise, people came up to her as she stood outside on the street and congratulated her. She had not expected this to happen. Ian appeared and shook her hand.

'You were fucking brave, Gracie,' he said, squeezing her hand before disappearing back into the crowd.

'I didn't think about that,' she said to Trevor, this detail occurring to her for the first time.

'Yeah, well,' he replied, 'a fucking good thing you didn't.'

While they stood there, Lucy Hurst was escorted out of the hall and placed in a car. She glanced around and saw Grace at a distance but did not acknowledge her. She appeared quite calm. Grace watched her being driven away.

'I guess I don't get to see her again,' Grace said, 'except in court.'

'Not unless you want to.'

'No,' she said, 'I don't think I do.'

Not long afterwards, Harrigan walked up to them slowly.

'How are you?' he said to her.

'I'm okay,' she replied. 'A bit light on my feet.'

He was silent for a few moments, looking at her, shaking his head.

'You should never have been anywhere near here in the first place. If I'd known any of that info sooner, you wouldn't have been.'

'Well, I'm here. I'm still alive to tell the tale.'

She tried to smile.

'You were lucky,' he said. 'You were lucky but you were brave. You deserved to be lucky. Now you've done that once, you don't ever have to do it again, do you?'

'No, I guess not,' she replied.

'You get debriefed before you do anything else. I'll need to see you back at the office when you're finished. And Trev, when you're ready — I need you now.'

'You almost had her shot,' Grace said after him as he walked away.

He stopped and came back to her.

'Is that what you're turning over in your mind? There's no in-between here. If I was going to finish the day looking at someone's body, it wasn't going to be yours. I don't have an apology for that.'

'It's not that. She wouldn't have cared if you had,' Grace said. 'She said to me, she didn't *want* to have to shoot me, didn't I know that?'

'Yeah. She had you on a tightrope. She had us all dancing around.'

'All she wanted to know was who she should shoot now. Because that was the only thing she had left to do. So what are we doing here? Have we solved anything? We're just playing some kind of game along with her.'

'Right first time, Grace. When you get to this point, it is a game and it's called survival. And you survived. Go and get debriefed. You need to.'

She let it go and he walked away.

'Do you always talk to him like that?' Astounded, Trevor dropped his own cigarette butt on the road beside Grace's small litter. 'No one else would fucking dare! You must be sleeping with him, Gracie.'

'No, I'm not. All we ever do is talk,' she said, watching Harrigan as he went up the steps back into the hall.

37

The day was not over yet. After the morning's proceedings had been wrapped up and he had allowed himself the luxury of a shower and a change of clothes, Harrigan stood at the front of the incident room watching it fill. He saw Grace slip in the door almost last of all, fresh out of her debriefing. People turned to speak to her, to shake her hand. She smiled awkwardly in reply. There was still a buzz from the morning; people did not seem to notice (or perhaps they had, what could he know) that both Trevor and Ian were standing quiet and withdrawn at the back of the room. Harrigan had talked to them a little earlier. He called for quiet just after Dea had walked into the room.

'All right,' he said, 'it's been a very long day. For some of you it's been a very long thirty-six hours and more and all you want to do is go home. So I'll be quick. I'll say first, briefly — probably too briefly — you were brave today, Grace, very brave. Everyone here thinks so. I don't want you to think it hasn't been noticed.'

There was some applause, she said 'Thanks' in her clear voice. He continued.

'I'm telling you this now because I don't want you to hear it from anyone else. We might even get bumped to second stop on the news. One of the area commanders was asked to step down last night. He's now got a date with the Police Integrity Commission and no one's expecting him back. I won't tell you who it is, you'll hear soon enough; it's not Marvin, I've got to say. As a result, there's been a reshuffle up top and while I was the last person to expect this because it's a jump up the ladder for me, I've been asked to stand in as the Homicide and Violent Crime Agency Commander as of nine o'clock tomorrow morning.'

There was a ripple of surprise throughout the room. He saw them watching him intently.

'Now, as you know, we've never fitted into the new structure, we're a glitch from times gone by. It seems Marvin doesn't like us being too independent on his patch. So I have to tell you — with me going, we're finished. This unit is disbanded as of now.'

There was a shocked and stony silence.

'Just like that? Is that it?' Louise's rough voice was the first to sound in the room. 'This job is the only thing that's keeping me going.'

'No one's losing their job. No one. If you want to, there are redundancies on offer. But there'll be jobs in the agencies or the local commands for you all. Whatever we can work out, there will be jobs and they'll be ones that you want to have.' Again there was silence. When he spoke again, he felt he was pleading with them. 'I told them this was a waste. I said, this is a good team, look at the results. They wouldn't listen to me. They'd made their minds up before I walked in the room.'

'You didn't have to take that job on, Harrigan,' Trevor called out. 'You could have said no.'

'I wasn't going to do that, mate. There's no point in me pretending I would.'

'Don't call me mate, mate,' Trevor said to himself.

'Now, Trev and Ian are going to take this case over to the Agency, to finish it off. I'm not leaving it with Marvin, I got that much out of them. And I'll be here tomorrow afternoon to talk placements with you all. Does anyone have any questions?'

He waited in the silence. They looked at him but no one spoke.

'So for all the work we've done, Harrigan, for you, for everyone,' Ian called out, 'all that happens now is we get shafted. And you let them do it.'

'There was nothing I could do to stop them. Nothing.'

Again there was silence.

'If you want to come down to the Maryborough now, I'll buy you all a drink as a farewell,' he said.

It was too late, they were leaving anyway, without speaking to him or even looking at him. They walked out in ones and twos, heading for the elevators. All he could do was go and sit in his office and watch them leave. Where Grace had gone, he did not know.

Trevor and Ian appeared, putting on their jackets. Harrigan went out to them.

'Where's Grace?' he asked Ian.

'How should I know? I thought if anyone would know that, you would,' Ian replied.

'There's no need for this,' Harrigan said almost angrily as they moved past him. 'When you're in the

Agency, you can both look for promotions. The prospects will be a lot better for you there. I'll make sure they are.'

'Yeah?' Trevor turned on him and spoke acidly. 'But they still weren't going to give me your job, were they? And do I know why? You fucking bet I do.'

They were gone in the lift with some others.

Dea was among the last to go. He watched her tidy her desk before she left, she was the only one who had. Everyone else had collected their coats and bags and left everything just as it was. Family photos, individual coffee cups, posters, football scarves remained in place. He walked up to her as she was picking up her bag.

'Do you know where they've gone?'

'I don't know. Out. The Maryborough, I suppose. Don't know if they want to see you down there.' She did not look at him. 'What happens to me?'

'I'll see you get a job, Dea.'

'Maybe I don't want one. It might be time to give it away. Might take one of those redundancies you're tossing around.'

She walked out without looking back or saying goodbye and then there was no one left. Isolation had sucked the air out of the room, he had to get out of there. He picked up his phone and rang Susie, telling her he would be on his way over to see Toby just as soon as possible. As he spoke, he looked at the vacant office, with its scattered chairs and empty desks, and thought that people asked too much of you sometimes. Shortly afterwards, he was driving in a slow traffic that was picking its way through the storm's aftermath, on his way to Cotswold House, relieved beyond description to have the day finished with.

* * *

Grace was stepping her own way through the chaos of the office, collecting her bag and her coat, glancing at Harrigan's empty office and asking herself where he would have gone. She had places of her own to go; they did not include the Maryborough where she knew everyone else would be writing themselves off. She drove over to St Vincent's Hospital, to the intensive care ward where Agnes Liu had been moved out of her goldfish bowl. Her son was with her, as usual. Agnes smiled in a pale sort of way from her mound of pillows when Grace sat down beside the bed.

'They rang you?' Grace asked. 'You do know?'

'Yes. Your Inspector rang me. A little while ago now,' Agnes said. 'Matthew saw it on TV as well. You've found her.'

'Yes, we've got her in custody. She'll probably be there for some time.'

'Was it her? The girl I told you about?'

'Yes, it was her.'

'I thought it would be. There will be people who'll blame me for this. I can hear now what they're going to say.'

'They shouldn't. She'll be the last person to agree with them if they do.'

'They will. They always do.'

'I won't be one of them,' Grace said, shaking her head.

'I'm going to recover,' Agnes said. 'I am going to go back into practice, even if it's only for a few days or even hours a week. I have to. It's the only thing I can do from here.'

'You'll do it, then,' Grace replied gently. 'You'll show them.'

Matthew Liu wanted to see her alone before she left and they went into a small, private room. His face was as thin and hollow as it had been the last time she had seen him.

'I saw you on TV,' he said. 'You went in there and you talked to her?'

'Yes, I did,' Grace replied and, in saying this, realised that she had crossed a boundary, that something about her had changed fundamentally.

'What was she like?'

'Small. Very small, just like you said. And very, very young.'

'Did she really tell you she wished she hadn't done it?' he asked, unbelieving.

'She did. And she meant it,' Grace replied.

'And she said that to you?'

'Yes, she did.'

'Is she mad? I can't see it.'

'She's nowhere you can connect to. Where she comes from is not somewhere you want to go.' Grace was surprised to hear herself sounding like Harrigan. 'She'll do whatever she does with herself but you mustn't let that touch you in any way at all. You can't let her destroy your life. Today's your very first day, Matthew. It's the first day of your life. You have to start from here.'

He broke down, shouting and picking up a chair and smashing it against the wall, and then weeping furiously. Grace stayed with him for as long as he wanted to cry before seeing him repair himself and go back to his mother's bedside. She needed to do this for herself, it took her out of her own head. She left them sitting together as the day finished.

She left the hospital and, in the evening dark, sat

in her car in the car park. In the darkness, she remembered the flash of white light she had seen as the bullets had crashed past her head and into the thick wooden door behind her that morning. If they had hit her, she would never have seen that light. The shaky memory of almost not being here rubbed like Velcro against the sense that she was here at this minute in time, still breathing, still thinking. A middle-aged man walked past her on his way to his own car and she watched him without curiosity. She had been changed by the morning, she could hardly describe how, only that now everything seemed brighter and sharper, more urgent. She took out her mobile and made a call.

'Hello, Paul?' she said to his answering machine. 'It's Grace here. I thought you'd like to know that I've just talked to Matthew. He's not good but he's okay, I guess. He's better than he was, which is something. I'm going to come and see him tomorrow as well. Anyway, I thought — if you wanted to — maybe you'd like to catch up with me some time. Since we're not working together any more, maybe we could go and have coffee or something. If you want to see me. Why don't you call? Up to you. Bye now.'

Yes, it's up to you, Paul. If you want me or my company, you can call me. Otherwise life was too short, just as Louise had said. Grace drove back to her flat, too exhausted to think of sleeping, ferociously hungry, jangled in her mind and no good for anything except solitude.

It took Harrigan longer than usual to get to Cotswold House, the traffic had been caught in a grid caused by uprooted trees and stranded cars. Susie greeted him at the door.

'Toby's waiting for you,' she said. 'He hasn't eaten yet. We thought you might want to eat with him. Would you like to do that?'

'A meal would be a life-saver just now, Susie,' he said. 'Thanks.'

She smiled and was gone.

When Harrigan walked into Toby's room, he was at his computer, surfing between news outlets.

Hi dad

'Hi, Toby. How are you?'

I'm ok Wot about u??

'I've felt better, mate. I'm glad the day is over and I'm still here to talk about it, and that just about everyone else is too,' he replied.

He stood behind Toby, massaging his son's shoulders, relaxing his own shoulders as he did so.

'You've heard all about it, haven't you?'

Yeah & Louise mailed m 2

'Yeah, I asked her to do that.'

Wot happens in gaol dad???

'Nothing very nice,' he said, frowning a little. 'Nothing we can do anything about just now.'

Is it like being me???? Being locked up like that???

'I don't know, Toby. All I can tell you is there's nothing weak about that girl. She can look after herself and I'm sure she will. I don't know if gaol is going to be too much different to the life she was living.'

He thought she would still be in the same space, just between four walls.

It has 2 be different dad Coz she won't be able 2 move The whole city was where she used 2 live Do u think she can talk 2 me from gaol???

'We can try and organise something for you if that's

what you want. You still want to do that? I can help you. I'll do what I can.'

Yeah I want 2 talk 2 her If she's locked up I can help her through it I know wot it feels like 2 be locked up like that I can talk 2 her

There was silence. Harrigan's hands worked at the muscle of his son's shoulders until Toby gave him a little shake to say stop. He stood looking at the screen over his son's shoulder.

I don't see the point dad Gaol I mean Is it going 2 prove anything 4 Lucy 2 be there?????

Harrigan smiled, more from exhaustion than anything else.

'No, mate, it's not,' he replied. 'It's not going to prove anything and it's not going to change anything either. But right now, it's all that's going to happen. Maybe she'll change in time, that's up to her. But she knew, Toby. She knew exactly what was going to happen today. Maybe she'll talk to you about it.'

She will She's always honest with me U can't say she wasn't

'No, that's true, she was. And that is something she is. She doesn't lie. Do you want to eat now? I'm famished.'

Yeah

They ate in the dining room. Susie joined them, helping him to feed Toby, talking with them. They did not mention the day's events. Afterwards, he helped put Toby to bed, settling his son down into some physical comfort. Harrigan was too stressed to stop and rest himself. Susie offered him coffee but he refused, needing something stronger. He drove to a bar in the city, a place he went sometimes when he needed the paradox of solitude in company. Here, he drank two neat whiskies quickly. Out of force of habit, he called in to check his voice messages, to see if there was anything he needed to know about. The barman appeared in front of him just as he hung up.

'Another one?' he asked.

'No, thanks,' Harrigan replied. 'That'll do me.'

Outside in the car park he rang her, but her mobile was turned off and he did not want to talk to her answering machine. He stood beside his car with his hands on his hips, thinking for some moments. 'Why not?' he said to himself and then drove to an all-night chemist where he bought mouthwash, something he loathed, and rinsed until he thought the taste and smell of whisky was gone. He drove to Bondi, through a city still littered with the effects of the morning's storm, houses with broken roofs and windows, barriers fixed around holes in the roads. He parked in the street outside her block of flats. There was a light on in the unit he guessed would be hers, but when he rang the buzzer no one answered. Various thoughts — that she had other company or did not want to talk to anyone just then, least of all him — went through his mind. He was close to turning away when a young, blonde woman arrived at the door, a keycard in hand.

'Do you think you could let me in?' he said, and showed her his warrant card. 'I need to talk to one of the tenants but I can't get an answer on the buzzer. I know they're in there.'

'No one's in any trouble, are they?'

She spoke with a European accent and he guessed she was a backpacker, passing through.

'No, this is just information.'

'I guess it's all right,' she said with a slow smile and opened the door. She glanced at him when he stopped at Grace's door.

'Gracie's in her music, that's why she can't hear you,' she said. 'But if you ring that buzzer, it'll light up on her wall. You have to wait until she notices you.'

'Thanks,' he said, willing her gone.

'I'm up here, if you don't have any luck,' she said with a grin and disappeared.

He rang the door bell, wondering how long this might take, but shortly afterwards he heard the security chain being unfastened. She opened the door to him.

'Hi,' she said, 'how did you get into the building? I didn't hear you ring.'

'This young German girl let me in. She turned up while I was at the door.'

'Bennie? I'll have to talk to her. She's not supposed to do that. Do you want to come in?'

'Yeah.'

He stepped into a small flat where everything needed for living was on display. Several CDs and a set of headphones were lying on a small couch. He tried not to look at the wide bed with its bright coverlet under the window.

'Do you want something to drink? I'm afraid I don't have anything alcoholic.'

'No, just some water will do, thanks, Grace.'

They stood awkwardly side by side in the tiny kitchen while he drank a glass of water.

'How are you?' he asked.

'I'm okay, I think. I keep finding it hard to believe it really happened. I sit there and I start thinking, is this true? Then I shake my head and I think, yes, it's true and I'm still here. How are you?'

'Me?' He stopped for a moment. 'That was one of the hardest things I've ever had to do. Telling everyone it was finished like that. I built that team up from nothing. They asked me to come back from a little country town to do just that. Now they've thrown it away. They didn't even give it a second thought.'

'Why not give it to Trev? He could have done it.'

'Why do you think? No, it's not even that really. No, this is them giving Marvin his little bit of blood on the way through. Just so I know I'm not getting something for nothing. Forget it. I didn't come here to cry on your shoulder.'

'That's okay,' she said. 'I didn't expect to see you. Not so soon anyway.'

'Well, I'm here.'

He put the empty glass down on the kitchen bench. He felt a wave of exhaustion roll over him.

'I don't know why I'm bothering you, Grace. I'm a dead man.'

'Do you want to stay? Dead or alive?'

'If you want me to.'

'Do you want to go to bed in that case? It's getting late and I'm pretty wiped out myself.'

She pulled back the covers on the bed and then gave him a clothes hanger for his suit while she disappeared into the bathroom. He hoped she would not come out to see him half-dressed in shirt and socks as he slipped jacket and trousers into the wardrobe between her spangled, shiny dresses and workday outfits. He got into bed and waited. She reappeared and undressed, tossing her clothes into the laundry basket. He watched her.

'You're lovely,' he said.

'Am I?'

She shook back her hair and lay down beside him.

'You don't have to say it. It doesn't matter if I am or I'm not,' she said.

It mattered to him although he did not say this. He

stroked her face and wondered why she did not take more pleasure from the way she looked. It might have occurred to both of them that they had not so much as kissed each other yet. He would have done so but his fatigue was overpowering. He lay beside her and slept. He did not even remember her turning out the light.

When he woke later, he saw by the illuminated clock that it was just after four in the morning. He got out of bed and went to the bathroom, staring at his face in the cabinet mirror as he flushed the toilet. He thought that he looked better than he should have expected to and perhaps there was life after death. If you had not been asked (or chosen) to leave straightaway, this was the time in the morning when you did it. Dressing quietly, sitting on the edge of the bed to do up your shoelaces, saying goodbye as the other person stirs, arriving home at five in the morning with enough time for a shower and a shave, a clean shirt and possibly even some breakfast before going to work.

As he came back into the main room, he saw Grace sit up quickly in bed.

'Did I wake you?' he asked.

'No,' she replied, shaking her head and lying down again, breathing a little fast. 'Bad dreams, that's all.'

He got back into bed and touched her forehead lightly.

'You don't let them in there, Grace. That's your revenge on them. They can't touch you.'

'She's not in my head. I'm keeping her out. I am.'

They kissed each other for the first time and made love without speaking in the partial darkness. Paul, having arrived at a place where he had wanted to be for some time now, encountered the firmness of her body under the softness of her skin. He liked this. He thought that this was the first but not the last time he intended to be here. Grace was pleased just to take him into her body and for that contact to be their only complexity before there might be other layers of emotion and memory for them to contend with. It was a slow lovemaking, shaded by their mutual tiredness. When they were finished, neither of them spoke. She lay with her head on his chest, listening to his heartbeat, while he placed his hand on her hair, stroking it. They slept again.

The next thing that broke into Paul's consciousness was Grace's hand on his shoulder, gently shaking him awake.

'What time do you have to be at your desk this morning?' she asked.

Suddenly, his eyes were open. Through the windows, he saw that the sky was a clear winter blue.

'Nine o'clock,' he said.

'It's ten to eight.'

He closed his eyes again and lay there.

'I don't have a clean shirt,' he said, and contemplated turning up to his new job, on a day which included media visits, unshaven and wearing a dirty shirt together with used underwear.

'You can have one of mine if you like.'

Her voice had a slightly sardonic edge. He sat up to see her smiling at him, her nakedness disappearing into a voluminous red kimono.

'Will it fit me?'

'You never know. I buy them to lounge around in so they're all too big for me. What colour would you like? I know. Grunge yellow. That would suit you.'

He lay down again.

'White if you've got it.'

A white shirt landed under his chin.

'There you go,' she said with a grin. 'You can iron it while I make some coffee.'

In a shorter time than he would have liked, he was standing in her kitchen showered and dressed and swallowing mouthfuls of coffee. The shirt she had given him was dangerously tight across his shoulders and uncomfortable around his neck. He had rejected her offer of a lady-shaver, thinking he would rather turn up unshaven than with cuts to his chin. The day-old underwear would have to be lived with.

'There's a barber I can get to, I should just have time for that,' he said, rubbing his chin. 'I might get him to brush my suit down as well. I'm sorry, Grace, I didn't want to have to rush off like this. Do you want to see me tonight?'

'Yeah,' she said, 'we can go out to dinner.'

'I'll call you, okay? We didn't even talk about what job you wanted.'

'Don't worry about that now, I'll talk to you this afternoon. You are going to be there?'

'Yeah, I'll be there. Even if everyone does hate me now.'

He kissed her once and was gone, like a disappearing act.

Grace sat at the table in a room which had become quiet and still. She fought the urge to light an early morning cigarette while she drank her cooling coffee. She reached into her bag and took out a letter offering her a placement in the intelligence task force attached to the Attorney-General's Department, hand-delivered to her at the front desk in the chaotic aftermath of Paul's announcement yesterday. It was a position she had applied for months ago and she had long since given up any hope that they would hire her. Suck it and see, who knew what it would lead to. At least it would take her out of the reach of the Tooth. In the meantime, there was Paul. Are we always going to be like this, Harrigan? You wanting to run in and out of my life when the job lets you? She stopped herself from arriving at any expectations. The same, strange lightness she had felt yesterday after the siege took hold of her. I am still here, I am still alive. She would take everything just for what it was. The present time, and the quality of the light outside, had never seemed more bright, more intense to her than now.

38

Grace's shirt tore across Harrigan's shoulders as soon as he reached forward to put his keys in the ignition and he had to spend most of the morning wearing his jacket. His new administrative assistant proved her worth by going out and buying him a wearable replacement at the first opportunity with no questions asked, only a sideways glance as she delivered it to him.

He had need of it. Just before lunch, he was asked to attend a meeting with the Assistant Commissioner and a range of other notables, including two crew-cut Americans wearing plain dark suits and thin ties who looked like nothing so much as religious proselytisers. They were accompanied by a plainly dressed woman from a national security agency and introduced themselves as 'the American cousins from the Embassy'. Harrigan reflected that his entrée to this meeting had been bought at the cost of shafting everyone on his team who had trusted him. The meeting began with one of the Americans tabling an extradition order for the Preacher Graeme Fredericksen as a material witness to the murder of Dr Laura Di-Cuollo. It had been received yesterday, they said.

Harrigan looked it over as it was passed to him. 'You may be a little late,' he commented.

'We're aware of that, Commander,' one of the Americans said. 'Your shooter has done our job for us.'

Harrigan perceived that the use of the word 'Commander' had the intent of flattering his ego. The implication behind this supposed compliment insulted him.

'The issue here is the Avenging Angels.' The woman from the security agency spoke up. 'We have been concerned they may be attempting to establish themselves here. That seems unlikely now, given the course of events, but, as you'll appreciate, we need to be certain.'

'Have been concerned?' Harrigan queried.

'Yes,' the other American said, 'we've been watching Fredericksen for some time now. Unfortunately — and we regret this — we were unable to anticipate the present outcome. But we have to say, Commander, we've been very impressed with the professionalism of your investigation. You've got some very good people there.'

Had some very good people there. He did not reply to this.

'A pity we didn't join forces before today. We might have had one less death on our hands,' he said instead in his neutral voice, referring — at least in his own mind — to Professor Henry Liu rather than the preacher.

'We understand your feelings on this point,' the first American replied, 'but you do have to understand that these are very dangerous people we're dealing with here. We were unable to say or do anything that might jeopardise our own investigations in any way.'

Harrigan did not feel the need to respond.

The man continued: 'Unfortunately, we weren't able to exactly determine Fredericksen's relationship to the Angels' inner circle prior to his decease. We know he was pretty close but we don't know how close. We were hoping he could name us some names. I guess we won't be able to ask him now.'

'No.' Harrigan's reply was untouched by any regret for the preacher's fate. 'Was he paid for Dr Liu?'

The agency woman received the question with the same neutrality with which it had been asked.

'Yes, he was. His financial transactions were paid through a merchant bank in LA, by means of a proxy.'

'We have that individual in custody now,' the first American added. 'He's helping us with our inquiries, as you put it over here.'

'Who was bankrolling this, as a matter of interest?' Harrigan asked.

'There are a variety of sources we've tracked down,' the man prevaricated. 'A small-arms manufacturer in California left a certain sum of money to another possible suspect we have in our sights. There are other benefactors as well.'

'My concern is that the Angels don't get a foothold here,' the woman said. 'We can't be complacent in assuming they haven't, irregardless of this turn of events. There are avenues we have to examine. We think it's best we do this now, while they're likely to be uncoordinated and may be considering going on the run.'

Harrigan took this to mean that they probably had established themselves in some way and that they might even have escaped from beneath the national security organisation's net of surveillance.

'I take it you'd like us to wind up our current investigation ASAP?' he asked.

'If you would. We'll pick up that angle of the investigation from here,' the woman said briskly. 'If you can charge this young girl you've got in custody without referring to this particular organisation, then we'd like that to end your involvement in the matter. We'll need to interview her but as we understand it, she knew nothing about their existence. Is that the case?'

'Yes, that's quite right,' he replied. 'She had no knowledge of that particular connection. She was acting from purely personal motives.'

'We thought not.' The second American spoke with a hint of contempt. 'She was the patsy.'

'I don't think I'd quite describe her as that,' Harrigan said.

'We can rely on your confidence in this matter, Commander? And that of your people?' the first American asked.

'Of course.' He smiled.

The meeting ended shortly afterwards, everyone unfailingly polite to one another to the end.

After the meeting, Harrigan went back to his old office to talk to everyone as he had promised he would. When he arrived, much of it had already been cleared out and it had the look of the abandoned territory it had become. There was the sense of a pervasive, collective hangover. Both Ian and Trevor were quiet, barely greeting him. They were in the incident room, stripping the images from the corkboard. Harrigan watched as Matthew and Henry Liu, Greg Smith and the Firewall's website disappeared into the shredder and were then emptied into the classified waste bag. Everything that had once cushioned him in this job was finishing, the more so when he spoke to them in his old office to tell them they had been warned off any further work on the Avenging Angels. They listened with an expected cynicism.

'That's no surprise,' Trevor said, 'they wouldn't want us traipsing around. So what do we do now? Just tie up the murder investigation and leave it at that?'

'That's about it, yeah,' Harrigan replied.

'It's nice of them to think we've got enough brainpower to do that. That shouldn't take too long, I guess,' Ian said. 'Not much to wrap up there.'

'I've got you positions at the Agency. I'm looking to act you both up at positions a level above the ones you're in now,' he said.

'What more could we want?' Trevor said. 'Do you want us to thank you?'

'No, mate. I want you to do your job and I'm sure you will. Where's Louise?'

'The last time I saw Lou, her eyes were disappearing into the top of her head,' Ian said. 'Why don't you ring her at home? Of course, she probably won't have dried out yet.'

'I will,' he said. 'Okay, thanks. I'll see you both tomorrow at the Agency.'

'We'll be there,' they said, and left his office.

He wondered if they would ever trust him enough again to have a drink with him.

Shortly after, Grace appeared.

'How are you?' he said.

'I'm fine. You need to read this.'

She handed him a letter which he read over with interest.

'You didn't need any help from me,' he said. 'This is a very good job you've landed. Very prestigious.'

'Do you think so? Not as prestigious as yours though, is it?' she replied, smiling at him, making him smile back. 'What happened to my shirt?'

'I'm afraid it's cactus, Grace. It lasted about ten minutes. I can get you a new one.'

'You don't have to do that,' she said quickly. 'It's just a shirt.'

'Yeah, I guess. Do you still want to see me tonight? Will you come and spend the night at my place?'

'I don't know where you live,' she said.

She thought, I don't even know who you are outside of this place.

He wrote his address on a piece of paper and gave it to her.

'Do you want to go out? I can get some takeaway if you like,' he said.

'No, let me do that. All right, I'll see you there. Seven-thirty?'

'Yeah. It'll be good to see you.'

She smiled and left. Yes, it would be. He would need her company, after today.

Grace arrived at Harrigan's house in the mid evening, walking down wide stone steps and then through the lush plants overgrown onto the flagstones, to see him through the open door to his lighted kitchen. She stopped in the doorway, watching him loosening his tie at the end of the day.

'Hi,' he said, seeing her there. 'You're here.'

'Yeah,' she said, hesitating a little.

'Do you want to come in?'

'Sure.'

She walked in and placed a hessian carry bag on his kitchen table.

'It's a nice place you've got here,' she said.

'Are you going to ask me how I can afford it?'

'No,' she said, surprised.

'People ask me that question. It was in the family, I inherited it.'

She shrugged.

'It's not my business. Why should I care?'

He walked up to her and stroked her cheek.

'I'm sorry,' he said. 'It's been a long day and I must be feeling got at. It's nice to see you.'

'Yeah.'

They kissed for some moments in the middle of the kitchen. Then he held her. She felt him relax against her, draw breath.

He put bowls on the table, she emptied the contents of the carry bag onto the kitchen bench, a collection of white plastic containers, together with whole limes and bottles of soda water.

'For fresh lime and soda,' she said. 'That's what I said I'd have if I got out of that place alive yesterday. So I am. That's for me. But you really need white wine for this dish.'

'What about beer?' he said.

'Yes. Beer is good.'

'What can I contribute to this?' he asked as he set out glasses for them both.

'Nothing,' she said shaking her head, 'this is from me.'

They ate in his dining room, a white-painted, high-ceilinged room with bare polished floorboards. She set the meal out and said how it should be eaten. He sipped cold light beer while he ate, and relaxed. They spoke little at first, there seemed to be no need for it.

'I like your mirror,' she said, after one of their silences.

He looked up at the wide mirror above the fireplace. It reflected the room they sat in, the hallway through the door and then the wide white room that he'd had built for Toby. The frame was a plainly carved reddish-gold timber.

'It was my aunt's,' he said. 'No one knows what sort of wood that is. But you look at it and it's beautiful. I've never seen it anywhere else.'

'Has it always been there?'

'Yeah, it has. She used to say it was hanging there when she was a girl. It arrived with the house, I think.'

'Looking back in time,' Grace said. 'Everyone in your family has been reflected in that mirror at some time or another.'

'That's true,' he said, glancing back up at it.

Things he would prefer not to think about or ever to see again.

'This is good food,' he said, 'I don't usually eat this well.'

'Yeah, they are good cooks. They know what they're doing.'

They had both finished eating but she did not ask to smoke. She sent a shiver down her spine, releasing tension, a gesture he was beginning to recognise. He thought of the shape and the line of her back. It was his turn to suggest that they should go to bed. He wanted to make love to her but he also needed the comfort of her body at the end of a rough day. He cleared the dishes into the ancient dishwasher while she stopped to scratch the cat's head.

'What an ugly-looking thing you are,' she said, as

Menzies batted his lumpy head ecstatically against her hand.

'He's another heirloom,' Harrigan said.

He turned out the lights and they went upstairs to bed.

In the darkness of the early morning, while his father slept with Grace, Toby Harrigan dreamed electronic words in his sleep. I'm here for you, you remember that, Lucy. Talk to me from where you are. I'm here in this body, you're there in that cell. I can reach you and you can reach me. Someone has to be there for you and it's me. Remember that.

In her cell, Lucy turned in her bunk, thinking not of the end of the world but of the beginning of time. Time starts for me now, Turtle, I have to find the ways to deal with what happens now, whatever that is. With knowing where I've been, what I've done, all that weight. I have to do that. You wait, Turtle. I'll do it because I've got no choice.

Grace herself woke suddenly, as though she had heard these very words when they were spoken in Lucy's mind, and drew in a quick, shallow breath at the memory of a young girl facing her with a gun in her hand. She felt the warmth of Paul's body next to hers and listened to her heart beating strongly with fright. She sat up. There was no one in the room other than themselves and nothing to fear. She looked at Paul, where he slept beside her. You don't have to be afraid of this closeness either, she told herself. Not all men are sleeping demons. She lay down beside him and slept again.

ACKNOWLEDGMENTS

For their time, advice, support and inspiration:

David Baldwin, head of Unix Services Group, Information Infrastructure Services at the Australian National University.

Dr Suzette Booth of the Child Protection Unit at The Children's Hospital at Westmead.

Julie Cremer, of Birchgrove.

Stephanie Haygarth, editor and writer, Canberra.

Ewan Maidment, of the Pacific Manuscripts Bureau at the Research School of Pacific and Asian Studies, the Australian National University.

John Symonds, biomedical engineer, of The Children's Hospital at Westmead.

NAVIGATING THE EDGE
JILL KNIGHT

Thirty-year-old Justine de Villiers has an ideal life — as a painter supported by her rich father. When her father's boat is found drifting off the coast of South Africa, with no sign of him, Justine is swamped by feelings of loss and grief. She is also swept away by an overwhelming sense of freedom.

Single-handedly she sails his boat, the *Pheonix*, back to Cape Town. The trip convinces her that this is what she wants to do with her life, and joining up with an old friend of her father's, Heron, who also becomes her lover, and an older woman called Andy, she sails to St Helena — Heron and Andy in his boat, Justine aboard the *Pheonix*.

Then a prisoner from St Helena — a man Justine knew in another life — escapes to her boat. Justine agrees to take him to Brazil. But the situation rapidly deteriorates — to the point where it becomes clear only one of them will survive...

In the tradition of *Dead Calm*, a great suspense-at-sea story with fast-paced, engaging characters, from round-the-world solo yachtswoman Jill Knight.

> *'... a rich cast of characters ... a touch of madness threatening to disturb calm seas'*
> — Courier Mail

THE EMPTY BED
PAUL THOMAS

Do you believe in love? Do you trust your partner? Nick Souter did — with good reason. He and Anne had something special. He didn't make a habit of going through her pockets but what's a man supposed to do when he's got a rotten cold and a wife who helps herself to his handkerchiefs? You can't blow your nose on an adulterous love note but it certainly took Nick's mind off his sniffles.

Secrets and lies can turn doubt into an obsession and a loving couple into snarling adversaries. Secrets and lies can kill. Anne's shocking death leaves Nick bereft — and the prime suspect. He seeks salvation in the truth but, as he of all people should have realised, what we don't know can't hurt us...

Acute and ironic, *The Empty Bed* is both a grimly funny self-portrait of a man watching his life unravel and an unnerving story of love and loss.

'Boy, can Thomas write...His fluency, wit and lucidity are up there with Carl Hiaasen and Nick Hornby'
— Sunday Star Times

'Lures you in and keeps you guessing...brimming with malicious wit'
— Shane Maloney

'Thomas's fifth novel finds him mining a darker and deeper seam...with touches of trademark ironic humour'
— Daily Telegraph